THE DEMON'S PET

DOMINO SAVAGE

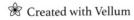

1

"Hey, omega, come give me a kiss."

I raised my head, staring through the straggled, dark strands of my hair at the smirking, obnoxious face of Zane, one of my worst bullies.

Then again, as the omega of my village, almost everyone had a reason to bully me, so rankings could sometimes be relative.

In any celestial wolf haven, we were expected to follow strict rules from the time we were born.

Without them, the pack would cease to function, or worse, the celestial enforcers, the archangels, would come to wreak havoc on any apostates.

And bless those who followed the rules.

I stared at the ground, chest painfully tight and heart ramming against my ribcage, and went over my possible options as Zane continued to taunt me from the other side of the road.

I didn't have to look up to know he was handsome. Blond. Tall. Athletic, though still slim.

All his life, things had been handed to him.

All because he was an alpha.

"Hey, omega, look at me when I'm talking to you."

I told myself to calm down, stay cool. It never did any good to escalate things in these situations. Even if I managed to fight off one alpha or beta, they would group up and enforce the pack dynamic.

And why not? They weren't at the bottom of it.

"Look at me, or I'm going to make you look at me," Zane snarled.

Alpha power. He'd use it on me, forcing me to bend to him.

We don't have to listen, something murmured inside me.

I'd always had this little rebellious voice that crept up at these moments to try to persuade me to go against the pack.

But if I stuck up for myself, they'd take away my ability to shift for a week, locking me in a collar.

The only moments of freedom I had were when I was allowed to shift and run through the endless acres of tall grass and wildflowers outside my cottage.

I'd seen collared omegas, and I had no desire to be one.

Not even the mated kind.

I'd rather die than be on a leash.

"You're an omega," my mother had said. "That means someone will always be in control of what happens to you." Her weary eyes, deeply lined and drained by her own life as an omega, begged me to accept it easily.

I never could.

From the second I'd found out I was an omega, I'd been fighting it. Ignoring advances from alphas. Fighting betas who were bullies.

Someone else running my life? I'd never allow that.

They'd have to gang up and kill me first.

Which wasn't impossible, since stoning got reinstated last year as a punishment for unruly omegas.

"I'm going to have fun punishing you for this infraction, omega bitch," Zane said, losing his patience. I could scent his stress in his sweat. My failure to submit to him had pricked his fragile, bloated ego.

"You stay right there," he snarled.

I stood but dropped my heavy groceries as I turned to face him.

As an omega, it was my job to do whatever a beta or alpha asked of me.

No limits.

Any refusal could be met with death.

With his shifter strength and deftness, Zane strode across the street and got to me in mere seconds. Before I could blink, he grabbed my hair, uncombed and tangled as usual (because what was the point of looking good for these assholes) and jerked my head back so I was forced to look up at him.

Tears bit at my eyes from the pain, and my neck flared in agony, but I held it all back and gave him the flat, unresponsive glare that I knew would deprive him of any enjoyment.

Any of the power he usually felt from putting someone down.

With a snarl, he shoved me away from him, so hard that I stumbled back and planted down on my ass in the dry grass beyond the sidewalk.

He circled me and then stopped as I realized others were coming to join us, their footsteps echoing on the pavement as their shadows danced toward us in the waning evening light.

"The mating ceremony is tonight," Zane said, bending over to grab my hair again. "If you want me to pick you, you'd better decide to be nice." He leaned his head in closer, closer, his lips coming in threateningly, slowly, as if he expected me to kiss him, opening his lips and letting his dog breath assault me.

I head-butted him, using the hard part of my upper forehead to crush his nose the way my karate teacher had taught me.

Before I'd been assigned my official omega status and was forced to quit, martial arts had been the best part of my life.

Zane's nose made a satisfying crack, and his blood spurted out on my shirt as he flew backward, landing on the ground but quickly pulled up by two of his lackeys.

"You bitch!" he hissed, swiping the quickly flowing blood from his nose even as I watched, mesmerized, as his shifter healing slowly moved the crooked bones back into place with little popping sounds, like a tent being assembled, the blood flow slowing.

In seconds, he looked normal again, except for the crust of blood around his nose.

"Typical omega, can't even hit that hard," he said, and several of his goons laughed.

The betas he ran with all looked the same to me. Handsome, built wolf shifters in their early twenties, with clean, expensive clothing and smiles built from other people's pain.

I smirked. "I'm not the one who called for backup."

His gaze darkened, and I knew I'd hit my mark.

One of the betas near me slapped me across the face for my impertinence. My heart stung more than my cheek as my face swung to the side.

I had grown up with these people. I wanted to be one of them. Ever since I'd been assigned to be an omega, I'd become nothing to them.

Less than nothing. Something to squash under their feet.

"How dare you talk to Alpha Zane that way?" Grayson, one of the betas, spat with a hiss.

"He's only alpha of the college," I grumbled.

I hadn't been allowed to go to school past high school. Educating an omega was seen as a waste.

I thought educating Zane was a waste when he could be perfectly suited to serving the community as firewood.

"And I'll tell your family alpha about what you did to him," Allison said, another beta who licked Zane's balls every chance she got.

"Come on, Cleo," Chris, a beta who never bullied omegas much despite hanging out with Zane, stepped forward, wringing his hands nervously. His red hair was damp with sweat as he looked between me and the angry alpha. His freckles stood out on his pale, wan face. "Just cooperate, please."

"Everyone else can accept their place here. Why

can't you?" Brittany, another beta, chimed in, throwing her perfect blond hair over her shoulder. "My little sister is a perfect omega. Pretty. Quiet. Seen but not heard." Her lip curled in disgust as her green eyes raked me over. "Look at you. You aren't even trying to catch an alpha."

She had that part right.

I wanted nothing to do with any alphas. Not the alpha of school, the family alphas, the alpha of the entire village, or even his son.

I'd be an old maid omega if I had any choice.

"What's so wrong with me?" Zane hissed, using his shirt to wipe away the rest of his blood as he lunged for me again, this time catching me around the waist and pulling me in against him. "I'm school alpha. The only one above me is the alpha of the entire village. You want to catch him?"

I shook my head, though I didn't owe him an answer. Any chance to reject an alpha was a good one.

He lifted a tangled lock of my hair, keeping me locked against him with his other arm and his alpha strength. "If you don't do something about this mess, you won't even catch a family alpha." He grinned, his leering eyes gleaming orange like a fall moon. "Then, after the mating ceremony, you'd be free game for anyone. Anyone's little bitch—"

I brought my knee up into his groin, but he jerked back, lifting his leg to guard against it while still keeping his hold on my hair.

He pulled me in against him again, and I yelped. I couldn't help it. I tried to never give these animals the satisfaction of seeing me bleed, but I had thick hair, and he jerked so hard he almost tore it out.

Something snapped in me, and I started fighting him in earnest then, scratching at his face, kicking out at him, not caring if he pulled out my hair as long as I didn't have to stand his touch for another moment. I let out a feral screech as I went straight for his eyes, wanting to tear them out.

I just wanted all this bullying to stop. To escape this stupid world that wasn't made for me.

"What's going on here?" A deep voice interrupted as a shadow fell over us from behind.

I thought at first it was simply the sun going behind clouds as it set.

But as I turned, I saw a radiant sunset blazing across the sky with burning oranges and pinks, cutting through mellow retro blues and hazy purple.

Something was blocking my view of the sun, casting the shadows, and I had to raise my hand to shade my eyes to see what it was.

"Shit, I'd forgotten archangels were coming for the

ordination before the mating ceremony," Chris muttered to Brittany as they both stepped back.

Zane let go of me, dropping me to the ground on my butt, and stepped back also. My eyes went wide and my heart dropped what felt like hundreds of feet in a second as I looked up at the most powerful being I'd ever seen.

His wings were huge, black, and extended from both sides of him in a threatening posture as he approached, the feathers on the end so long that the tips dragged on the ground, making an ominous swishing noise.

I'd heard angels put their wings out to demonstrate their authority, but I'd never thought I'd see it.

And those wings. Pure, abyssal black. What did that mean?

Somehow I tore my eyes away from the wings to look at the actual man. There wasn't anything too outlandish about the rest of him.

He wore a white tee, which skimmed a perfectly muscled but lean build with wide shoulders and powerful arms, slim hips, and long, toned but muscular legs encased in dark jeans. He also wore work boots.

He looked to be in his mid-twenties, though looks could be deceiving.

Oddly enough, his arms were covered in tattoos, like

humans sometimes had. I hadn't expected an angel to have them.

Shifters considered their human forms temples to house the animal god inside them. They didn't defile them with piercings or tats.

But looking at this guy, with his wings and tats and power, I just felt the sudden desire to be everything he was. To have everything he had.

His eyes fell on me, and I took the moment to study his face.

Suddenly, I couldn't breathe. Sheer masculine perfection hit me like a wall as I noted his strong brow ridge, thick brows, and piercing dark eyes with long lashes. His nose was long and straight. Not a small nose, but a beautiful one.

It complemented his hard, masculine jawline and stubborn chin and contrasted his soft, full mouth that turned down at the corners in a permanent frown.

A frown that deepened as he appraised all of us. His wings drew in to a semi-tucked position as he walked forward, and I saw that his hair was a golden brown, falling in rough, tousled curls over his forehead. He had the kind of highlights that came from days in the sun, rather than a salon.

The idea of this harsh-looking person in a salon

made me giggle despite the gravity of the situation and the fact that I was in the presence of an actual angel.

Someone with far more authority than anyone in this stupid town.

"Something funny, mortal?" The angel arched a thick brow, drawing to his full, much-taller-than-me height.

I immediately sobered. "No."

His gaze lingered on me for a moment, and the dark, heated brown of his eyes reminded me of dark rum.

It looked equally intoxicating.

No. No way. I couldn't have thoughts like that. I didn't fall for alphas. And angels were like the alphas of alphas.

I'd die before I perved on one.

But his abs did look like they'd be so hard under that shirt...

Fuck. I wanted him.

I felt his eyes on me again. Then, as if he had to tear them away, he looked to Zane and folded his arms.

"I asked you a question."

"I—I'm sorry, what? I forgot," Zane said. Sweat dampened his forehead, and all of the betas around me didn't look too reassured by the fact that their alpha wasn't acting so alpha right now.

The angel was deathly quiet, save for the slight

rustle of his feathers as his wings moved slightly. They were upright and folded, arching out from behind him and falling in straight lines to the ground, making him look more like a classic biblical angel.

He cocked his head, and the cracks in his neck punctuated the ominous silence. "I hate bullies."

"Sam, stop," a voice called out from farther down the street, and I looked up to see three more angels standing behind him, their wings various shades of white to gray. None were black like his.

The small, rundown street around us with its small, modest buildings and shops looked like an odd backdrop for such powerful, beautiful, celestial creatures.

The giant wings drew me most. More badly than I wanted to eat like a pound of chocolate by myself, I wanted to just reach out and touch a single feather of Sam's wings.

He'd probably puke if touched by a lowly omega.

"Get out of here," Sam said. "Go home and prepare for the ceremony, all of you."

Zane and his cronies scattered, running down the street as fast as their shifter feet could carry them, leaving me alone on the pavement with these guys.

But what kind of angel had black wings and tattoos?

Sam nudged my foot with his, his lip curling in disgust. His long lashes shaded his eyes, making them look even more dark and sinful. His lips pressed into a tight line. "Stop staring at me and go, you idiot."

"I'm not an idiot," I muttered, unable to stop myself. Oh no. Oh holy shit, I was fucked. I'd just spoken back to an angel.

I'd always been told my mouth would get me into trouble. Oh well, maybe if these angels obliterated me, I wouldn't have to go to the mating ceremony.

The angel went silent and still above me, and it felt like a dangerous sign.

But my stupid mouth wasn't done. The rage inside me at being mocked by this gorgeous, powerful creature had stung me right to the core.

"And I may be an omega, but you're not my alpha, so you can't tell me *shit*."

One of the other angels stepped forward with a gasp. "Mortal, do not—"

Sam put up a hand. "Shut it, Os."

Os, a gorgeous angel with dark skin and wings tinged purplish-gray, stepped back and out of sight as Sam continued to glare down at me.

His lips slowly curled slightly at the ends, much to my shock, and his eyes lit with something I didn't like.

"Your alpha, hm? Don't tempt me." His eyes ran over me, and his brows came together in consternation as he took in my disheveled appearance.

Worn clothing from the thrift store. Uncombed hair past my shoulders. No makeup. Deep circles under my eyes.

"Sam, we've got to go. The village elders..."

"I know, I know. They want us to confirm the alphas here with celestial blessings in front of the congregation." Sam's perfect nose wrinkled in disgust as he looked at the town around him. "Why do the celestials allow places like this? They're positively medieval."

"We can't interfere in their religious beliefs," Os said, shaking his head. His hair was purple and long, pulled into a half ponytail to keep it out of his eyes. "Even if they seem extreme."

I looked up at him and noticed his eyes were purple too. Soft, like lilac growing on a branch in spring.

I liked him immediately but was too nervous to say anything to him. I still couldn't believe I'd stood up to Sam.

Sam, who might have actually saved me. I couldn't tell if it was an accident or not.

"Come on, Sam, let's go," Os said, the other angels waiting a dozen or so feet away.

The sun was setting. The rays of the sun were desperately reaching above the purple crests of the mountains that surrounded our little valley, and soon it would be dark.

I did love this place, with its woods and wilds and mountains.

I just hated my place here.

I wished I were born one of these angels, with all the power and privilege in the world.

But my fate was set, and I knew better than to hope for more.

I was an omega. The village omega. The lowest of the low. That was all I would ever be.

Sam watched me for a couple more seconds, then turned to leave with his friends, casting just one more wayward glance over his shoulder at me before they moved away down the road, headed for the center of town.

Town hall and the city park where the ceremony would be held.

I needed to get home and figure out a way out of this town before someone put a collar on my neck.

Before the door of the cage I'd been born in slammed shut.

2

"How dare you attack Alpha Zane?" my dad said as his hand lashed out and made stinging contact with my already sore cheek.

My head whipped to the side, and in our dimly lit, rundown house, I saw my mom cringing back into a corner.

Typical.

I brought my eyes back to my father's. They were brown, unlike the vivid blue of mine. Huge, bushy brows dominated a florid, furious face, and his cracked, slack lips spat saliva as he continued to yell at me.

I held my cheek, my heart hammering for vengeance, my soul crying for justice.

And all of me knowing it was pointless.

I could explain what happened, and everyone would

still blame me because I should have done nothing while the alphas and betas did whatever they wanted to me.

That was an omega's place.

"I'll be glad for the mating ceremony," my dad said, his hand out to the side and twitching as if he couldn't wait to use it again. "To be rid of you."

He was a weak beta until he married my mom and gained the title of family alpha. As she was already an omega, that was the default.

With his lack of control, his bullying tendencies, and his willingness to displace all of his anger and rage onto me and my mother, he definitely fit the alpha mold, at least in my experience.

I wondered what other villages were like outside our haven.

Sam, that scary-looking but tremendously hot angel, had called us medieval. But why? Didn't other havens do things the same way we did? It was the gods' will after all.

But something about the way he looked at me, at all of us, with disgust, like we were beneath him, stuck in my craw.

I swallowed, watching as my dad turned and headed for the door.

"I'm going to go apologize in person and try to make

amends for this. You, young lady, will prepare yourself for the mating ceremony." He waved his hand at me, then shook his head in disgust.

When the door slammed behind him, my mother turned to me, wringing her hands, wearing a nearly threadbare dress.

We'd never had a lot of money, thanks to my father's gambling at places outside the haven.

Only alphas could travel outside the lands of the pack.

Omegas had to stay close, so they could be "protected."

Protected. What an absolute racket.

"You've never defended me," I spat at my mother, grabbing the worn railing of the wooden stairs that led up to my tiny room. "Never once, in my entire life." I touched my cheek. "How could you? I'm your daughter."

She wrung her hands again, made as if she were going to come over to me, and then stopped. Her cheeks were flushed. Her blue eyes welled with tears. "What could I do? I'm an omega."

I nodded because I knew it to be the truth.

What could she have done? Still, it hurt that she had never even tried.

"You need to stop fighting," she called after me. "You

need to stop getting involved when alphas are dealing punishment—"

I stomped partially back down the stairs to look at her, my combat boots almost splintering the ragged wood. "By punishment, you mean when they gang up to bully kids just because they're omegas? No. I'm gonna fight." I grinned. "And I'm going to fight this mating ceremony, because I'll be damned if I have to accept a life like the one you live."

I felt slightly bad as I saw her face fall, but I couldn't care anymore. She let me be beaten and bullied, all because she worried for her own skin.

She was still a shifter, though she'd been assigned the omega role. We were still strong, though not as strong as alphas, who were often picked because of physical strength.

But we weren't that much weaker. We didn't need to take as much punishment as she did.

But as she always did with the tough things in life, she hung her head and stepped back. "I'm sorry, Cleo, for failing you."

I couldn't bring myself to say anything as I walked back up the stairs to my room, feeling heavier all over but mostly in my heart.

I opened the door to my room and surveyed it. A small oak dresser with a mirror. A desk with drawers. A wooden floor with no rug. A small bed with a straw mattress, threadbare sheets, and a scratchy quilt.

Our pack wasn't about luxury. We were about staying hidden and sustaining our own pack however we could.

We made most things ourselves, through pack woodworkers and craftsmen.

And the best crafts were never wasted on an omega.

I liked my room, though. It was a way to be away from everything. No bullies. No alphas asking me to submit. Even my father seemed to respect my space when I came here.

I flopped on the bed and stared at the ceiling, making out faces in the stucco above me.

I needed to get out of here. I looked over at the small window, which looked out on a wheat field next to a large pasture.

Maybe if I went that way and just kept running... But then the border enforcers would just find me and bring me back for my own good.

But if I went to the ceremony...

I shook my head. The idea of standing in a white dress while the alphas assessed me, each choosing the mate they wanted, while I had no say in it because I should just be grateful to find an alpha to protect me...

It was all so ridiculous because, if they kept all the alphas in check, I wouldn't need to be protected at all.

But I wasn't allowed to bring up issues like that. Not if I wanted to stay out of the stocks, which were used for public shaming.

I sat up on the bed, pressing my hands into the scratchy quilt my mom had sewn for me. I walked to the window and looked down over the waving gold curtains of wheat swaying in the last light of the sun.

The moon would rise soon, and the ceremony would start.

I glanced at the white dress hanging on the door to my small closet. I should put it on. Comb my hair. Fucking try for once to at least attract the least terrible alpha.

The problem was I hadn't seen a single boy who'd been given the title of alpha that hadn't turned into a bullying, conceited little snot.

Even the ones I'd thought highly of before had turned into something else with the title of alpha.

For some reason, there were no alpha females. I found that odd, but I'd been constantly reassured that women were considered and just not found to be the right match due to the will of the celestials.

Still, it seemed weird to me. The women of the pack were strong and resilient like the men. In wolf form, a female beta was as strong as a male beta. But alphas, once blessed by the celestials, had power that set them apart from other wolves.

The whole situation was hopeless for an omega like me.

I shoved open the window and threw one leg over the windowsill, climbing out and clinging to the frame as I looked beneath me. It was only about ten feet down, and there were soft bushes that would break my fall, so I jumped, hoping for the best.

The bushes cushioned me enough that my butt only felt a dull thud and my head was jolted, but I was otherwise unharmed by my fall.

I glanced up at the window, still open.

I'm sorry, Mom. But you let me down too.

I was nobody's slave. I was going to get out of here.

My wolf had always been a fast runner. There was a chance that some of the border enforcers would be assigned as guards at the ordination meeting before the mating ceremony. This might be my chance to run.

If I was fast enough, if I found a gap where they couldn't reach me, just maybe I could escape.

Where I was going or what I was doing, I didn't know.

My decisions at the moment were guided by sheer desperation and a lack of options rather than reason.

I crouched on the ground and focused, letting the scents on the wind reach me and thinking of my wolf.

She'd come to me on the full moon of the year I'd gotten my period. She was another presence inside me, quiet and calm. I felt her, but never with words. A touch of celestial power inside me.

"Let me shift," I murmured.

My back hunched as I felt my spine change. All my bones popped and cracked, but there was no pain due to the magic of the gods inside us. The ability to transform matter. My snout elongated, giving me fierce canines and a nose that could smell for miles.

Many scents assaulted me instantly as my hands turned to paws, and dark-brown fur sprouted all over me, finishing my transformation into my wolf.

I was larger than a normal wolf but not the size of an alpha who'd been ordained by the celestials.

Tonight, before the mating ceremony, the celestials would bestow "blessings of power" on the chosen alphas, sealing their fate as more powerful than anyone else.

I hated seeing their smug faces.

Then the celestials would leave to continue on their rounds to other havens, and the mating ceremony would take place.

Quick as lightning striking, I bolted forward, eating

up the ground with long bounds as I ran, ignoring the wheat thrashing against my face, and enjoying the grainy smell of the air around me.

It smelled like fall. Like spice and the bonfire burning outside the chapel where the ordinations would take place. Like grass beginning to bed down for colder weather. Like stress from the wolves who were uncertain what would happen tonight.

Like fresh air and flowers and weeds and trees and so many things I loved smelling with my wolf nose.

As I broke out of the field, wide, rolling acres of lush green grass met my gaze. Far past them in the distance, purple mountains. And past that, a large gray wall of thick smoke that was impossible to see through.

The veil, as we called it.

If one were able to pass through it, they'd enter the mid-realm. If they kept going and reached the dark realms, they'd be just one step from the final abyssal realm, hell.

And if you reached there, demons were sure to torture you so much you'd wish you were dead.

All the celestial realms were on this side of the veil, including the shifter havens and the nine sky realms the celestials inhabited.

Just beyond the veil lay the fae wilds and barrens.

Mostly neutral ground, if forbidden. And beyond that... I shuddered to think about it.

Pushing away my fear of what lay beyond the veil, all the stories of evil creatures and torture I'd been told, I kept running, my paws gaining purchase on the lush grass, my eyes pointed on the mountains. I would get through them just fine, probably avoiding any orcs or trolls. But when I reached the veil... I had no idea what would happen.

All I had was my wits and my strength, but if no one got in my way, it felt like I could do anything.

I'd survive on roots and bark if I had to. Take any job I could.

Anything to avoid an alpha's leash around my neck.

I raced over the acres of grass, wind on my fur, eyes bleary from the speed, heart pounding in anticipation of this perhaps actually working.

After all, the alphas would already be getting ready for the ordination ceremony. Everyone wanted to look their best for the celestials. Why should they guard the border? Who cared if one little omega escaped?

I reached the border, where lush grass met hard, light-brown dirt, and was just about to jump over it when I heard footsteps behind me.

My paws dug into the dirt, and I ran harder, blood rushing as the footsteps sped up, getting closer.

No, no, please no, I prayed, running forward in what I knew was a fruitless endeavor. One of the border guards or, worse, an alpha had sensed my escape and was chasing me.

They won't catch me, I thought. *They can't.*

But as I kept my head down and tried to be as aerodynamic as possible, I could feel prickles on my spine at the sounds of them slowly but surely catching up.

Out of nowhere, something huge and silvery-gray came flying through the air at me, grabbing me by the scruff and knocking me sideways, rolling over and over with me until we both stopped.

Fuck, I was caught.

3

I struggled, emitting a growl, but the alpha holding my scruff shook me hard, jarring my brain in my skull as I slowly lost the capacity to retain my wolf form due to pure confusion and shock.

He released me but put a paw on my back, keeping me down.

I lay on the ground, still clothed because the magic that allowed us to transform allowed us to stay clothed as well. The celestials had made sure it was that way due to requiring modesty from their adherents. Thus, our clothing transformed and hid like the rest of our physical form when the wolf rose to the surface.

I growled at my attacker, trying to roll over so I could glare at him from beneath my matted hair, but human hands roughly grabbed my shoulders and yanked me to my feet.

I guessed he must have transformed too.

When I turned, I saw the furious son of the village alpha. Bran.

I should have known from his silver fur.

He was tall and thickly muscled, with short dark hair, grey eyes, and freckles on his plain but handsome face.

He kept his hands on my shoulders as he started to frog-march me back in the direction of town.

I fought him, trying to kick out at his shin or throw my hand back to hit his groin, but he simply sighed as if this were a huge annoyance and threw me over his shoulder like I weighed no more than a sack of beans.

"Stay there," he said. "I don't want to have to hurt you."

As the pack alpha's son, second in command of the whole village, I hadn't seen Bran that often.

"I was assigned to your residence tonight because I was told you would probably run."

"You were there the whole time, and it took you this long to catch me?" I snarked. "I guess alphas aren't that fast after all."

He was quiet, unbothered by my barbs, but let out a little grunt. "Why can't you omegas just make it easier on yourselves by accepting the rules? If you wouldn't make trouble, it wouldn't follow you."

I ignored him, hanging limply over his shoulder, pretending acquiescence while I plotted my next move.

"You didn't have to be such a hellion, Cleo. And yes, I know of you. You refuse to be groomed or polite in a way that would give credit to the gods."

"I don't know why the gods would care if I'm hot or not," I grumbled.

"It is the way things are," he said. "The system works the way it is. Most omegas are really happy with the current system."

"Maybe because they know complaints lead to beatings."

He let out a snarl. "I've never beaten an omega."

"You're a unique alpha, then," I muttered.

He stopped moving for a moment, as if I'd given him something to think about, then continued walking again, carrying me like a sack of flour.

Gods, I hated alphas.

"It's not exactly easy being an alpha. I have a lot of responsibilities, and—"

"I'd trade you in a second," I said.

He was quiet for a few more steps. "I believe you." He let out a sigh. "Nevertheless, we are what we are, and as long as we stay this way, the celestials will bless us.

You don't want to be selfish, do you, Cleo? The whole haven could be destroyed if we lose the celestials' blessing. You don't want us to be attacked and tainted by demons the way humans and other creatures disloyal to the celestials have been, do you?"

It was my turn to stay silent. I had nothing good to say about the celestials. At this point, I might as well take a chance on some demons.

I grimaced at that because I'd been told my whole life the horror of what demons could do, and it far superseded the abuses I suffered here.

So far.

"Please, just try," Bran said, upping his pace to a jog as he pulled me off his shoulder and carried me in his arms like a princess.

I hated it. I still felt like a piece of baggage. Something others could move from one place to another without any regard for what I would want.

But I was aware of how many other girls and women in the village would be jealous to be in the arms of the son of the alpha of the pack.

He wasn't half as bad as Zane, but I still couldn't stand him.

Anyone who went along with this system without resistance was on my bad side.

"You never know," he said, looking down at me. "You

might find a very powerful mate, and things might change in your world."

I laughed ruefully. "If any alpha had given a shit about me, he would have intervened sooner when I was getting the shit kicked out of me all over the place. When I was getting assaulted—"

His gray eyes met mine, and there was real regret there. "Omegas should be protected. It's true. Maybe an alpha wanted to intervene but couldn't. Maybe he finally can."

I blinked up at him, wondering if he was saying what I thought he was saying.

"I've always noticed you, Cleo," he said. "There's fire in you. I admire that. If molded to the right situation—"

"I can't be molded," I said. "I'm a person, not a lump of clay. My heart is the way it is. I won't be molded."

He nodded. "Would you accept me as a mate?" He slowed his jog when we were still a good distance from my house in the worst part of the village, but I could see it in the distance as we walked around the wheat field rather than through it.

His wolf buddies were following us a little way behind.

I swallowed, looking up at him to see if he was joking. But his gray eyes were dead serious.

So I considered his question earnestly, because he'd

caught me in a serious infraction and hadn't beaten the life out of me as any other alpha would.

Perhaps a life with him, as the mate of the pack alpha's son, would finally protect me from bullying. Make me immune to the misery of being the omega I was.

I would stay home every day, cook and clean, and as long as I behaved, my life would be safe and comfortable.

As long as I behaved...

"I don't think so," I said, almost sorry to turn him down, if he was truly even asking.

I was still a little astounded that such a powerful alpha would even want me.

"Why?" I asked. "You don't even know me. How could you want me as a mate?"

He cocked his head, and his smile almost charmed me. "I like a challenge."

I wrinkled my nose, frowning at him. "I'm not a game or a challenge. This is my life. I genuinely hate being ruled over. No part of me feels like an omega. And a collar would feel like a chain."

He nodded. "Then what will you do?"

"Fight," I said.

He let out a weary sigh. "So you'd rather be a pack whore than the mate of an alpha?"

"I'll bite off the next dick that comes my way without consent," I muttered. "So no, I don't think so."

He stopped, looking down at me with what felt like genuine sorrow in his eyes. "I don't want you to die, Cleo. It's a waste of so much fire and energy. You're special. I can feel that sometimes, even watching you in the congregation."

"Kinda creepy that you're sitting up there eyeing potential mates when you're overseeing religious services."

"I can't help it," he said. "If you just tried, you'd be beautiful, you know."

"Try to get more attention? Not likely," I said.

I didn't know why, but I felt comfortable talking with Bran, despite his position and me barely knowing him.

He kept walking, and when we got closer to my home, he stopped, waving away his other wolves as they gathered around him.

Shrugging, they headed off, probably toward the chapel where the ordinations would take place.

He set me down, then rested his hands on my shoulders gently, holding me in place. "Will you at least think about it? It'd be a good life. Better than any other you could hope for. And you deserve it, after everything."

I just stared at him, still shocked by this turn of events.

He released me with a sigh, stepping back from me. "Don't run again. There are border guards near where I caught you. If you run again, you're going to have it worse than you ever have." He took a few steps away. "And, Cleo, please behave at the ceremony. Please think about your future, and your family, as you consider what to do."

Then he shifted into his wolf and bounded away, probably late to the ceremony.

"Hmph," I muttered to myself as I cast one more glance longingly at the horizon where the sun could no longer be seen. It was twilight, and the purple haze over everything cast it in a more romantic light.

My village was beautiful.

I would miss it.

But despite what Bran said, I was definitely going to try and run away again, and I'd fight like hell at the ceremony. I couldn't stay here, even if my rank moved up in the system. I'd always be an omega, and I'd never been able to submit.

Something in my heart just felt wrong about it all.

I slumped into the house, irritation rising in me when I saw my mom's face sag in relief as she paused in folding rags to watch me come in.

I walked over to help her fold the laundry because

she was older, after all, and I didn't mind the chores of an omega.

Plus, my head was still rushing with Bran's words.

I could be the mate of an alpha. I would have power over all those who hurt me...

But I would still never be the owner of my own life, the captain of my ship.

It wasn't enough.

When I was finished helping my mother, she pulled me in for a kiss to the forehead, and I didn't fight her because, despite everything, I couldn't hate her.

She was just part of this messed-up system, and while sometimes I could be furious with her, I knew I was only displacing my real rage.

Her crimes had always been of omission, and what power did she have to intervene anyways?

I pulled away from her and tried not to slump as I headed up to my room.

Right now, all the alphas would be meeting with the celestials, and the celestials would lay their hands on the alpha's heads and bestow blessings, approving each alpha to have power over those he ruled.

They would drink fine wine, and there would be hymns, and all the betas would cheer.

And no omegas were allowed there.

No, we were supposed to be home preparing for the

ceremony instead, which would happen at midnight, when the moon was high and full.

Fuck.

All the newly anointed alphas, and any previously anointed but unmated alphas, would have the chance to then reward themselves for their ordination by choosing a mate.

I was just supposed to sit and look pretty and show off just how far I could bend my neck bowing for them.

I'd seen omegas that looked ready to snap themselves in half to catch the right alpha's attention.

I glanced at the closet where my dress was hanging, flapping slightly in the breeze from my still-open window.

It was simple and sack-like, with a sash around the middle. My mother had never been much of a seamstress, and I'd told her not to make too much of an effort.

I'd called it a shroud because, for me, the day I found an owner (no matter how they called it a mate) would be the death of everything that mattered in me.

My heart. My soul.

My independence.

To distract myself from the pain, I pulled out an old paperback from the box full of books I kept stored under my bed. Every time the thrift store in town (which sold human goods from before the great divide) had a book, I spent part of my measly allowance to make it mine.

Books had always been my lifeline. I'd always had a quick mind, always been eager to learn, and when they prevented me from going to the haven's small college after my omega assignation, books were my savior.

I'd always loved them as a child.

Stuck up here in my room after so many punishments, I'd found solace in beautiful words.

Of course, I'd started reading classics because those were cheap or free from the village store most of the time.

Les Misérables had always been one of my favorites, a tale of redemption and humanity and kindness and mercy toward those less fortunate or less powerful.

I also loved *Anne of Green Gables*, where I got to live adventures with a little red-headed girl whose imagination helped her escape as much as mine did.

When I got a bit older, I found young adult novels and romance novels and fantasy novels.

The paperback I'd just pulled out was a fantasy romance with heroes that believed in the humanity and strength of their heroines.

They treated their mates like equals.

If only I could have something like that.

I opened the book and began to flip through the pages and felt all my worries slowly fade away as I melted into the story.

All worries, all cares, all thoughts of being a hopeless omega drifted away, and I was another person. Someone who had a chance to fight for what they deserved.

I paused when I got to the first appearance of the villain.

He had large black wings. I blinked, remembering Sam at the village. Damn it, there had been four angels, but I had to be obsessed with the one with tattoos and a terrible attitude.

He'd called me an idiot. That still stung.

But the more I read, the more I couldn't stop thinking about him, and when the hero and heroine got to the first love scene, for some reason, my brain conjured an image of me and Sam.

Him pinning me to the wall, kissing me, powerful wings extended behind him.

And I was enjoying it.

I tossed aside the book and shook my head, thinking the stress of the day had just made me crazy.

I wasn't going to kiss anyone, let alone an angel.

I turned on my side and snuggled into my pillow, gazing at the window as I slowly began to fall asleep.

Sam's sleepy, sloe-eyed gaze was the last thing on my mind as I drifted off.

The next thing I knew, my mother was shaking me, her hand on my shoulder, her words blurry through my still-sleepy brain.

"You need to get up, Cleo. Come on, it's time for the ceremony. Your father's outside..."

The nervousness infusing her tone made me push myself up with a groan, and I eyed the dress and nodded.

For now, I'd go along. But soon, I'd show them all what I thought of the omega program and every alpha in this gods-damned town.

4

My scalp ached, my legs felt horribly naked, and I didn't like or recognize the woman in the mirror, but I'd somehow managed to shower and groom my hair into a presentable enough state to avoid another beating from my father.

He never held himself accountable for what he did to me. He always said it was his job to "help me glorify my calling."

Calling? What kind of calling led to omegas having to stand in a line like cattle at an auction?

Wistfully, I glanced at my box of books on the bed behind me, wishing I could just stay here and read the book on top of the pile, an exciting pirate novel by Johanna Lindsay. Sure, her heroes could be a bit questionably rough or dominant, but they challenged the smart, strong heroines around them and pleasured them senseless.

And her gorgeous landscapes would always remain in my mind, though she had passed long ago in the human realm.

I'd rather be tied to the bow of a pirate ship than go to the mating ceremony.

Maybe no one would pick me, I thought hopefully, opening the door to my room and closing it behind me.

Down the narrow hallway, my mother's bedroom door opened, and she beckoned me toward her.

Father had already left for the ceremony after ensuring I wouldn't embarrass him.

I raised an eyebrow at her, still stinging at her betrayal, but sighed and walked forward into her room where she gestured for me to sit on the bed and then shut the door.

"I just wanted to talk to you a bit before the ceremony," she said, raising her hesitant, lined eyes to mine. Her graying brown hair was pulled back in a bun, and she was wearing a modest blue dress. As an omega, one should never try to draw extra attention.

"Fine," I said. "Since I'm about to be sold off and you might not see me again."

At the end of the ceremony, the omegas were "carried" off by their alphas to their new home, and then the alphas would send betas or servants for the omega's things.

I hated all of it.

She swallowed nervously, twisting her hands in the rough covers next to her. Unexpectedly, pity hit me, and all I could feel was sadness for this woman who had never fought the cage she was in.

Because she'd never thought there was a point to it.

And what I hated most was that, deep down, I knew she might be right.

"It'd be easier for you if you could be kind and sweet," she said hopefully. Her eyes darted nervously to the side. "Look, try to catch the eye of a higher alpha." She swallowed. "I wish I'd been slightly less demure to maybe catch the eye of a higher alpha." Her eyes gleamed. "You still can."

I sighed because my mother was still truly broken.

Her dream wasn't to be free. It was to have a better owner.

I let out a calm breath and held my tongue. Despite everything, I didn't want to cause her more pain.

I loved her, though I might have hated that I did.

"I also wanted to talk to you about the actual mating," she said. "Since I might not get another chance."

I resisted the urge to roll my eyes. I'd read quite a

few human romance novels, which contained detailed love scenes. Though we were part wolf spirit, we spent most of our time in human form, so I figured the sex shouldn't be much different.

My mother started to sweat and wiped a bead off her forehead before she put up a hand. She straightened her forefinger and kept the rest in a fist. "His thing, it'll get hard and stick out... like this."

Oh gods, make this stop. I would have done anything to run away at that moment.

Her other hand made a loose fist with a space in the middle, and she slammed the forefinger of her other hand into it.

"He will want to go into you... like this. Do you understand where he will go?"

I nodded.

She moved her finger forward and back a few times, and the whole thing was so awkward I felt like I was having an out-of-body experience.

"He'll do this for a few minutes, and when he's done, it'll go soft." She removed her forefinger from her other fist and showed it slowly curling down, limp. "Like that." She gave me a radiant smile. "Then it's over. Not so bad, right?"

My eyes were wide, my throat tight. She had to be kidding.

Um, didn't you miss a few fucking things? Like a fucking orgasm or any sense that I'm a person and not an inanimate fist made for fucking?

This was not the thing to say to me before the ceremony, but based on my mother's blissful look and self-satisfied nod to herself, she believed she'd done her duty.

All I could feel was an ache in my heart at the state of things between her and my dad.

And some regret that I'd ever come in to talk with her.

She didn't even ask any questions, then just stood, folded her hands in front of her, and walked out.

"Are you coming?"

I don't know, I thought. I might try running again, because being torn apart by border guards would be better than enduring hundreds of years of what she described.

We lived a lot longer than humans did. Not as long as immortals, like angels.

That was a long time to feel like an object.

But my brain still hadn't come up with an escape. I'd known this was coming for years, but I kept telling myself I'd find a way out.

But I'd been beaten down for so long. They took my

martial arts. They turned my friends against me. They took me out of school.

It was a slow, long process meant to remove my humanity and my inner wolf's strength, and when I didn't fight back, it felt like it worked.

But where was there even to go for me? No other supernatural community would take me.

The undead hated shifters, and they were in the dark realm anyway, except for the more sophisticated vampires in the mid-realms.

Humans lived mostly in clusters between shifter havens, unable to see our enclaves due to enchantments placed by the celestials.

And angels lived in complex communities in the heavens.

The fae claimed the barrens that were left when humans were chased out of inhabitable areas, and now didn't allow anyone into their territory.

They were even more protective of their wilds.

If I went among the humans, like other supernaturals who tried to hide among them, and was caught, the penalty was death.

We were supposed to leave humans alone.

And truth be told, I loved our little haven, the way time seemed behind. Before I'd been assigned the role of omega, I'd loved my friends and teachers and town.

But now, as an omega, I could never love this place, because if I wasn't suffering, someone else would be.

I couldn't be happy standing on someone else's pain, and to be honest, I didn't know how anyone else stood it either.

I followed my mother down the creaking, half-broken stairs of my cottage and out into the night.

It was dark, and the moon was full, with only a few scattered, hazy clouds in the great, dark-blue canvas above us. The moon shone so bright the stars looked faint around it. I stared at it and felt a strong call from my inner wolf.

Let's run, she said, more through feelings than words. *Let's run in the woods and smell the leaves and feel the wind.*

I felt her in my skin, ready to rise, a prickling sensation that was making my hairs stand on end.

Then I heard another inner voice, more distinct. The one that always got me in trouble when it showed.

Come on, let's go take on those shitty alphas. Should be able to kill at least one before we go down.

I couldn't help but agree, though it seemed stupid. Every time I fought, I just got kicked down even harder than before.

But deep inside me, something wanted to fight, and even if I didn't know what it was, I agreed with it.

The wolf spirit in me stirred in response, but I could

feel her reaction. She wanted to bend to the pack, to stay with the pack. And as omega, she would bend her head to any alpha.

So what was this thing in me that wouldn't?

As we walked to the ceremony down the dirt side road by our cottage, I saw many others coming out as well.

Young girls and women in omega white, representing purity. Alphas in long black robes. Beta males in blue and females in red.

Everyone in their place.

People excitedly buzzed all around us, speculating on who would pick whom.

I heard girls behind me discussing which alphas were the most handsome at the ordination ceremony and who they would want to be picked by.

Females could only be betas or omegas, but alphas only chose from omegas for some reason. Beta females weren't considered as in need of protection and thus could "settle" for a beta male, who would, at marriage, become alpha of their home.

I wished I'd been made a beta. Then I would have been spared this humiliating outcome.

In my head, I dreamed of being like Bruce Lee in one of my favorite martial arts movies, pulling out a weapon and taking out a whole room of people, all alphas.

Then I shook my head. I needed to stop having stupid fantasies, but they were all I had.

I looked around and caught the eyes of one of my childhood friends, Ben, a blond-haired beta I used to sit with at lunch. He looked away from me, turning his nose up slightly.

He hated me, not because I was an omega, but because I hated it.

Everyone hated me because I kept putting a fucking wrench in the "plan" when I was supposed to put my head down demurely and satisfy an alpha.

But for now, I kept my head high, marching toward the ceremony as we all moved onto the main street, people flowing together from side streets like streams into a river.

The excitement was building. I noticed other omegas around me from the other side, the nicer side, of our village. They glowed with anticipation, though I could scent fear on some.

Tuning into my wolf, I focused on the scents around me. Perfumes made at the village apothecary. Cottons and linens and silks because people wanted to show off.

There were torches all along the road, so the smell of

smoke was thick in the air, along with the spicy scent of fall.

Something dead yet rich-smelling all at the same time. Mulch and dead leaves and fallen apples.

I let the river of people carry me to the brightly lit chapel next to city hall, which had a huge field in front of it, at the center of which the ceremony would take place.

Standing at the doors of the chapel was Bran, one of the newly anointed alphas. The other alphas were standing on the steps, still keeping themselves raised above all of us so we could appreciate them in all their glory as we walked forward.

Bran glanced my way, and his grey eyes were unnerving even as his gaze was interested and warm. His hair was carefully groomed, and his tall, muscular body looked well in the robes of an alpha.

So why did I feel nothing for him?

I was a little jealous that the angel I'd seen before had put his hands on Bran's head.

I wanted to knock my own head at my wayward thoughts. If alphas were bad, then surely angels, the alphas of all alphas, had to be the worst.

Sam was probably pompous, cruel, stuck-up, and abusive like the alphas here.

It was good that he was gone, though a slightly

hollow feeling in my heart said that not all of me felt that way.

Sure, I'd only met him for a moment, but something about him would resonate with me for a long time. The way he looked at me like something he was studying, not just something beneath him.

Then he'd called me an idiot. I needed to remember that, after all, and keep Sam out of my mind.

I was probably just trying to distract myself from the imminent threat of sexual slavery, though if I called it that, I'd be blasphemous.

Everyone else had accepted what the gods wanted for them. Why couldn't I?

But I would always remember the day the alpha of the pack had laid his hands on my head and declared me an omega.

My life ended that day.

I glanced away from Bran, overwhelmed by the painful memory, and my mother nudged me in the side eagerly.

"Did you see that? The alpha's son, who will be alpha over the whole pack one day, looked at you. You've caught his eye!" She smiled. "Well, I was pretty in my day too. I'm glad I could at least pass something good on to you."

Once again, I managed to keep my mouth shut and not retort something cruel. She was a victim in this also.

"I'm not interested in any alpha," I said. "Even Bran. Maybe especially Bran, since his dad is at the head of this."

My mother let out a hiss. "Don't say that. Don't let anyone hear you say that. If you reject the alpha's son, you'll be stoned. It's the highest honor to be considered. To reject him is to betray the pack."

I swallowed. That did raise the stakes a bit. I wanted to live free or die trying, but stoning? Seeing all the people I once loved trying to hurt me so badly I died? I wasn't sure I could take that.

I kept my head down and followed the others until we got to the steps and they began to separate us and direct us to our groups.

I didn't say anything as I was ushered to the group of omegas, all huddled together and wearing white. Some were looking around with slumped shoulders, their eyes haunted like mine, but most were giggling, eager, nervous, and gorgeous.

I looked down at my simple, shabby dress. My long dark hair hung limply beside my face. I was slightly taller than average, and any curves I had were hidden under my sack of a dress. I was pale, my only good feature my bright-blue eyes that almost seemed to glow at times.

Otherwise, I couldn't have been more unremarkable, at least in my opinion.

But as I looked up at the alphas, all standing in a group to look over us, I saw more than one leering at me. Apparently, I'd made more of an impression than I'd thought.

Zane was there, and he sent me a quick sneer before turning back to the others. Maybe he wasn't planning on picking me. A girl could hope.

"They're all so handsome," said Lulu, a blond, pale omega next to me.

"I hope Bran picks me," Sara, an omega with dark hair and warm brown skin, said next to her.

I locked eyes with Sara. We'd always gotten along, though omegas stayed inside so much that we'd rarely seen each other outside of church.

She gave me a nervous smile, and I felt a warm feeling of kinship with her.

I hoped Bran would pick her as well, if that was what she wanted. He might be the least awful of her options.

"Who do you want?" Lily, another of the omegas, asked, looking as though she'd had to work up the courage to ask me.

I could never be cruel or snarky to anyone truly

nervous, so I resisted the urge to tell the other omegas that I'd rather fuck a whole field of rutabagas than any of the alphas currently eye-fucking us right now under the guise of religious ceremony.

The whole thing was so fucking unfair.

I thought of Sam again, for no fucking reason, then pushed him, once again, out of my mind.

"Ooh, you do like someone," Dolly, one of the omegas I really couldn't stand, chimed in. "Look, she's blushing."

"No, I'm not," I said fiercely. I kept any sexual arousal or sexual thoughts fiercely tamped down since alphas, with their keen noses, would take note of such things, think you might be in heat, and act as they thought appropriate.

Another thing omegas were just supposed to tolerate until they found an alpha.

"I'm excited," Sara said, thankfully drawing the attention away from me as I gave her a grateful smile. I felt like a bag of wet garbage and didn't want to spread it on the others.

They were innocents in this too.

"Why are you excited?" I couldn't help asking Sara as the others went back to talking about which alpha was hottest.

"Honestly?" Sara pushed her gorgeous dark hair

back. "I'll have more freedom. I can go and have an escort and not worry about attacks."

I was surprised we were even calling them attacks. I'd always been told it was just alphas being alphas. They had such strong hormones that they couldn't fight their own horniness, so it was our job to try and keep as asexual as possible, both in dress and appearance, if we didn't want to be blamed for "tempting them."

"I just want one man of my own," Sara said. "A happy-ever-after. Pups. Not to be harassed by random alphas anymore." Her eyes darkened, and I put my hand in hers, giving it a squeeze.

I understood her.

She gave me a grateful smile this time, and then we separated hands as the pack priest who was officiating the ceremony came over to us, the rest of our families having found seats on the chairs that had been set up on all sides of the huge grass area.

As omegas, we were led into the field where the grass blades were lit with silver from the bright moon. My wolf was alive, sensing everything, ready to break out at any moment.

We were directed to all hold hands in a circle and move together around and around as the alphas watched from a line they'd formed in front of us.

The whole thing felt surreal. As I kept my hands

clasped in the hands of the women next to me, I could make out so many faces that were familiar to me, watching with pride and sometimes surprise.

I guessed they, like me, never really expected me to be here. I'd been causing problems for so long.

When we stopped, we moved into a line, twenty feet between us and the alphas, and our families sitting back twenty more feet in rows on all four sides of the field.

Torches flared at the corners, and lamplights glowed from the street and the entrance to the chapel.

Everything seemed almost magical, except for what was about to happen.

The officiating priest stepped forward.

"This is a special night for the pack," he said. "Tonight, we honor the alphas who have accepted their difficult, burdensome position in our pack, to be protectors and leaders."

The crowd clapped loudly, some hollering, though it was discouraged. The alphas all glowed with pride, standing tall in the moonlight in their stupid robes.

"And we also honor the omegas," the priest said. "The most important role in our community." He raised his hands to the sky. "Since wolves existed, omegas have been the most crucial part of the pack. Though it may seem cruel, without omegas, wolf packs in the wild have been known to die. This life we all live is difficult and frustrating, but with omegas, all of us have a place for our cares to be heard, somewhere to place our burdens." The priest looked at all of us with a doting look that made me want to vomit. "And something we want to protect."

I felt like I was going to crack my teeth I was grating them so hard.

"Omegas, you are special. Never forget that. If an alpha loses his temper with you, always be sweet to him. Never raise your voice to a beta or alpha, no matter what they may need from you. Be pleased, knowing you are honoring your pack and even your gods with your sacrifice. Though, with such amazing alphas as we have this year, who could even call it a sacrifice?"

That drew a laugh from the crowd, and murmurs and shouts of pride.

My heart felt like it was trying to commit suicide by ramming up against my chest.

My vision blurred with pure rage at this man's description of what was expected of me.

"Omegas are naturally gentle, nurturing," he said, walking down the line in front of us and looking us all over. "Kind. Sweet. Natural mothers."

I was suspended in the fifth year of school for throwing a boy down a hill because he wouldn't let me wrestle with the guys because I was a girl, but sure. Naturally gentle.

I rolled my eyes.

He came to a stop in front of me. His thin, gaunt face had cruel, dark eyes in the center of it that no patronizing smile could disguise.

"A doubter?"

I just stared at him.

"All those struggling to express their natural omega traits will be guided, either by their alpha or a higher alpha." He whipped around away from me, his hands behind his back. "However, please remember that your duties extend far beyond simply pleasing your spouse after you are mated."

I barely managed not to roll my eyes again, not wanting any attention.

Honestly, I was pretty pleased by my restraint.

"You are to be his comforter, counselor. Accept and understand his rages, his difficult moments, because you can never know the burdens an alpha carries."

Everyone grew solemn, pitying the poor alphas.

"After all, the alphas protect the pack from threats, and it is up to all of us to support them, but omegas most of all, for that is their gods-given role."

"What threats?" I couldn't help saying. Oh shit, where had that come from? I wasn't supposed to ever speak back to an elder, let alone a priest, let alone anyone.

"Other packs," he said. "The celestials protect us from demons, but the alphas ensure no other rogue alphas ejected from other havens can come to take anything from us."

"When's the last time an alpha had to deal with a threat that wasn't another of our alphas?" I spat out, unable to help it anymore. "How is it honorable to protect us from yourselves when you're the problem? Why should we choose one of you to hurt us just so we aren't hurt by all of you? If alphas are so great, why can't they just stop fucking around and hurting people?"

I clapped my hand over my mouth, eyes wide, as I realized I'd just sworn in front of the entire pack.

Fuck.

"How dare you insult our alphas?" the priest said, coming forward and grabbing me by the neck. "Without our alphas, this entire village wouldn't exist." His eyes glowed red, a sign he was losing control as an alpha, but I didn't care. I kicked out at him, trying to catch him in the jewels.

"Omegas carried the alphas inside them!" I yelled back at him as he struggled to keep hold of me while being actively kicked by me. "They carried the stones to the church. They built houses. They tended children.

They've carried this world on their backs, and you think they need some shithead who can't even control himself to control them? I don't fucking think so!"

Damn it, damn it, this was all going wrong. I was going to get in huge trouble at this point.

The priest shoved me back so that I hit the ground on my butt, and I knew there would be grass stains on my dress—not that I cared about it.

I glared up at the priest furiously. If I had to listen to one more stupid word about how awesome being a slave was, I'd spit in his fucking face.

Part of me wished I could be docile like the omegas around me, able to bow my head and step back and await my fate.

Sara sent me a nervous glance, but I shook my head at her, and she moved back into place.

The priest approached ominously. "You have always been an unruly omega. You have never accepted your place. Perhaps tonight is the right night for a stoning ceremony, since you've decided on blasphemy rather than an eternal mate."

Eternal mate. Eternal slave owner. I wanted to puke.

"You can call it what you want, but you're selling us off to the highest bidder under threat of rape or worse," I said. "If I say no, or am not picked, I'm fair game, aren't I?"

"If you refuse to help one alpha contain his urges, then you will be available for group use, yes. But you may not hate it. You may actually enjoy it," he said, crouching, grabbing my chin, and forcing me to look up at him. "Omegas are always asking for it with their pheromones, after all."

He stood, letting go of my chin and shoving me aside at the same time.

No one did anything about it, as usual. Everyone in the crowd watched in wonder.

"No one is going to choose you anyway," he hissed at me. "So you might as well prepare yourself—"

"Hold on," Bran said, stepping forward. "You step away from her. I'm selecting her as a mate."

5

I looked up at Bran, so shocked I probably went paler than the full moon above us.

His smile was pure, well-meaning condescension. "I can tame her. I'm sure of it." He reached out a hand to me, helping me to my feet. The other alphas behind him looked upset, particularly Zane, much to my shock.

Had more than one been planning on picking me when all of them knew I hated them? That only made this whole thing sicker.

He moved closer to me, raising my hand to his lips. Odd prickles moved up my skin, and I wasn't sure if that was a good or bad thing.

"Choose me, and I'll protect you," he said, eyeing the priest, who was stepping back now, looking nervously at

Bran and his father, who was seated in the front as pack alpha.

Bran's father looked much like him, and he was watching us with hard eyes as if displeased by all of this.

"Well, it's a little unconventional, but I suppose we can start the choosing now since the son of our alpha has decided it," the priest said warily.

"I do," Bran said, easily stepping into the role of authority that had been handed to him.

I had to admit it, I was impressed by how he was handling this. Maybe it wouldn't be the worst thing to be mated to an alpha, if he could just see me as an equal.

Maybe he could help me escape, or we could leave this place together. He'd stood up to the priest. Maybe he liked me, not as an omega, but as me.

Maybe this was the start of our romance novel.

Something inside me still felt sick with dread, but at least my outburst wasn't ending with stoning.

Bran reached out to stroke my cheek, and I let him. The first time I let an alpha touch me without resisting him.

I tried to lean into it, to see if I could feel anything that made my heart less icy about the proposition of belonging to an alpha.

But I wasn't sure.

Bran gave me a nod, as if he felt he had my full agreement, and then moved down the line in front of Sara.

He took her hand and brought it to his lips as well.

Her eyes flew wide in confusion, and she looked over at me.

Bran gave us both a doting smile as he turned to face the part of the congregation in front of him.

"It is my pleasure to announce that the celestials have given us a new dispensation as alphas. From now on, an alpha may mate as many omegas as he can support. There is no longer a restriction on owning only one omega."

Did he just say *owning*?

I glared at him as he continued to explain to all of them that strong alphas, like him, would be able to bless and protect more than one omega and that the gods had given their blessing.

In the congregation, people whispered with shock, and the wind blew through the mostly quiet clearing.

I almost wished the celestials were here so I could ask them about this stupid new rule that only benefitted alphas, when only alphas had been in the meeting with them to hear about it.

"I demand you call back a celestial to confirm this change," I yelled, my hands in tight fists, my anger turning infernal when Sara let out a gasping sob of shock.

She was one of those omegas who'd tried to gracefully adjust to this situation, but this seemed to be too much for even her.

The idea of sharing a mate... when mates were supposed to have a sacred connection.

Her father stood, a good beta who'd become alpha of her family but never used his power for bad that I'd seen. "This is not in the book of precepts!"

"Many things are not," Bran said, turning to face him with folded arms. He looked around at the other alphas. "Besides, it's just what the angels told us, isn't that right, alphas? And we have to do as the celestials say."

He walked to Sara. "This one I will take as my true mate. Gentle, kind, in need of my protection." He touched her chin, and she didn't jerk away, though I saw that she wanted to.

It was so sad. She'd wanted Bran, and now she had to share him.

Bran walked in front of me, taking me by the shoulders. "This one, she's feisty, impossible for anyone else in the village to control. She'd be stoned without me, after turning down an alpha. Something is wrong with her mind, and she can't accept her place as omega, though her position deems her a blessed daughter of the gods." He puffed his chest and looked around solemnly, as if announcing he was about to run into a burning building for all of them. "I can keep her in her place."

The others applauded tepidly, barely rising above the hum of the cicadas in the wet grass.

I think they were hoping for a stoning.

He leaned into me, keeping his hands on my shoulders. "Do your best for me, and I promise to always protect you." His lips got close enough to graze my ear. "I know you're difficult, but the fire you'll bring in bed should be worth all the trouble. So much fight in you—"

That's when I made the biggest mistake of my life.

I kneed the alpha's son right in the crotch. Unlike Zane, he hadn't been my sparring partner before I was forced to quit, and he didn't know how to dodge quickly enough.

I felt my knee hit soft but firm flesh, sort of like a small, hard plum that smashed against me, and then Bran let out a howl and crashed to the ground.

"She's ruined me!" he yelled, tears streaming down his face as he held his crotch and rolled back and forth on the lawn. I could have done a lot worse to him.

"I'm castrated!" Bran howled as the pack medics ran over to him.

I was hauled out of the line by one of the alphas, but

my eyes were on Bran, and I couldn't help feeling guilty, if he really was ruined.

We were all part of this fucked-up system.

He was crying now, sobbing, which wasn't very alpha of him.

The medics nodded to his father, signaling that he would be fine, and I wondered how such a high-ranking alpha could be such a baby about pain.

I'd been hit so many times I barely reacted now.

"The stocks," the priest yelled, and the next thing I knew, I was frog-marched over to the town square, across the dirt road in front of the chapel, and locked in a pair of lonely stocks in the middle of the town park where everyone could see me.

Then everyone went back to the ceremony, leaving me in the lamplight of the square, my hands caught in holes to my sides, my head hanging down in the middle, resting on the bottom of the main hole.

My hands rubbed against the rough wood as I tried to escape, and it only led to painful splinters cutting into my skin.

In the background, about a hundred yards away, the ceremony continued, punctuated with cheers.

When they were done, they were probably going to stone me.

"Fuck."

"That's not very celestial," a voice said sardonically. The voice was smooth, deep, laconic. Like melted chocolate and brandy to my ears.

I tried to look up and see, but the stocks prevented me from looking up very far.

All I saw were black robes until the person talking knelt in front of me.

I gasped when I recognized dark eyes and golden-brown hair, Sam's face so close I could make out the tiny pores on his perfect nose.

"What are you doing here?" I asked, shocked to see him. "Weren't you supposed to leave with the other celestials?"

He didn't answer me, just studied me with those beautiful eyes and then looked over the stocks.

"What did you do to deserve this?" he asked.

I ignored him and let my head fall limply forward. At this point, I could be sassy, but why bother? I had probably already earned myself death with my actions.

"I didn't leave because they told me they might need an executioner," he said, answering my question. "They didn't say why."

My head flew up, as much as it could at least. "An executioner?"

He nodded slowly. Silently.

Suddenly, the black wings made sense. I'd heard

rumors of an angel that had joined the others. Black wings. The angel of death.

Yeah, he probably wasn't going to help me.

"Can you get me out of here?" I begged. Couldn't blame a girl for asking.

He shook his head. "Celestials don't interfere with personal haven affairs." He moved back and sat on one of the benches near the stocks. "We give rules, and you follow them. As easy as that."

"Well, one of your new rules sucks," I spat. "Because, apparently, alphas don't have enough privileges, so now they can have multiple mates, and—"

"Multiple mates?" He cocked his head. "I haven't heard of that happening in a haven yet. Very celestial, though."

I grunted. "You say that like you aren't one."

He was silent.

"What do you mean, very celestial?" This was an absurd conversation to be having, but it distracted from my imminent demise, so...

"Oh, you know, most celestial communities have some kind of sex-cult vibe. It's practically the way to identify a celestial influence," Sam said placidly. "Is there a male claiming to talk to a god or the gods? Well, the first thing he's probably going to do is declare that he can have multiple wives, or concubines, or whatever they call them."

"You have a pretty cynical view of celestials for being one of them," I muttered.

He was silent again.

I couldn't help relating to him, though. All the things I'd thought were ridiculous seemed ridiculous to him too.

Yet celestials like him and his friends were the root of my problems.

All the gods could go to hell as far as I was concerned.

"What would you even do if I let you out of there?" he asked, cocking his head. Gods, he looked beautiful, even in those robes.

I felt my body reacting to his presence, his smell, like burnt incense, spicy and smoky at the same time.

That beautiful body.

His wings weren't out. I supposed when he was alone, he went incognito.

"Where are your friends?" I asked.

"Off to ordain other alphas," Sam said almost apathetically.

He leaned back on the bench, crossing one leg over the other, and tilted his head back so that the breeze caught his hair, ruffling it and tossing it over his forehead.

It was a beautiful picture and not a bad last thing to see before I died.

"So you going to tell me what you did so I know whether or not to agree when they tell me to kill you?"

"It might not be me," I muttered. "And besides, we don't need an executioner. We do our own executions."

"I wonder why I was told to stay behind, then," he said cryptically.

"So you kill people?" I asked.

He nodded lightly, seeming unbothered by the topic.

"But I'm the one in stocks," I muttered.

He grinned at me, even his teeth perfect. "Life isn't fair, pet."

Okay, now I wanted to punch his lights out.

I looked away from him, annoyed by all of this. My heart was strained, my chest tight, my forehead damp with cold sweat.

I talked a big game, but I really feared the stoning.

"What happens next?" he asked indifferently.

"I kicked the alpha's son in the crotch, so I'll probably get stoned," I said.

I thought he might have let out a snort of a laugh at that, but it was stifled so quickly I couldn't be sure about it.

"Wish I could see that," he said. "It's sure to be interesting."

His words bit into my heart. All alphas were evil, and despite their promises of protection, all of them seemed happy to hurt us.

He stood. "Well, it seems they won't need my services, so I should probably catch up to my... friends." The way he hesitated before "friends" made me think he didn't like them very much.

Fair. They were probably dickbags like him.

"Bye," I said sullenly.

He stood to leave, then paused, coming in front of my stocks again and kneeling in front of me. "I would save you, pet, but it's against the rules. Your whole pack could be destroyed if I interfere in things."

"I wouldn't care," I muttered, but it wasn't true. There were some people I still liked there.

"This is why I said you were an idiot," he murmured.

"What?" I glared at him with all of my power. "I'm not an idiot. I'd be an idiot to go with Bran!"

"You're an idiot for not seeing so many things," he said. "You're an idiot for not... waking up."

Then he did something unexpected. He leaned in... and kissed me.

His lips were so hot, so soft, and so experienced, his tongue darting out to tease mine open.

It seemed too odd to kiss here, unnoticed by the town, in the dark, in the stocks. But not being able to move, being so close to my upcoming nightmarish death, my body had never felt more alive than it did when he kissed me.

I let out a muffled moan as his tongue parted my lips and slid inside. His hand moved up to stroke my cheek lightly, pushing sticky strands of hair back, and he deepened the kiss, his tongue slipping deep inside as he held us together.

I wanted my hands free to hold him, to run them over his incredible body. I was instantly wet. I wanted things it was foreign to want.

Like this man, deep inside me. I wanted him to do to my body what he was doing with his tongue. Coax me open, please me, fill me... My thoughts raced, impossible to hold on to against the storm of his hold on my mouth.

I was melting, melting, heating...

And then he pulled back, and though I could barely breathe for my gasping, he seemed completely calm.

But in his burning brown gaze, there was something, as he raised a gorgeous thumb and slowly, thoughtfully, ran it along his lower lip, wiping off his mouth.

"Thanks, omega," he said, getting a leering grin as he stood. "Didn't want you to go completely to waste."

Anger flared inside me, combining with the heat and frustration he'd caused in me to swirl into an inferno of hate.

I'd been treated badly almost my whole life, but I'd never been this angry.

I hated my family. I hated Bran. I hated this whole damn town.

But most of all, I hated this man who had come to take advantage of me even when I was about to die.

What kind of monster did such a thing?

Deep down, I hated how much I had fallen for all of it and how much I had desperately wished to keep going.

He let out a sigh. "Shame, though. Well, if they don't manage to kill you, I'll be back tomorrow." He stood, and his wings unfurled, black against the already dark night.

Then he walked out of my line of sight, and I heard and felt whooshes of air as his feathers rustled, probably carrying him up and into the sky to torture someone else.

I listened until the swishing couldn't be heard anymore, meaning he must be gone.

And for some odd reason, my heart twinged painfully at the thought.

I was alone once again.

But as I sat there, my body was still oddly as hot as he'd made it when he kissed me. He'd left me with an odd sort of energy that I'd never felt before. I didn't know if it was because I was so gods-damned angry at him or because he'd turned me on so hard, so instantly, that my body had yet to catch up.

Even now, I realized that what he'd done was wrong. I was in the stocks. He didn't even ask.

Then again, I'd probably been eye-fucking him. Maybe he pitied me.

And what did he mean he'd be back if they didn't manage to kill me?

Alphas and betas would be throwing huge rocks. Yeah, I was going to die.

But as I hung limply in the stocks and tried to imagine what Sam had looked like flying in the sky below the full moon, I couldn't bring myself to hate him for long.

After all, his kiss had felt so good that my blood was still dancing inside me.

I might be about to die, but thanks to him, it felt like, at least for one moment, I'd lived.

6

My anger only built as I knelt there in the stocks, listening to the cheers as the ceremony proceeded.

I wondered if any alphas had chosen multiple mates and gotten away with it yet.

Probably. They got away with everything.

I jerked against the stocks again, only succeeding in getting more splinters in my skin, which was ragged and bleeding from struggling.

It was hopeless, so I finally slumped down, accepting my fate. For now.

The stocks carried the same enchantment as the collars the celestials had given the alphas to prevent shifting if a shifter was unruly.

They would probably put one on me when they came and got me.

I stared out at the empty park, the bench where Sam had sat, and scented the air, which was full of incense, smoke, and celebration.

The omegas who had been picked were probably drinking wine with their alphas to symbolize sharing a union.

Then tonight...

I shuddered to my core as I thought of the thing my mother had described.

Was that truly how celestials condoned sex?

Deep down, I knew the answer. We were brood-mares and scapegoats, so who cared if we ever felt pleasure?

The only pleasure I'd probably ever had was what Sam had given me, and I wouldn't even live long enough to taste it again.

Or read another romance novel.

Or run in the woods.

My heart felt wrung out by despair. I half regretted fighting back, due to everything I was about to lose.

But I also knew I couldn't change who I was. A fighter, to the last.

So why was I born here where I would never be able to fight?

Finally, the ceremony ended, and a huge round of

applause swelled above the gathering and hovered ominously in the air.

And then silence fell, and I heard the priest speaking. And people began to walk into the woods around the chapel. I heard their footsteps scatter in different directions, though not to go home.

They were looking for stones.

What better way to celebrate a bunch of new couples than a bloody lynching?

Stupid Sam for leaving me there. Proof all alphas were useless.

My heart was pounding, my blood still dancing with that odd, burning heat I'd felt ever since he kissed me.

It had only grown stronger since he left, maybe due to adrenaline or rage at being left in the stocks.

I wasn't sure.

I only knew that the footsteps were returning to the main grassy area, and thuds were resonating all the way to me.

Big-ass rocks, obviously.

I hung my head again, wondering if there was any point in praying. But if there was one thing I'd learned in my twenty-two years, it was that I was utterly alone.

When the thuds slowed and then stopped, eager whispers swelled into words of excitement, the feeling in the air that of humans gathered around a particularly bad accident.

Fuck my life.

The footsteps came closer, crossing the street over to the square where I was locked in stocks.

I could feel the heat of the crowd, their shouts and cheers growing louder and louder. Their thudding footsteps.

It was over.

The priest reached over and unlocked the stocks, and two alphas who were ordained last year pulled me out of the stocks and jerked me onto my feet. Then one put his arm around my neck to hold me while the other took a collar from the priest.

It was black leather with a small silver medallion with a wolf's head in the center, and it buckled on easily.

I felt the wolf in me recede, hiding, my strength draining me, my increased sense of smell and sound fading away.

I sucked in a breath, struggling against the alpha's hold on my neck, but he kept me locked tight until the collar was checked and rechecked, and then I was shoved forward onto the hard cobblestones behind the stocks.

I was hauled to my feet by two alphas that grabbed my arms on either side and dragged me forward.

Just to be extra annoying, I went limp, dragging my legs to be as heavy as possible. One of the alphas simply growled and picked me up, throwing me over his shoulder to carry me effortlessly.

Stupid alpha strength.

I kicked against him fruitlessly for a moment, more wild animal than person, and then slumped. I'd need my strength more in a minute, when I tried to run.

Unfortunately, while some of the pack came to get me, the others decided to set up a giant metal stake in the middle of the grass. The chairs had been moved back and made into two circular rows for those who wanted to watch.

Some of the pack, the more sensitive types, had gone home.

The rest were standing in front of their seats, piles of rocks sitting in front of them at uneven intervals.

I met their eyes as the alpha carrying me set me down and started locking my hands into the shackles attached to the stake in the ground, which allowed me limited movement but no way to escape.

I would be totally helpless. I guessed Sam wouldn't need to be back to finish the job.

The shackles dug painfully into my splinter-cut wrists, but I still jerked back against them as hard as I could, struggling to get free.

I'd been a dog on a leash all my life, but only now had I fully been reduced to one.

A rock hit my back, and I whirled around to see a small child, smiling at me then up at his parent as if he'd done something awesome.

I sent him a glare.

The priest stepped in front of me to address everyone while our alpha watched from nearby.

"Today, we bless this omega and remove her sins through this just punishment. May her spirit be revived without the flaws she was born with. May the gods receive this omega's spirit... or send her to hell where she belongs. We, the pack most blessed by the celestials, will carry out their holy will in order to sustain the blessings from the gods and repel all demons."

While he spoke, I looked around at the people, some of whom I'd known from birth, solemnly holding stones. Some had eyes that gleamed with mirth. Some looked like they couldn't wait to get vindication.

And some, to their credit, looked horrified and reluctant.

But they were holding rocks nonetheless.

I met the eyes of my first-grade teacher, a sad omega with a wary blue eyes. She tossed her rock up a few inches into the air and caught it again, her stare locked on mine.

I looked away, unable to bear it. I'd really liked her, and I couldn't picture her being a part of this.

But she would be, and so would most everyone else, based on the look in their eyes. It was a creepy expression, almost robotic. But they would do this. Because they thought it was saving their pack and honoring the gods.

"I'm not finished," the priest said, looking sternly at the child who'd thrown the rock.

"Though each of you may find this unpleasant, know that it is what this blessed omega has chosen, and it is our duty to carry out the consequences of her choice. To do otherwise is to anger the gods, to invite demons over our borders, and to eventually be destroyed."

Loud boos and jeers rang out at that statement.

I could hear thuds from people who were holding and throwing their rocks up and down in their hands.

"I will step out of the stoning circle, and then the stoning will commence. May this restore your honor in the afterlife, I pray sacredly to our gods. Amen."

He stepped over to the crowd, reached down, and picked up a stone from the pile of them, and his dark eyes gleamed with malice as he drew back his arm.

I thought he'd be the first to throw, but several rocks came at me at once, too fast for me to dodge them all.

I jerked to the side to escape one thrown at my face and felt another one hit my ribs, glancing off my breast with stinging pain. I turned to glare at the person who'd thrown it, and another rock hit me in the back as a large one made contact with my leg. It became sort of a game, trying to dodge the right rocks and use my more durable body parts to shield my less durable body parts.

The pain wasn't too unbearable yet. People were still testing their throws, and some rocks weren't even hitting me.

This stoning was halfhearted at best.

But it still stung, looking into their faces and seeing shame, even as they picked up another rock.

My teachers, my neighbors, the kids who had been my friends, all picked up rocks and began throwing them, more earnestly this time.

Was this really going to continue until I was dead? If so, what was the point of just taking this?

I reached for one of the rocks that had hit me, drew my arm back, and threw it right at the pack alpha who was standing near the church stairs.

He stepped to the side, and it missed him, but my act incited more violence from the entire pack. How dare I strike out at him?

But as he stared me down and I met his eyes with rage, I let out a snarl.

"Do you feel like an alpha right now? Do you feel like a big, tough man?"

He turned to walk into the church, and I noticed Bran standing to the side, shaking his head.

"You're just going to watch?" I yelled at him. "Fuck you!" I grabbed another rock and threw it at him, but unfortunately, he caught it.

I grabbed another stone and threw it at my teacher, who'd already thrown several my way, and it bounced off her head, leaving her in shock with a significant bruise.

Good.

Let them all feel the rocks they were sending my way. Until I died, I would be throwing them too.

I wasn't fast enough, though. For every rock I threw, three came my way, and it increased as everyone got angrier, more emotionally involved in the moment.

But I was the angriest, and I began throwing stones as fast as I could, using what strength I had since I was collared and my wolf was restrained.

"Stop this!" the priest yelled as I lobbed a rock at him that he somehow managed to dodge. "This is blasphemy!"

"What are you going to do, stone me?" I lobbed another, hitting him in the shin as he nearly tripped over his fancy robes while trying to dodge.

I flung more stones at those who'd hit me, and the priest stepped forward, holding a particularly large rock.

"You no longer deserve salvation or any forgiveness or blessing. All of your pack will now reject you, and may you forever burn in hell."

He held the rock aloft as he walked closer to me, then threw it in a way that there was no way to dodge given my position and shackles.

It hit me in the thigh super painfully. I gave him an acidic glare.

"I reject you." Bran's deep voice echoed in the clearing as he threw the rock he'd caught back at me.

It hit me in the cheek.

"I reject you," a small boy-child said, throwing his rock as well.

Suddenly, there was a chorus of everyone reciting their rejection, and rocks started flying as never before.

It felt like being caught in the worst kind of hailstorm, pain exploding all over my body in every place I could be hit.

I let out a howl as a large rock hit my head, making everything go dark for a second. Another large rock knocked me forward onto my face. I covered my head as they continued to fly, pelting my legs, my arms, my back, my ass, and the back of my head.

I'd never felt so much pain before, like being punched from so many directions. Emotionally, I was a wreck. At first, I'd felt pain at this betrayal, this utter rejection.

But right now, white-hot rage was all that built inside me, and it felt like my blood was beginning to literally boil.

I began to pant, heat rising within me as rock after rock dented my body. The rocks were getting bigger, thrown harder, and I wondered how much longer I could go. How would I die? What would crush me?

A giant stone was lobbed, crushing my lower leg, and I felt the bones snap. I screamed and rolled over to check it and caught a rock right in the face, knocking me back.

They were coming in a flurry now, and I felt a bone in my cheek shatter with another hit, and then my orbital bone snapped. Lightning-sharp pain rocketed through me, and all I could do was lie on the ground on my face as I felt my body continue to be broken.

I hate this. Just let me kill them. Let me live so I can kill them all.

Anyone who would do this to anyone, for any reason.

This stupid mob.

Something was burning inside me now, and I wondered if my body was releasing some kind of hormone to usher me into death.

But it kept getting hotter. It was hard to breathe, almost so distracting I couldn't feel the stones.

"Fire!" someone yelled. "I smell smoke!"

I looked around and noticed odd, smoky tendrils rising from my skin, everywhere on my body. *What the fuck?*

"It's her!" someone said. "She's burning!"

"A witch!" another screamed. "A demon."

"I'm not a demon or a witch, you fucking nightmares!" I shrieked back.

But an odd thing was happening. The heat was increasing, and when I looked at my hands, I could see tiny flames licking along the surface of my skin. But I wasn't burning.

My entire body felt hot, intensely filled with energy, somewhat like the energy when I'd kissed Sam.

As though my anger had taken physical form and was leaking out of me as it multiplied.

I really had no idea, but all of a sudden, I felt the bones in my leg reforming, my cheek and eye as well.

It didn't even sting, even as I saw the smoke rising and more flames along my skin.

Soon, I was engulfed in fire and stared in wonder as

I stood, rocks pinging off me as my body continuously healed.

"How is she not dying?" someone screamed.

"She's on fire! Put it out!"

Someone ran, probably for water, but looking down at my hands, unburned but consumed in fire, I was pretty sure water wasn't going to take care of this.

It actually felt good, kind of cooling on my skin, like flowing silk.

It seemed as if I were hallucinating as I stared at my flaming body. Even my clothing wasn't burning.

But the rocks didn't hurt where they hit me, and somehow I was healing rapidly.

What the fuck was happening?

I was still distracted, staring at my body, rage flowing through me that this was even happening, when a rock hit the back of my head.

I whirled around to see my father standing there with wrath in his face, his hands clenched, having just thrown the stone.

He glared at me. "How dare you disgrace us, even at this moment? You can't even die like a member of this pack!"

My mother stood next to him, and in her hands was a rock.

I realized it then. What I was to them. I'd never been

a daughter or even a person with her own thoughts and feelings.

I'd always just been something that would either grow up to make them proud or shame them.

My mother's eyes were wide as she stared at my flaming body, but though others were running for water, she just stood there, pale and gaping.

The way she always did.

Most people were still throwing stones, but a few were now running forward with buckets of water, throwing them at me.

The fire covering me only hissed and climbed higher in response. I knew they weren't trying to save me, so I supposed they were trying to put out the fire so it wouldn't spread.

Gods damn it, what had I ever done so wrong to be born here?

My hands clenched into fists, and I could still feel the cool flames between my fingers.

Fuck them. Fuck all of them. Now they have to die.

I felt a wave of energy emanate from me, like a sound wave, and all the rocks currently in the air were knocked backward forcefully.

I looked at the rocks on the ground and raised my hands, somehow knowing they would rise too. They did, all around me, some marked with my blood.

Spinning, I sent the rocks out and flying toward the crowd, where people dodged back, screaming.

I levitated several more rocks, feeling more waves of energy burning inside me.

Had this been what Sam meant by waking up?

Because it felt like a part of me that I'd always suppressed had awakened, and it was pissed.

It was surreal looking down at my own body, covered in flames, and then at the rocks floating around me in circles ominously, along with other debris.

As this storm continued to spin, it gained traction and started pulling in larger objects.

"A demon!" the priest yelled over the whir of the spinning wind I was causing and the cracking of the flames and the screaming of the crowd. "She's demonic! Demon-tainted! Everyone, run for your lives!"

People started to flee, knocking each other over, trampling each other in the process.

Ha. That was a sight to see. I suddenly felt powerful, maybe for the first time in my life. I waved my hands, sending rocks at the fleeing villagers, hitting those who had struck me hardest.

But I didn't realize the village alpha had somehow come up behind me, quiet as the wind. He stood outside my whir of objects and raised his hand.

"Obey, omega," he commanded.

I felt my wolf, even suppressed, wanting to bow to him.

But I also could still feel where I'd been hit by the rocks.

I'd never trust anyone in this village again.

"Never!" I said.

The priest came forward, pulling something out of his robe. "I never thought I would have to use this on a member of my own congregation." It was a small crystal bottle with clear fluid and the celestial emblem on the front, wings crossing over a heart.

"Holy water!" he yelled, throwing it forward onto me.

Oh gods, it burned. It actually hurt, which meant I was technically, at least in part, a demon.

The irony didn't miss me, considering I'd been called a hellion most of my life.

But still, how did I not know there was a demon inside me? One of the very things this village did everything to protect itself from?

I didn't know what to think of myself.

The priest hit me with more holy water, and it burned my skin like acid. The intense pain doubled me over, and I nearly fell forward. The objects in the air slowed slightly, though still levitating.

But while the priest had me distracted, the village alpha had snuck up behind me with a large rock, it seemed, because I felt something huge crash down on my head, and then everything went black.

7

"So they didn't manage it, as I thought."

A deep voice pulled me out of the achy, heavy darkness I was swimming in, and as I opened my eyes and blinked around me, I realized I was in the pack jail.

And across from my cell, sitting on the main interrogator's desk, was Sam.

I looked at my wrists and saw I'd been shackled again, this time with cuffs on a long chain that buckled to the wall, allowing me only to move around the cell to sit or lie on the bed.

It took me a minute to recall everything because my head ached, but even that made me remember that someone had tossed a rock on me and knocked me out.

Because I'd exhibited demon powers.

"Aren't you tired of bothering me?" I rolled my eyes

at Sam and turned over to look at the cold gray concrete wall of my cell, the hard, lumpy straw mat beneath me barely counting as a mattress. Then I turned back around to see his reaction, unable to stop myself.

"Well, if my company is unwelcome..." He slid off the desk and stood up, looking almost tall enough to reach the ceiling.

"How tall are you?"

He ignored me and walked over to pace in front of my cell. Despite his calm expression, his movements seemed somewhat agitated.

His gorgeous brows were furrowed, his hands behind his back as he walked. He was wearing a black outfit that looked nothing like the robes the alphas were wearing.

Chains ran over his shoulders and crossed in the middle of his chest, then wrapped back around to his hips, silver and gleaming. He wore a long-sleeved tunic that was wrapped tight by some type of black bandages, and the tunic came to midthigh, revealing tight pants with black bandages that showed off heavily muscled legs.

At his hip, in an elaborate black and silver sheath, was a katana.

Damn, I wanted one.

I kept moving my eyes down and noticed his black

leather boots, which had black and silver spikes at odd angles. His gaze, as I studied him, held a challenge.

"Like what you see?" He taunted.

"No," I lied.

"Liar," he said, and there was a smile in his voice.

My lips twitched as well. Despite the situation, there was something compelling about him. Then I remembered everything that had happened between us and turned back to the wall again.

"What's wrong? I'm so ugly to look at that you prefer concrete?"

I said nothing.

I heard his footsteps move to the desk, which creaked as he probably sat down on it. I didn't look to see.

"So you're here to kill me?" I asked, my heart racing.

"That's why they called me, yes."

"How do they even do that? Call an angel."

"We have our ways," he said. "Among them are birds, magical bond highways, and other forms of communication with other communities."

"Seems good to be a god," I muttered.

He was quiet again at that.

I decided to be quiet as well. What point was there in getting to know someone who was going to kill me?

That would only make the whole thing more painful for both of us. Not that I cared if I hurt him.

Not that he had a heart to hurt.

He'd left me to be stoned last night, after all, after forcing a kiss on me.

"What happened last night?" he asked in that calm, smooth voice that intoxicated my senses like mulberry wine fresh from the village sommelier.

I decided not to tell him.

"Did my kiss help?"

I turned over to look at him, eyes wide like saucers. "You forced a kiss on me. How would that help me?"

"I didn't force it."

"I was in stocks!" I yelled.

He frowned, looking put out by my accusation. "I know when someone wants me. And when I came forward, you didn't move back. And when I kissed you, you didn't struggle, you moaned and let me in and—"

I covered my ears, making my shackles jingle. "Shut up. That's not consent, you idiot."

"You wanted me. I know it."

Damn it, if I got out of here and got my powers back, he'd be the first one I attacked.

Smug bastard.

"Let's say I did do something bad. Who would

punish me?" He cocked his head, and a gorgeous lock of golden brown fell across his flawless forehead.

He had a point there.

"Another celestial?" I asked.

He snorted. "You really don't understand them at all. None of you country bumpkins do."

"Them? You mean you and them?"

He was quiet again.

"So how did you get the executioner job?" I asked caustically. "Were you so heartless you were perfect for it?"

He laughed, a cold, empty sound. "Yes. But also because I enjoy it. And no one else wants to get their wings dirty."

"Dirty?"

"You know, when an angel commits mortal sins, his wings darken."

I swallowed because I had no idea, and I figured he was probably only telling me this because, in the morning, he would kill me.

I looked at the tiny, barred window to my cell and stood as much as I could to look out of it.

The village was quiet and sleeping. No one was waiting outside the jail.

No one gave a shit that I was here, which made sense.

"Your wings are black," I said. "What does that mean?"

He grinned. "Think about it."

I tried. I wasn't sure which mortal sins he committed to be that way. I was a bit curious how many murders it took to go completely black.

"How many people have you killed?" I asked.

"Countless," was his reply.

"And you enjoy that?" I asked. "You get off on it?"

He didn't answer that, just got off the desk to roam around the jail as if he hadn't even heard me. Angels really did move to the beat of their own drum.

I still couldn't believe I was talking to one. The closest thing to a god in our world. The only higher gods, the elder gods, never visited, leaving the archangels to do their work.

He moved over behind the desk he'd been sitting on and opened a drawer, pulling out a large book. "Ah, pack law. Interesting."

"You would know," I said sullenly. "You and your kind set the rules."

"It's not exactly like that," he murmured, licking his finger and continuing to flip through. "Hmm..."

Still a bit dizzy from my head injury, I got back onto my bed and rolled onto my back to stare at the ceiling.

A sudden pain throbbed, and I put a hand to my

head. When I looked up, I caught Sam staring at me. As I caught his eyes, he quickly looked away, ignoring me completely and going through the book again.

I reached up to my neck, wondering if I still had on my wolf collar. I did. But there was another collar there, too, making my neck feel crowded. I touched it, but it was a choker and I couldn't get a good look. I could feel the leather strap and that there was a smooth, cabochon stone in the center, but other than that, no idea.

"You went demonic last night," he said. "One of my angel friends put that collar on you, and then they told me to stay and perform the execution while they moved on once again."

"They leave you behind a lot?"

He shrugged. "I don't mind it." He smiled, those perfect white teeth flashing. "I like killing."

My heart clenched. This beautiful man was going to kill me.

"Did you want to hurt them?" He cocked his head again, still holding the book.

"Yes," I said, though saying it was all some accident and I never wanted to hurt anyone would have probably gone better for me.

I just wasn't a very good liar.

He nodded. "Good." Then he went back to flipping

through the book as though he were in the library on a lunch break, not waiting to execute me.

"How soon?" I asked.

"Sunrise," he said.

"And what is this collar?" I asked. "Does it keep my demon suppressed?"

He nodded.

"Great," I said. "I finally unlock enough power to level the playing field, and I'm about to get murdered before I can even get revenge."

"That is frustrating," he said coolly. "As I said, pet, life isn't fair."

"I'm not your pet," I spat.

His eyes slid to mine, dark like melted chocolate, with a ring of molten gold at the center that I hadn't ever noticed before. "You might not find it a hardship."

I grimaced, shaking my head. "I'll never live on a leash. I promised myself that."

He frowned at that but shook his head and sat down in the chair behind the desk, leaning back and putting his booted feet up on the interrogator's important papers. "I'm busy. Try not to distract me. It's for your own good."

"What? So you can kill me easier?"

He ignored me, so I went back to resting on my cot,

wishing I at least had a book so I could read one more before I died.

I jolted when the door to the jail opened and sat up to see Zane walking in alone, still wearing his alpha robes.

Zane's hands were in tight fists as he faced me. "You've ruined everything. You could have been my mate."

I shrugged at him. "Well, I guess there's at least one positive to this whole execution situation."

Zane's face went an unpleasant shade of red that clashed with his blond hair. His blue eyes were fiery. "You can't ever hold your tongue, can you?"

I took the Sam approach and ignored him, staring at the ceiling.

Zane walked to the wall and grabbed the large ring of skeleton keys the jailer kept hung there. Then he started toward me.

I sat up on the bed in alarm.

Zane, apparently aware of the no-interference clause, glared at Sam. "You gonna get out of here? I got business with this omega."

Sam raised an eyebrow at him as if he were a flea under his boot. "Go ahead. It has nothing to do with me."

"You should leave," Zane urged.

"I was commanded to stay here and keep an eye on her until the execution. I specialize in demons, see? And I have to watch this one." He smiled unpleasantly. "So please, do whatever you want with her. Act like I'm not even here."

Zane hesitated a moment. Even though they were both tall men, Sam had a few inches and at least forty pounds of muscle on him.

"You can't interfere, can you?" Zane asked. "It's against the rules."

"Utterly," Sam said. "Be my guest." He gestured to the cell.

"No!" I yelled. "Don't let him in."

"I told you, pet," he said. "I can't intervene." But there was something in his eyes as he watched us, his gaze lingering before he turned back to his book.

Zane unlocked the door and stared at me like I was a steak and he was starving. His face was still red, his hands still clenched, but there was a heat in the air I didn't like. A tension in his body, wickedness in his eyes.

I'd been bullied enough to know the different kinds of bullying.

This was going to turn sexual. In front of a kinky angel who'd probably enjoy watching.

Fuck.

"Get away from me," I said, kicking out at Zane as he came within range.

Zane shoved his hair off his sweaty forehead as he came forward, trapping me against the cot by standing far too close.

I tried to get up, but he pushed me back.

I heard Sam stir at the desk, but when I looked up, he was only reading his book.

Of course.

Zane grabbed my chin. "You're going to die anyway. You might as well choke on my dick while you're at it."

I snapped my head to the side to bite at his finger, and he pulled back just in time. I tried to follow it up with a punch, but the shackles restrained me.

"It's a waste," he said. "You could have been a beautiful omega. Your strength could have been an asset in aiding an alpha. And now you're going to die."

He pulled his robes over his head and threw them to the side, then began unbuckling his belt. "Well, at least you won't go to waste."

Because my legs were free, I kicked out at him, but he grabbed me by the shoulders, jerking me up and holding me against the wall, pinning both hands in one of his just high enough that my toes could barely scrape the ground. I kicked, but he pushed my legs aside, moving between them as he started to fiddle with my muddy, torn white dress.

"Fuck! Fuck, get off me!" For a split second, I almost asked Sam for help. I looked over and saw him staring as if he were wondering if I would.

But I wouldn't give him the satisfaction of turning me down.

"Fuck you, Zane," I said, spitting in his face. He raised his hand as if to hit me, then turned to look at the angel, unsure that would be allowed.

"I don't want to mar your pretty face more anyway," he said. His hand sprouted wolf claws, and he tore the front of my dress, slowly, like undoing a zipper. I tried to kick, but my legs were helpless. With his hands holding mine above my head, all I could do was dangle as his mouth came closer, closer.

"I wish I could go slow and take the time to really enjoy your pain and fear. I wish I could pause to savor every scream. But I don't have time, so—"

He tore my dress fully apart, leaving me in my bra. I tried to spit at him again and began fighting in earnest. Even dangling, even with two collars, I was going to fight.

I heard something scrape at the desk but couldn't see over Zane to know what was happening.

I felt Zane's hand touch my side, and then he was

pulled away from me, and I fell on my hands and knees at the sudden lack of contact.

I looked up to see Sam was in the cell, looking so tall as he shoved Zane back by the shoulder, pushing him into the wall the way Zane had pushed me.

Zane only had a moment to stare at him in shock and confusion before the metallic sound of a sword being drawn from its sheath startled both of us.

Before Zane or I could react, Sam spun his sword so he was holding it up like a dagger, and, quick as lightning, he slammed it into Zane's face, right through his open mouth. The wall behind him made a crunching, grating crack as the sword impaled itself there.

My whole body went light with shock. I'd never seen anything so violent.

Slowly, dreading what I'd see, I stood, looking over at the wall and Zane, who was shaking there, spasming, his mouth gushing blood, his head completely impaled on the sword embedded in the stone behind him.

Zane choked, let out a strangled sob, and lurched against the sword, but his body just kept jerking as blood ran down his chest.

To my horror, I saw his weight on the sword was slowly cutting through his soft palate, up toward his nose, as his eyes rolled back in horror.

Sam smiled at him, watching him as though Zane

were a watercolor he'd painted. "I wish I could go slow and take the time to really enjoy your pain and fear. I wish I could pause to savor every scream. But I don't have time, so—"

He yanked his sword out, and a spray of blood went with it as Zane fell to the ground, seizing a bit before lying still.

Sam looked at his sword, then pulled a dark cloth from inside his tunic and wiped the blade down, then spun it in a fancy motion and put it back in his sheath.

I just stood there, splattered with blood, wondering what just happened.

"What... what did you...? Why...?" I couldn't find words for anything. I had no idea how things had gone so sideways. When I saw violence, it was always targeted at me.

"It's nothing personal," Sam said. "I just hate rapists." He held up the book, open to a page with red underlines. "And attempting to rape a prisoner is against the precepts, even in this backwards 'haven.' So we're good."

"Good?" I yelled. "Good? He... Oh gods, you shish-kebab-ed his face!"

Sam turned to me in consternation, folding his arms over his impressive chest, his sword swinging at his side.

Despite the horror of what had just happened, he was completely unaffected by it.

"I can't believe you're angry at me for saving you," he said, rolling his eyes. "Anyway, please be quiet because I have some studying to do before my friends show up in the morning."

I heard a gasping, wet, choking noise from Zane, which instantly panicked me, sending me back onto my cot.

Sam looked over, bored, as Zane went quiet again.

"Agonal breathing," Sam said. "Just a reflex."

"You... you killed him," I said.

"I told you. Rape is against the precepts." He grinned. "I apply punishment."

He looked supremely pleased with himself.

"But you can just... just murder someone?"

He nodded. "Absolutely. I do it all the time. Now, as I said, please stop bothering me. I really am trying to work something out that might suit both of us."

I cringed. I couldn't imagine anything that could work for both of us. This cruel man who felt nothing even when dealing out incredible pain would be ending my life.

What would work for us?

I looked at Zane, his bloody body and mutilated

face, then back at Sam, calmly reading behind the desk again. "Can you at least... move him?" I begged.

Sam sighed, rolling his eyes like he was extremely put upon, but he stood, walked over to Zane, and dragged him by the leg out of the cell, leaving a trail of blood behind him.

He dumped Zane somewhere outside the building, then came back with the keys and locked my cell again.

"What about his family?" I asked.

"Not my concern," Sam said. "They let him be like this. They should know the consequences of having a rapist for a son."

"And if they don't?"

He shrugged. "No one goes against the celestials. Well, maybe slayers. But we're not likely to meet one of those here."

"Slayers?"

He sat back at the desk. "I told you I'm working on something. Let me focus. I won't ask you again."

So I did, scooping my ruined dress off the floor to cover myself.

He sighed, then grabbed a blanket off a nearby chair and tossed it over to me. "At least cover yourself. It's distracting."

"Sorry for being a distraction," I muttered, pulling the blanket over me.

But as it warmed me, and the shock of what Zane had almost done began to fade, I realized I truly was safe.

Someone had finally helped me.

I glanced at Sam, wondering just who this crazy angel was and whether he would truly kill me in the morning.

8

"So that's her?"

An unfamiliar voice jolted me out of my light slumber, and I sat up to see there were now four people in the jail.

The window showed it was very early in the morning, and the horizon was an eerie gradient of light-to-dark blue, as the sun hadn't yet risen fully.

I tried to be subtle as I rolled over to stare at them.

"She's bloody," an angel with ash-blond hair that looked nearly gray said with a sneer, walking over to the cell. His light-brown eyes flashed at me. "Why is there blood everywhere?"

"Sam was here all night," a higher, smooth voice said as a tall man with very delicate features and soft black hair curling around his face to about his collar came forward. He was a few inches shorter than Sam but still very tall. His irises were silver-blue. "That's the only explanation needed."

Unlike Sam, this man wore armor, a shimmering, lightweight plate of some kind, that had shimmering links of chain mail at the joints and a tunic over the top. He looked like a crusader.

He cocked his head at me. "You're just lucky that blood isn't yours."

"He does like killing things," I muttered back at him, earning a confused look.

"She talks to us like normal," the black-haired one said, turning to his compatriots. "She isn't afraid at all."

The last figure was the one I'd seen with Sam the day of the ceremony. Os. He had gorgeous dark skin, elegant features, and beautiful lilac eyes. His purple hair was tied into a loose ponytail and hung down his shoulder. Os, the black-haired angel, and the blond angel all wore the same light plate armor in various iridescent shades.

I was a little confused by it since they'd been in robes when I last saw them.

Os stood in front of the others and rested his hands lightly, almost delicately, on the bars.

"She isn't afraid of much, this one. Sam and I met

her yesterday before the ceremony, when she was mouthing off to an entire group of alphas and betas."

I just glared at him, unsure of what else to say.

I *wasn't* afraid of them. I didn't really know why. I supposed that because I didn't know them, there was no way they could hurt me the way I'd been hurt my whole life by people I loved.

When you loved someone, it hurt so much worse when they attacked you.

"I'm not here to hurt you," he said.

"That's Helios," the black-haired one said. "Our diplomat."

"Helios? Why?"

"It's a codename," Os said. "Call me Os, though. Helios is too long."

"She won't be calling us anything," the dark-blond angel said. "She'll be dying."

I heard a *tsk* from Os.

"Gabe, stop," the black-haired one said. "There's no need to taunt her."

"I don't need your help with etiquette, Mor."

Mor shrugged and went behind the desk to bother Sam, poking him in the shoulder and seeming to tease him about something quietly, while Os and Gabe moved in front of my cell, blocking my view.

They couldn't have seemed more different. Os with his warm smile and Gabe with his severe frown.

The only thing they had in common was being good-looking and masculine, along with their outfits.

Os was slightly shorter than Mor. They still all towered above me. Probably all six feet or over.

Os gave me a sunny smile. "I'm sorry about Sam," he said carefully. "For whatever he did to put blood there."

"No need," I said bluntly. "He saved me."

Gabe's eyes narrowed. "There's no need to intervene. It's forbidden—"

Sam held up the pack book of precepts. "What I did was perfectly legal."

Os shrugged at Gabe like he should have known better.

Sam stood, walking over and shouldering them both rudely out of the way to stand in front of my cage himself.

Gabe looked ready to kill Sam, but he allowed Os to pull him back.

Sam put his hands on his hips, and I'd never seen him look more handsome. I hated that I had to die at this beautiful man's hands.

"I'm going to keep her."

"What?" Os turned to face him as Gabe and Mor gasped in shock.

"I've looked at the by-laws. It's perfectly legal." He held up the book. "The stupid idiots in this pack decided that any alpha can claim any omega. An angel, like me, is higher than any pack alpha. I can claim her."

I wanted to yell at them that I would never be claimed, but for once, I kept my mouth shut.

I'd seen what it was like on the end of Sam's sword. I had no desire to experience it if it could be avoided.

What did he mean by "keep me," though?

"She's demonic," Gabe said, his voice hard as concrete as he faced off with Sam. They were each other's equal in height and stubbornness, jaws jutting as they squared off. "She must be destroyed."

"I'm allowed a pet."

"I'm sorry, what?" I asked, utterly confused.

"Don't interrupt, human," Os said. "Sam's trying to help you."

"No, I'm not," Sam said flatly. "But she'd make a good pet. I'm keeping her."

Mor put his hands on his hips, glancing between his companions. "There is a pet clause in our contract."

"You can't take a human pet," Gabe said, nearly spitting with rage. He wasn't nearly as handsome when he was angry.

"She's not a human," Sam said. "She's a wolf. A dog." He shrugged nonchalantly. "So I'm taking her as a pet."

"You're allowed..." Gabe pinched his nose. "As an archangel, you're allowed a companion animal. It's true. Things can be lonely, but—" He looked over at me. "That's not an animal."

"You're right. It's not," Sam said, folding his arms. "It's a demon. A useful one."

"How so?" Gabe said, eyeing the collar around my neck for some reason. "You said she isn't the one we're looking for."

Sam shook his head. "She's not, but she can help us root out other demons. She's a succubus. She'll attract them. Make them easier to find among the congregations."

"What do you mean?"

"Demons will be drawn to her," Sam said. "Then we can find them easier. You know any demon with any significant power is good at hiding it."

"You said she was a common kind," Gabe said. "The brimstone only turned yellow. That means a common demon."

Sam nodded. "That's why she'll make a good pet. Not dangerous enough to be a threat, but good demon bait. Trust me, we can use her."

Gabe frowned. "I don't trust you. But if it were anyone but you, I'd think you were only being soft on her." He smiled cruelly. "Well, being tied to you is an even worse punishment than death. So she's to go on your rounds with you?"

"Yes," Sam said. "And if I can't train her to meet my needs, I'll find another pet."

Mor walked over to Gabe and whispered in his ear, though I could hear him. "Anything that keeps Sam a bit saner isn't a bad thing."

Gabe considered that for a moment, clearly the leader. "I still don't like it."

Os stood up. "I can go with them."

"No," Gabe said shortly.

Mor laughed. "Not possible. Without you, Gabe will be making mortals lose their beliefs in the gods wherever he goes."

Sam stood. "It's my decision. You can't gainsay me."

"I'm the leader here," Gabe snarled. "You came in out of nowhere, and we're just supposed to accept you because—"

"You know damn well why you have to accept me," Sam said, stepping closer, getting nose to nose with Gabe as the blond angel backed up. "Because I have the blood of a celestial from the ninth realm, and yours is only from the fifth." Sam glared at all of them. "None of you can challenge me."

He stood then, walking out of the jail with a

purposeful stride, without even so much as a "see you later."

"He's got a point," Os said to the others. "None of us can kill him, regardless, because his power is higher, and his father is—"

"I know who his father is," Gabe snapped, looking over at me. "You better not get us in trouble, girl. Will you behave?"

I stared at him for a second, then turned back to the wall, uninterested in this farce until Sam got back and explained what he meant by keeping me as a pet.

"That means no," Mor said with a laugh. "I like her. She's got spirit. She'll make a good pet for Sam."

"Are we really just going to allow this?" Os asked. "A person as a pet?"

"What else can we do?" Mor asked. "What Sam wants, Sam gets. I can't even remember the last thing he wanted other than to bloodily kill things. We should give this to him."

"Is anyone going to even ask what I want?" I yelled at them, rolling over again. "I'm the one most affected by this."

Gabe sneered as he walked over to me. "You're just a worthless sinner who can't even obey the gods. You deserve death, and—"

"That's my pet," Sam said, pushing the door back

open as he entered again. "I wouldn't speak to her like that if I were you." His words were calm, but the ice in his eyes promised death.

I screwed up my brows. The last thing I needed was this executioner angel defending me. I'd seen him shish-kebab Zane. The guy wasn't normal. At all.

Gabe looked like he wanted to make something of it but stepped back. "As you wish, Samael. But we'll be keeping watch. And when we meet up with you again, I expect a report on her training."

"Training?" I asked.

Gabe ignored me. "If she truly isn't serving us, and if I hear about anything weird that might hurt our reputation with the locals, I'll find a way to kill you myself."

"You and what army?" Sam retorted. Then he turned back to me, his brown eyes gleaming with gold at the centers. "So what'll it be, pet?"

"She has to wear that suppression collar at all times," Gabe said.

"Which one?" Sam asked.

"The one suppressing her demon. You can take it off if you're in need of her powers, but when this is over, when we've found... what we need to find, you will have to kill her, as you would any demon."

Sam just nodded.

So much for helping me.

And what was a succubus? I wasn't very familiar with demons and hadn't heard of that type.

"You can take off the wolf collar," Gabe said. "When you're in certain territories, it might be best if she had a lupine appearance."

Sam nodded.

"And leash her," Gabe said meanly.

Sam nodded again. "She'll be a proper pet."

"Only Sam would think to do this," Mor said, shaking his head. "But all right. We must get to the pack bordering the fae wilds soon. I have to get out of this stupid armor."

Os nodded. "I hate when they make us dress up."

I had no idea what to say to that, so I just listened as they got together in a cluster to discuss a few more things, then started to head out.

"Good luck with the pack leaders," Gabe said to Sam. "How are you going to explain this?"

"I'll just tell them I'll be punishing this unruly omega much worse than death while she's with me." He grinned. "That should satisfy their bloodthirst."

The angels nodded and left, and the jail only held Sam and me.

"What's a succubus? What do you mean I'm yellow and common?"

He gestured to my collar. "You can't see it, but your

collar is special, used only by celestials to detect certain types of demons. It's our job to remove demons from celestially blessed communities, after all. The cabochon is made of brimstone, and it turns colors based on exposure to demonic power."

"And mine is yellow, so I'm a succubus?"

"No," he said.

"What? But you said—"

"I don't answer to anyone," he said. "So do you accept my offer?"

"Can I say no?" I asked.

"Sure," he said. "I'm a firm believer in personal freedom. If you'd prefer to die, my sword would be happy to feed on your energy..."

"It feeds on—"

"Or... you could come with me and see some new places and maybe learn some things about yourself."

"I'm not going to be your sex slave," I said. "You'd have to kill me first."

He raised an eyebrow. "You'd be the first begging me *not* to fuck you, but sure. I told you. I hate rapists. You might change your mind—"

"I'm not fucking a celestial."

His eyes got a wicked glint, as if he knew something I didn't, but his lips simply curved up in the slightest of smiles. "Your answer?"

"What did he mean by leash?"

"A magical tether," he said. "I can set the length. The magic of the gods works through will, and mine is incredibly strong. I will make sure you can't escape me or go very far from my side."

"How will I sleep? Pee?"

He folded his arms, flexing impressive biceps. "I think all you should be asking is whether you want to be dead or not."

I sucked in a huge breath and let it out in a sigh. "You're going to kill me at the end anyway. Why should I help you?"

He stepped closer to the bars of my cell, and I did as well. He reached up to brush my cheek with the back of his hand, then pulled back abruptly.

"I offer you only one thing, the same thing I'm searching for."

"And that is?"

"Vengeance," he said, standing so close I could smell the spicy scent of incense I'd noticed when I kissed him.

Even as I hated him for offering me only a leash, I couldn't resist a certain inexorable pull toward him.

My body wanted him, even if my heart and mind knew better.

He said he wouldn't rape me. Surely, he had options, but that didn't stop most rapists.

But he was right. I did want revenge. I wanted redemption.

And maybe I could escape him, find somewhere I belonged, and not even get killed in the end.

Or maybe I could win him over... find his soft side.

I remembered his cruel mocking of Zane as Zane died horribly and quickly dropped any hope of this monster having a soft side at all.

In all likelihood, he was hiding something, and he was using me.

But what choice did I really have?

"I need time to think," I said.

"You don't have it. I just looked outside. The sun will rise soon, and the pack will start arriving for the execution. We need to be out before then."

"But you told Gabe you'd smooth things over," I said.

He shook his head. "I'll leave a note. No one here would dare question celestials. But the alpha here hates your guts. I don't want to have to fight and kill him in front of the pack. It wouldn't be good for people's perception of celestials."

"You don't really act like an angel," I said quietly. "Not like the others at all."

"Thank you," he retorted, walking over to the desk to pick up the ring of keys.

"So, omega, what will it be?"

"My name's Cleo."

"Cleo, my pet, what will it be?"

I looked down at the floor and then up into Sam's eyes.

His looks, the feeling of power around him, everything bespoke angel. But those eyes, the way they burned, made me feel like I was facing a demon after all.

But the whole world was out there waiting, and even if all I did was get to see it and have my vengeance before I died, then that would still be more life than I had in the morning.

"I'll do it," I said.

Sam nodded, putting the key in the lock and turning it. "Good choice, pet."

9

As I walked out of the jail behind Sam, I still couldn't believe this was happening.

I'd been rescued, sort of.

By the bad boy of the celestials.

I'd also learned a bit about him in the process.

He was from the ninth celestial realm, which was the highest in the sky realms.

And the other angels couldn't go against what he said.

Which meant I was probably totally at his mercy, as a mortal and his pet.

But he took off my wolf-restraining collar immediately, which I appreciated.

"Which direction is your house?" he asked, as morning light beamed over the mountains.

"Why?"

"We need to get your things. Some clothing, anything important to you," he said.

Well, that was oddly thoughtful for a psychopath.

I led him to my house and, when I got there, lost my nerve just before I opened the door.

"What do you need?" he asked. "I'll go in and get it. If I see your parents, I'll explain. They're probably upset over this whole business."

"No," I said. "I guarantee they aren't. They've always hated me."

He gave me a long, cool look, then nodded and opened the door to the house without even knocking.

"All I own are my books," I said. "But we probably can't bring them. I need some clothes, if we don't have somewhere to stop for more."

"I can procure clothes for my pet," Sam said. "I'm not a complete incompetent. I can buy you books as well."

"My books are special to me," I said. "You asked what I wanted."

He pursed his lips and gave me another extended stare, then nodded. "I'll be right back."

Apparently, my parents slept like the dead because he was out and shutting the door behind him without any fussing.

He walked over to me, putting a small black fabric

bag in his pocket and handing me a pair of jeans and a tee shirt he'd grabbed.

"Where are my—"

He pulled out the small sack again. "It's enchanted so that anything I put in it is stored in the void and thus takes up no room here. Your books and things are inside. I'll carry it for now."

My eyes were wide as he tucked the little sack back into his tunic. I'd never heard of such magic.

"Did you want to say good-bye to your parents?" Sam asked.

I shook my head. "They had stones in their hands last I saw them... before they started running."

He gave me a sadistic grin. "Did you hit them at least? Once you sent rocks flying?"

"How did you know that's what happened?"

"I guessed," he said cryptically, walking toward the wheat field where I'd tried to escape before.

"Look, I don't get any of what is happening. You kissed me in the stocks, and you brutally murdered Zane. Why should I trust you?"

He sent me an impatient look over his shoulder, then shook his head. "You ask the most idiotic questions."

I gasped. "That's so rude!"

"I never said you should trust me. Only that death

was your other option. Now be quiet while I decide what we're doing next."

I muttered to myself, feeling my wolf rising within me beneath the surface. Maybe I could still run from this guy.

"I have an execution not far from here. In a reserve at the base of the mountains to the west." He put his hands on his hips. "Put on those clothes. I think we'll have to fly."

"I can fly?" I looked down at the clothes, then the wheat field we were in the midst of. "Where am I supposed to change?"

"Here," he said. "It's the best I can do in terms of privacy."

"Look away."

To my surprise, he did.

I quickly changed, then balled up the bloody dress and tossed it to the side.

He grinned, looking down at my tee, which was black and read: *Warning: Possessed.*

I'd bought it as a joke at the thrift store in my extra rebellious days.

I supposed it was true now. And the jerk had picked it on purpose to remind me of that fact. I wasn't going to give him the satisfaction.

I looked at the wheat field ahead of me, then felt my

wolf rise, and I wondered once again if I couldn't just take off on him.

After all, he planned to use me and then kill me when all of this was done. I couldn't be won over by him simply bringing my books.

"Now, as to flying—"

In an instant, I felt my wolf take over, not liking this guy at all, and before I knew it, I was sprouting fur, bones popping, and running on all fours as familiar smells assaulted my nose.

I vaulted forward as fast as I could, dodging side to side in case Sam was chasing me. But to my surprise, I didn't even hear his footsteps behind me, as though he wasn't even moving.

His loss.

But just as I reached the edge of the wheat field, my entire body stopped abruptly, jerked back as if every cell was commanded to stop at once.

It hurt, like reaching the end of a leash, but instead of a pull on my neck, it was all over my entire body.

I fell immediately, losing my footing, and stayed right where I was, my wolf wary of facing that punishment again.

What had even happened?

"Idiot wolf," Sam said, striding over to me, looking

pissed. He wore a white tee shirt and jeans instead of the badass chain ensemble he wore at the jail.

That must have been his executioner apparel, and he'd changed in the seconds while I'd run.

"What was your plan even?" he asked, putting his large hands on his trim hips and staring down at me like I was the world's biggest idiot. "If you got past me, just exactly how long would you last out there, an omega wolf with a collared demon inside her?" He walked over to me and looked down imperiously.

I let out a groan and shifted back into my human form as I rolled onto my back to stare at the early-morning sky.

I was exhausted.

"And we have to go find another pack where you need to do an execution?" I asked.

He cocked his head, dark eyes narrowed. "At this point, I'm wondering if I should take you at all." His eyes moved out to the mountains on the horizon. "The clan we're visiting is at the base of that hill. Their territory extends into the mountain. They have an abomination they need me to deal with."

"Abomination?" I asked breathlessly, still trying to distract from the fact that I'd just tried to escape.

"Something that shouldn't exist but isn't exactly a

demon," he said. "Well, no help for it. We don't have time to walk."

His wings extended, huge and black, out of nowhere, casting a shadow over me as he shook them out.

"Where do you put those?"

He raised an eyebrow. "I'm a god. I manipulate matter. Hiding my wings is easy."

He flapped a couple times, lifting into the air, and looked down at me from about ten feet up.

Stupidly sexy angel, golden glints in his hair catching the morning light and his perfect skin beaming.

His tattoos were showing again, giving him that badass look that drove me crazy.

I wanted to turn away before he caught me staring, but I also had no idea how this was going to work.

I raised my hands. "So, what, are you going to carry me?"

His lips curved up on one side meanly, and he took off, straight up into the air. At about fifty feet up, he began flying forward.

So he was leaving me? "Wai—"

I yelped as my body flew forward, dragged by an invisible force, my feet dragging over the grass beneath. I stared up at Sam, who was flying forward, a slight smile on his face.

So he was just going to drag me?

I moved my limbs around, but nothing mattered. I was moving in tandem with him, and there was nothing I could do about it.

I hadn't even seen him set the tether.

Gods were scary.

"Sam!" I yelled. "You're going to ruin my shoes!" The grass was scraping over my sneakers as I tried to dig into the ground. "Go up!"

He said nothing, just kept flying forward, and ahead, I saw a giant boulder in the field, rapidly approaching.

It was a bit like being beneath a giant parasail, strapped in and trapped into going where it went.

And I was about to become a pancake if I hit that rock.

"Pull up, pull up, pull up!" I screamed, covering my face as the rock came close. My attempts to dig my feet in did nothing.

At the very last second, when I was sure it would be too late, Sam must have flown up because I was jerked up and over the rock just in time to not die.

My heart was pounding so hard I thought I might be having a heart attack. Now ten feet off the ground and still tethered to Sam, I glared up at him.

I heard a laugh.

That sadist.

Then he took off even higher, and I watched my feet lift off the ground as if my entire body were attached to a kite that was dragging it.

Oh gods, what a time to realize I hated heights.

Or maybe I just hated being dragged through space with no control by a psychopathic angel who kebab-ed alphas and kept shifters as pets.

Was I his first?

I tried not to look at the ground, which was far beneath me now, as Sam moved up into the clouds.

I tried to relax, putting my hands out like I was a superhero from a human TV show.

I looked up at Sam, but he wasn't watching me, or laughing, for once. He was simply focused with deadly stillness on something ahead of us I couldn't see yet.

His vision must have been amazing.

Slowly, we began to lower again as the sun came up and beamed over the world, lighting the grass with emerald green as we approached a tall wall of trees at the base of the mountain.

Sam got lower, lower, and touched down gently, letting me get my feet for a second before he came down himself.

I put my hands on my knees, slumping forward and gasping to catch my breath.

"Never... do that again," I said breathlessly. "I could have... died."

"Nonsense," Sam said, shaking his wings and folding them back in until they were curved around him like an arching cape. "Why would I take a pet just to kill it? That wouldn't make sense."

He brushed off his arms, flexed, cracked his neck, and put a hand to his chin. "I'm trying to remember what the cougars think of the celestials."

"Cougars?" I asked.

"Any big cats in the area would be here also, but the alphas are cougars."

I thought for a moment. "I mean... robes are always good."

He snapped. "Thank you. Robes." In an instant, black robes covered his body with an ornate silver chain around the middle as a belt. On his feet were simple black boots.

He started toward the tree line. "The community is hidden behind these trees. Come on."

I slumped toward him, my body feeling tight and sore from the effort of tensing for so long and being dragged with him.

"Can't you at least, like, maybe carry me next time?" I asked.

Sam stopped, turned to me with his brows furrowed,

and sighed. "I don't need you getting ideas of romance like women do when carried like that." His mouth quirked up. "Then again, I didn't know you wanted to be in my arms so much. I'll keep it in mind."

He started toward the tree line again, and I stared at him, mouth agape.

He had to be kidding.

My hands tightened into fists as I stomped after him. "I don't want to be in your arms. I just don't want to be flung through the air like I'm being catapulted."

"At least you're not dead," he retorted.

"I almost was, thanks to that rock, asshole!"

He chuckled again. "I had plenty of time. I told you. I'm not going to just take a pet to let it die." He exhaled. "Now shift into your wolf form before we go into this village."

I shook my head. "No way. The cougars are our enemies. We fight like literal cats and dogs. Bad idea." I'd been warned since a long time ago to avoid any cougar I saw near our territory and to call village elders to deal with it.

We just didn't get along on an elemental level, despite sharing a belief in and reliance on the celestials.

"Fine," he said. "They'll still smell wolf on you, so stick close." He grinned. "Very close."

"I'd rather be eaten by a cougar," I muttered.

"Your choice," he said simply.

I would never get used to this angel.

As we reached the trees, I looked up at the towering blue-green pines that stretched at least forty feet high.

Sam led the way between two of them, and I gasped at the scene that opened up before me.

There was a canopy of treehouses supported by huge oaks that had to be extremely old. Beneath them, small cabins stood on the ground in small groups, made of rough-hewn dark-brown wood.

The fancier houses were definitely in the trees. Which made sense. Cougars liked high places.

"Interesting place," Sam said. "I like it."

He walked forward into a clearing of dirt littered with pine needles and let his wings unfurl again.

"There must not be very many of them," I said.

"Some of them live in the wilds, in the mountains," Sam said. "I just need to find the leader. They don't form a pack exactly—"

I heard a slight rustling and looked up to see a giant cougar winding his way downward, delicately treading over tree branches and landing on the ground in front of us, staring with beautiful amber eyes.

"The others are hiding," it said from fanged lips.

"I am a celestial," Sam said, as if the wings didn't give it away. "Here for the abomination."

"The execution," the cougar said. "Come with me."

The cougar padded across the clearing to a small shack with a chain link fence around it. "In there." Then the cougar moved back, slinking toward the treehouses again. "Do as you must."

The cougar then slipped into the shadows and was gone.

"Well, that was quite a welcome," I said sarcastically.

Sam sent me a glare. "Whatever this is, they don't want anything to do with it."

"They don't seem fond of celestials either," I said.

Sam shrugged. "Not everyone sucks celestial asshole as much as the wolves. Most of them put up with us as a necessary evil and stay out of our way as much as possible." He put out a hand, motioning for me to stay back. "Whatever this thing is, the cougars fear it."

"I can—"

"Until you're further trained, you're of no use to me," he retorted, cutting me off. "After this execution, I'll have time to explain more. Stay put."

I looked at the shack just as a low moan reached us. I heard something brushing the walls of it, rustling like... feathers?

Then a roar shook the entire clearing, making needles fall from the trees.

Whatever was in that shack, it was giant, and it was furious.

Sam crept closer and put a hand to his hip, where his sheath appeared out of nowhere. Smoothly, in one motion, he drew the katana he'd used to kill Zane.

It was shiny and clean, as if it had never killed anyone.

Sam put a finger to his perfect lips, pinned me with a look, and then moved in front of the doors and yanked them both open.

10

Sam went inside, and another huge roar shook the clearing, making more pine needles fall.

No one came out of the treehouses. No one wanted to see Sam put this thing to death.

What kind of creature could it be to be called an abomination and cause these powerful shifters so much fear?

Despite Sam's warning to stay back, I crept around in front of the doors and peeked through the crack by the hinges, trying to see what was inside.

There was a huge animal with a golden pelt, a leonine body... and wings? Giant white wings lashing out against the sides of the shack.

I heard the jingle of chains and saw what was keeping this animal from tearing all of this down. His paws were chained. His head was that of a lion, matching his body, and his wings... looked like celestial wings.

"A griffin," I murmured. "I thought they were a myth."

Sam looked over at me and frowned, a twitch in his jaw the only sign he was super pissed at me for disobeying. "Get back, pet."

I ignored him, coming closer to the giant chained beast as its wings flapped again, trapped against the low ceiling and walls.

The creature's eyes were deep, clear blue and solemn and angry at the same time.

Sam moved forward, reaching out a hand, and the griffin snapped at him, showing off giant white fangs and massive teeth.

Sam scowled, made a closing motion with his hands, and the griffin's mouth snapped shut as if held by invisible chains.

So this was the power of the ninth realm. If he simply wanted it to be, it was so.

I envied him.

"Calm down, boy," Sam said. "I'm not going to hurt you."

The huge animal moved nervously, looking like it would have lashed out again if it could.

"I need to go talk to the elders," Sam said, making a motion as if to say the griffin could open its mouth again. "This isn't an abomination."

"It has wings," I said. "Doesn't that mean you have to kill it?"

Human planes had long ago stopped working. Celestials ruled the skies, and they jealously guarded their kingdoms and palaces.

Even in the wolf world, we knew that any creature born with wings would have to be reported.

Sam thought for a long moment. Then he turned on his heel and left the shack, his footsteps echoing on the soft dirt ground outside.

I heard his wings flapping, probably taking him up into the trees. Apparently, he didn't think I needed any more explanation than that.

I walked forward, toward the huge animal, admiring his golden-brown pelt. "Well, aren't you beautiful?"

I reached out a hand to touch his wings, unable to stop myself. When he didn't move away, I put my hand on his huge shoulder, stroking the fur there.

"If it helps, he was supposed to kill me too, and he didn't," I said, stroking the griffin's fur, which was soft, thick, and velvety. "So he might not kill you."

The griffin's blue eyes studied me, intrigued.

In an instant, the fur beneath my hand vanished,

and the air blurred around him. I moved back as I saw a man sitting on the ground in front of me, wearing only blue boxers. His chains lay on the floor, abandoned now that he'd shifted out of his much larger griffin form.

He was tall, probably six-six, and handsome in a boyish, jock kind of way.

He had a five o'clock shadow outlining a powerful jaw and broad shoulders tapering to long, perfect abs.

He stood, walking toward me, as I backed up against the wall of the shack. I could shift right now, but what was the point?

He put a hand on either side of me, trapping me against the wall, and he leaned in to inhale my scent.

He smelled like clean mountain air and pine trees in winter.

Feeling like I was being examined by a giant cat, I sat back and let him. His eyes moved to my collar and narrowed in confusion.

Then he stepped back and rubbed the back of his head. "I'm Griffin," he said.

"You are a griffin, or your name is Griffin?"

"I have been Griffin since I was born," he said simply. He leaned in to sniff me again. "Dog? Wolf?" He breathed in deeper, and his eyes went dark. "Demon." His hand moved to my throat, though he didn't squeeze yet. "Does the celestial know?" He shook his head. "He looks like a demon himself. Anyway, I'm getting out of here. I expected someone else to come, and that's why I waited. But I'm not letting that guy kill me. Not before..." He trailed off, looking away. "Anyway, I don't want to hurt you, so just be quiet and—"

I sucked in a breath to yell for Sam, unsure what this creature wanted from me.

"Shh." He closed his hand tighter, choking off my breath so I couldn't make a sound. "I told you I don't want to hurt you, and—"

The doors to the shack swung open again, and Sam stood there in all his fallen angel glory. Except he wasn't fallen at all. He was in charge.

Griffin looked at him, then continued to press my neck.

"Go ahead and do it," Sam said coolly, though I could hear a razor-sharp tone in his voice. "Show me who you are. So I don't have to hesitate when I kill you."

Griffin stepped back, his face wary.

"Why did you stay here chained if you could shift to escape at any moment?" Sam asked, eyeing the chains.

"I agreed to this," Griffin said. "None of us wanted this, but no one wanted to displease the celestials." He sucked in a breath. "But I can't die. So I planned to escape. That way my community gets credit for giving me up, but I don't have to die."

Sam folded his arms and paced around Griffin, who seemed to inherently understand the power emanating from the celestial. "There is no rule about executing creatures with wings. Merely reporting them."

"I know what happens to creatures who are reported," Griffin said. "Regardless, I would never be at home here. I make everyone nervous."

"Wings do that," Sam said, walking around Griffin in a slow circle still. His boots thudded on the coarse wooden floor. "Who are your parents?"

"I do not know," Griffin said. "I was adopted."

"That's for fucking sure," Sam muttered. He turned to look at me, then the doorway. "I don't need this."

"He wasn't going to hurt me," I said. "He was trying to protect his friends. He can sense I'm—that I have a demon in me."

Sam whipped around to look at him. "Can you? Well, that's useful."

I didn't know what to say. I liked this guy, despite his threat to me. I also related to him having never fit in where he was born.

But it seemed his people were sad about his execution, rather than gleeful like mine were.

"What do you sense about me?" Sam asked, standing before him with his hands on his hips.

Griffin inhaled the air deeply, and his blue eyes flashed.

"Angel," he said simply.

"Good," Sam said firmly. "Your winged form, it can fly?"

Griffin nodded.

"I need a mount for my pet," he said solemnly. "Can you do that?"

Griffin blinked as if he had no idea what Sam was offering. He ran a hand through his blond hair and looked down at the chains. "You can spare my life?"

"I can do whatever I want." Sam tapped his boot on the ground impatiently. "But if you want to die, by all means, let us proceed with the execution."

I was starting to think Sam wasn't such a bad guy after all.

"I'll be collaring you," Sam said. "Just in case. You aren't a griffin. Not exactly. Until I can determine what, I need to make sure any excess power is stifled. You will be able to shift and keep your strength. What do you say?"

I wanted to tell Griffin that making any deal with Sam was kind of a devil's bargain, but I understood the desire to not die.

But a mount? Did that mean I would be riding a griffin?

"Not a problem," Griffin said. "I give the kids rides all the time."

"I'm not a kid," I muttered, my hands clenching into fists.

"You're small," Griffin said simply, staring down at me. "Bite-size."

"Sorry I'm not huge like you guys," I said. Compared to these guys, I was barely taller than average.

"We need to go," Sam said. "The longer we stay, the more they'll question me not killing you. We need to be decisive."

"What are you going to tell them?" Griffin asked. "My family—"

"I'll tell them you're no longer their concern and currently the property of celestials."

"I'm no one's property," Griffin said, blue eyes flashing.

Sam shrugged, reaching for his katana as his sheath appeared at his side. "Your funeral."

"Wait," I said, stepping forward. "Sam, you can't just keep saying you own people."

"Yes, I can," Sam said stubbornly. "I just did."

"Griffin, he isn't as bad as he seems," I said, causing Sam to glare at me as though I'd just insulted him. "He won't treat you... like property."

"How long have you been with him?" Griffin asked.

"Uh... one day," I said.

Griffin laughed, a slightly mocking edge to his tone. "Then you have no idea what he's capable of."

"Probably not," I admitted. "But what choice does either of us have?"

Griffin looked at the ceiling, frustrated, his huge muscles flexing. "I suppose you're right."

"Your animal is so beautiful," I said, softening my tone. "It would be a sin for anything to happen to it. Or you. I can already tell you're a good person."

Griffin laughed. "That obvious? Well, I am." He put his hands on his hips and stared at Sam. "I'll do it. For her." He waved a hand at me. "I don't like her being alone with you."

Sam's lip curled in a sneer. "Like I would get ideas about some human-dog hybrid."

His words stung me to my core, and Griffin looked over at me, shocked.

Sam turned on his heel and left the shack, pine needles crunching under his feet. "We need to leave."

Griffin's eyes watched me with apologetic softness as we walked out into the clearing.

"Wait," Sam said, holding out his hand and staring at it. In a twinkling of light, a collar appeared, and Sam held it out to Griffin. "Put this on."

Griffin fastened it around his neck. "What does it do again?"

"Binds any demons within you."

Griffin reared back. "There are no demons in me. I would never—"

"Put it on, then," Sam said simply.

Griffin clasped it around his neck, then shifted. I saw Sam closing his eyes, murmuring quiet words.

Then he opened his eyes and gazed upon Griffin's winged lion form.

"I've created a magical tether. If you get more than fifty feet from me, your very cells will stop where they are. Understand?"

Griffin's eyes widened, but he nodded, his mane bouncing in the warm morning air.

"Get on," Sam told me, unfurling his wings, which shone like glossy obsidian in the bright sunlight that filtered through the trees around us.

I walked to Griffin, unsure about all of this. After all, he was a person. I didn't know if this was treating him like an animal, and—

Before I could hesitate more, I felt Sam's strong hands reach around my waist and lift me easily onto Griffin, who was so tall I was still about six feet off the ground.

I wrapped my hands in the fur, which was so soft and silky I could have lain down and fallen asleep on it.

"Come on," Sam said, lifting into the air, his giant wings making whooshing noises, sending pine needles and dust everywhere. "We still have a long way to go."

11

Griffin stretched out his huge wings and beat the air a few times to test them. Then he leaped forward into the air, and his wings caught him, lifting us upward, toward the sky.

We rose and rose above the tree line and up over the mountains, so beautiful and pristine beneath us.

I took a moment to look back over my shoulder and saw cougars far below, watching us leaving.

I looked farther back and saw the rolling green hills and yellow wheat fields of several wolf havens.

Then I turned forward and saw only blue sky and then the veil, a huge wall of purple smoke blocking everything in front of it.

"Have you seen beyond the veil?" Sam called back to us.

"No," Griffin and I said simultaneously. Griffin flew so smoothly that I barely had to hold on to feel safe. His back was so wide, so soft.

"Well, try not to freak out," Sam yelled. "It might not be the way it was described to you."

I sucked in a breath as we flew higher, the angry purple clouds showing hints of pink and gray as they rumbled in front of us, moving like shifting sands.

I'd been told the mid-realm was a disaster. A war-torn, mostly abandoned conglomeration of cities ruined by human greed and climate change. I'd been told that there was only a bit of inhabited land and that most places were overrun by supernaturals much worse than shifters.

It was a dangerous, lawless, dirty and polluted place, and anyone who escaped there and made it through the veil was sure to wish they were dead.

That was if they weren't tortured to death by demons first.

I dug into Griffin's fur and buried my face against him as we hit the cool wall of clouds that made up the veil. The air felt silky but charged.

We flew for several seconds in pure gray mist and then broke out into the open air again. Holding on tight to Griffin, I chanced a look down.

And frowned.

It didn't look much different here than it did before the veil.

Large swaths of green grass and wildflower-covered hills stretched beneath me, with a little stream running between them.

In the distance was a village with buildings much like the ones I'd grown up around.

I widened my perspective, looking out farther, no veil to limit my view.

I made out cities far in the distance with rising, rotted skyscrapers and industrial areas. I saw lakes and rivers and forests filled with trees.

It didn't look utterly uninhabitable or demon-infested. Sure, I couldn't see that far, but it seemed not too different from the shifter lands.

Were these truly the fae barrens? Did those forests hide the fae wilds?

Mountains rose behind the large industrial area, hiding what was behind it. I was sure I was only seeing part of the mid-realm, but it was so thrilling to see so much more than I ever had.

I gripped Griffin's fur harder, wondering if I would pass out.

I thought there would be only barren, burned land and clouds of smoke with wandering demons.

This world was beautiful and open, and I wanted to explore every minute of it.

"Don't misunderstand," Sam called back to us. "This is the nicest part of the mid-realm. After this, it does get darker. But whatever you've been told is an exaggeration. The celestials need to keep the shifters in line and supplying them with power, after all."

"With power?" I murmured to myself. None of this made any sense.

Suddenly, I just felt very tired. The sense of dread I felt going through the veil had left me, and the confusion of everything just made it too hard to think.

Not to mention, I'd been stoned, attacked in the jail, and dragged over here without even a night's sleep.

My body was collapsing from pure exhaustion, and I fell forward on Griffin, feeling like I was lying on fluffy blankets. I nuzzled my face in. "Good kitty," I murmured, hoping he wouldn't let me fall off if I went to sleep.

"Stop that!" Sam yelled out, hovering in the air with small motions of his wings as he looked back at us. "You stay awake. I can't risk you falling off."

"I was nearly executed!" I yelled at him. "I had a bunch of stones thrown at me, nearly died, used up all of my healing ability, got collared, and then dragged over here to ride a griffin and find out everything I knew is a lie! Of course I'm passing out!"

Griffin began to fly downward, gently so it didn't feel like a sudden drop.

"Stop that!" Sam yelled. "We don't have time to stop here. It's a bad place for it."

"I can feel her tiredness," Griffin said. "We can't go farther unless you're going to tie her down."

"Not a bad idea," Sam said mockingly. "There are... This is not the place I would recommend we stop."

"It's beautiful," Griffin said.

"I want to stay here," I murmured.

"Frustrating, stupid pets," Sam said. But then he looked at me and seemed to understand I was truly too tired to go farther. "Fine, we'll go down and tie you onto the creature and resume our journey."

"But where are we even going?" I asked.

"That's not for a pet to know," he snapped.

Then he dove downward, pinning his wings and then unfurling them just above the ground to catch himself, flapping a few times as he made purchase in the soft, thick grass.

Griffin landed soon after, and Sam walked over to put his hands up to catch me as I leaned over and fell off into his arms.

To my surprise, he held me closer for a moment, and

I could feel his breath on me as I lay there, seconds from sleeping.

"I should tie you onto this beast," he said. "I really should." He looked around him. "This isn't safe."

I forced my eyes open and looked around. "What are you talking about? It's beautiful."

I could hear the babble of a brook nearby. There were wildflowers in the grass.

Sam set me down, and I stumbled slightly, then sat down in the grass.

"I'm just going to rest here," I said. "Just like... an hour or two."

Sam glared at me, then at Griffin, who just shrugged.

"It seems like she's been through a lot, bro," Griffin said. "Have mercy, come on."

"I'm not your bro," Sam snapped, eyes blazing, biceps flexing as he folded his massive arms and retracted his wings until they disappeared. "Fine, I'll just have to protect all three of us until morning. In minotaur country. No problem!" He threw his hands up and stomped away to study the stream.

"Minotaurs?" Griffin asked. "Seriously?"

A sharp glare from Sam over his shoulder was the only answer Griffin got.

"Come on, aren't you a god?" Griffin asked, walking

over to Sam. Apparently, he had no fear for his life at all. "Make her a house. Let her sleep properly."

Sam glared at him, then nodded. "Fine. But if you're going to be bossy, then I might change my mind about this execution after all."

"I don't think you will," Griffin said, glaring down at him. "I don't think you're as bad as you say you are."

Sam breathed in very slowly, then let it out. "I could kill you in less than a second, and I would feel nothing about it. So think that over before you question me again."

Griffin froze, then nodded, stepping back with his hands up. "I'm just saying I could feel her exhaustion when we were flying. You need her for something, or you wouldn't be protecting her."

"I'm not protecting her. I'm—"

"You need her," Griffin said. "And she won't be able to do jack shit if she doesn't get time to recover. I could feel her heartbeat through my fur. It felt weak, and—"

"Fine!" Sam said, waving his arms as wood came flying from nowhere, spinning around as other objects appeared. He was creating them from out of thin air.

Slowly, wood became walls and floors and a roof, and a small, perfectly formed house settled down with a thud, shaking the grassy ground beneath our feet.

It was just small enough for two.

"You can stay outside," Sam said to Griffin. "You go in," he said to me.

I was about to thank him for putting work into sheltering me when his lips turned up in a sneer and he pointed to the sign above the door, which read: *Dog House*.

My jaw clenched, but I was too tired to argue. "I guess that means you won't be coming inside either, then," I said.

"Of course not," he said. "Too long in close quarters and you'll get ideas that are bad for both of us. I guarantee it."

"Don't count on it," I shot back, though the truth was I already wanted him. "Egotistical jerk."

His eyes ran over me, and it was hard not to be turned on by the sheer force of such attention from such a gorgeous man.

"I don't want you," I spat.

"Your expression says the opposite," he retorted. "So do your underwear, probably."

My jaw dropped, and Griffin stepped forward, swinging a punch at Sam.

I gasped, wondering what would happen, but Sam dodged to the side easily, looking at Griffin as if to ask if he was crazy.

"So you do want to die," Sam said, reaching for his sword.

"Don't talk to her like that," Griffin said. "And don't harass her. You'll have to kill me if you do."

"Don't threaten me with a good time," Sam spat back.

"Both of you, just stop," I yelled at them. "Look, I have no idea what's going on. But I don't care what that guy says to me, and I don't need you defending me, Griffin." I swallowed. "I barely know either of you, and I just found out I'm a demon. So I'm going to rest and hope this is all just a dream when I wake up."

The men just watched me in stunned silence as I walked into the doghouse, a comfy bed awaiting me on the right side.

Curling up on it, I didn't care that Sam had labeled it a doghouse or taunted me. I wasn't worried about minotaurs or being beyond the veil.

Even though the world was different than I had ever expected, as I drifted to sleep, I had never felt so safe.

Hopefully, I wouldn't wake up to havoc.

12

I woke up with the sticky, hazy, tired feeling of sleeping during the day.

A cool breeze blew through the cracks in the small house, bringing with it air scented like exotic wildflowers. Running water babbled nearby, bringing everything back to me.

We'd flown through the veil, and I now had an ally and "mount."

I would never let someone ride my wolf form, so I was a little surprised by how willing Griffin was.

Looking around the tiny house, small enough to almost be a dollhouse, I wondered why Sam hadn't made it bigger.

And what did he mean by if I stayed in close quarters, I would get ideas that were bad for the both of us? The hell?

I had some self-control. I'd said no to every alpha that had tried.

No man could compete with the fictional characters in my books.

But I had to admit that something in my body got excited at just the thought of seeing Sam again.

That handsome face, the wicked glint in those eyes, that incredible body...

Something in me liked him. Had since I first saw him.

Since I first kissed him.

I honestly had no idea about Sam. What he wanted from me. Why he'd taken me as his pet when he so clearly disdained me.

Why he'd chosen Griffin as a mount.

I rolled over on my bed as I heard voices not far from the cabin.

"Honestly, Samael. Doghouse? Did you have to?" a light, high voice said. It was familiar somehow.

"She was tired."

"You know that's not what I meant." The voice continued, chiding a little less gently this time. "Sam... you can't treat just any creature like a pet, truly."

"Why not? She is one. So is he."

"Who is *he*?"

"Ah, that's right. You haven't met Griffin yet. He's sleeping down in the shade by the stream."

"And why are you in minotaur country? You know what will happen if we're caught."

There was a silence fraught with hidden meaning.

"She was complaining," Sam said, as if that explained everything.

"You can't have two pets. Gabe is going to freak out if he finds out about this—"

"That's why I called you. You can have a pet too."

The other voice was quiet for a moment, and all I could hear was the rustling of the grass.

"I don't need a pet," the voice said.

My brain was racking itself trying to remember who it was. I could swear I'd heard it before, multiple times.

"It's a winged lion, Os," Sam said.

That answered my question.

"And you think I would have an interest in that why?" Os retorted.

"He doesn't have to be your pet. Just claim he is."

"Why should I?"

"We both know you owe me one after that business with the—"

"Gods yes, fine, just stop talking about it. I assume you're taking him to the usual place?"

There was silence, so Sam must have nodded or shaken his head.

"Fine," Os said. "I'll go with you until that point. Then it's not my problem anymore."

Sam was quiet.

"Promise me," Os said.

"I promise nothing," Sam retorted. "Do you even want to meet Griffin first? He's a mount for Cleo currently."

"The dog, you mean?" Os said, mocking the way Sam said it. "Cleo now?"

Sam was quiet again. "I can call her what I want. She's mine."

I heard something like Os slapping his forehead and a long sigh.

"You can't just own creatures," Os said. "That poor girl was going to be executed for practically nothing. That's the only reason I backed you up against Gabe."

"Where is Gabe anyway?"

"He and Mor are still in the fae wilds," Os said.

"Gabe loves it there."

"Mor hates it," Os said. "But Gabe needs a partner to keep him in line when I'm not there. They might join us later."

Sam just let out a grunt.

"All right, where is this Griffin character?" Os asked.

"You found him in cougar territory, I imagine? That was where you were headed when we split."

"Yes," Sam replied.

"Good enough," Os said. "I like the cougars. Honorable. Unlike the wolves, they have a moral code that supersedes simply asking for whatever they want from the celestials."

"They still reported him as an abomination. He's not," Sam said.

"Hm," Os said. "Take me to him."

I heard their footsteps echo past the cabin, toward the stream. I slowly pushed the door open and poked my head out.

I saw Sam walking next to Os, neither of them with their wings out, and let out a sigh of relief.

Os was the diplomat. He'd been nice every time I saw him. I felt better having both him and Griffin around.

I went back into the house to pull my tee shirt down and finger-comb my hair into a less-tangled mess. In my jeans and sneakers, I couldn't have looked less like I was trying to impress.

Which was good because I wasn't. Who on earth would try to impress that psychotic angel who only thought of me as a dog?

I hadn't kept my self-respect after so many years of abuse to simply lose it falling for some rogue celestial.

He might have saved me, but he was still one of them. And he seemed as eager to use anyone around him to his advantage as any other celestial.

I heard voices rise, and I stepped out of the tiny door to walk into the cool afternoon air.

The warm sun shone down, heating my skin, even as a cool, humid breeze blew over me, refreshing my senses.

This was a beautiful place, and I had no idea why Sam hated stopping here. As I walked down toward the stream, I saw Griffin in his lion form, lying down with wings tucked.

Sam and Os were approaching him.

I jogged toward them, not wanting to be left out.

"Sleeping Beauty is awake," Os said, looking over at me. His deep-brown skin glowed in the sun, his purple eyes so beautiful I could stare into them forever. There was kindness in his face as well.

"Hey, wake up," Sam said, kicking Griffin in the side.

"Stop it!" Os said, immediately facing off with Sam.

"He's hard to wake," Sam argued as Griffin stirred and woke, making a catlike yawn that showed off his powerful fangs.

But despite his size and teeth and claws, I got the feeling Griffin wouldn't hurt a fly if it could be avoided.

He shifted to his human form, and Sam must have given him clothes because he now wore a gray tee and jeans.

His eyes moved around, and when they rested on me, he smiled. The royal blue of his eyes was gorgeous beneath the blue sky. His blond hair was windswept and short, and his jaw could have cut diamonds.

Os's features were slightly more feminine. Wide eyes. Full lips. A beautiful V-shaped jaw.

In height, Os was below both Sam and Griffin but taller than me.

All three of them stared at me as I approached.

Yesterday, I'd just been an omega in a wolf pack. Today, I was hanging out with three beautiful guys who hadn't tried to attack me.

Not too bad, even if one of them did consider me a dog.

One thing that still bothered me was that Sam had kissed me and told me to wake up before he'd saved me from Zane.

But since then, he hadn't wanted to touch me. Even to carry me in the sky. He'd only lifted me down from Griffin. Otherwise, he'd avoided me.

And I didn't like it, though I wasn't sure why.

Griffin strode forward, all wide shoulders and towering muscles. He brushed a lock of my hair back that was blowing in my face. "You feeling any better?"

I nodded then, before I could resist, hugged him. "Thank you for sticking up for me."

He gladly gave me a hug back.

I heard a low growl and saw Sam approaching rapidly, his hand on his katana sheath, which looked odd with his tee shirt and jeans.

"Stop that," he said, pointing at us. "We don't have time for that."

I pulled back from Griffin, who frowned and folded his arms. "What are you going to say about it? She's only a dog to you. Why do you care who hugs her?"

Sam's eyes flashed, and I could almost swear his black irises with gold at the centers turned red for a second. But it could have just been an odd effect of the sunlight catching his eyes at a certain angle. "She's my pet, not yours."

Griffin let out a low growl. "I don't like any of this. You can't have a human as a pet."

"She's not human. She's a shifter," Sam said, as if that made it better.

"Shifters have a human side too," Griffin said, advancing on Sam. "This isn't going to work if you aren't going to treat us as such."

Sam just glared at him, looking like he was picturing how many ways he could dismember Griffin and get away with it.

He probably was.

Sam then gestured to Os, who was standing behind him and walked forward to extend a hand to Griffin. "This is Os. Short for Helios."

"We've met," Griffin said faintly, and then for some reason, his handsome face went completely red.

"Have we?" Os tapped his chin. "You would think I'd remember." He beamed at Griffin. "Regardless, I'm delighted to make your acquaintance."

Griffin finally took Os's outstretched hand, shaking it in his much bigger one. When he released the angel's hand, Griffin's face was redder than ever. He turned away from us, fanning himself. "It's hot out, isn't it?"

Sam just rolled his eyes and muttered something. "I'm going to get food." He looked between us. "I'm going to remove my tethers. You both have to swear to stay with Os." He looked around us shrewdly. "This isn't a place where we can split up."

"Can I run in my wolf form?" I asked, pleading. It would feel so good, especially in this beautiful place. There was a small, shaded woods area across the stream where I could have sworn I heard a small waterfall where the stream came down from a nearby mountain we'd flown over.

I was dying to explore it.

Sam didn't answer us. He was already walking away, his wings unfurling, obsidian in the sun.

Then he took off, up into the clouds, disappearing out of sight.

I put up a hand to shade my eyes, shocked he'd just left us like that.

"Couldn't he just... use his god powers to get us food or something?" I asked Os.

Os shook his head. "Two options. Either he lied to us completely and is doing something else, or he really is hunting down food in a nearby town. Sam is odd about using his celestial powers. When he can avoid it, he'd rather not."

Interesting.

"Your wings," I said. "Why are they purple? Sam's are black..."

Os smiled at me, flashing perfect white teeth. "We all have secrets." He gestured for both of us to come over by the house, and he waved a hand, making the air shimmer around us.

When the shimmers fell, a small camp appeared, complete with logs for seating and a small unlit camp-fire with a pot hanging over it.

"We travel a lot," Os said by way of explanation. "I'm good at setting up a camp."

Griffin came over to sit on one of the logs, sending a look of longing at the stream.

"Come. Let's talk for a minute," Os said, patting the log next to his as he sat down.

I walked over to sit, and as I did, my stomach growled, making me realize I truly was hungry.

"What will Sam bring back?"

Os shrugged. "One never knows with that guy."

"He doesn't seem right in the head," Griffin muttered. "Why do the celestials keep him around?"

"We needed a slayer," Os said.

Griffin perked up. "What do you mean?"

"You know, the demons have dedicated slayers for their kingdoms. The celestials... we lose authority by killing. It's a job no one wants, and Sam signed up for it. With his power, we couldn't really refuse him."

"How often do you have to kill?" Griffin asked.

"Just when it's needed. Like in the case of abominations. But, well, we have to give the havens what they want. And sometimes things truly are a danger. You two are anomalies."

I wasn't so sure about that, but I hoped he was right. The thought of Sam killing innocent creatures made my heart sore.

"Sam isn't your regular celestial," Os said. "Normally, we took turns with executions, but he's happy to take all of them. He insists on it." Os flushed as he looked down at his hands. "I think he might enjoy it."

"I think he does," I muttered.

"That's right," Os said. "You saw him kill. How was it?"

I shook my head because I didn't want to think about it.

"Now, about you," Os said, looking over at Griffin, who kept stealing shy glances at him. "Why did Sam save you?"

"Griffin wasn't hurting anyone," I said quickly.

"He should have been reported to the celestials," Os said. "Sam called only me instead."

I had no idea about that.

"Who knows why that guy does anything?" Griffin asked, shaking his head.

"Nonetheless, if I want to keep you out of the hands of the celestials, you'll have to be my pet. Like Cleo is Sam's," Os said. "For me, it'll be in name only." He wrinkled his nose. "I have no desire to actually rule someone."

Griffin nodded eagerly. "I will protect you with my life."

Os looked slightly taken aback, then laughed

awkwardly. "Probably not needed, seeing as I'm a demigod, but I'll keep it in mind."

Griffin seemed somehow disappointed.

How did he know Os?

And more importantly, what was going to happen to me once Sam got back?

"I want to go for a run," I said, standing and stretching. "Anyone want to come?"

Os frowned. "Tell you what. I'll set a long tether bond."

"A what?"

"A link so that if you're in trouble, I can know and come right away."

I looked at the pristine, wild land around me, the bubbling of the stream soothing my ears. My inner wolf wanted nature, now.

I was finally free from my home.

"It's not like Sam's," Os said. "It's more to join us so I can see what you're seeing than to restrain you." He sighed. "You'd do best not to wander far in minotaur country."

"What are they?" I asked, a chill moving up my spine at the way Griffin and Os looked at each other in response to my question.

"Demigods," Os said. "This is their territory. Technically, if we're here, then..."

"You don't want to know," Griffin said. "I've seen one break into the cougar territory. Took three cougars to take him down." He shook his head. "I was too young to fight when it happened."

"So they're bad," I said.

"They're just mindless fucking machines," Os said. "Half human male, half bull god. All instinct and sexual hunger."

"So they'd attack me?" I asked.

"They wouldn't see it that way," Os said, folding his lithe arms. "They'd see you being in their territory as permission." He shook his head. "Even the celestials don't know what to do with them. There aren't many left, and they cause problems whenever they wander outside their territory."

"How do they... make other minotaurs, if they're all male?" Griffin asked. "That always bothered me."

Os smiled unpleasantly. "This place is beautiful and abundant. They rely on other creatures wandering into their space. Almost any creature can be impregnated by a minotaur, though carrying the offspring to term is fatal for the mother. Or father."

Griffin's eyebrow rose. "So they..."

"Aren't particular," Os said. "But as I mentioned, there aren't that many of them. You're unlikely to run into them. Most of their time is spent grazing and rutting, even with each other."

I wrinkled my nose. "Awesome."

"Well, that's why their territory is all the way out here," Os said. "As far away from most creatures as possible."

"Sounds like they should be eradicated," Griffin muttered.

"It's not for us to decide what lives and dies, unless we are called to protect our subjects," Os said. "Many different creatures came into being when the supernatural realm merged with the humans in the mid-realm, during the great divide. As long as something isn't a demon, we let it be, unless they leave their territory."

Griffin snarled at that. "I'd say something that impregnates unwilling creatures, knowing it will kill them, is more of a demon than any devil in hell."

Os shook his head, looking nervous. "You don't understand demons. They make minotaurs look like plush ponies."

"She's a demon," Griffin said, pointing at me. "What about her?"

Os cocked his head, his purple hair falling to one side over his shoulder. "I don't know. She's mostly wolf. But yes, given what happened, she's probably part demon."

"How does that even work?" Griffin asked.

Os studied me coolly for a moment. "I do not know." He sighed. "Sam is taking a huge risk in this. I don't fully agree with it, but it's not for me to say." He put his hands up. "I'm just the diplomat, here to make sure everyone gets along."

Maybe it was just me, but the way Griffin was beaming at Os, it felt like he already wanted to get along splendidly.

Perfect. I could leave them alone and go for a run.

"I'll be back," I said. "I'm just going to be in that little woody area. I think I heard a waterfall. I still have some blood to wash off."

"You want me to come?" Griffin asked, putting his hands on his legs to stand.

"No," I said. "I'm sure Os has a tether on me."

Os closed his eyes for a moment. "Yes. Now I do."

The next second, I changed into my wolf, letting my bones quickly pop into place as fur sprouted. Then I was off.

I splashed through the stream, letting it clean me as I swam through the deeper areas. It tickled my fur, and the water was so clear I could see the speckled gray rocks at the bottom of it. I swam and then walked out of the water at the other side, where it got shallow at the bank. Then I darted into the shade of the woods.

Tall, leafy trees made a canopy above me, and I ran along the riverbed until I reached the base of a rocky hill, where water was flowing downstream.

I wanted to taste the water but wasn't sure if it would be safe.

I moved around large gray rocks that littered the area and looked up through the trees to see sunlight streaming through.

Then I lay on all fours, just enjoying the cool ground beneath me. Plants stood at the edge of the water. Beautiful purple lilies with blue centers. Vivid red flowers that reminded me of daisies. And a light-pink plant I didn't recognize with tiny sprays of hot-pink blooms.

Bushes with yellow berries. Trees with rich gray bark tinged with brown and heavy canopies of verdant leaves.

It smelled like wild rose and violet in the air, plus soapy green notes from the plants near the water.

I could have stayed there forever.

I couldn't hear Griffin and Os talking in the distance, though I assumed they were getting acquainted.

Above all, it was just nice to have some time alone.

Though, my thoughts kept wandering to where Sam was. Where he'd flown to. He hadn't wanted to stop here. Was it really because he feared minotaurs, or was he supposed to be somewhere?

I felt a bit bad for delaying him.

Then I remembered the "Dog House" sign and all guilt flew away like so much pollen on the wind.

I lay there relaxing and only stirred when I heard something moving in the brush.

All senses on alert, I slowly lifted my head in wolf form, scenting the air.

I caught something odd and musky. Not quite human.

I looked up as a large figure appeared out of the bushes to my right, about twenty feet away.

The beast was so tall, I had to crane my neck to look up at it.

Its head was part bull, part human. It had a blunted snout with a bull nose, bull ears, and a large flat face.

Other features, like its eyes, looked almost human. They glowed green as it looked at me.

It was hugely muscled, with fur on the edges of its limbs and tanned human skin in the middle. It had rippling, impossible muscles. Human pecs. Human abs, covered in thick fur from the waist down. It stood on two huge, hoofed legs that extended back like a satyr, with huge black hooves at the bottom.

Hooves that stirred the grass as it began to breathe hard, looking as if it wanted to charge me.

I stayed still for a split second as it studied me, hoping it would simply think me an animal.

By the look in the thing's eyes, I realized even that didn't make me safe.

This had to be a minotaur.

I took off, springing off my back feet lightning fast, bounding through the trees and back over the water.

Os would know what to do, right? My heart was pounding as though it would explode, and my entire body was wracked with fear as I ran forward, splashing through the stream loudly and running up toward the camp.

Os and Griffin stood as I reached them, and I didn't even have time to explain before a bellow rent the air, and the minotaur burst into the clearing.

The beast was sweaty from its chase and even more terrifying in the sunlight outside the trees.

Its furred human hands clenched into fists as it stomped toward us.

Os moved in front of me and Griffin. "Let me handle this."

"Move, celestial," it growled in a low, bellowing voice. "You know the rules. Give me the mortals."

Another minotaur came out of the woods, crossing the stream to stand behind the first.

A third followed, then a fourth. They were huge and apparently moved in groups.

Or maybe they'd just heard the bellow of the first one.

The one in front licked his lips, rubbing his hands together.

"Two of us can breed. Excellent."

Griffin looked at me at the same time I looked at him.

"I can take one," Os said. "Four? Doubtful. I'd have to kill them, and—"

"Angels don't like killing," Griffin said.

"No," Os said. "It weakens us." He sighed, raising a hand. "But I'll do what I have to. Get ready to fly off with Cleo if things go bad."

"I won't leave you here," Griffin said.

The minotaurs approached slowly, ominously, their hooves clacking against the stones in the riverbed.

"You know the rules, celestial," the minotaur in front said. "I won't tell you again. Give us the mortals."

13

We heard flapping above, and I glanced up to see Sam flying in, looking like a dark shadow against the sky as he hovered above us, observing the situation.

"Minotaurs are demigods," Griffin said. "A lot to take on even for a celestial."

I wondered for a moment if Sam might just leave us there as punishment for being stupid enough to stop in the minotaur area.

Then again, if it was so unsafe, why had he left us here?

The minotaurs began sniffing and then looked up in the air where Sam was hovering, flapping occasionally.

The next second, Sam dove down toward us, landing smoothly. He unfurled his wings to the sides and moved forward threateningly.

"I knew we shouldn't have stopped here," he said as he moved in front of us all.

"You can't kill us," the lead minotaur said. "This is our territory. Give us the mortals." It looked to me. "At least the girl."

I guess they could tell what I was even in wolf form.

"I want him," one of the minotaurs said, pointing at Sam. "He smells good."

One of the other minotaurs agreed, while Sam put his hands on his hips and looked up at the sky like he was praying for patience.

"Os, lead Cleo and Griffin to the clouds," he muttered.

Os's light-purple wings unfurled, and he took off upward. Griffin shifted right after, turning into a gorgeous golden lion with bright-white wings.

I shifted out of my wolf form, keeping a wary side-eye on Sam and the minotaurs as I did so. The scent of musk in the air was getting stronger.

"Not fair," one of the minotaurs said, trying to walk past Sam to get to me and Griffin as he lowered to a crouch and I grabbed his fur to climb up onto him.

"Come on," Os said from above us. "In the air, *now*."

I was barely on when Griffin took off, moving upward.

Os beat his purple wings, flew fifty feet up into the air, then paused, and we all looked down at Sam.

"I feel bad just leaving him down there," I muttered.

Griffin grunted in assent. "Can he really take on all four?"

"Sam?" Os let out a laugh. "It's nothing to him. He loves slaughter."

Griffin made a grimace of distaste that was almost comical in his lion form. "Who could love ending someone's life?"

I stared down at Sam, who was unsheathing not one, but two katanas. One sheath was the black and silver one I'd seen in the jail.

The other sheath was red and sparkled in the sun like it was made of crushed rubies. When the katana was drawn, the hilt glittered with red jewels between the black rope that crisscrossed over the grip.

"Okay, I wasn't going to say anything about this guy having a slayer sword, but two? That's just insane," Griffin said.

"What are slayers?" I asked as we watched the minotaurs advance on Sam.

"The most powerful, brutal demons in existence. They protect their territory from celestials the way we protect ours from demons."

That all sounded odd. If demons were so bad, why did they need to kill celestials to protect their territory?

There was so much I needed to learn, and it was clear that the tiny wolf haven I was raised in was unaware of all of it.

"Sam had two swords when he came to us," Os said. "His father is... Well, he's from the ninth celestial realm."

Griffin let out a low whistle. "So he has elder god blood. Makes sense. Power just emanates off him."

"Should we go help him?" I asked.

Both turned to look at me, puzzled.

"I'm not a bad fighter," I said. "I did martial arts, and my wolf form is strong—"

Both Griffin and Os just laughed, making me irritated.

"Don't get me wrong," Os said. "I'm sure you're strong. But no wolf can take on a minotaur."

I touched the stone at my throat, feeling oddly nervous as the minotaurs got closer to Sam.

He was huge, muscled, but those creatures had to be ten feet tall, and there were four of them.

"I'm not *only* a wolf," I said, holding the collar. "Os, if you took this off..."

"I'm not going to risk you exposing yourself as a demon just for minotaurs," Os said, shaking his head.

"That needs to stay on, or you could hurt even yourself."

That made me shut up instantly. But my stomach was still in knots over Sam. Not that I should care about that stupid, rude, psychopathic angel.

But no one should be impregnated to death.

"Sam's got this," Os said. "I was only worried when he wasn't here."

"Aren't you a celestial too?" Griffin asked. "Why is he stronger than you? You're both gods."

"Demigods," Os said. "Archangels aren't fully elder gods, or we wouldn't be able to visit this realm."

"Ah," Griffin said, looking mildly confused. His huge white wings beat up and down, stirring up the air and seeming to almost go to the beat of my heart.

Sam appeared to be shit-talking down below, though it was hard to hear above the whooshing of Griffin's wings.

Os noticed me leaning down to try and hear, and he waved a hand. "I can magnify the sound."

"Come on," I heard Sam yell, spinning a sword once in each hand as he approached the first minotaur, about ten feet in front of him. "Show me who you are."

"He says that a lot," Griffin says.

"Because he won't be punished for killing if there's a mortal sin being committed."

"But the minotaurs have a right to anyone on their territory," I said. "Right, Os?"

Os shook his head. "Not exactly. The person they want to mate with is allowed to try and defend themselves."

"Are they attracted to celestials?" Griffin asked as one of the minotaurs made a crude epithet to Sam, making all of us grimace.

"I don't know," Os said. "A lot of things are attracted to Sam wherever we go, regardless of his terrible personality."

"I heard that," Sam yelled from below, looking up to glare at us.

"It's just that most things can't defend themselves from a minotaur. But Sam can."

"Do they realize that?" Griffin asked.

"Probably not," Os admitted. He looked at both of us, his purple wings beating the air. "He's going to start soon. So if you don't want to watch, I suggest you look away—"

But it was too late. With a yell, Sam had moved toward the minotaur closest and, with one clean slice, cut the monster's right arm off.

Blood sprayed from the wound as the monster let out a bellow, and all three of its friends closed in.

It was hard to even see Sam in the melee, as all the

minotaurs jumped him at once, but his two swords were constantly moving, and I heard bellows of pain as more limbs fell and more blood sprayed.

I didn't even know what belonged to whom as Sam cut off legs, arms, and heads, and minotaurs fell to the ground, spraying blood in all directions, painting the stream and the ground around it in crimson.

One minotaur was down, a headless torso facing blankly up at the sky as blood flowed from all four severed stubs where arms and legs had been.

His limbs, and those of his friends, floated slowly down the stream as the water ran even redder.

Two minotaurs were still fighting, and Sam moved between them, so fast it was hard to watch. He slashed off one's remaining arm, then crippled it by taking its legs, then took the head off the last and fourth one.

Soon, all of them lay still in the stream, in various pieces, and Sam stood among them, wings pulled in, bloody swords in both hands.

I almost wished I'd been closer to watch it.

Griffin slowly flew down with Os next to him, and when we reached the ground, I quickly slid off. Griffin turned back into his human form just in time to fall on his knees and loudly vomit.

Sam's wings disappeared as he turned to face us, bending to dip both his swords in the water. He cleaned them with a cloth he took from his pocket and then slid them into their sheaths. Then the sheaths disappeared.

Most of the minotaur bodies and limbs had flowed downstream and past us, but Sam grabbed a remaining leg and held it up with the hoof pointing at the sky.

"Steak, anyone?" he asked, grinning, his entire body splattered with blood, golden-blond hair matted with it.

His muscles were straining beneath the tee, his chest heaving with exertion, and despite his bravado, I knew the fight had taken more from him than he was letting on.

As Os gagged at the steak suggestion, Sam just shook his head at us and tossed the leg aside, pulled his shirt off over his head, then stepped out of his pants and moved upstream where there was a deeper spot in the water.

He submerged himself and came up cleaner, splashing water over his face.

I was just trying not to look at him in tight black boxer briefs.

As he cleaned himself, moving water over his huge biceps and rippling chest and abs, I had to work hard not to drool, despite all the violence that had just happened.

I was attracted to this angel. I had been since I'd met him. He knew it, and I knew it.

And by the way he met my eyes and smirked, he could tell exactly what I was thinking right now.

I hated how well he could read me.

And he'd been right. Before, when I'd claimed not to want him, I'd been lying.

I guess I was just one of the many who'd found him sexy, as Os had said.

Since we were all fine, and Sam was still smirking at me as his hand moved over his perfect abdomen, I whirled and stomped away from him over by the campfire to check on Griffin.

Griffin wiped his mouth, still looking horrified by what had happened. "So much blood. That angel really is a demon. It was like feeding them into a woodchipper."

I walked over and brushed his hair back, trying to soothe him as he bent forward and gagged again.

Os walked out to meet Sam, probably to get their stories straight for when they were questioned about this.

I looked at the bloody stream, where some minotaur parts were still bleeding, caught on rocks, staining the beautiful plants on the banks.

I hated that this had to happen.

But seeing Sam in motion... that had been amazing.

I kind of wondered what was wrong with me that I'd found it thrilling rather than repulsive or nauseating.

I didn't want any creature to have to die... but since they would have killed us...

Looking over at Sam, who was rolling his eyes at something Os was saying, I could only feel grateful toward him.

Not that I was going to say as much, since he'd only throw it in my face.

Griffin stood with my help as Sam came forward, still shirtless but wearing loose black pants.

His dark eyes met mine, flashing with hints of gold. "No one was hurt before I got here?"

I shook my head, looking at the others.

"Where did they come from?" Sam asked.

I flushed. "I went for a run, in wolf form."

"I thought as much," Sam said. "I had hoped to avoid them..." He shook his head. "The elders won't be happy about this. They like the minotaurs."

I raised an eyebrow at that, but Sam just shrugged.

"Well, pet? They didn't hurt you, did they?" His tone was casual, but unless I was imagining it, his eyes were actually concerned.

All that bloody violence, had he done it for me?

I considered it only for a second, then laughed inwardly. No way. If he hadn't loved killing so much, if it had in any way inconvenienced him, he probably would have sent me to them himself.

What were pets for if not being useful, after all?

But he was still watching me, tall and shirtless and still, waiting for my answer.

"I'm fine," I said, nodding.

Sam nodded back quickly and then walked over to one of the logs, motioning for Os to join him.

As Griffin came to my side, the two angels put their heads together and began discussing something quietly.

"Come on. Let's go upstream a bit," Griffin said. "Away from all the blood. I'm going to throw up again."

Probably a good idea, though, for some reason, I hated taking my eyes off Sam.

14

Griffin held his head as he sat on a log facing away from the stream, where all the blood was slowly diluting into the water, any traces of Sam's bloody fight disappearing.

"The way he just slaughtered them... like they were nothing," Griffin said, shivering slightly.

"I saw him kill before too," I said.

"How?" Griffin asked, deep-blue eyes filled with horror.

"Right through the head," I said, and Griffin went even paler. "Never mind, let's not talk about it."

Griffin nodded. He looked over at Os, who was listening to Sam intently. "What do you think of the other angel?"

"Os? He seems nice," I said.

"Really nice," Griffin said, giving him a dreamy look.

"And you're going to be his pet?" I asked. All of this still seemed surreal.

Everything moved so quickly.

A part of me still felt like, at any moment, they'd all call me a worthless omega and I'd be shipped back to my pack to be stoned again.

Even if I was never punished, I'd die a slow death in that town on someone's leash.

Griffin nodded. "Do you miss your family?"

"It's only been like a day," I said.

"I miss mine," Griffin said. "I was adopted, but they loved me as their own. As a lion cub, I suppose I looked a lot like a cougar, so I was brought there by a stranger and left there. I got my mane and wings later, and..." He trailed off. "Well, we all knew what had to be done."

"Hey, it could be worse," I said. "You're here. With friends."

"I barely know you," he said.

"You got any other friend options?"

He laughed. "All right. Friends. I liked you the moment I met you anyway."

I smiled back at him.

"Seriously, though, I worry about you with that guy. Os seems nice, but Sam..." Griffin shook his head. "Anyone who can kill like that isn't right in the head."

"Someone had to kill them," I said quietly.

"What was it like for you, before you were taken?" Griffin asked.

"I wasn't taken, exactly," I said. "Sam gave me an option."

"Oh yeah, what was the other option? Dying on the end of his sword?"

I nodded.

Griffin sighed. "I suppose it's not his fault the rules are what they are. He still seems to use them to his benefit."

"I think that's smart," I said.

"You still haven't told me what it was like in your wolf haven," Griffin said. "I've heard bad things..."

I pressed my lips together, trying to think just how to approach this. I didn't really feel like ranting and complaining.

"I was an omega," I said quietly. "Village omega. So I was everyone's scapegoat, and everything that came along with it."

Griffin cocked his head. "The omega system is messed up, but omegas are usually treasured. Protected. Not attacked."

I gave him a smile that was more of a grimace. "Depends how cooperative you are with what the alphas want. Some alphas are real bastards."

"Good for you for saying no, then," Griffin said. "You didn't deserve anyone trying to hurt you."

I didn't know what to say to that. All my life, I'd been hurt by various people and told it was my fault and I deserved it.

It was very odd to be around people who defined me as something other than my position in the pack.

"So... the thing about omegas being naturally submissive isn't true?" Griffin asked.

"No," I said. "It's just because they make us."

"I had wondered," Griffin said. "Cats are fairly promiscuous and don't pair off in terms of alphas and omegas. They are tightly knit as a community, though. As much as we hate the wolves, I had always thought of the alpha and omega program as old-fashioned and romantic. That omegas were just born needing to be protected, and alphas stepped up to do the job."

I snorted. "Not really the case. Or maybe it's just that I have a demon in me." I caressed the smooth, cool stone on the collar around my neck.

"Don't take this wrong, but it seems like defying the alphas of your village was worth risking death. Yet you took Sam's deal, and he seems far more dangerous than they are."

I blinked. "Well, I still have a chance to escape him

and find a life out there apart from being an omega. If I'd died that morning..."

"And you think he actually would have killed you if you refused?" Griffin asked. "Because it doesn't seem like you did anything wrong, in my opinion. Executing you would have made him a monster."

"Celestials can't be monsters," I muttered, glancing over at Sam, who, as always, was too sharp not to notice someone looking. "They're always right."

Sparks moved over my skin instantly as his eyes met mine. Then he quickly turned his attention back to Os, though I still got the sense that somehow he was watching me.

"Yeah, well, there's something not right about that celestial if you ask me." Griffin's eyes tensed and jaw hardened as he watched Sam scoot in slightly closer to Os to show him something on the palm of his hand. Like he was outlining a route on a map.

"I don't like having him next to my master," Griffin said with a snarl. If he'd been in cat form, I'd swear his hackles were rising.

Sam looked over at us and grinned slightly as he moved a lock of Os's hair back over his shoulder.

He then winked at Griffin.

Os looked up at Sam with an odd, confused smile,

then went back to discussing whatever the topic at hand was.

I grabbed Griffin's arm and jerked him back onto the log. "Let them finish. I'm sure it's fine. That sadist is just trying to get a rise out of you."

"He is a sadist, isn't he?" Griffin muttered. "That's what I don't like about this. It's fine to kill if you have to, but you shouldn't like it." He shook his head, and quiet footsteps approached as Sam's smooth, deep voice flowed over us.

"So it would be better to be forced to do something I hated?" Sam cocked his head at Griffin, and a lock of wavy gold fell over his forehead. He looked absolutely pissed.

"You done talking to Os?" I asked, standing up and brushing my jeans off, hoping to head off a confrontation.

Sam's perfect lips lifted in a sneer as he looked me over. "What about you, pet? Offended by my enjoyment of killing?"

I thought for a moment. "No. Intrigued by it." Then I walked past him, trying to act more confident than I felt.

I'd escaped my village. There was a demon inside me. I was making friends and seeing more of the world than I'd ever been able to access from my cage.

It was starting to embolden me.

I moved over to sit by Os and then leaned back, soaking up the sunlight. If Griffin and Sam wanted to argue, I wasn't going to get involved.

But instead, I noticed Sam still watching me as if he didn't know what to make of the fact that I wasn't disgusted by him on principle.

He almost looked disappointed.

I shook my head, leaning back to stare at the sky again. The sun was blinding, so I shaded my eyes, and the bright-white clouds looked fluffy enough to sit on.

The whole world felt so much bigger now.

Sam walked over to me and put out a hand to help me off the log. I took it because, despite him never calling himself my alpha, there was an instinct in me to simply follow him.

Even if he was probably the last person I should trust.

But all I knew was that while I was by his side, nothing terrible had happened. And a whole new life was opening up because of the chance he'd given me.

Despite all of his rough edges, just due to the chemistry between us, I got the wild thought that it actually might be possible to fall for this angel.

Not that I would.

"Come walk with me for a moment. We have to talk,"

he said, releasing my hand the moment I stood. My hand almost missed the tingle of his electric touch.

We walked through the stream, the cool water soaking my shoes, though I didn't mind it, and into a grove of trees near where I'd seen the minotaur.

Hopefully there weren't any more in the vicinity.

Sam put his hands on his hips and faced me. He'd put on a new white tee shirt and jeans that weren't splattered with blood, and his skin was clean from the stream.

Looking at him, you'd never know everything he'd done in the past two days.

He looked down his perfect nose at me as if still trying to gather his words. Then he pinched the bridge of his nose.

"You need to stop looking at me like that," he said, letting his hand drop to the side and cocking a hip as he looked at me.

"Like what?"

He sighed. "Like you want me. Like you trust me. You're just my pet. I should have set this out at the jail, but watching you with Griffin, hearing you defend me, I need to make some things clear."

I gave him a nod.

He put his hands on his hips and paced in front of me. "I'm used to traveling alone. This is an aberration.

I'm still figuring out what you are and what to do with you. For now, you're a useful pet." He took a step closer. "But just because I showed mercy to you doesn't mean I'm someone to look up to. I'm using you, nothing more. Don't get ideas about why I protect you."

I shrugged a shoulder. "I didn't even think you were protecting me in particular."

"Don't fall in love with me," he shot at me, gold glinting at the centers of his dark eyes.

My jaw dropped, and a pile of offended protestations was about to fall out. "You egotistical—"

"Jerk," he finished for me. "I know. But I know my effect on women... on people, and I'm warning you now. There isn't a heart for you to find. I'm not something broken to be fixed. And if you try to dig deeper inside me, you'll only find more darkness."

I just stared at him. The audacity. Sure, I'd found him attractive. One would have to be blind and frigid not to. But falling in love? I'd only just gotten my freedom back.

"Who gives a flying fuck about love?" I retorted, glaring at him as fire lit in his eyes that only stoked the fire burning in me. I raked my eyes over him, the way he did to me. "Sure, I'm attracted to you. But I'm also attracted to Griffin and Os."

Sam let out a low growl at that, for some reason.

"But I'm not here to date or fall for anyone," I said, my hands clenching into fists as I took a step toward Sam.

He held his ground, though I could tell he was shocked I was challenging him.

"I may be your pet because death was my only other option, but don't you ever think I'm easy." I laughed caustically. "Fall in love with you? Unlikely. How could I love anyone who puts me on a leash?"

Sam stared at me for a long moment, then exhaled. "As long as we agree."

He turned to go, and hurt was still lashing through me for some reason. Being preemptively rejected just sucked.

It was not because I was already getting feelings for him. It was just because he kept confusing me.

"Why did you kiss me?" I shot at him, realizing too late that Griffin and Os could probably hear us.

My heart pounded at my own boldness as Sam's broad shoulders turned and he faced me.

"I never said we couldn't fuck," he said. "I kissed you that night for reasons I can't explain until we're somewhere more private." He looked around us. "We're too close to celestial haven territory. I can explain more later."

"So we can have sex, but I can't fall in love with you."

I cocked my head. "And why would I want to have sex with you anyway?"

He came closer, grabbed me by the arms, and pulled me in.

Though I should have been scared, heat exploded in me just at the closeness. The way he was holding me.

The fire in his eyes.

"There are things we can't discuss in front of Os and Griffin." He released me. "Just don't fall in love. That's all I'm going to ask." He looked at my collar. "I'll even take that thing off you, once you can control yourself. I'll only ask you one favor when all of this is done. Do we have a deal?"

"What is the favor?"

"I can't tell you," he said.

"Why did you save me?" I asked. "I'm a demon. I just don't get what you could want."

His lids lowered slightly. "I told you. I can't tell you that now."

"Ugh!" I wanted to stomp in frustration. "Fine. I obviously won't fall in love with you. You're a sword-waving psychopath who kissed me against my will in the stocks!"

"Still going on about that, are you? Still denying it was the hottest moment of your life?"

My cheeks burned, flaming red in all likelihood. "I didn't consent."

"Fine," he said, hands tightening into fists. "Not a mistake I'm going to make again, you little virgin." He took a step back. "But you're going to have to experiment with a few mortal sins if you want to see what kind of demon you are. If you want to have more power—"

I blinked. "Mortal sins?"

He looked past me, and I realized Os and Griffin must have been noticing.

He lowered his voice. Gods, he had a sexy voice. "I just wanted to warn you about where we're going," he said. "Fae barrens in the mid-realm."

Excitement burst in my chest. "Fae?"

He nodded. "The warriors there won't like that you're a demon, if they happen to figure it out despite your collar. You must stay close to my side, at all costs."

"I'm on a tether," I said. "It's not like I have a choice."

"I haven't put one back on," he said. "If you run, I can catch you. I was only being strict back at the haven because if you ran and the wolves caught you, there would be no way to save you."

I blinked at that, then grinned at him. "So you do care."

His gaze was hard. "I care about one thing you might be able to do for me. That's all."

"Can I ask one question?"

"No," he said flatly.

"But you seem to hate celestials, even if you're a celestial—"

"I said no," he said. "Now come on. I just wanted your promise that you would stay close in fae country. If I tether you, they'll feel the magic of it and might ask questions. It would be best if you acted as if you were by my side of your own free will."

"Why?" I asked. "Won't it look bad that you hang out with a demon?"

"They won't know you're a demon at first," he said. "And they won't like that I have a shifter on a chain. They see shifters as holy animals, blessed by the celestials. The fae worship nature and love animals. They'll see you as something interesting because shifters are rarely seen in the mid-realm."

"Really?"

"Really," Sam retorted.

"Fine," I said. "I guess I can stay by your side and play nice."

"This is the last stop on the way to my place. I promise to reveal everything I can there, when it's safe. If you can just trust me until then—"

"I do," I said.

"Fae have some odd customs," he said. "I may say things you hate. But—"

"I get it," I said. "Stay close, fate worse than death, blah, blah, blah—"

"One of the warriors might offer you escape, if he thinks I'm unfairly using you," Sam said. "You must refuse."

"Why?" I asked. "Jealous?"

"Because they *will* find out you're a demon at some point, and you won't like how they deal with it." He pinched the bridge of his nose again. "Don't you get it? I'm trying to protect you."

Before I could say something snarky about him caring, he fixed me with a glare.

"Fine, fine," I said, throwing my hands up. "I'll ignore the fae warriors and play good little pet. Happy?"

Sam grinned, a dimple flashing by his perfect lips. "Yes."

He strode back through the stream, over to Os and Griffin, and I couldn't help hating how everything was always on Sam's terms.

I might have been free from my other life, but I still had to listen to whatever Sam said, or I might die in this dangerous world.

It was hard to shake the feeling of being an omega when I had to agree to being a pet.

Sam turned back to me. "If you truly can't resist leaving me for some offer from a warrior, just know that I'll find you, and that warrior will die a bloody death. That is certain. I need you, and I won't let you go."

I swallowed, realizing I was more a prisoner than even I wanted to acknowledge.

But at this point, there was no one who could save me from Sam, even if I needed it.

He was the most powerful of the celestials, a man of secrets and scorn and sadism.

And I was his pet for the foreseeable future, whether I liked it or not.

He wasn't just warning me for my own safety now. He was threatening me, and it made rage bubble up.

But I suppressed it because the only way I had was forward.

"I hear you loud and clear," I said, following him as he continued across the stream. The sun beat down on us, making sweat bead on my forehead.

"Ready to leave?" Os called.

"Fae territory," Griffin said, grinning at me. "I've never seen it."

I sucked in a deep breath, gaining energy from the smiles of my two new friends.

I might be chained to a psychopath, but for the first time in my life, I wasn't alone in facing what lay ahead.

"Okay," I said, jogging over to them. "What are we doing there anyway?"

"Killing an abomination," Sam said, his shadow rising over me as he caught up with the group. His wings shot out on both sides, gleaming black in the sun.

The urge to touch them hadn't gotten any weaker.

He pinned me with a look, then took off into the sky.

As Griffin shifted into his giant winged lion form and knelt for me to climb onto his back, Os unfurled his wings and waited.

We flew up together into the huge blue sky. Sam started flying forward toward an area of ruins amidst clumps of exotic trees.

The fae barrens.

I wondered what kind of monstrosity could be strong enough for the fae to need help, since I'd heard fae were almost as strong as celestials themselves.

Would Sam actually have to kill this one rather than save it as he had me and Griffin?

My heart pounded as we flew forward, the future racing toward me whether I was ready for it or not.

15

We landed on the edge of the fae barrens we were visiting, and as I slid off Griffin's back to the ground, my jaw dropped.

It smelled gorgeous here. Humid greenery and fresh roses and wildflowers filled the air, along with notes of mint and other plants.

There were trees and plants everywhere, growing amidst the ruins of large buildings. Small, rounded dwellings sat amongst the trees, looking like flat, wide trees themselves, with a body of bark and leaves covering the roofs.

Some were barely ten feet square, others closer to twenty.

There were many of these little buildings and then, up at the far end of the community, aged stone steps leading to a courtyard. At the center of the courtyard stood a large iron cage with blackened bars.

Inside, an odd, blurry black shadow moved like an insect swarm, though I could make out a large, humanoid figure within.

But I didn't have long to look at the faraway cage because Sam led us to one of the larger dwellings and rapped the wooden door with the back of his knuckles, tapping his booted foot impatiently as Os joined him from behind.

Griffin and I stayed back a few steps, waiting uncertainly.

Someone opened the door, and I could barely see them as their chest was at the door's short level.

A smooth, dark hand with long, slim fingers and jeweled rings extended, slowly curling a finger at Sam.

Sam waved for us to follow and ducked his head low to go in.

"Will there be room for us?" Griffin asked dubiously, ruffling his blond hair with his large hand.

Os simply laughed and waved for us to follow, entering after Sam and disappearing from sight.

"We have to trust them, I guess," I said. "At least for now."

"I'll come to watch out for you, then. And Os."

I grinned at him. "You're really going to have to do

something about your protective side, aren't you? I'm a pet."

He nodded. "I can't help it. I just want to prevent bad things where I can. I've always been that way."

I supposed that wasn't the worst thing.

Griffin ducked to go in, and even I had to duck slightly as I walked into the small house, but as I looked up when I entered the room, I realized some sort of spell had been cast on this place because it was huge on the inside.

Sam was talking to a tall, handsome man in the center of the room, the one who must have beckoned us in.

The man's deep brown skin glowed against ornate blue robes with pink swirls over the front.

He studied me as a woman came up from behind him, with skin so pale it was almost pearlescent. Another man with pale skin followed her as well. They wore robes of yellow with orange flame overlays, and the gemstones on their fingers matched.

The furnishings in the room were also beautiful. Tapestries in bright colors hung on every wall, and the room was shaped like a hexagon, each side about fifteen feet long.

At the center sat an ornate wooden chair with gold

leaf along the frame and a blue silk cushion in the center.

The man with black, blue, and pink robes sat in it, crossing his feet and showing off elaborate silk sandals.

His eyes were vibrant periwinkle, gorgeous and vivid. His features were elegant, and his ears were elongated and came to delicate points.

No wings, though. I had always wondered if the fae would have wings.

The two other fae stood behind him, their hands clasped in front of them.

"I am Zarris," the man in the seat said, cocking his head at us. His long black hair was tied into a simple ponytail, and he appraised me with those startling purple-blue eyes that were soft like velvet but glowed, almost as if they were backlit. "High priest of the fae of the East Barren." He waved elegant fingers behind him. "These are my attendants, Vera and Soris," Zarris said. "Do not make any overtures. They are gem bonded."

"Gem bonded?" I blurted out, too curious to stay still.

Sam sent me a look of warning, but Zarris smiled.

"I am familiar with you, Samael, as we've done business before." His eyes moved over to me and Griffin. "However, you've brought me something very interesting."

Which one of us was he talking about?

"You, girl, come here," Zarris said, beckoning me.

I hesitated, looking at Sam, and a smile crossed Zarris's handsome face.

"You would defy a high priest of the fae?" His tone said it would be very stupid to do so.

"This is Cleo from the Lark pack in the celestial havens," Sam said. "She is my..."

Yes, how are you going to describe this? I thought meanly.

"My consort," Sam said simply.

Zarris grinned. "You will want shared accommodations, then. Are you bonded?"

I looked over at Sam again. What was bonded?

Sam shook his head.

"So she can entertain overtures from my warriors, or perhaps even myself?" Zarris's eyes gleamed even brighter at the concept, but Sam took a half step in front of me.

"She chooses to be with me for now," he said. "But I don't own her."

Yeah, he does, I thought. But I kept my mouth shut because I didn't know anything about these people, and Sam seemed to know them all.

Sam folded his arms. "You know Os. This is his pet, Griffin."

Zarris smiled, lifting a hand in greeting to Os, held in an odd symbol with his thumb and first finger extended.

Os merely nodded.

Griffin looked confused, overprotective, and ready to run from the room all at once.

"A griffin, hm?" Zarris said, standing to walk around Griffin.

"No," Sam said. "It's just his name. Some kind of shifter. We're still figuring it out." He exhaled slowly, in a way that finally caught the fae's attention and sent him scuttling back to his chair to face Sam. "You have an abomination. Tell me about it."

"Of course, celestial one," Zarris said, though there was a hint of sneer in his voice when he said celestial. "The creature is out in the cage. Some sort of void creature, though we're not sure what. That cage prevents him from escaping back to the void to evade punishment."

"How did he get here?" Sam asked.

"We do not know," Zarris replied. "But what we do know is that he murdered five people in the middle of the night."

"Tell me more," Sam said.

"We took in a small family of wood fae, because

we're closer to kin than not, and they were seeking shelter."

"The fae are always generous in offering shelter."

"Well, with access to our own fae dimensions and unlimited space due to our magic, it would be unreasonable not to," Zarris said, resting back in his chair. "This family was assigned to a small house. A mother, a father, and three children. In the black of night, we smelled smoke. All we found were the smoldering ruins of the home and five bodies. That creature was hovering over them in cloud form. Though, he can also look like a man."

Sam nodded. "Might be a void walker." He lifted his head, his dark eyes clear and sharp. "Lead me to him."

"He might try to attack you when you do attempt an execution. The cage binds him, for now, but you can't go in with him without risking attack," Zarris said. "He is a coward who strikes and runs to the void in a moment's notice."

"If he runs to the void, then I'll follow him there," Sam said nonchalantly.

Zarris grinned. "That's exactly why we called you instead of Gabe. Your willingness to do anything is much appreciated."

Sam merely nodded. "I'll kill him, for the usual tithe."

Zarris nodded.

Tithe? That was new to me. Had Sam been paid to execute me and Griffin too? What a racket.

I'd heard an old human saying once that if you did what you love, you'd never work a day in your life.

Sam had picked the right job, then.

"I have to talk to him," Sam said. "Alone with Os."

"Very well," Zarris said. "I can take your friends to their accommodations."

"They're coming with us," Sam said. "They will have to stand back while we discuss things with the abomination, but then we will all go to our accommodations together."

"I understand," Zarris said. "It might take several days to deal with such a complicated creature." Zarris stood, and his attendants followed him outside.

Other fae were poking their heads out of cottage doors, and I wondered if all of the insides of the houses were so glamorous and spacious.

We followed Zarris over the soft dirt paths that connected the parts of the village, and Sam and Os moved in front of the cage as Zarris stepped back to stand with us.

He moved in closer to me, sniffing the air subtly.

"Keep your distance, Zarris," Sam called out tersely. "I told you she's with me."

"Picky, picky. Celestials are so possessive, even when not bonded."

"I'm sorry, but I don't know much about fae," I said quietly. "What do you mean by bonded?"

Zarris looked delighted by my question and, ignoring a low growl from Sam, moved over to me and put my arm over his to escort me as we walked in a circle around the area with the cage.

Griffin followed closely after.

"My dear, we all have magic deep inside us. We draw it from the planet where we are born, from every living creature and every element. And we can choose to join that magic to another, sharing each other's strengths. That is what I mean by bonded."

"That's pretty cool," I said. "So that's when two fae become a couple?"

"Two fairies, yes," Zarris said.

"Do you have wings?" I blurted out. After all, every day with Sam might be my last, and I was dying to know.

Zarris smiled warmly, and beautiful, iridescent butterfly wings unfolded from behind him, glittering with pink and blue. "Our strongest power comes from gemstones, which radiate energy from deep within the earth." He showed me his hand. "I resonate with sapphires, turquoise, and pink tourmalines, along with rose quartz and pink spinel." He wiggled his fingers, making the stones twinkle. "Which do you prefer?"

I looked among the rings and pointed to one with a vibrant pink stone at the center surrounded by vivid light-blue stones that seemed to glow.

"Ah," he said, removing it from his hand. "Mahenge spinel and Paraíba tourmaline." He handed it to me. "You're excellent at sensing power in gems. You might make a good fae yet."

I laughed. "I can't become a fae."

"No," he said. "But you could bond with one and still share in their power." He made no attempt to take the ring back.

I handed it to him, taking one last glance at its beauty. "I don't think that's possible. Thank you, though."

I glanced over at Sam and Os, who were discussing something with the void creature in low tones I couldn't make out.

But it spoke in a low rumble that Sam seemed to be able to understand somehow.

An angel of hidden talents.

Zarris pulled me to the side a bit and took both of my hands in his gently. "Time to be honest with me, little one. What is a blessed creature like you, with wild nature inside you, doing with that sadistic wretch of an angel?"

I choked out a laugh, not able to help my shock. "You don't like him?" I asked in a whisper.

Zarris's eyes narrowed. "Who would?"

Sam kicked the cage, his voice rising as the creature let out a growl.

"Still, you need a monster to deal with a monster," Zarris said.

"But he's a celestial," I said.

Zarris shook his head, making his silky ponytail shimmer. "Not all celestials are the same, pet."

"I hate that name," I said quietly.

"Noted," Zarris said. "I meant it as an endearment, nothing more. Come. While Sam is working, you can meet one of my warriors. He can show you around." He turned to his female assistant, who had been following us quietly. "Fetch Zadis," he said.

She nodded, and the male attendant stayed with her as she left.

"That's really fine," I said. "Sam's going to be done at any moment, and—"

"But he will be busy," Zarris said. "In the meantime, my half-brother can—"

"Your half-brother can what?" Sam's flat voice reached us as he whirled to face us, stomping over authoritatively with Os trailing behind him, sending dubious looks back at the creature.

"Nothing, celestial," Zarris said, giving Sam an obsequious smile. "Let me show you all to your accommodations."

"I want to stay with Cleo," Griffin said, but Os shook his head.

"We will room separately," Os said.

"Noted," Zarris said, walking forward down the damp dirt path around the square. He took a side street and moved down it to a small house next to an overgrown oak tree. "For you, Helios, and your Griffin."

Os looked embarrassed for some reason, but he gestured for Griffin to go in first.

Griffin hesitated, his royal-blue eyes searching mine to see if I was okay with this. I gave him a quick nod, and he went in, giving me a wave as he disappeared.

We were all tired and hungry, and hopefully settling in for the evening meant we could eat. My stomach growled as we followed Zarris down another side road to a small house next to two pine trees with sloping, overgrown boughs.

Sam gave me a look that darted down to my stomach then up to my eyes, and he glowered. I just shrugged. What he did expect after almost a day without food?

"Here we are," Zarris said. "The second of our finest guest homes."

Sam opened the door and looked inside. "It'll do."

"I presume you will want to be among my people later?" Zarris asked.

Sam nodded, not saying more. Then he took my shoulders and gently moved me under the doorframe and shoved me into the house.

He followed after me, slamming the door behind him.

"He's already interested in you, damn it," Sam said, pushing his hair back with one hand. "What, do you want me to fight the high priest of the second-most powerful fae colony in the barrens?"

"No," I said, confused, as I looked around the home and saw a familiar hexagonal shape. The furnishings were simpler, with paintings of wildlife and simple tapestries of blue with dark gold threaded into nature scenes.

There was a hallway to the right that probably led to the sleeping areas.

The main room had a partitioned area with a simple kitchen with human goods like a microwave, fridge, and dining table. Plus an oven that looked old-fashioned.

"They are used to human visitors," Sam said. "Hell, they welcome it."

"But they bond to each other," I said.

"And outsiders," Sam said. "And anything that will screw them. They bond, take your magic, and—"

"By share magic, you mean?" I asked.

Sam glared at me, lifting his taut jaw. "What did he tell you?"

"More than you have," I muttered.

"I'll get us food," he said. "You can lie down if you want to."

I watched him, his broad shoulders and back straining that white tee shirt, his ass in those jeans, just taking him in.

He really was gorgeous.

"Stop staring, wolf," he muttered, opening the fridge and not even turning to look at me.

If it weren't for that damn mouth...

"I'm going to take a nap," I said, darting into the kitchen to grab an apple from a fruit bowl I'd noticed.

Sam just ignored me and continued to pull things out of the fridge. "I'll call you when dinner's ready."

The hall split in two directions, probably heading to bedrooms at either end. I picked one direction and strode down the hall to a small room with a bed covered in pink silk with green silk pillows. The walls were a gentle cream. No windows.

I fell back on the bed, letting out a sigh of pure relief. It was soft. We were safe. Sam was cooking.

Everything was fine for the moment.

I closed my eyes and almost drifted off to the sound of trees rustling above the house. But then I stirred, jarred by the sound of voices.

It was Os talking to Sam.

I sat up, listening intently.

"Griffin's making food," Os said in a voice he was clearly trying to keep quiet. "Where's Cleo?"

"Sleeping," Sam said flatly. "What do you want?"

"That thing in the cage. Is it... you know, what we're looking for?"

I didn't hear Sam say anything in response.

"You know we have to find it. It's the only reason the celestials are putting up with you joining us on patrol at all."

"You know damn well I can pull rank on anyone who questions me."

"You know what I mean, Sam. We all know why you're here. This is important. This is the safety of the whole world we're talking about."

"I know."

"The Morningstar—"

"I know!" Sam's tone was sharp, though his voice was

quiet. I thanked my excellent wolf hearing that I could even eavesdrop.

Sure, it might have been kind of wrong. But since both of these angels wouldn't hesitate to kill me...

"It's not the Morningstar," Sam said. "At least, I don't think so."

"But the prophecy... it's someone hated—"

"I told you to be quiet. It's someone hated without reason. I still need to investigate the reasons they hate this void creature. It appears to have committed murder, but I'm not so sure. But no, it's not the ultimate weapon. Now leave me alone."

"Why are you keeping Cleo?" Os asked. "If you were just trying to save her, you could release her here. The fae would care for her."

Sam must have ignored him because I heard nothing.

"She's mine," Sam finally responded. "And I'll kill anyone who tries to take her from me. That's all you need to know."

"And we're all just supposed to let you do whatever you want with her? She's—"

"Unless you want to fight me, yes," Sam retorted. "Now let me cook, Os. Go back to your lion. He likes you."

Os sniffed. "I don't care about that. I'm on a mission."

I heard Sam laugh.

"There's still time for fun on a mission," Sam said.

"And do you plan to have fun with Cleo?"

"Only if she begs," Sam said. "Now leave me. I have food to make."

I heard Os's weak protests, and then the door opened and shut.

I fell back on the bed, staring at the cream-colored ceiling, my heart racing.

What was the Morningstar? Would Sam even tell me about it if I asked?

I was learning so much about the celestials, but so far, I had more questions than answers. Did they always get tithes? When did Sam start working for them? What was this ultimate weapon they mentioned?

Was the entire world in danger?

My racing thoughts overwhelmed me, and I tried to clear my mind as I rolled over on my side and pulled the covers over me, ready to sleep.

When I woke up, I could decide whether to confront Sam about everything or just keep my mouth shut for my own good.

16

A knock on the door startled me, jolting me from sleep.

I pushed up on the silken covers, noticing that I must have kicked my pants off as I slept. My tee shirt was riding up, exposing the edge of my bra.

I quickly pulled my shirt down and yanked the covers over me. "Come in," I said, knowing it would probably be Sam with dinner.

I was still starving.

The door swung open, and Sam stood there, shirtless, to my surprise.

My jaw gaped, but he simply leaned against the doorframe, watching me with those mysterious eyes shaded by long lashes.

My eyes couldn't resist running down his muscles,

his hard, square pecs, those abs so defined I wanted to run my tongue over them.

As a wolf, my high sex drive had always been confined to my heat, which was only once a year.

At those times, I was desperate but sequestered, so as to not tempt others to sin.

And none of the alphas in my village had ever made me feel anything but disgust for them.

But Sam's naked chest, long, muscled arms, and the trail of hair down his hard stomach into his jeans made something in me stir, tightening my chest and making it hard to breathe.

Sam moved into the room, shutting the door behind him. I looked up in time to see him push one hand through his tousled curls, raking them as his eyes pinned mine, making it impossible to look away.

"Like what you see, wolf?"

I felt like I was dreaming.

"No," I spat, lying. I hated this person. He killed without mercy. He was probably using me.

But I was still turned on by him.

He took another step forward, hooking his thumb in a loop on his jeans, tugging them down and showing a perfect V-line running into his pants.

"Liar," he growled, taking another step forward, towering over me with his powerful body as he looked down. Slowly, his tongue licked his lower lip, his eyes burning with that ring of gold in the center of the darkness.

Just what was this creature? No angel should have been able to make me feel like this. So sinful.

Sam's head cocked slowly, and he bit his lower lip, pulling it through his teeth carefully, the tension in the air growing so thick I would have given anything for it to break.

In the next second, almost faster than I could see him move, he was on the bed with me, crawling over me until his hands were propped on either side of my head.

Spicy incense. Musk from that beautiful body.

It wasn't the wolf in me calling out for more. It was something else.

Something much deeper... and wilder.

I wound my arms up around his neck, but he quickly pulled them away, gripping them in his hot hands as he shoved them together and pinned them above my head with one of his hands.

His eyes were hard as they stared at me, and he looked down at my tee, narrowing his eyes for a second before grabbing the front of it in one large hand and tearing it away like it was tissue.

It was clear that, even in bed, Sam was more alpha than any wolf.

I gasped, but he kept my hands trapped as he lowered his mouth to kiss the tops of my breasts. I jerked at the new sensation, at the pure pleasure of his touch. He moved up to my neck, ignoring my attempts to kick out at him, leaving a searing trail of kisses up my neck, my shoulder, and then up to my ear, where he bit down lightly on my earlobe before sucking it into his mouth.

Damn, I was wet. I had no right to be. I hadn't asked for this. It was wicked, sinful.

I was his *pet*.

I tried to kick him away out of the pure shame of it, out of knowing, for a lifetime, I was supposed to save myself for a mate.

He shoved my hands down tighter, as if to make the point of who was in control, but his other hand reached out to grip my chin, forcing me to look up into his eyes, which were filled with molten lust.

Sex was in the air, and my body was aware of it, practically writhing beneath him, begging for more, even as my mind knew I should stop this.

If this man—no, this god—gave me an orgasm, I would never be the same.

And he'd told me to never fall in love.

He held my gaze, a muscle ticking in his jaw, his chest heaving. I looked down to see his hard member pressed to my hips, so big I wasn't sure how I could take it.

"Look at me," he said sharply, and I did. "Would you deny both of us when it could be so good?"

I nodded quickly. This was wrong.

His hand moved down to the apex of my legs, trapped under him. He had to reach behind his leg to touch me, but he did, smoothly gliding over my panties up to a sensitive part at the top of my sex.

He rubbed over it, sliding over the wetness and the silk covering me, and his eyes seemed to eat up my reaction as I arched back in response to the pleasure his heated touch brought.

Nothing should feel this good, I thought.

"I won't let you rob us both," he murmured, leaning over to whisper against my lips, his breath hot against my face. His finger moved faster, faster, and I felt something building in me, tighter and tighter, making my body feel hard to control. I bucked against him, but he simply moved his hand away just as I was about to go over some interminable edge, making me whimper.

"Shh, pet, I'll make it better," he said quietly in that rough, low voice that drove me crazy. "Just a little more torture first."

To my shock, he tore away my bra like it was paper. Then he shoved my hands up as he moved down my body, putting his lips directly over my left nipple. As he sucked the sensitive nub into his mouth, I arched again, uttering an oath.

"The only god's name you should mention is mine," he hissed.

"Sam," I cried out as he flicked his tongue out against my nipple and then sucked it to caress it before dragging his teeth gently along the edge. Each move made heat sear me down to my center, causing my body to buck with pure shock.

The sensations were like nothing I'd ever felt before.

If I'd known someone could make me feel like this, I would have sinned before.

Sam moved to my other breast, using his hand to tweak the nipple of the wet one that was now exposed to the air, sensitive and cold without his touch.

As his mouth licked one nipple and his hand tortured the other, he began to move his hips against me, stroking that incredible hardness against my wet heat, building the fire inside me even higher.

I could barely breathe, barely think. I was so overwhelmed in pleasure. But I also had the feeling I was awakening to something. Something I could never ignore now that I'd felt it.

Sex could be so *good.*

I bucked against him as he bit lightly on my nipple, the pain just the slightest edge on the pleasure rushing through my body. I never wanted this to stop. I bucked against him harder, but he was so big, so strong, so unstoppable, and there was nothing I could do but hold on.

"Sam," I uttered, feeling the tension in me tighten until I felt like a violin string begging to be plucked. I felt panicked, like something was supposed to happen but it wasn't. I thrashed side to side, trying to shake his hands.

I needed him, needed something, but he just sat back, looking down at me as the room began to swim, blur, and disappear.

"Oh no, no you don't," I muttered. "Don't you start this and not finish it."

I grabbed for his hands, but he was motionless now, just sitting atop me, watching me.

"No, I can't." I bucked and writhed. "Please." Something had to happen. I couldn't stay like this.

Even if this was a dream, it was cruel for it to end like this.

But the room continued to blur, then go black, and when I woke up, I was tangled in the sheets, my hand down my underwear, the sheets covering me clumsily.

And Sam was standing at the door, watching me,

wearing that stupid white tee shirt that showed off his powerful chest.

I looked him over. No sign of an erection.

It truly had all been a dream.

I'd never been so humiliated.

And he was studying me with that hard-to-read expression, so I had no idea how long he'd been there or how much he'd seen.

Yet I still had an odd ache inside me, like something was tense because it hadn't relaxed yet.

"Can I tempt you?" Sam asked in a low voice, leaning against the frame, much like he had in the dream.

I stared into his handsome, cold face, wondering how I could even have gotten such ideas about him.

I didn't even like him, and the feeling was mutual.

I should have known it was a dream.

"What?" I asked.

"With dinner," he said, giving me a smirk as he turned to leave the room.

My heart dropped. Whatever he'd seen, it had been enough to know something. Groaning, I reached for my jeans to pull them on and go out and eat.

I was starving, and at least I could satisfy my hunger in one way.

Even if it was going to be the most awkward dinner of my life.

17

When I entered the small area where there was a dining room and kitchenette, Sam set a bowl in front of me with some kind of thick brown soup.

It smelled amazing.

"Beef," Sam said. "You're not vegetarian, are you?"

I shook my head.

"The fae have used magic to create synthetic meat, just like the original version. Humans were on the verge of lab-created meat before the great divide." He eyed me. "I figured, as a wolf, you would be a meat eater."

I nodded, then eyed the soup suspiciously. It seemed a little odd to eat something cooked by the demon that I was just dreaming about.

He shoved the soup bowl closer, making it slosh slightly. Then he sat in a chair across from me.

"You're not eating?" I asked.

"I'm fine," he retorted.

My stomach clenched with hunger, so I scooped up a bite of the soup with a simple spoon that had been next to my bowl. Immediately, spices exploded over my tongue, filling my mouth with warmth, every ingredient the perfect texture and packed with flavor. "Oh my gods, so good," I practically moaned.

I looked up as Sam moved in his chair slightly, looking vaguely uncomfortable.

I ignored him, eating more of the soup until the bowl was almost gone, at which point Sam got up and served me another one, sliding it over without hesitation. He brought me a glass of juice as well, which tasted of fresh oranges.

The entire time, he just watched me.

"You can cook?" I asked, pushing away the bowl when I was finally finished. I let out a satisfied sigh. "That might have been the best meal I've ever eaten."

Sam smiled, just a tiny crook at the corner of his perfect mouth. As I looked at his face, it was hard not to let images of my dream flood my brain. Those lips on my breasts, those hands pinning mine...

Sam's smile fell, but his eyes glimmered with intensity. "You were dreaming when I woke you."

I nearly choked at that and put my hands over my face. "What did you hear?"

"Now, isn't that an interesting reaction?" he asked, reaching over to pull my hands down off my face before he sat back once again. "I heard nothing."

I blinked. My cover wasn't blown.

"But based on your level of redness right now, I think it's something I *should* know."

I felt even more blood flood my face. Traitorous body. Even now, we wanted him. Wanted to finish what he'd started in my dream.

"Was it about me?" he asked, leaning back in his chair and appraising me like a lion might a cornered gazelle.

"I... No," I said.

He leaned forward then, placing his elbows on the table. It creaked. "Tell me the truth, pet."

"Why should I?" I sputtered, desperately stalling for time to avoid the truth. It felt like this angel could simply tear me open and spill out any part of me. I deserved to have some secrets.

And I refused to see the smug look on that face if he did find out what I'd been dreaming about.

"You haven't told me anything," I muttered. "Who you are, where you're from." I picked up my spoon and jabbed it at him. "How you can cook."

His smirk fell, and his handsome face was stone-cold again. "You learn a lot when you raise yourself. Now, answer my question."

"You raised yourself?" I asked.

He nodded.

"So the gods of the ninth realm are bad parents?" I asked.

He was quiet, but a muscle ticked in his jaw. "I wasn't raised there."

More and more mysteries. I'd already gotten the feeling that Sam wasn't a normal celestial, and his conversation with Os had confirmed it. But who was he exactly?

The longer I was with him, the more I wanted to know.

"I won't tell you more, pet. Now tell me about the dream, because I *will* figure it out."

I blinked and dropped the spoon back in the bowl, realizing I probably was caught. I stared down at my hands as I flattened them against the table.

"Was it about me?" Sam asked quietly.

Damn. My face went even redder.

"Did you have a dirty dream about me, you naughty little virgin?" Sam made a low noise that might have been a chuckle, but I couldn't be sure. I refused to look up at him and give him a view of my ruby-red cheeks.

I'd never had a dream like that before. Never. And it had felt so real I didn't know how I would ever look him in the face again.

"No shame in it, pet," he said gently, reaching out and coaxing me to look up at him. "So what did we do?"

I turned away from him again and heard his chair push out in response as he stood.

He moved around and stopped behind me, then lowered and placed his hands on the table just outside of mine. He leaned down slowly to whisper in my ear. "What was I like?"

Just the feel of his breath made hot sparks run through my body, the emptiness aching again. "I... You were..."

"What?" he asked, his voice intoxicating like wine again, as his finger came up and grazed the sensitive spot where my shoulder met my neck.

I jumped slightly from the shock of it. "Stop that. I can't focus."

He straightened, moving back over to his chair. "I hadn't expected this. I knew my effect on you would be strong, as it is with everyone. I hadn't known it would happen this fast."

"That what would?" I asked. "What do you mean, so fast?"

He shook his head lightly, but there was a slight

flush on his high cheekbones. "So tell me what you dreamed."

I moved my hands off the table and into my lap, fidgeting nervously. I could still feel where his breath had brushed my ear, where his hand had grazed my neck.

And gods help me, I wanted more of him.

"It's not a good idea for us to be together, pet," he said, making my entire body go tight.

How could he tease me like that if...? Well, it was all my fault for having that dream.

I went rigid and sat up straighter, deciding to go back to my room and finish this by myself.

"I want you, Cleo," he said, as if trying to mollify me, but my ego was already wounded. "I'm your master. It would get messy. And there are... things you don't know."

"I can't know if you won't tell me."

"They aren't for a pet to know," he said, raising an eyebrow at me. "Did you think my inquest about your dream was an invitation? Pet, something happening between us is a terrible idea."

I nodded.

"But I'm still dying of curiosity to know what I was like in your dream."

I shook my head, too embarrassed now to even want to talk to him. He didn't want me. He didn't—

"I'll tell you what," he said smoothly, darkly. "An exchange. You want to know what I'd really be like in bed. I'll tell you if you tell me what you thought I'd be like from your dream."

My hands twisted in my jeans, but I couldn't help it. I was still horny, and I wanted to know what he'd be like in bed. If only so I could go imagine it while I got off in a minute.

Something had awakened in me, and there was no chance of it going back to sleep as long as he was around.

Gods damn it, if only he'd—

"You were rough," I said, barely able to choke it out. "You... were rough, and I liked it."

His eyes met mine, and I could swear I saw a flash of red in them. "Oh, pet. You're in so much danger, and you don't even know it."

"Why?" My breath felt light and fast, like I was waiting for something.

"Because you tempt me beyond all reason," he murmured. Then something in him seemed to snap back to his normal, cold self, and he pushed away from the table. "I... It would be imprudent to talk more about this now," he said, pushing away from the table abruptly.

"I'm going to the other bedroom, across from yours. I need to rest, and—"

"No fair," I sputtered, anger bursting through me like fireworks that he would cut things off like this. "You said you would tell me what you're like. We had a deal."

He just eyed me quietly. "I didn't say when."

Clearly, he just wanted to tease me. To wind me up and show me he didn't need to make any kind of bargain or ever hold up his end of the deal.

Just like he didn't want me when I so clearly wanted him.

I fled before he could, running down the hallway to my room, slamming my door immaturely and locking it so he couldn't get in.

Not that he'd try to.

Why was this happening to me?

Despite my anger at him, despite the interlude of dinner, I still wanted him. I couldn't stop aching for him.

All of this was so wrong. I was an omega. I was his pet. I should have been thinking about how to survive and find my way in this world and escape Sam's sadistic grasp.

Instead, I was pissed he didn't want me.

Very well, regardless of how wrong it was, I would have him in my mind, and I would get this heat out of me so I could think straight once again.

My body was coated in a fine sheen of sweat by the time I'd tossed my clothing off and lay on the bed, naked except for the sheets pulled up to my waist. My breasts were exposed to the cool air, which kissed them as Sam couldn't.

I hadn't dared to masturbate back in my village. There was no privacy in the home, and my dad or mom could walk in at any moment.

Not to mention, it was prohibited as a sin by the celestials.

But right now, I didn't give a single fuck about rules. I'd escaped that place, hopefully forever.

And it was time to take my pleasure in my own hands, literally.

I slid my hand down between my legs, as Sam had in my dream, my fingers twitchy and nervous. I touched the spot he had in my dreams, at the top of my sex, a tiny pearl.

As I moved my hand over it, pleasure sparked through me, and my body jumped. I moved my finger, stroking and caressing, and put my other hand to my breast.

This was the right place.

I closed my eyes, pretending it was Sam doing it, even as a flush at my own wickedness burned through me. But even though I stroked and arched and tried to picture him, it wasn't the same as my dream.

I wasn't even sure what exactly I was seeking.

I let out a quiet cry of frustration.

I just didn't know how to do this well enough. I'd never wanted to.

Gods damn that angel.

"Cleo."

I jumped at the sound of Sam's voice, lower and raspier than I'd ever heard it.

"I will keep my side of the deal," he said, and there was a sound like his nails biting into the wood of the door. I had to be imagining it.

In my mind, I could see Sam on the other side of the door, hard and hot and as desperate as I was.

But I knew I was just imagining it.

"I wasn't fair to you," he said in a low voice. "So I'll help you now, even though it's dangerous for me."

I stroked to the sound of his voice and had to bite down to keep another cry from moving out at the sheer pleasure. How much stronger it felt to touch myself when he talked.

How had he cast this spell on me?

"Use two fingers," he said. "Move them over yourself, pushing one fingertip down, then the other. Alternate, and don't stop, as I tell you what I'd be doing to you."

I gasped but did as he said, feeling the tension in me slowly, finally begin to build.

"You have no idea," he choked out. "If I were in there, I wouldn't be able to hold back."

I pictured it, and the sensations rose again, making my body buck.

"I'd pin you down, and I wouldn't stop pleasuring you till you passed out in my arms. I wouldn't be able to stop, no matter how you struggled, as long as you were coming." The desperation in his voice turned me on, forcing my pleasure even higher.

"Sam," I grated out.

"I'd touch you everywhere," he said. "Those breasts, they'd be mine. In my mouth, in my hands. Your little clit, I'd be sucking it, no matter how you screamed for me to stop. I'd lick it and suck it, over and over. I'd find every spot you could come from and tease you until you came, just to watch your different orgasms. I'd—"

Heat erupted in me, and I cried out as what must have been an orgasm washed over me, making my muscles clench and release as feelings unlike anything I'd ever known before engulfed my mind, my heart, my soul.

This was being *alive*.

Waves of pleasure moved through me, and my body

went rigid as I arched back, closing my eyes as stars erupted from the pressure behind my lids.

When I finally relaxed, my body felt heavy, exhausted, and enervated. I sat up, pulling the sheets up over me, my heart pounding like it could fly out of my chest.

Wrapping the sheets around me, I got up to go over to the door, which I opened.

Sam wasn't there.

I peeked down the hall to see him striding toward the front door of the tiny house, his shoulders straight and strong.

Had he really just been dirty talking behind the door?

Had he been... helping me?

He turned back to face me, and his expression was cool and calm, a light gleam in his eyes the only sign that something in him was still burning.

Just like, despite all the pleasure of my orgasm, something was burning in me.

Something that wouldn't be satisfied until we were together, and it felt like both of us knew it.

"I'm going out," Sam said. "You get some rest." He put his arms out, and a black coat appeared on him, a trench that went to his knees. He reached in one of the pockets and pulled something out, which he put on a small table by the door. "Here, your void sack. It has your books and clothing."

I took the small black sack, which felt silky despite looking like it was made of coarse fabric. I wondered where he'd gotten it, since it seemed related to the kind of creature in the cage outside.

But I doubted he'd put up with me asking him about it right now.

He opened the door to leave.

"Wait, Sam—"

He paused, staring at me with those unfathomable eyes, abyssal darkness with a golden ring.

"I'll be back in a few hours," he said. "Don't leave the house."

"But you didn't even eat," I said, taking a step toward him.

His eyes raked me, a familiar wickedness flaring there. The corner of his lips turned up. "Yes, I did." Then he turned and left, his coat flapping behind him.

I walked back to my room with the void sack, both glad and infuriated that he'd given me time to read.

Already, I felt both nervous and excited for his return.

Something had happened between us. Something that couldn't be reneged on. And when he got back, I was going to get to the bottom of just what was going on.

18

There was a small bathroom attached to my bedroom, with a small porcelain bathing tub and an ornate showerhead attached.

It was easy enough to work, probably because these houses were for those used to human plumbing.

It felt good to be clean, but the entire time I rinsed off, every square inch of my skin just felt too aware that Sam hadn't touched it.

And my mind was obsessed with replaying those moments he'd been outside my door, "helping" me.

Why had he done that? To keep his word?

All I knew was that it had been the most amazing feeling I'd ever experienced.

I opened the void sack and dumped the contents on my bed, watching dozens of books and several outfits fall out. I smiled as I sorted through the clothes.

None of them were mine, but Sam clearly had rifled through my drawers enough to know the kind of things I liked.

There were black combat boots, black jeans, and shirts with funny pictures and comments like the ones I enjoyed hunting at the thrift store for used human goods.

Tears bit my eyes as I remembered how hard it had been to find things like this in our haven. How often my dad had torn my clothes and told me to dress modestly in dresses, like other omegas.

I changed into my clothes, picking out a shirt that read: *Danger: Uncaffeinated* and noted that Sam had even gotten the size of my underwear and bra right.

Weird.

I looked in the mirror and noticed how much better my face looked.

My skin, normally pale, was flushed with health. My blue eyes were extra luminous, and my hair was still wet but long and shiny.

My features had never been of much interest to me. The alphas seemed to like my face until I opened my mouth, but I wasn't sure what the fuss was.

My eyes were too round, too easily startled-looking.

My lips were full, my cheekbones high, my jaw a bit stronger than average.

Nothing I'd ever cared about much.

Besides, making myself as ugly as possible had always served me well, at least in deterring sexual attention from alphas.

But right now, I felt like I didn't have to hide anymore. Not like I was some great beauty, but I didn't need to hide behind straggly hair, like a girl emerging from a well in a horror movie, to keep unruly alphas from getting ideas.

My hair was tangled, and it took a while to finger-comb it since I had no brush. It looked like it would dry in long, dark waves.

I smiled at my reflection in the mirror. Would Sam notice the difference?

A knock on the door interrupted me, and my heart leapt in my chest. Had he changed his mind? Was he back?

I walked over to the door, fully changed and hair only damp, and looked through the tiny stained-glass window.

I didn't recognize the man standing there. He was tall and built, with long black hair, pale olive skin, and blazing green eyes. His features were so delicate as to almost be pretty, but his strong, stubborn chin and straight jaw counteracted them.

"Hello?" He stepped up to knock again, maybe seeing me through the window.

I wasn't sure what to do. Whether to answer without Sam.

But then indignant frustration welled up in me. Sam *left*. He didn't have any say in what I did.

I might have left my pack to be with him, because I had no other choice, but he didn't own me.

I opened the door and stood in the doorframe with my arms crossed, hoping I looked intimidating.

After all, I was still a wolf shifter, and nothing was stopping me from transforming.

The man was taller than me by half a foot, but a smile lit his face as he looked me over.

"A real wolf shifter," he said, looking at me like I belonged in a museum. He cocked his head and took a step back to appraise me. Then his eyes landed on my collar. "You are suppressed?"

"No." It was the truth, at least about my wolf form.

"I am Zadis," he said, putting out a hand to shake mine. His grip was warm and strong, and he released me slightly slower than might have been proper.

"Careful," said a blond fae passing by, arms linked with a brunette friend. "Zadis has a thing for shifters."

The pair disappeared between cottages, and I looked back at Zadis.

"So you're Zarris's half-brother?" I asked. I supposed there was some resemblance in the delicate features.

Zadis nodded. "Fae and other supernaturals have intermixed with humans for centuries, here where America used to be. We come in all colors. We share a mother, whom I favor. Zarris favors his father."

"I see." I folded my arms again nervously. "Look, Sam isn't here, so—"

"I know," Zadis said. "He will be busy conducting interviews, pursuing his investigation. I thought, in the meantime, we could get to know each other."

My cheeks heated because I got the feeling that the way this fae warrior wanted to get to know me was more than friendly.

And Sam had warned me not to get too close to them.

But Zadis seemed nice, and what could happen when Sam probably wasn't far away and Griffin and Os were nearby also?

"What did you have in mind?" I asked.

"Just a walk in the woods," he said.

I wrinkled my nose. "Where?"

"Past the other side of our village are some beautiful

fae wilds, cultivated by our horticulturists. You'll love it. It might even inspire you to shift."

His green eyes lightened to almost a moss color in his excitement, and I laughed. I didn't hate being a wolf, if it didn't come with being an omega, and shifting might be kind of fun...

And I'd never met a man like this. So polite, so kind. Instantly treating me like an equal while still showing interest.

Not harassing and pushing me away like Sam.

I still felt confused about how he could just walk out after practically giving me an orgasm.

My cheeks must have reddened because I felt Zadis staring at me even more intensely, as if trying to make out what I was feeling.

Unlike the other fae who wore robes, Zadis wore a dark-green tee shirt and black jeans, plus sneakers. His broad shoulders were relaxed, and he shoved his hands in his tight pockets.

"Look, I'm not going to hurt you. Ask anyone. I love humans and shifters. I think they're so interesting. I even dress like them." He spun in a quick circle. "Way sexier than robes, don't you think?"

I laughed. "So if your brother is the high priest here, what does that make you?"

"Something like a prince?" He grinned. "Though, I

suppose I'm what you'd call a nerd about humans and other rare creatures, so I'm not very prince-like." He reached out to take my hand, grabbing it, to my shock, and pulling me with him away from the house.

I barely managed to pull the door shut behind us.

"Come on," Zadis said. "I promise you're safe with me."

I pulled my hand away from his, blushing furiously despite my best attempts not to. "I just don't like being forced to do anything."

He froze, studying me for a moment, then nodded. "I am sorry." He reached out a hand. "Come with me?"

I looked down at his hand, then shook my head. "I'll walk normally."

He grinned, a pleading look in his huge green eyes, as he wiggled his fingers at me again. "Come on, we're going to be friends, aren't we? And friends build their bonds."

"Bonds?" I asked, ignoring his hand and falling into step beside him. "I did want to hear more about that."

"Fae bonds," he said. "We believe that our innate powers can be linked to one another, shared and made greater through our connection. The highest being the bond between bonded mates."

"What are bonded mates?"

He cocked his head, then looked forward, picking

up his pace so I had to almost jog to keep up. "I have to keep some mystery if this relationship is going to work."

"It's not going to work," I said, drinking in the fresh, mulchy, humid air as we walked along the paths around the village. Tall trees rose on all sides, sending fragrant green scents to my sensitive nose.

"Why not?" he asked, walking backward as he faced me.

Gods, he was beautiful. I preferred Sam with his dark, wicked eyes and harsh beauty, but this man was a close second for now.

Just talking to men who didn't see me as only an omega was incredible.

The world was truly opening up for me. I'd really escaped.

Whether Sam would let me live to tell the story was another question.

I looked around, keeping out a keen eye for Sam. It was late evening now, and the sun was setting, casting pink and red rays over the orange clouds above the tall trees surrounding the fae village.

"I... I'm sort of stuck with an angel," I said. Then I cursed myself because that was probably exactly what I wasn't supposed to say.

But why should I listen to Sam anyway? He kept

everything secret yet expected me to just trust him, even when he admitted to using me.

I knew I was being a bit petty in ignoring Sam's order, but a new world was opening to me, and I couldn't just hide inside and wait for it.

Zadis let out a sigh. "That angel... You shouldn't be with him."

"Why not?"

Zadis's eyes flashed. "He is not a worthy partner. He is a disgrace of a celestial. He used to..." He shook his head, as if remembering he wasn't supposed to be talking about something. "Regardless, you can do better. In the mid-realm, a full celestial wolf is impossible to find."

"You can find regular wolves?"

He nodded. "With other kinds of magic. Werewolves that are bitten rather than born. The occasional hellhound makes it here from the dark realms." He studied me again with that keen gaze that made me heat from the inside out. "But you... you have an animal god from nature in you. The blood of the ancients."

"I suppose," I said.

"The celestials keep you all so sequestered because they know you're special."

"Well, we're descended from them, right?" I asked.

He just slanted me a glance. "The celestial program

has been... interesting. That's for sure. Do you believe in them?"

I didn't know how to answer that, and he seemed willing to let it go when he saw my expression.

He led me off a side path and into the woods by the village, sitting on a long, mossy log, patting it next to him for me to sit down.

I did, enjoying the fragrant trees and shrubs and the sunset peeking through the canopy above us.

For a moment, all I felt was peace.

And it set in. I really was free from my village. From my past life. From being an omega.

"What is it like in your village?" Zadis asked excitedly. "I hear it's old-fashioned on the other side of the veil."

"We know what the human world was like," I said. "And we have some human goods that get brought in by the alphas once in a while. But I know nothing of this new world since the great divide."

His eyes darkened for a moment. "Yes, much has happened since then. Since the supernaturals came out of hiding to demand their share of the earth. The celestials all disappeared, and we thought celestial shifters were extinct until we realized the veil was just keeping them from us. No fae is allowed to travel past the veil without having at least some celestial lineage."

"They keep us safe from demons by patrolling the borders," I said quietly.

He shuddered minutely, shaking the log. "Understandable. They don't bother us much. The loving, bonding nature of the fae repels most demons. They aren't interested in us because we desire a connection to nature and each other more than power."

"They want to corrupt those watched over by the celestials, apparently," I said. "Plus, if you don't need protection, then why is Sam here?"

"That devil." Zadis shook his head. "He's worse than any demon. He..." He frowned. "I shouldn't say more. It's forbidden. If Os or another celestial heard me speaking ill of an angel with blood from the ninth celestial realm, I'd be in huge trouble. So I'll just speak generally. The thing Sam has to kill isn't a demon exactly. Just demonic. But it needs to die, and Sam has a renowned reputation for killing. But we don't believe in the divinity of celestials the way that shifters and other celestial-blessed creatures do above the veil. We understand their archangels' power, which is quite similar to that of our strongest warriors. But we prefer not to get our hands dirty dealing death to demons."

I grinned. "That's some good alliteration."

He grinned back. "Thank you."

I liked this guy. I couldn't help it. So I decided I

should help him avoid a beatdown or a possible sword in the face. "Look, I'm with Sam, whether I like it or not. And he said he'd bloodily murder any fae warrior who tried to take me from him."

Zadis sat up straighter. "Then you are his prisoner?"

"It's a long story," I said.

"I have time, and it's a beautiful night," Zadis said, putting a hand on my leg. I moved it, and he simply smiled guiltily. "Can't help it. I want to bond with you so badly."

He was flirting with me, I realized with a sense of something like wonder. Flirting. Alphas didn't bother to flirt with me as an omega. They skipped right past it to trying to push me down.

"I'll tell you my story if you tell me more about bonds," I said.

"Deal," he said. "Though, it will be better if I show you over the next day or two."

I cocked my head, considering it for a second. Bird cries sounded in the distance, eerie and echoing. A lush breeze blew through, bringing the scent of leaves and flowers and even a hint of far-off smoke.

"I come from a small, quiet village in the havens," I said. "A wolf shifter pack. We make everything we can ourselves, through farming and crafting, and our alphas find and import anything else we need." I let out a dry laugh. "Whatever they decide we need anyway."

"Go on," Zadis said softly.

"Have you heard of the alpha and omega program?" I asked.

Zadis shook his head. "No... but I am aware of alpha and omega dynamics in other, non-celestial races."

"Well, in my village, after you reach puberty, you are assigned the title of either alpha, beta, or omega. You can guess which I am."

"Alpha," Zadis said. "I can feel the power radiating off of you."

I shook my head. "Omega."

"Even more special," Zadis said. "Without omegas, I've heard wolves die in the wild."

"Not special," I said sharply, pain lashing through me as the memory of the day I was ordained flashed through my mind. "In my pack, it means torture. It means anyone can do whatever they want to you. Any alpha can claim you. Anything they want to do... they can."

Zadis watched me carefully, concern glowing in his emerald eyes. "I assume that didn't sit well with you. I knew from the moment we met that you didn't like to be told what to do or controlled."

I nodded, relieved to be understood so I didn't have

to go into more detail. Already, I had a tight feeling in my chest just from talking about it.

This time, Zadis put a hand on my knee gently, comfortingly, and I didn't remove it. "Tell me how you came to be here."

"I... broke the rules." *Don't tell him you're at least part demon.* "And Sam was called to be my executioner."

"What was your crime?" Zadis asked, looking nervous.

"Let's just say I rejected the alpha's son in a pretty rude way."

Zadis's mouth firmed into a hard line. "If he was trying to force something on you, that's hardly cause for execution. Unless it was his execution."

"It is if you're an omega in a celestial-blessed pack," I said. "At least in my haven."

Zadis was quiet for a long moment as bird calls sounded in the distance, and I savored the beautiful scents and the pure freedom of the moment.

Right now, no one could tell me what to do or where to go. Maybe I could even run.

Sam's dark eyes, glinting at me before he left, removed any thoughts of doing so.

That sadistic angel would definitely catch up, no matter where I went.

But for now, I was free.

"So I assume Sam refused to execute you," Zadis said. "Since you're here with him." His eyes widened in alarm, long lashes fluttering. "He's not... I mean... You aren't being coerced to—"

"No!" I shook my head, my cheeks burning once again.

"Good," Zadis said. "Because I'd have to kill him."

I looked up at Zadis then, so handsome in the light of the torches that were being lit all around the roads of the village.

It was the first time a man had offered to protect me without asking for anything in return.

I was stymied.

"Don't get me wrong," Zadis said. "I'm no angel. But I can't stand seeing a woman forced to be with someone she doesn't want."

"No," I said. "Sam and I made a deal." The other option was death, but I decided not to mention that.

Zadis turned to me suddenly, taking my hands in his. "I think this is fate. I've been wanting to meet a celestial shifter my whole life, and you come into my village. And you need protection, which I can offer. I want to bond with you, to share powers with the wild animal inside you. Can you at least think about it?"

I blinked at the whirlwind of emotions that moved

through me at his words. I nodded because I had no idea what else to say.

This man was unlike anyone I'd ever met. Plus, Zadis stated his intentions clearly, and Sam only lied or refused to tell me things outright.

"I'm serious about you," Zadis said, squeezing my hands lightly in his large, warm ones. "And I will share my power with you as well."

Sam wasn't serious about me. Then again, Zadis didn't know I had a demon inside me.

Choices, choices.

"I'll think about it," I said, pulling my hands away and standing up. "We should probably get back." I didn't want Sam to start hunting for us.

"But I haven't told you about bonds," Zadis said. "Promise to go out with me tomorrow while your angel is hunting leads, and I'll tell you all you need to know."

I thought for a moment. I liked this guy. Like me, he thought the celestials were less than worthy of worship. I wanted to know why he thought that.

And I wanted to know about fae bonds.

And my wolf wanted to be out in the fresh air.

"I'll let you know," I said. After all, I was a demon wolf on probation, not a normal woman who could date.

But that seemed to be enough for Zadis, and he

nodded. "Just one more thing before we go back. Can you shift for me?"

I stared at him, shocked by the question. "Seriously?"

"Please, please, please," he said, clasping his hands together. It looked so silly for a big warrior to be doing that I nearly laughed at him.

"Fine," I said. "Just for a second."

But before I could, I heard voices calling out in our direction and jolted away from Zadis, putting at least a few feet between us as we stood there.

It was Os, followed by Griffin. Os was wearing some kind of purple tunic with silver embroidery over tight purple leggings and soft slippers. With his light-purple hair and eyes, he looked gorgeous as always.

Griffin wore a blue tee shirt and jeans, and his hair was standing up in all directions as if he'd been napping. He was panting from exertion, his eyes wide with worry until they met mine and relaxed.

I had no idea why he was so protective of me.

Os looked at Zadis with disapproval. "Sam won't like you being here."

"Sam doesn't have to know, does he?" Zadis asked lightly, though there was an edge to his tone.

Os frowned. "I will not keep it from him."

Zadis moved closer to Os, putting a hand on his

shoulder and leaning in, his voice taking on an ominous, serious tone that he hadn't used at all with me. "The fae don't allow those on our land to keep prisoners. If he has her against her will—"

I heard Griffin snarl and step forward, but Os merely put up a hand, waving him back, utterly unperturbed by Zadis's approach.

"It is official celestial business," Os said, turning to glare at the much-taller Zadis. "And it would be best for your personal health and safety if you didn't even fucking look in her direction."

I was shocked by the crassness of Os's language, but Zadis wasn't, though he took a step back.

"Even you won't tell me what to do in my village, Os," Zadis said. "Especially while under our hospitality."

"She isn't for you if you want to live," Os said. "I can tell you that much."

Zadis sent me a look as he headed back toward the road that led into the village. "We'll see about that. She's not for Samael either, if I have anything to say about it."

When he was gone, Griffin turned to me. "We should probably get back."

"Sam left us a note to check in on you," Os said, sitting on the log and heaving a sigh of relief as he did so, like a balloon letting out air.

"I could have taken him," Griffin said stubbornly.

"It's not your job to protect me, Griffin," Os said sternly. "We're just doing this for Sam's benefit. He wants you as part of his... Never mind. You'll see soon enough."

Griffin frowned at that.

"We can't make things too awkward with the high priest's brother while we're here taking care of this," Os said. "We don't always work with the fae, but we get along. No need to escalate tensions."

"He escalated tensions when he brought Cleo out to the woods. Alone. And asked her to shift," Griffin said.

I shrugged. "I don't mind. I like shifting. And Sam left me with nothing to do."

"It's dangerous here. Don't you get that?" Os asked, his purple eyes flashing like high-grade amethysts. "Did Sam not warn you?"

"He did," I said. "I just don't see anything dangerous about this place. They bond with one another. They care deeply about equality and would never have omegas. It's better than the place I was raised. And no fae has called me an idiot or forced a kiss on me, unlike..." I trailed off as I realized neither of them knew about those things Sam did.

Flushing violently, because apparently my redness was going to be permanent, I folded my hands in my lap.

"I'm going to kill him," Griffin said, standing.

Os grabbed him by the wrist and easily jerked him back down to sit on the log, though Griffin was much larger.

"Damn, celestial strength is scary," Griffin said, rubbing his wrist.

"I'm sorry," Os said, looking genuinely apologetic as he brushed long, purple hair back over his shoulder. "But Sam has his reasons for everything he does. He saved Cleo's life." He looked over at me. "When did he force a kiss on you?"

"Back... in my village." I didn't want to say in the stocks because I didn't really want to explain.

"Hm. And has he done anything since?"

My cheeks were impersonating tomatoes. "Not against my will."

"If he does, come talk to me," Os said. "He shouldn't force you."

I nodded.

"I still want to kill him," Griffin said.

"Os is right," I said. "That was a weird situation." And I'd liked it. "He already said he wouldn't do anything to me now."

Os sent me a grin. "And you don't like that?"

"No," I sputtered. "I... I don't care what he thinks. I'm just glad to be free of my village and all those bullies."

Os lowered his voice. "They may adore shifters here, due to their love of nature, but they can't stand demons. If one finds out what you are..."

I swallowed, bitterness filling me at the thought that even if Zadis liked me, he wouldn't truly like that side of me. "It's not my fault there's a demon inside me."

Os sighed in commiseration. "I know. And it's awful. But it is what it is. You'd be in danger getting involved with a fae. If you get close enough and you get discovered..."

"I get it," I said, somewhat bitterly, standing with my hands in clenched fists. "I get it. I'm just wrong wherever I go. Too alpha to be an omega, too demonic to be celestial..." I shook my head. "I just shouldn't exist."

I started back down the path to the village, watching my feet and listening to the mulch cracking beneath me. The sounds of the forest at nighttime.

I could hear Os and Griffin catching up, calling out for me, but I ignored them, feeling too irritated to talk to anyone anymore for now.

It just seemed I couldn't get things right no matter what I did.

19

I was walking fast when Griffin caught my hand.

"Cleo, come on. Talk to me at least." He waved for Os to go on without us, and he did, with a heavy sigh.

"I'll go find Sam," Os said. "See if I can help wrap this up sooner."

I turned to Griffin, tired and irritated by being interrupted with Zadis.

It had been the closest thing to a normal date I'd ever had, and I was enjoying it.

"You really should be careful of that guy," Griffin said, pulling me past some trees to a clearing in the forest where the last rays of the sun were streaming through. We were far enough from the main part of town that no one could overhear us.

I yanked my hand out of Griffin's and whirled to face

him, ready to take all of my rage out on him.

When I saw his sweet, worried, handsome face, I couldn't bring myself to do it.

So I tapped my foot and took a deep breath to gather my patience instead. "I'm tired of you and Os, and even Sam, thinking I'm your business."

"Well, you are," Griffin said. "Sam's business, I mean. I don't know much about what happened before you came to my village with him." He sighed. "But if I'm being overprotective, it's only natural. We're in way over our heads here."

Something in me just snapped.

"You think I'm weak and in need of protection?" I pointed to the collar on my neck. "This represses my demon, but I can be all wolf, right here, right now. You want to go, kitty?"

"Cheese and crackers, no!" Griffin said, wincing. Apparently, that was the closest he could get to a curse at this moment. "I don't want to fight you, Cleo. I just don't want you to be unsafe by overestimating yourself."

"I don't overestimate myself," I growled, pacing up to a stiff Griffin and jabbing my finger hard into his chest so he stumbled back a few steps. "Everyone else under-estimates me. Why is it? Because I'm a woman, an omega? I'm getting a bit sick of your protectiveness, given that you're all fine watching me with Sam."

Griffin rubbed the back of his neck in frustration. "I'm not fine with you being with him. You're a kind person, Cleo. I could sense it instantly when you accepted my animal, though I still had worries you were going to help execute me. But you called my lion beautiful. Not everyone reacts that way. Some think I'm a freak. So yes, I'm protective of you because we're friends. But also, isn't it natural?"

"What makes you think you can even protect me?" I asked, putting my hands on my hips stubbornly. "We're both shifters, but I'm also a demon."

Griffin put up a shushing finger, looking slightly silly. "Don't say that. You don't know how people feel about demons here."

"Yes, I do. I know how people feel about them everywhere, and they're wrong," I said. "At least about creatures like me that seem to be a mix of some kind. I don't want to hurt anyone or wreak havoc."

He took a step forward. "Do you even know what to do if a man comes on to you?"

I merely glared at him, remembering all the alphas I'd thrown off of me over the years.

Then again, Griffin hadn't been there to see me fight, ever. But just the assumption he made that I was weaker than him pissed me off.

"Here, pretend I'm doing it and show me." Griffin

reached out toward me, and lightning fast, out of pure rage, I grabbed his arm, moved my hips quickly in front of his, and hinged downward, sending him flying over my head.

He went crashing into the dirt, sprawling on his back in shock, and sliding a few feet before stopping against a tree, where he let out a grunt of pain. "Okay, you're strong." He pushed himself up, brushed himself off, and put up both his hands in a placating gesture. "My bad. I should have asked if you could fight first."

My chest was heaving from the throw. "It's almost like you don't know I was stoned because I kicked the alpha's son in the crotch. And I fought every alpha who tried to assault or degrade me every year since I hit puberty. I took martial arts but then got kicked out for being an omega. But I kept practicing by myself. I'm strong. I could beat almost every alpha who attacked me. I could stop them, even if I wasn't allowed to attack harder. The only thing that stopped me from hurting them more was the knowledge that there were always more alphas, and more wolves backing alphas, and always more punishment waiting. Always too many against one. No one to help me." I finished, panting, and Griffin stared at me with eyes that were glistening in the low light.

He came forward and pulled me into a hug, and I

didn't realize I was crying until I felt his shoulder grow wet beneath my face as I buried it against him.

I was so tired of fighting alone. So tired of being underestimated. So tired of control always masquerading as protection.

So tired of no one holding me with strong, warm arms like this while caring for me.

Griffin was so tall and so broadly built I felt completely safe nestled in his hold. There was no attraction between us, and I'd never once felt Griffin look at me that way.

But it felt like, for the first time, I might have a true friend.

He pulled back slightly, keeping one hand around me while the other wiped a tear. "I'm so sorry, Cleo. I never knew you had it so rough. I did know you did something to get in trouble. I didn't know you were such a fighter."

"I'm sorry, Griffin," I said. "I overreacted. I'm just tired of people underestimating me."

He smiled down at me. "It's awesome that you know martial arts. You'll have to show me sometime. Make me more deadly." His eyes crinkled, and I could tell he was trying to make me feel better.

"You couldn't hurt a fly," I murmured, coming forward to put my head on his shoulder again.

It was so odd to find a huge man comforting.

"I could, for you or anyone I cared about," he said.

I looked up at him. "You already care about me? I've only ridden on your back and spoken to you a few times."

"I told you. You thought my animal was beautiful. Even those I loved had a hard time accepting me. I knew you were a good person from the first time we met." He gave me a firm squeeze, lifting me off my feet and making me giggle. "And now we're going to be good friends."

"So touching," a sarcastic voice cut in, and we looked up to see Sam approaching from the direction of the village, wearing the black trench coat over his tee and jeans. His hands were in the pockets, and even in the low light, I could see his eyes were burning as he appraised us both. "So I hear from Os you escaped with a fae warrior, and when I come to rescue you, you're getting it on with the cat. Excellent." His tone said excellent was the last thing this was.

Gods, he was tall. Almost as tall as Griffin but with a build that was more to my taste, with broad shoulders and lean muscle and that *face*.

That beautiful face.

"Stop staring at me and get back to our place," Sam

grated out sternly. "It's impossible to work with you out causing problems."

I glared at him. "I wasn't causing problems. Griffin was—"

"She was just talking with that warrior," Griffin said. "Nothing harmful."

"Any interaction with a warrior has the potential to be harmful for her, but go ahead. Justify yourself harder. I'm sure it'll work." Sam's jaw ticked.

Griffin gulped. "Even though nothing was happening between them, I thought I should talk to Cleo about some self-defense—"

"Cleo is already an adequate fighter," Sam retorted. "I've seen a demonstration myself. I also fail to see how that led to embracing."

"It's called a hug," Griffin said, apparently having had it with Sam's anger. "Friends do it. You ever had a friend, Sam? What about a brother? Come on, man."

Sam's eyes flashed, and for a second, his face went paler and his expression slackened. But it felt like I'd imagined it since it only took place in a fraction of a second, and then his face was back to cold stone.

"I owe you nothing, Griffin. You're lucky to be alive." Sam walked over to us and grabbed my hand, ignoring me as I tried to jerk away from him. "We're going home."

Home. That was odd. Staying with him. Sleeping down the hall from him.

Trying not to have dirty thoughts about him. Since I hated him.

"Cleo, are you okay to go with him?" Griffin asked, following after us.

"Go harass Os," Sam said. "If you want to go get in his pants, you don't need to try and get in Cleo's."

So that's what this was all about.

Sam was *jealous*. At least that's what I would think if Sam was anything other than a death-loving psychopath.

Griffin let out a snort. "I'm not scared of you, angel—"

"You should be."

"Be that as it may, I'm not trying to get in Cleo's pants. That's not... my taste," Griffin said.

Sam slanted him a look, then nodded. "Keep it that way."

"Possessive, aren't you?" Griffin asked as we walked past torches and curious fae back to our cottage.

"Of course I am," Sam said. "She's my pet. Unlike Os, I'm a very attentive owner."

Griffin folded his arms. "Os just doesn't treat me like I'm beneath him."

Sam opened the door to our cottage and pushed me inside, then stepped in front of me.

I would have stopped him, but I was kind of enjoying this caveman bullshit, to be honest.

"She's mine," Sam said. "And the only thing you'll be beneath is the ground, if you lay hands on her again."

"Cleo's my friend," Griffin said, nearly growling. "And that means if I want to hug her or hold her if she's sad, then I will." He looked over Sam at me. "You okay for the night, hon?"

I nodded. No matter what, I didn't feel Sam would hurt me because of something like this.

If I was a misbehaving demon maybe, but not this.

Griffin nodded then, and there was warm concern in his eyes as he looked at me. "I'm going back to my place, then."

"Os is still... investigating," Sam said tightly.

Griffin sagged. "I thought as much."

"He has his way of diplomacy. I have mine," Sam said. "A word of advice, Griffin. Seek to get in his pants, not his heart. Os can be colder than I am, in his own way. You'll only be disappointed."

Griffin's hands tightened into fists. "Then you don't know him at all." He whirled away and stomped off then, genuinely angry, and I wanted to go after him and ask more about Os.

It felt like Griffin knew him from somewhere.

But right now, other things were pressing.

Like Sam, who had shut the door to our dwelling and was now advancing on me, forcing me down the hallway as I stared up into his imperious face, intimidated by the sheer size of his shoulders.

When we reached the door to my bedroom, which was closed, he shoved his hands on either side of my head with a loud *bang*, trapping me, and brought his face down in close to mine.

His breath smelled like fresh mint and herbs, and the rich, spicy incense of his skin filled my nostrils.

Every time I was around this man, power just seemed to emanate off him in waves, making it hard to think straight.

I clenched my hands and legs slightly as a wave of arousal moved over me, and Sam seemed to notice, his lips turning up in the slightest of smiles.

"Even when I'm mean to you, you like it," he said, coming in close, brushing my neck and shoulder with his warm breath as the heat of his body loomed only inches away.

It felt like I would light on fire if he touched me.

He moved back to my face, his beautiful eyes darting to my lips as he came closer, closer. His lips nearly brushed mine, and it was suddenly hard to breathe, to think, to do anything but want this man on top of me and possibly—no, definitely—inside me.

"You want me even when I'm mean, far more than you want Griffin or any fae warrior. So remember that no one can make you feel like I do." He moved slightly over to my ear and flicked his tongue out over the lobe, and I had to suppress shock at the pure pleasure of the sensation.

I wanted him to touch me so much more.

But he pushed back from the wall with a heavy sigh, almost looking ashamed of himself.

"You tempt me, pet," he said. "You make me lose myself, both to anger and to lust, and I'm not used to it." His mouth firmed into a hard line. "I'm the master of both, usually." He let out a breath, deflating slightly, and shoved a large finger in my direction. "Be safer tomorrow. I don't want to hear about you hugging Griffin or going off with a fae warrior."

"Griffin isn't into me. Don't you get that?" I yelled at him, frustrated for him teasing me and pulling back yet again. "And I'll go wherever I please and with whomever I want, since you aren't going to give me what I want from you."

His eyes hardened. "Who said I wouldn't?" He sighed. "But I shouldn't." He ran a hand through his hair, tousled by the night air. "We *will* talk about this tomorrow, Cleo. I'm tired and still have things to do." He turned to go down the hall toward his bedroom. "If you need something, too bad. I'm unbotherable for the next hour."

That's what he thought.

He opened the door to his room and disappeared inside, leaving me alone with the house and my books.

I could have read in peace, which I would have been happy to do only a week ago.

But instead, I was curious.

It wasn't like him to just go hide from me in a room like that. There was something in his face when he said it. Something...

The sparks between us had been flying. He was as turned on as I had been. I knew it.

He said that he wasn't totally against giving me what I want, not that I was sure what that was anymore.

Sam was the first man who made me interested in sexuality, and it was hard to tell why.

After all, things had been complicated from the beginning.

So maybe if I went to him, if I prettied myself up and really asked him, or even brought up the fae warrior again if necessary, he could give me what it felt like I ached for deep inside.

I wanted to experience something like I'd seen in my

romance novels, and I felt like Sam could give that to me.

It was probably a terrible idea, but when thinking with my bottom half, I didn't care much.

It was an almost irresistible want. Seeing Sam show up made it instantly clear how different my feelings were for him than for Griffin or even Zadis.

Something inside me flared to life when he was by my side.

Something that had been there since I first saw him in the street.

I walked to my room to freshen up, brushed my hair, pinched my cheeks, and put on something a little more revealing. A pink tank top and short black shorts. Then I padded down the narrow hallway to Sam's bedroom, where light streamed from under the door.

So he was still up.

I sucked in a breath, gathering my courage. After all, he might reject me again, but then I'd be no worse off than before.

Hopefully.

I raised my hand to knock on the door and heard a muffled groan.

I panicked instantly, thinking he might be hurt, and grabbed the handle to shove the door open.

Luckily, it was unlocked. I'd never heard Sam make a

noise like that, so I was sure he was really hurt.

But as I shoved open the door and saw him, several thoughts immediately ran through my head as I let out a shrill scream of shock.

1. Never bother a celestial when he says he's "unbotherable."

2. Men masturbating sometimes make sounds oddly like they've been injured.

3. Sam wasn't a celestial. At least not *only* a celestial. Because the person staring at me in utter shock, while lying back naked and stroking their cock, didn't look like Sam at all.

He had long, sultry red hair in a dark shade like blood about to clot. Glowing red eyes that seemed larger than usual.

Horns, black and sinister, curling up out of his beautiful hair.

Long, pointed ears and a white tint to his skin that hadn't been there before. Little flushes of pink to add contour to his cheeks, making him look almost otherworldly.

The face and body, that was all Sam, though his coloring was different. Paler and more ethereal and flushed with pink.

We stared at each other for a tense second, and then his face went bright red.

"Get out!" he yelled, grabbing a blanket to cover himself.

I yelped and ran for it, not even slamming his door in my rush to escape.

Holy shit, what just happened? What did I just see?

My cheeks were flaming like someone was pressing a hot iron to either side of them, and the image I'd seen upon opening the door was burned into my brain.

Sam, if that's who he was, lying back on those pillows, gorgeous muscles on display.

It had been the most erotic thing I'd ever seen in my life.

His beautiful hand over that huge cock. Liquid leaking from the tip. His chest taut and flexing, his abs rigid, his long legs spread.

I wanted to memorize it, even though I had no right to see it, so I tried to put it out of my mind.

I locked my door, but I doubted it would save me when he came to talk to me.

I'd just caught a celestial masturbating when I wasn't supposed to, and I'd also just realized that celestial wasn't what he appeared to be at all.

I'd seen his *horns*.

Heavy footsteps pounded down the hallway toward me from Sam's bedroom.

Yeah, I was probably a dead wolf walking.

20

When the footsteps reached my room, the lock jiggled as someone, presumably Sam, tried to wrench it open.

Then, to my astonishment, I saw the lock slowly turning to an unlocked position, and the door swung open, Sam pushing it with one hand.

He was back in his usual form, with mussed golden-blond and brown curls and those dark eyes with the golden ring.

His bare upper body, full of those traditional tattoos, gleamed with sweat, and I watched a drop slowly move down and over his abs, wishing it was my tongue that could do so.

His tattoos had been missing in his other form.

My eyes followed down to the waistband of the loose gray sweatpants he was wearing.

Oh no. I'd always been a goner for gray sweatpants.

Sam took another step inside, and I cringed back on my bed, knowing there was probably no way to escape from him.

He put his hands on his hips in a cocky stance and glowered down at me as though he didn't even know what to do with me.

Then he ran an elegant hand through his waves, mussing them further.

"Cleo," he said firmly. "What did I tell you about not bothering me?"

I glared at him, fire sparking in me. "What part of me, ever since you met me, made you think I would listen?" I asked back.

Shit, I was probably going to die, but he had to admit I had a point. Defying authority was practically a sport for me.

He let out a sigh. "I wasn't planning to tell you yet." He turned away from me, looking at the ground, giving me a view of his broad back and its spectacular muscles.

Then he whirled to face me again, this time with folded arms. It was the first time I'd seen him feeling even vaguely uncomfortable.

"This is my fault, so you can stop cringing back like I'm going to hurt you," he said. "I know I'm a cruel person, but have I hurt you, physically at least?"

I shook my head slowly.

"If I'd wanted to, I would have by now. But as I said before, I need a favor from you."

"What favor?" I asked.

"Again, I can't tell you much until we get to our next destination. Where we can have privacy."

I looked around us at the empty room. "Aren't we private now?"

Sam's expression darkened. "I don't trust the fae. Now that you've caught their attention, they could be spying on us."

"I see," I said, a small shiver going up my back at the thought. "But I don't think Zadis is like that. He's really nice..."

Sam took a step closer, glaring. Damn, he was intimidating up close. So much beauty. So much power. "You don't know that fae. Don't assume you do just because he's putting on a good front."

"He's honest and upfront, unlike you," I said. "He told me he's serious about me, and—"

Sam's eyes widened in shock and then narrowed in a glare. "He said that?" He turned to go. "I'm going to fight him."

"What?" I squeaked, running after him. I reached out to grab him, but there was no shirt to hold on to.

Sam spun and trapped me against the hallway wall,

one hand on either side of my head. He seemed to like having control of me that way.

I'd be lying if I said it wasn't hot. At the same time, I knew if it was anyone else, I'd be making meatloaf out of their crotch.

"You aren't getting this," he hissed at me. "You're this innocent little celestial who knows nothing about this world, but that's okay. You have me to guide you, if you would only listen and stop waking up my fucking incubus!"

I blinked at him in shock. "Incubus?"

He pushed off the wall and away from me and headed into the kitchen. He didn't say anything, so I guessed he just assumed I would follow.

I did.

When I got to the kitchen, he was drinking a glass of water and staring out the window over the small sink at the dark night, torches glowing in the distance.

He turned to face me, leaning against the counter with his hands planted on the edge of it.

My eyes fought not to wander down to his sweatpants.

"I knew wolves were horny, but this is really something else," he muttered.

Damn, how did he always know?

He folded his arms and crossed one leg over the

other, still leaning back. "As an incubus, knowing what you want is one of my abilities. I can sense your desires. But even if I had no powers, it's so obvious on your little face, you virgin."

I gasped. "Why do you keep saying that like it's a bad thing?"

"I keep saying it so that both of us remember what a bad idea it would be for us to get sexually involved, no matter how many come-hither looks you send me."

I thought back to the day Sam fought the minotaurs and talked to me in the trees after. "But you said that I just couldn't fall in love with you, not that we couldn't... couldn't..." I flushed bright red, unable to say it as he had.

"When I said we could fuck?" He cocked his head slightly, and an errant curl fell over his forehead.

I nodded.

"I was trying to scare you. I know you celestials are raised from birth thinking about a soul mate, and you aren't allowed casual sex, so I thought if I told you there was no chance of commitment, you'd back off. But you still look at me like you want to tear my pants off."

"I have a thing about sweatpants," I mumbled.

He looked down at himself and then grinned. "I do look good in them." His expression sobered. "But we need to do something about this. Because if you keep looking at me like that, my incubus is going to come out again."

"Do the others know? Does Os know?" I asked. "The celestials, they—"

"Whether they know is one thing. Whether anyone can do anything about me, even if they do know, is another. Even if someone knows my history, they won't dare bring it up." He looked to the side. "That doesn't mean I want the fae to know any of my weaknesses." He sighed. "Besides, they hate demons. That's what I keep telling you."

I thought back to Zarris, how he was rude about Sam's history, alluding to something bad.

I decided not to mention it for the moment. It would probably only make him madder.

"So you're part demon?" I asked. "Why would it be a weakness?"

"It's only a weakness if they know exactly what I am," Sam said. "And most won't meet an incubus in their lifetime."

"But... you're a celestial," I said. "From the ninth realm."

"Half of my blood is from the ninth celestial realm," he muttered. "But I have no love for anyone there."

"Then why do you—"

"I don't have to give you my reasons," Sam snapped.

"So... why is it me that's making you turn into an incubus?"

"Celestials age much slower than other creatures," Sam said, pacing now in front of the sink, his hands clasped behind his back. "I didn't manifest my celestial side till I was fully grown as a demon. Then I took this form. My incubus... it hasn't been a problem. I feed using bloodlust instead of sex and—"

"You feed on bloodlust?" I asked.

His eyes narrowed, glittering like black diamonds and gold. "I said I didn't owe you any answers."

"But you're telling me halfway," I said. "That's almost worse than no answers at all."

"I guess I better leave, then," he said, turning as if to go.

"No," I said. "Please. Look, if it's my fault your incubus is coming out, just tell me how to stop it."

He leaned back, ruffling his hair again. "I'm not even sure. I've never struggled with this before. But when you look at me like you want me... when you feel pleasure from what I do... it's almost impossible not to take my demon form... and give you what you're begging for."

I flushed, but something heated and excited filled my chest. "Why don't you, then?" I asked.

He sneered. "Like I'm a defiler of virgins."

"You're a demon," I retorted.

"Not anymore," he said. "I retired. I'm a celestial now." He gave me a smug, superior look that made me want to bring his incubus out just to bother him.

"So what's wrong with your incubus coming out?" I asked. "Look, it went away."

"While I might be able to maintain an erection while *some* people are staring at me with abject fear, you are apparently not one of them." He rubbed the back of his neck, exhaling roughly. "Damn it all, Cleo. What am I going to do with you?"

I wiggled my eyebrows at him. "You could start my sex education, incubus-style," I joked.

He gave me a look that said he didn't think I was very funny. "You don't want to do it with an incubus, virgin. Incubi can see your deepest, darkest desires, and make them happen, whether you like it or not. Incubi are ruthless, nearly senseless when feeding. They just feed on pleasure instead of blood, like vampires."

I swallowed, thinking for a moment. "So you can read my mind?"

"No, but I can feel what you want," Sam said. "Even when I try to block it out. I don't know why."

I scratched the back of my head, erotic thoughts of Sam masturbating running through my mind. "I mean, none of that sounds too bad."

"You would pass out most likely," he said. "Look, just

trust me. It's nothing to mess with." He started to leave the room. "If you leave me to deal with it, and promise to actually not bother me this time, I'll get the frustration out and hopefully suppress my form for a good while."

I glanced down at the crotch of his sweatpants. "I could help you deal with it."

Dear gods, what had gotten into me, being so forward?

Horniness. Horniness had gotten into me.

"I would make a terrible lover, regardless," Sam said, frowning. "The celestial side of me is ruthlessly possessive and jealous. The incubus side is insatiable. I know you haven types. You want to walk on the wild side, but—"

"I don't," I said. "I've never wanted another man before."

A flush brushed the top of his high cheekbones, making him look adorably flustered, though it was still a very slight expression compared to anyone else.

It probably took a lot to break him.

For some reason, I wanted to see it.

"We are... We shouldn't..." He looked away. "I didn't think you would still want to after..." His eyes met mine, deadly serious. "This doesn't have a happy ending, pet."

I swallowed. "I didn't have a happy ending in mind." I grinned. "Well, except, you know..."

He shoved his hand through his hair again, apparently a nervous habit. "This is such a terrible idea."

"But I'm... I could help you," I said. "And I promise, no feelings. I get it. I won't fall for you."

His eyes narrowed. "I've heard that before. And unlike some incubi, I don't get off on hurting people."

I blinked. "But you actually kinda do," I said.

"I mean hurting people emotionally. If I hurt someone physically, they deserve it. And yes, I enjoy it. I'm part incubi. I feed on sensations. Pain is one of them." He raised an eyebrow at me. "I'm not the prince you're looking for, princess."

I wrinkled my nose. "Princess?"

He shrugged. "That's what you are to me. Spoiled, sheltered..."

"I was bullied my whole life," I said.

"You've never been tortured or hung by your skin for weeks while being flayed, have you?"

I shook my head, nauseated just at the thought of it.

"I've seen things you couldn't possibly imagine," Sam said. "You haven't even been to any of the abyssal realms, also known as the dark realms."

I was quiet for a moment. "No, but I want to know about them."

He shook his head. "No." He planted his hands on his hips and faced the window again. "I'm not doing it. It's going to blow up in our faces." His jaw clenched so hard I could see it from behind. "I will overcome this. It's only a matter of time."

"But aren't you hungry?" I asked, coming up behind him.

I didn't know how I felt the power to be so bold, but I'd never wanted someone so much.

And I wanted to help him, even if it was just an excuse.

Slowly, tentatively, I tried to wrap my arms around his waist.

He turned and pushed me back, gently removing my hands.

"I'm a celestial now, almost all of the time. I feed on adulation."

"But most people despise you," I said.

"It's still attention," he said.

"And wait, what do you mean the celestials feed on adulation?"

His lips firmed, and his eyes said he'd said something he didn't mean to.

He moved toward me, and even though I got the feeling he was just trying to distract me, it worked. He backed me up to the counter and put a hand on either side of me, looming over me.

I looked to the side, feeling his warmth, the heat of his gaze. "Why do you keep doing that?"

"Because I can't figure you out," Sam said. "And I like to keep you still when I'm studying you." He let out a sigh and put his head on my shoulder, shocking me. "I just don't get why you have this effect on me. I feel many people want me. My incubus doesn't ever feel like he's jumping out of my skin. Only with you." He shook his head. "It's an unnecessary complication."

"What can we do about it?" I asked.

He pulled back to look down at me, and my shoulder still tingled where he'd been.

"If you want to be with me, and you're truly willing to accept that I will never feel anything for you... there is something we can do."

"What?"

"I can keep taking care of it, but it's not going to satisfy my inner demon, honestly." He thought for a moment. "I haven't had time to really think about it, and I thought this all could wait until we got to my place. But perhaps this could work for both of us."

"What could?"

Sam grabbed my hand and pulled me in against him, his hand tightly wrapped around my waist. "You need to start exploring vices anyway, if you want to start accessing your demonic powers. I need to know what you are, and I can't feel that yet. Not when you're this suppressed."

"Because I'm a virgin?" I asked.

"No," he said. "Because you've been living all your life under silly rules that expressly kept you from ever accessing your inner powers as a demon." He put up his hand. "Let's see, what do celestials say is a sin?" He counted them off on his fingers. "Sex. Eating too much. Loud laughter. Murder. All the fun things."

"Murder is a fun thing?"

He glanced down. "You should try it sometime."

"No thanks," I said, wrinkling my nose.

He gave me a funny look but dropped it. "Regardless, you give up your power when you deny yourself everything you want. You have to start taking it all back. That means sexual exploration at the very least."

"Ah," I said. "But how does that work for both of us?"

"I get fed," he said simply. Then he shook his head and pushed away from me to walk away. "No, I'm not thinking straight. That is the stupidest idea I've ever had. We just have to stay farther apart until we leave this realm and get to my place. Killing that void creature should satiate my bloodlust at least."

I stared after him, shocked and bereft. My legs were

practically trembling with anticipation, and he could just walk off like that?

"Then should I sexually experiment with Zadis?"

Sam stopped dead, then turned to give me a glare scarier than any before. Which, with Sam, was really saying something. "What. Did. You. Say?" His tone was quiet, deceptively calm.

"You said it," I said, so nervous I was surprised my voice wasn't shaking. But Sam was right. All my life, I'd been kept back from the things I wanted.

And now there was something I wanted right in front of me, and I'd be damned if I didn't at least try to take it.

"Said what?" His tone was rage and ice all at once. For someone who couldn't get feelings, he sure did get jealous. Maybe that was his celestial side coming through.

But why should he care? All he wanted was a favor.

"You said I need to unlock my powers. Zadis is willing to help me."

Sam breathed in and out once through his nose, like an angry bull. "There will be all manner of men, or women if you like, ready to assist you at our next destination. Why him?"

I looked at him honestly. "Because it can't be you."

"Damn it, Cleo," he rasped, saying my name like an oath. "I told you, you tempt me beyond all reason."

I took a step toward him. "Then lose your reason," I said. "Come with me."

He froze as I reached him, his huge body stock still as I raised a hand to stroke his cheek.

He jolted back, looking at me like I'd burned him.

He grabbed my wrists, locked them together over my head, and spun me to the fridge, slamming my hands down against it. "Not like that. If we're together, it will be raw, perhaps even violent."

"You won't hurt me," I said, looking into those dark, fathomless eyes that shone with gold.

"I'll ruin you," he said. Then his lips closed over mine.

21

I was kissing *Sam*. And it wasn't like that night in the stocks.

It was hot, urgent, just on the edge of vicious, as his teeth rode the edge of my lip and bit down just enough to make me squeak in shock.

But his tongue flicked out over the sore spot, making pleasure flow through me, filling me with warmth as he thrust into my mouth in an experienced move that had me parting my lips instantly.

His tongue explored slowly, making heat rise exponentially as he stroked the most sensitive places of my mouth, thrusting slowly in and out in a way that made me clench my legs, thinking of other things.

"Already overwhelmed, little wolf?" Sam asked, pulling back to look at me while keeping me pinned.

"Yeah right," I said, though I was panting. I leaned forward to catch his mouth again, but his lips slammed into mine, holding me back against the fridge.

He insisted on taking control, thrusting his tongue harder in against me and making me let out a muffled groan. His tongue twisted together with mine, teasing it in an erotic dance that had me wetter than I'd ever been.

I wanted my hands free. I wanted to entwine them in his gorgeous wavy hair, hold his face, but if this was how he wanted it, the only way he'd accept it, then I'd take it.

And I had a feeling that after he had me, I would never be the same.

He pulled back again, panting, and I noticed a fine sheen of sweat on his skin. His eyes flashed red when they met mine, and he grunted and closed them. Then he took a deep breath, and when he looked up again, they were their usual dark color. "This isn't working. You drive my incubus crazy."

"Let your incubus out," I whispered, still hazy just from the kiss. A few men in my life had forced kisses on me. But this, what Sam could do with his lips, the things he could say without saying anything...

It was amazing.

I wanted so much more. I wanted to see him in incubus form, losing control. Both of his forms were so hot.

He chuckled, brushing back my hair. "So eager, little wolf." He moved forward to kiss the sensitive spot just under my ear, and I gasped, arching back and writhing as much as his hold on my hands would let me.

"Oh gods, that's intense," I gasped out as he sucked and licked, then sucked harder so pain sparkled over my skin, covered by pleasure as his tongue stroked over it, his lips kissing it better.

I could already tell what this would be like with him. Pleasure and pain. Heat and fire.

Both of us trembling, trying not to go any faster.

"I could never... show you my incubus in this kind of situation," he said, panting. "I told you it's not safe."

"Not ever?" I asked, staring up at him.

He shook his head. "I told you. I'd be out of control."

"I don't believe you," I said, looking up at him stubbornly.

His lips pressed over mine almost savagely, and this time, when he claimed my mouth, he owned it. I could barely breathe, but I didn't want him to stop.

When he pulled back, my legs were trembling.

"You can't scare me," I rasped out. "All I want is more. It feels so good."

His eyes flashed red again. "Maybe I'll bring my incubus out whether I want to or not." He released my hands by my sides and stepped in close, pressing our bodies together as he reached up one hand to stroke through my long hair. "You're so beautiful, and you don't even know it."

My eyes flashed at him. "I don't want to know it. It's done me no good. Only brought me trouble."

He looked me over, nodding understandingly. "Beauty is dangerous, and you are gorgeous, no matter how you try to hide it. But as long as you're with me, I'll protect all of you, your beauty included."

Pain pinged my heart at his unexpected sweetness, and suddenly, I just wanted him to be rough again.

"Can we go to your room? My room? Any room?" I asked. "It's getting hard to stand..." I glanced down at my trembling legs, and he grinned.

"Usually, I would make a game of this. See how long I could torture you until you can't stand anymore, till you'd fall to the ground without me holding you, till you couldn't feel anything but the sheer need to orgasm." He exhaled. "But not tonight."

To my shock, he bent, shoved his shoulder into my waist, and picked me up, fireman style, carrying me down the hallway like a sack of potatoes.

Small potatoes.

I thumped his chest playfully. "This is not how you're supposed to do it. It's not princess style."

He just laughed. "I'm a demon, not a prince."

My heart raced in anticipation, and I got even a little bit wetter thinking about what would happen when we got to his room.

He opened the door and practically threw me on the bed, dropping me roughly. But my landing was soft on the mattress, amongst the luxurious silk covers.

He landed over me, trapping me with his hands at either side of my head.

"So possessive," I said, laughing.

"Always," he said. "I warned you about that."

I leaned up, feeling bold, and nipped at his earlobe. "I'm not good at heeding warnings."

"I know," he said in a low growl. His eyes flickered red and black before settling on black again. "Why do you do this to me?"

"I don't know," I said. Then I wrapped my hands around his neck and pulled him down for another kiss.

As our lips pressed together, it was gentler this time. Until his tongue came out to twirl with mine again, making that low, slow heat build in me.

I was practically aching between my legs. How could I get any wetter? But Sam didn't seem in any hurry to be done kissing me.

He kissed down my neck, over my ear, sucking the sensitive lobe and biting it lightly, dragging it through his teeth. He kissed over my shoulder, then down the front of my neck, coming dangerously close to my décolletage before coming back up to my lips, claiming my mouth in yet another harsh kiss.

I hadn't known just kissing could do this. The longer he kissed me, the more rabid I felt. Everywhere he touched was blessed with pleasure. Everywhere he kissed was set on fire.

If I wasn't obsessed with this man before this, I had a feeling I would be now.

I'd never wanted anything from anyone. But right now, I wanted everything from Sam. The ache in me, like something tensing, was building as my entire body kept tightening and then relaxing into his touch.

I mewled helplessly against his mouth, trying to thrust my hips up against him, unsure of what I was after.

"Shh," he whispered against my lips, before kissing me again. "I won't go fast with you."

I broke away from the kiss, gasping. "I don't think I can get more turned on."

He raised his head, and the cocky, dark smile he gave me made my sex clench. "So naive it's almost adorable." His lips moved down to my neck, softly kissing and licking, as my hands dug into his strong back. I jumped against a sensitive nerve he found and looked down to see him looking up at me in triumph. Then he flicked his tongue out against the place again, as if just to demonstrate that he had control over me.

And he did. Gods, he did. I felt like a puppet in his hands. Just by kissing, he made my body feel like something foreign to me, something he could convince to do anything. The moans coming out of me, the way I kept arching, grabbing him, kissing him back...

It all felt so wholly unlike me.

It also felt like finally being myself, touching a deep inner part of me that I'd always kept pressed down.

I let out a growl as I tried to reach down for his waistband to show him what I wanted.

He grabbed my hand and glared at me, putting it above my head as he put the other with it as well. "If you're going to be bad, I'm going to have to punish you."

My eyes went wide. "What?" I began to stutter, wondering if he was going to stop. "I just... wanted to do something for you."

"I don't feed like that," he said. Then his hand reached for my top, and he lifted it over my head, using it to tie my hands quickly.

I looked up, wondering how he'd done that, but I didn't have time to think about it much because his hands were moving toward my bra. Was he going to—

He pulled down one cup and lowered his face to it, looking at me once more for confirmation.

Oh gods, no one had seen me like this. It felt so forbidden, so dirty. If I had my hands free, I would have covered myself.

"If you want to escape, little wolf, just say so. But if you want to keep going, I'm not going to stop until you've come."

"I... I..." I looked to the side. "It's just so embarrassing."

"Nothing about this is embarrassing," he growled. "Nothing here is shameful. We are alive. This is life, the very basis of life."

"Do we need protection?" I asked.

"I'm not going to fuck you," he said.

"Then how will you feed?"

He looked at me askance. "I don't feed from my own orgasm. I feed from yours."

My eyes widened again. This man was really something else.

His mouth went lower, closer to my nipple, and gods, he looked sexy from that angle, almost predatory, his huge, naked shoulders flexing, his breath warming my nipple as I let out a tortured gasp.

"Please, Sam. Do something, anything."

His lips closed over my nipple, encasing the sensitive tip in hot warmth and wetness that made me arch back at just how good it felt.

But as usual, Sam wasn't in a hurry. He swirled his tongue slowly, languidly around my nipple while watching me with those seductive eyes.

I'd never felt so watched before.

I writhed, I bucked, but nothing got him to stop licking and sucking, until my nipple was a tortured peak that couldn't take any more.

Then he moved to the other. When he'd finished torturing it with pleasure as well, I felt like I was falling apart, desperate, writhing. Missing something, though everything he did felt like the only heaven I'd experienced.

"Hurry," I said. "Get it over with." I wanted to feel that orgasm I'd felt in my room.

"I said I'd make love to you," he growled. "I didn't say you could tell me how to do it."

"But I'm ready to come. I swear. Touch me—" I knew I was pathetic, practically begging, but I couldn't help it. If I didn't come soon, I felt I would break.

"You said you wanted to help feed me," he murmured, licking my nipple again. "Not all orgasms are equal. Let's make this a big one."

I arched against him, only getting more sensitive everywhere the longer we went. "What do you mean a big one?"

"I'm going to edge you," he said. "I told you. Incubus.

I won't make you pass out, and I won't fuck you, but I'm going to take you to the edge of your limits, and by the time you come, you're going to think you're going to die the feeling will be so strong. You're going to dread it, beg me for mercy, and that, my little wolf, is when you will come for me."

I blinked but had no further time to consider his extremely hot words because his hand was trailing down, down, to the top of my shorts. He lifted his head to look at me, waiting for me to nod, and then shoved his hand down between my legs, cupping at first.

I mewled because, in simply holding me with that big, hot palm, he couldn't touch me with more pinpoint precision just where I wanted it.

Where I needed it.

His fingers palpated, pressing down into my folds and stroking lightly, gliding easily along my wetness.

"You're soaked," he said, lifting his hand for me to see it.

I turned away, flushing violently, but he reached out his free hand to tilt my face back to him, forcing me to watch as he licked my wetness from his hand, slowly, as if it were the most delicious thing he'd ever eaten.

His eyes gleamed at me, red at the centers now. "Never be ashamed of your desire, Cleo. It's the most beautiful, normal thing in the world."

"For an incubus, you sure can be gentle," I said.

"Wait and see if you still say that in a minute," he said as his hand moved back down to my sex.

This time, two of his fingers rested over my clit, pressing lightly. I jerked instantly, the feeling like lightning moving through me at this first touch on the most sensitive part of my sex.

He stroked lightly, slowly, patiently, watching my eyes. He moved in circles, and I closed my eyes and tried to hold on. Colors danced behind my eyelids.

He moved in lines, then drew something that felt like the alphabet. Every time I would arch back, close to that incredible sensation I'd had before, he would pull back his finger, give me a secretive smile, and go back to kissing my breasts.

My whole body was shaking, trembling, and soaked in sweat as he continued, and I realized he might have a point.

My legs were nearly numb yet shaky from being so tense, my breasts were on fire in the best way. My clit was swollen, getting even more sensitive. And he had already figured out the motions I liked and was now torturing me with them, bringing me to the edge quicker and quicker, then stopping and leaving me hanging in an almost painful way.

Tension had built in every part of my body, and I was

breathing heavily. I couldn't take it anymore, even though it all felt so good. He kissed my lips, my breasts, my shoulders, wrapping me in a whirlwind of pleasure that just kept my tension rising higher and higher.

If he kept this up, it felt like soon I would leave the atmosphere and not be able to breathe anymore.

And he looked as though he had no intention of stopping.

Gods, this was going to be strong. I could feel it in my trembling leg muscles, in my clenching core.

And for a moment, I was almost afraid of it. Like it was a freight train rushing toward me. Even though his finger swirled on my clit, even as pleasure rose to a fever pitch, like a ringing note, I almost felt afraid to come.

I writhed helplessly and felt his hand on my hands, pressing me back and holding me. With so much built-up pressure, it felt impossible to stay still.

I need to come. I need to come.

Finally, as his finger stroked me slightly and he lifted it above my clit and paused, he sent me a wicked, teasing look, and I knew exactly what he wanted.

And I was too desperate, too out of my mind from his teasing to care anymore. I didn't know if it had been minutes or hours or if I was going to die when I came.

"Please, please, Sam."

"Come for me, pet," he murmured against my ear, his hot breath taking me even higher.

His finger pressed down on my clit as he spoke, then jerked slightly to the right, and I came instantly, pleasure overwhelming me in waves strong enough to drown me.

He held me down as I jerked through it, even though I wanted to hold him. He watched every minute with that intense expression, as if he couldn't even blink or miss a second, and that only made it hotter, made my body buck and writhe like never before against pleasure so great I could barely conceive it.

More than even before, this release felt like *life*.

I felt alive and whole and somehow healed by him. Even if he was just trying to feed, or make it the best orgasm ever for him, I'd never forget the way he watched me. Learned me. Pleased me so hard I thought I was going to pass out and die.

And this was him being gentle?

He sat back finally, licking the tips of his fingers again, his abs flexing, his eyes red, his beautiful face pleased as could be. "Thanks for the meal."

I couldn't talk yet. Couldn't really formulate words or full thoughts. My body was still wracked with aftershocks, my muscles almost sore from how hard everything had clenched and released, surging with pleasure, almost against my will.

Realizing he'd released my hands, I pushed myself up shakily. The difference between this orgasm and the other one had been day and night.

He'd been right.

And as he sent me a wicked look that said he knew he'd just proved his point, I realized with something like dread that this was only the beginning.

What had I gotten myself into?

22

"Meal? Seriously?" I asked Sam, finally composing myself as he pushed off the bed and stretched, showing off perfect muscles.

He shrugged. "We both know what this was. Helping each other." He cocked his head. "Don't you feel your inner demon more strongly?"

I blinked. "What do you mean?"

He looked like he was fighting hard not to roll his eyes at me. "That little voice that pops up sometimes, telling you to do things that seem to be the opposite of what you're doing or what you 'should' do as a celestial."

I felt the blood drain from my face. "That's my inner demon?"

He nodded, still flushed and looking so handsome it was hard to breathe.

Had we really just done that together? After such an intense orgasm, the lust was starting to retreat, and in its place, slight shame began to rise in me.

Oh gods, I had been horny.

"Don't you dare go getting all celestial and guilty on me," he said sharply. "Nothing we did was wrong." He shook his head. "Sex is a powerful thing between two beings. Of course the celestial gods want to control even that." His dark eyes met mine, no longer wine-colored. "But this is our right. To have pleasure. To not just survive but *live*."

I had never thought of it like that. Then again, I hadn't been attracted to anyone before him.

"Is it just your incubus making me want you?" I blurted out.

He scowled at me.

"Not that you're not gorgeous. I just mean, is there some kind of spell? Some special ability you have to draw people to you?"

He nodded. "Not a spell. Just being hot. Most incubi are. Becoming a celestial didn't seem to do anything to dampen my appeal." He looked down at his tattooed arms. "I got all of these because I hated my celestial skin. I wanted to hide it as long as possible. But they didn't dampen my appeal either."

I grinned. "So you can't escape from being hot?"

"From being wanted," he said, giving me a look that was more thoughtful than usual. "Something you might understand."

"Yeah," I said. "Seems a bit like being an omega. Everyone wants to fuck you or, in my case, bully you."

"They wanted to fuck you too," Sam said flatly, standing and grabbing a shirt to pull over his head. "You just didn't let them. Good for you."

I stared at him blankly. "Thank you?"

He nodded. "We need to talk about tomorrow."

It felt a little odd, getting back to business after what just happened between us. But he was right. He'd fed. I'd gotten my lust satiated and even increased awareness of my inner demon too.

Hopefully, she'd show up soon.

I'm right here. You just never listen to me.

I went rigid.

Sam lifted his head. "You're hearing it, aren't you?"

I swallowed. "Maybe."

"The more in touch you get with it, the less it will feel so separate. But as you are part celestial, the two different sides of you will always be at odds."

"You would know," I said softly. "You're part both as well."

"Yes," he said. "Though, it's different."

I sighed. "I have felt this voice before. Telling me to fight. Telling me I didn't have to listen to alphas."

"Why didn't you listen?" Sam asked.

"Because I didn't want to die," I said.

"So you don't trust it."

"What?"

"Your inner demon." He lay back on the bed next to me, dressed in a tee shirt and sweatpants now, as he tossed a blanket over me to keep me warm. "The voice said you didn't have to obey alphas. That you could win. Why didn't you listen?"

Gods, he was right.

"I thought it was just a crazy wild hair. Something that could get me killed. Delusions."

"You're stronger than you think," he said. "I knew that when I saw you fighting that alpha when I visited your village."

"You called me an idiot," I retorted.

"You are," he shot back. "For letting them hurt you."

I thought back to that day and sat bolt upright, grabbing the blanket around me. "Is that why you kissed me? To awaken my demon?"

He looked at the ceiling, as though my question didn't even warrant a response.

"Is that why you were kind to me? You could tell we both had inner demons?"

"My demon isn't an inner demon. It's just less dominant than my celestial side, so I spend most of my time in this form."

"Do I have another form?" I asked excitedly.

He smirked. "I guess we'll have to see. When I can trust you enough to take your collar off."

"Why can't you just take it off now?" I asked.

"When you keep threatening to run off to Zadis?" His expression darkened. "I don't think so."

He had a point.

"But how am I going to learn to use my powers or awaken my inner demon if I always have my collar on?"

"You can still hear your inner voice and become more aware. But it would be dangerous to take your collar off. Even for you."

"Why?" I asked. "I wouldn't hurt myself."

"Not on purpose," he said. "But you've been running around with something inside you, and until we know what that is, and how to train you in controlling it, your life could be at risk."

"Why? What kind of demon do you think I am?"

"I haven't the slightest idea," he said, continuing to stare at the ceiling while my heart was beating rapidly.

"Why did you tell them I was a succubus if you're the one who's an incubus?"

He let out a sigh, as if growing impatient with the

topic. "If we ran into someone who could detect demon magic, they would sense incubus, and that would allow me to hide what you really are."

"Which is?"

He refused to say more. "The demon inside you has always been suppressed by your inner celestial. As we wake it up, it might be angry since you haven't listened for so long. You fought back. That's good. It's part of that inner demon. Rebelliousness, freedom. Those are traits demons value, just as celestials value power and faithfulness. We want to wake your demon, but not give it full power until it calms down. Otherwise, it might destroy you."

"But you have no idea what it—"

"Cleo, we need to talk about tomorrow."

He's hiding something.

There was my inner demon again. So he was right. What we did together strengthened her. Strengthened a part of me.

I'd always thought sex was this forbidden, scary thing alphas did to omegas only when mated.

But if it was anything like what I'd just done with Sam, then I really looked forward to doing it with someone I loved one day.

You don't have to love them, my inner demon added helpfully.

I snorted at that, making Sam finally look over at me.

Then he turned back to the ceiling calmly. "I'm glad you're able to have more open discourse with your inner demon. Now, about tomorrow. I'll be out conducting interviews, and I don't want you going anywhere with Zadis."

I rolled onto my side to stare at him, still covering myself with the blanket. "You don't get to tell me who to spend time with, even if I do have a collar on."

Sam's eyes flashed, and he sat up. "If you feed on me, you can't possibly feed another."

He never said that before we started, so in my mind, he couldn't change things now.

"I thought this wasn't serious," I said. "Just casually helping one another out."

"There's nothing casual about sex," Sam spat. "It's deeply intimate, no matter how you want to think about it."

"I..." I ran my hand through my hair, mussed and tangled from thrashing on my pillow. "I don't want to think about it. I just couldn't help it."

And the demon lying beside me was never going to have feelings for me, so I needed to stay as distant as possible.

No matter how much I might be coming to like him.

"I don't think exclusivity is too much to ask," Sam said.

"You didn't ask it," I said. "You never said that was a condition of what we did." My hands felt shaky. I didn't want to owe him anything.

I didn't want to belong to anyone, at least in that way.

"I'm not looking for a mate," I said. "If there is a demon inside me, then I just want to live independently. Take care of myself."

"And how are you going to do that?" Sam asked. "You have no money and no idea of anything to do with this world."

He had me there.

"I... I hope you'll keep training me," I said.

"I will," he said. "I'll even take your collar off later." His jaw ticked. "But I can't believe you're still thinking of Zadis, after what we—"

"I escaped the celestials," I murmured, twisting my hands in the blanket. "I won't belong to anyone again."

"You're my pet," he reminded me.

"Yes, but I agreed to that in name only. Yes, you are in control of me, but that has nothing to do with what we just did. We did that together as equals. Not as master and pet."

"Ha, you aren't even close to being my equal," Sam

said, standing and looking angrier than I'd expected. "Go read. I don't feel like being around you right now."

It stung, but I didn't blame him. I gathered my things and went to the door. "Sam, you said not to get feelings for you. How was I supposed to know you wanted to be exclusive? I'm just not ready for that—"

His eyes narrowed on me, looking almost like a hawk's eyes, sharp and glaring with that golden ring. "That's fine. And we don't have to do that again. And if you want to, you know my requirements. I only feed exclusively. I won't share my meal with another. Feelings have nothing to do with it."

"And I'm only a meal to you," I spat back. "So why does it matter?"

He glared at me, and I realized we weren't going to get anywhere with this. "I can't be here watching you, so I suppose you'll have to come with me on my interviews."

The thought of going around the fae village cheered me. Plus, it would be hard to say no to Zadis if he came by.

It wasn't as if I were actually thinking of him or wanting him.

It was just that I wasn't going to give Sam control in ways we hadn't negotiated.

Good girl, said my inner demon.

Sam's jaw ticked again. "Maybe I shouldn't have awakened your inner demon so quickly."

I folded my arms. "She would have awakened at some point on her own."

"You'd be dead if not for me," he growled.

"So what, you want me to grovel? You know I'm not like that. You saw me in a jail after almost getting stoned, and I still didn't grovel."

"And yet I still underestimated the difficulty in dealing with you," he shot back.

Fury rose in me. I was tired of being called trouble when I was just standing up for myself.

"You didn't think I was difficult a moment ago," I said.

He sneered. "A moment ago, you threw yourself at me."

"Fine," I said, stomping down the hallway. "This was a mistake. It didn't work. Thanks for showing me how sex works, Sam."

"You don't even know the first thing about sex, you little virgin!" he called down the hall.

I whirled to face him. "Yeah, but maybe I will soon."

"You wouldn't dare," he called back. "You touch Zadis, and I swear he's dead."

"You don't get to tell me who to have sex with," I said, utterly frustrated.

"You're mine!" he shouted back. "When and if you get your collar off, do whatever you want. Regardless, I'm not stopping you. I'm just telling you the consequences. As always, you will do what you like. But if you want to avoid bloodshed, avoid that fae, and do as I tell you in general."

"Ugh!" I slammed the door behind me. So like a man to act different until he started trying to own you like everyone else.

It's not exactly the same, my inner demon said.

Oh yeah? How so? I asked myself.

He told you he was possessive.

He can be possessive when he has a lover, I thought back. *If he wanted terms, he should have said them before we did what we did.*

We both got what we wanted.

I heard nothing more, perhaps because it already felt so weird talking to myself.

I opened one of my books and flopped onto my back, not looking forward to waking up the next morning and seeing Sam again.

But at least we'd be out together, and I wouldn't be here ruminating about what we'd done together.

Do you actually like Zadis? My inner demon asked.

I didn't. I didn't even know him. But I couldn't help being rebellious. There seemed to be nothing wrong with him. I wasn't going to flirt with him to provoke Sam.

But if he was kind, I wasn't going to avoid him either.

If I was going to survive as a demon's pet, I needed all the allies I could get in this new world.

23

The next morning, Griffin showed up wearing red fae clothing, a grimace on his face. Pink embroidered swirls covered the long tunic and pants, plus red boots.

I smothered a grin at his discomfort. "Sleep well?"

Os pushed in front of Griffin before he could answer. His light-purple eyes looked like freshly bloomed lilacs in the morning light. The morning air was crisp and cool. "Where's Sam? We need to get started. The creature is causing problems."

"Don't we still have interviews to do?" I asked. "Sam! They're here!"

A tired-looking Sam showed himself, dressed in the ninja-esque black outfit he'd worn in the jail, complete with spiky boots and chains across the front.

His executioner outfit?

"Don't we still have interviews to do?" I asked.

"We will still have to do the execution today, regardless," Os said firmly. "And that outfit helps impress the seriousness of the topic on those we interview. Besides, I'm glad we're wrapping it up soon. We have good ties with the fae, and they don't like being questioned. It's best if we just get it over with and leave."

Griffin grunted, folding his huge arms. "I don't agree with this. Whatever hurry we're in, whatever relationship we have with the fae, that creature deserves a fair chance."

"I'll do what I can," Sam said. He put his hands at both hips, checking that both his red and black sheaths were there. "Then I'll do what I have to. The sooner we leave, the better." He narrowed his eyes at me. "Cleo here is getting ideas about Zadis."

"At least he's nice to me," I muttered.

Os gave me an impatient look. "Cleo... if you aren't going to listen to Sam on this, listen to me."

I didn't really feel like being lectured by any of these people since they didn't even know what happened between me and Sam last night.

"Let's just go," I said, pulling on a blue sweatshirt I'd been carrying on the way to the door. I was wearing simple jeans, Converse, and had my hair tied in a high ponytail that trailed down to my midback.

Sam watched me carefully as we walked into the early morning air. As usual, the aroma of flowers and leaves filled my nostrils, along with a cool mulch scent. Smoke was wafting from the small chimneys of the little homes, and we wove around them toward the main square of the village where the cage with the creature stood.

I stayed back a bit from the others as Sam approached the cage and the fae who were arguing in front of it.

Zadis was gesturing wildly, and the fae across from him was shaking his head. It looked like Zarris, his brother. Seeing them next to each other, I did notice a resemblance in the long, elegant nose and sharp brow they shared.

When they saw Sam, they immediately stopped and waved him over to them.

Behind him, in the cage, the shifting cloud that almost looked like billions of tiny black particles moved in a shape somewhat like that of a tall man.

As it shifted, I felt something unsettling, cooling me and lifting the hairs on my arms.

Meanwhile, Zadis turned to face me, sending me a smile as Sam spoke with Zarris, a stern expression on his face.

Was Sam still mad about yesterday?

I lifted my hand in a wave to Zadis and felt Griffin lean in over my shoulder.

"Look, Cleo, maybe you should listen to at least Os on this," Griffin said nervously.

"You should," Os said, patting my arm as he went over to join the conversation with Sam.

Their voices rose, but I tuned out what they were saying to walk around the large iron-barred cage.

I didn't see how this huge, shifting black shape couldn't just escape. Then I remembered Zarris saying the cage was enchanted.

As I moved around the enclosure, I felt like I was being watched and looked up to see the dark swarm moving, following me.

"Who... are... you?" said a deep, unearthly sound that only vaguely approximated a voice.

I glanced at Sam and the others, who'd moved a few feet from the cage while arguing.

"What... are... you?" that sound, I thought the creature's voice, asked again.

I had no idea how to answer.

Griffin was behind Os, watching over him like an angry bodyguard as the men talked. He didn't appear to hear anything.

I put a hand on the bars and jerked back as the black particles rushed toward me with a hissing motion.

"Sorry," I murmured. "Not trying to invade your space. I know how that is."

The black particles seemed to almost buzz in place and pulled in tighter, showing almost the shadow of a tall man. It cocked its head at me.

"Don't talk to it," Sam snapped at me, grabbing me with an arm around my waist and lifting me well out of the way of the cage with one easy swing. He set me down. "Do I have to constantly keep an eye on you?"

I glared at him. "I was fine. We were just—"

He put his hands on his hips. "Don't talk to it. Promise me."

I shook my head. "I can talk to who I want. You never said I couldn't when I agreed—"

"We can't talk about it here," he said sternly. "Go back to your room and just read, Cleo. Can you promise me that at least?"

I resisted the urge to glance over at Zadis. "I can't."

Sam sighed, folding his arms. "I'm just trying to keep you safe. You get that, don't you?"

"Said every man who has ever tried to control me," I hissed back.

"What's going on over here?" Zadis asked, smiling as he looked down at me. "Surely, this angel isn't upsetting you, Cleo?"

"No," I said, flushing deeply at being caught between

the two of them. I looked up at Sam, who had his hand on his black katana as he stared at Zadis with rigid posture.

Zadis merely flicked his eyes down to the sword and back to Sam, his stare mocking. "I'm not afraid of you."

"Then you're stupider than you look," Sam retorted. "Which is saying something."

"Guys, guys," Os said, stepping between and pushing them back. "Stop this. We can all get along. We—"

"He doesn't believe that thing over there killed an entire family," Zadis said. "He should have completed the execution the day he came."

"What I don't get is why you have a void walker in a cage," Sam said. "How did he come to be in your community in the first place? He claims he was kidnapped."

Zadis went slightly paler. "He lies. He lies to save his life, after he killed others. Perhaps, since you can relate to him, you're willing to give him leniency and go against your longtime allies, but—"

"You listen here—" Sam lunged past Os to grab Zadis by the front of his black tunic. "You could be the one I execute—"

Zadis pushed back as Os grabbed Sam and pulled him off the fae. "Be careful, celestial. There are things that can kill you."

"I know," Sam said, glaring as he put his hands on the hilts of his swords. "I've already met two of them."

Zadis paled slightly, looking down at the swords. "I knew about the one, but..." His eyes met Sam's. "You're a monster."

"I do what I have to," Sam said. "Now, I'll kill that thing for you, if it needs killing. But first, do you need killing? How do you have a void walker here?"

Zadis frowned. "You were going to talk to the villagers—"

"After hearing you and your brother out, I'm pretty sure it's just between us now. The rest of the village doesn't even know what happened that night."

Zadis whirled away from him, his black hair flying in an elegant arc as he strode away, back to his brother. He wasn't wearing human clothes today and looked more fae-like with his large, almond-shaped green eyes.

He still sent me a wink over his shoulder as he went.

Zadis appeared to be complaining to his brother about Sam, and Zarris appeared to ask him where else they could find something that could slay void creatures.

"A lot of this world seems to be about killing," I muttered to Os and Griffin as Sam went back over to continue the conversation, following Zadis.

"About what you can kill, yes," Os said. "Listen, Cleo. I've been wanting to talk to you because I feel Sam isn't doing a good enough job preparing you for how different the world is on the other side of the veil."

"To put it lightly," I muttered.

"Come on," Os said. "Let's you and me go for a walk. Griffin, can you keep an eye on things? Make sure Sam and Zadis don't kill each other or start war in the mid-realm?"

Griffin nodded, though he looked reluctant to leave our sides.

"Griffin, I'm a celestial," Os said. "One of the most powerful beings in existence. I can protect myself and Cleo, though I appreciate your care."

Truly a diplomat.

Griffin nodded again, still seeming unhappy about the situation. But Os was determined to take off with me and linked his elbow through mine, pulling me down a path between houses. We met up with a path that wrapped around the outskirts of the village, and Os decided we should walk and talk there.

"Listen, Cleo," Os said. "I know Sam is rough, and I may be the only celestial to believe this, but I do believe his heart, however broken it is, is in the right place."

I didn't say anything. I wanted to go back and talk to that black swarm creature. I wanted to know what a void walker was.

But I also wanted to hear Os out first.

"I know that life on the haven side of the veil was not ideal for you. It wasn't like life in the sky realms, where I was raised. But still, the protection that exists in the havens—"

"What protection?"

Os gave me a smile that was less than pleasant. "Sorry, was your village ever pillaged by demons? Invaded by vampires?"

I swallowed, shaking my head.

"That's because of the protection celestials provide in patrolling your havens and protecting the veil."

"Oh."

"After the great divide, humans were free game for all the supernaturals who emerged to take the earth back. Shifters were the most treasured of the humans, and they were taken up behind the veil, sheltered by the celestials who were descended from the gods who created shifters."

"I see." I was still better off in this world.

"So I'm glad you're free and no longer being abused. I'm sorry your haven wasn't functioning as expected. But this world... someone like you, someone raised in a celestial haven, will be a target. Rarely seen here. Sheltered—"

"I'm not sheltered."

"How do vampires kill?" Os asked, letting my arm go

to walk in front of me confrontationally with folded arms. "What do you do if you meet an ogre with bloodlust?"

I blinked.

"You're strong, Cleo, or Sam wouldn't have taken you with him. But you don't understand this world, and until you do, it would be best if you listen to Sam."

My hands clenched into fists. "I don't trust him. How can I? He murders for a living—"

"It's his job, yes," Os said. "To be honest, I do not know him that well. He joined up with our squad this past year, and I hadn't met him before. But he has been honorable, isn't snobby toward certain creatures like Gabe is, and always keeps things interesting."

"Hm."

"And I've never seen him kill someone wrongly," Os said. He let out a sigh. "This might be the first. This creature... I do pity it. I don't know how it came to be here. But now that it has killed a family, including fae children, it can't be allowed to leave."

"Look, I get it," I said. "I'm in danger. This is a new world. Sam's my only guide right now. But..." My cheeks flushed, hard. "Things are complicated."

"He made a move on you, didn't he?" Os asked, letting out a disappointed sigh. "I'm sorry, Cleo. I thought better of him."

I rubbed the back of my neck. "No, I sort of... made a move on him."

"And he said yes?" Os's eyes went wide, a darker purple in this light. "I've never seen him do that before, and he's been propositioned by literally every creature, it feels like."

And now I knew why.

I knew Sam's secret.

Did Os?

Os gave me a knowing look, which told me he at least had some info on the situation.

"I get what you're saying. You're warning me against Zadis, or—"

"I'm warning you that this entire world is far more dangerous than anything you've experienced. There are no laws, just separate communities of creatures with their own rules and morals. And strength is the law of the land. What you can kill and what you can't kill."

"Okay, can you answer a few questions for me?"

Os looked impatient but nodded.

"What is a slayer?"

He grimaced. "The only demon who can kill celestials. They protect the demon abyssal realms the way celestials protect the havens above the veil."

I swallowed. "And Sam has killed two of them?"

"Sam has blood from the ninth celestial realm," Os said, as if that explained everything.

Of course, I knew of the nine kingdoms that rose above the havens. I could look up and see them high up there at night.

I didn't know why Sam being from the highest kingdom mattered.

"He's hard to kill," Os said simply.

"I see," I said.

"And he can kill everything, with very few exceptions."

"Hm."

Os stared at me like I was missing something. "That's a very good ally to have, in my opinion."

I blinked. "Oh, right."

"So please at least try and get along with Sam, as long as he isn't doing anything bad to you. If he does, you know you can come to Griffin or me. But please don't bother escaping or doing something stupid. You're far more in danger without him than with him."

"Why?" I asked, clenching my hands into fists. "I just want to make my own decisions, rather than waiting for someone to tell me how everything works. I thought I escaped. I want to live—"

"I know," Os said. "And one day, when you know everything you need to know about this place and you've unlocked whatever abilities you have, it might be different."

I went quiet at that.

"Cleo, why do you think the fae are here, so close to the veil, rather than deeper in the mid-realm?"

"I don't know."

"Because they hate demons," Os said. "If Zadis finds out... I shouldn't even be talking like this outside."

"You were fraternizing with them, weren't you?" I asked. "Do you hate Zadis?"

"I don't, but—"

"I'm Sam's pet," I said. "I can't escape, but—"

"He's helping you, Cleo. That's all I'm trying to say."

"He's using me," I spat back. "I don't need you to defend him. You don't know anything that's happened between us. And I will spend time with who I want, as long as it's not hurting anyone."

"Speak of the devil," Os muttered as Zadis appeared from between two houses and grinned down at us.

"Finally," he said. "Cleo, would you do me the pleasure of joining me for lunch?"

"Yes," I said at the same time Os tried to say no.

Os glared at me as if I were trying to make his life more difficult.

I wasn't. I just liked this prince and wanted to spend

more time with him. And after a confusing night with Sam, I deserved to make my own decisions.

Zadis grabbed my hand in his and pulled me away from Os before Os could say more.

"If you tell me I'm not allowed to spend time with a guest, please know I'll be terribly insulted," Zadis said to Os as we left.

Os merely watched us with a slitted purple gaze.

24

"What were you two discussing?" Zadis asked, pulling me along with him until we reached a large circular building with an ornate door.

He opened it and pulled me inside. Then he settled on a comfy, large cushion on the ground that served as a chair and gestured for me to do the same on a cushion next to his. "Welcome to my home."

It was beautifully furnished with paintings of nature and gemstones on the walls and ornate furniture that was a mixture of human and something a little more eccentric.

Zadis gave me a smile, and his green eyes lit like green flames. "Finally, I get you to myself."

I flushed lightly. "Ah, yes."

"It's very hard to find a human around here," he

said, putting his hands behind his head as he leaned back. His black robes hid his body, but his arms, where they peeked out, were toned and firm. His jaw was hard, his nose straight. He was handsome... He just wasn't Sam.

"Well, that's a pretty blush," Zadis said. "I hope it's for me."

I didn't have the heart to say it wasn't.

"I did hear humans and human shifters were rare," I said. "I never knew that."

"Interesting," Zadis said. "What did you think the world was like outside the veil?"

I thought about it for a moment. "I don't know. I guess I pictured chaos and danger... but also adventure and magic."

"Magic, indeed," Zadis said, holding out his hand for me to look at the array of sparkling gemstone rings on it. "Which of my stones is your favorite? I'll show you some magic with it."

I blinked. "Seriously?" I'd never seen anything but shifter magic, which mostly involved shifting.

"Sure, come closer. Pull your cushion over here."

I dragged it over by his and sat in it as he shoved his hand in front of my face again.

"What do you think?"

I looked at the rings on his hands, the sparkling

beauty there, and noticed a huge red stone surrounded by little white ones. "That. That's my favorite."

He smiled, then closed his palm and held it tightly. When he opened it, a tiny red flame danced on his palm. "Ruby. Gives fae the power of fire." He closed his palm, and when he opened it again, the fire had disappeared.

I smiled. "It's beautiful too."

"Stay here with me, and I'll shower you with rubies," he said, giving me a smile that almost anyone would have found charming.

However, I still did owe Sam that favor, no matter how angry I was with him right now.

"I'm afraid I can't," I said.

He pouted, sitting up straighter. "Come on, Cleo. Is he keeping you hostage? From the moment I saw you with him, you looked miserable."

I blinked. He'd noticed?

"You're special," Zadis said. "The most special creature those rotten celestials created."

"Because I'm a shifter?"

"A wolf shifter," Zadis said. "The strongest and most noble of the beasts."

"I don't know about that," I said. "There might be shifters in the mid-realm."

"Demon-tainted shifters," Zadis said, his lips

sneering up at the corners. "Disgusting creatures with nothing to recommend them." He sighed. "Cleo, you're still pure and untainted. If you go past our village and deeper into the mid-realm, you will meet creatures no innocent wolf like you should ever meet."

Irritation made my hackles rise. "I'm not that innocent."

"Oh, come on," Zadis said. "Look at you. You're probably even a virgin. Don't celestial shifters wait until mating?"

"I... Yes." I was blushing violently now but stood, ready to leave. "You don't have any right to talk about such things with me. And I'm going deeper into the mid-realm because Sam—"

Zadis grabbed me by the arm, stopping me. I glared down at him, but he gentled his grip and let me go, stepping back with his elegant hands raised.

"Listen, Cleo. You're better off here with me and the other fae. Only demons, vampires, and worse wait for you if you continue."

"Sam's a celestial," I said. "You seem to forget that he's not going to take me around demons. He kills them."

Zadis was quiet, and I could tell there was something he couldn't tell if he should say out loud.

"What?" I asked, frustrated. "If you have some

reason to hate Sam, tell me. If not, I'm going to assume you're just gossiping, like they did about you, and leave." I sighed in frustration. "I came with you to get away from drama, not cause more of it." Maybe I would go see if Griffin was up for some sparring. I needed to get some tension out, stat.

"I'm sorry, Cleo," Zadis said, stepping in front of the door to block my exit. "I didn't mean any harm. Look, I'm not part of your religion. I don't see the celestials as gods. And Sam? He and I aren't inequitable in power level." Zadis shook his head. "But fine. I won't talk about him anymore. Will you at least stay and have tea with me?"

I sighed, then walked back over to plop on the cushion I'd been sitting on. "Fine. But only because I don't feel like seeing Sam again."

"Trouble in paradise?" Zadis perked up slightly. "Does that mean there's a chance for me after all?"

"I don't know," I said. "Look, I'm not exactly into someone who only wants me because of my species."

"Why not?" Zadis asked. "You're also beautiful and fiery—"

"You barely know me," I said.

"I'm trying to change that," he said. "It's kind of like meeting a mermaid for me. I can't help but want you. You're so different."

I wrinkled my nose. "That's just making me an object. A rarity."

He shook his head. "No. I swear. But if you studied mermaids all your life and got to meet one, and they were beautiful and sweet and had amazing taste in gemstones, you'd be interested too, right?"

"You're a prince," I said. "Aren't you expected to be with a fae?"

He cocked his head. "There's no limit to whom I can be with."

"Hm," I replied.

I glanced around his room, noting that the walls were a pale blue and the room was circular, like his brother's. But I also saw stairs leading down, so there must have been another floor.

He caught the direction of my gaze and smiled at me warmly. "Something interesting?"

"I just didn't know there were basements in these little homes."

He smiled again. "We have vast areas underground. We had to live there at first, when humans had the world. It is nice to be in the sunlight again."

"And why did humans give up the world?" I asked, wanting to know if it aligned with what the celestials had taught me.

"Because they nearly killed it, so the supernaturals

took it back," Zadis said. "The humans covered it in plastic and ugly buildings and chemicals. The vampires live in the ruins of their cities. Fae and elves won't live anywhere near those areas. They're still so poisoned."

I thought about those humans for a moment. Why they did what they did. How they lived.

In the celestial haven I was raised in, we sometimes got human goods, and I was fascinated by them. By how far their technology had gone. Apparently, some vampires were still selling human tech and such from their areas.

I shivered at the thought of vampires.

"If you go with Sam, you'll be going into danger," Zadis said.

"I know," I said. "But I don't have any choice." I twisted my hands in my lap, not sure who to trust.

I liked Sam. After what we did together, after seeing his incubus and letting him... do that to me, I just felt confused about everything.

My biggest worry was what would happen if I stayed with him. Would he wind up hurting me?

Did I have any other options?

I liked Griffin and Os, but I barely knew them as well.

"I can see you're hesitating. Good," Zadis said. "Now

tell me what Sam has on you, and I'll tell you how I can rescue you from his clutches."

I laughed, resisting the urge to touch the collar around my neck. "I don't think that's possible."

Zadis looked at my collar anyway. "The fae don't acknowledge slave bonds. If you're his prisoner—"

"It's complicated," I said. "Besides, after growing up in that haven, I could never go back. I'd rather do anything but that. And when Sam took me with him, I promised him a favor."

"He may well kill you," Zadis said. "You understand that, right? Celestials don't really care about anyone but themselves. He will get what he needs and then abandon you. This situation, whatever he has offered you, is temporary. And what does he plan to do when he has to go slay someone in a realm you can't go to? Think clearly, girl."

"Don't call me girl," I snapped.

He paled slightly, offended. "Why not?"

"I'm twenty-two. I'm a woman."

He snorted. "A girl. To me. But fine. I'll call you Cleo."

I stood because I couldn't see this going anywhere beneficial.

"Wait," Zadis said. "I'll get tea." He moved over to the kitchen, and I leaned back on the cushion, listening to the sounds of him presumably preparing tea while my thoughts wandered to that swarming black creature in the cage.

Sam seemed reluctant to kill it. Plus, what was a void walker, and why was Sam accusing the fae of bringing it here?

Nothing made sense.

And I kind of wanted to sneak out and see the creature again. See what it would ask me. See it take that odd humanoid shape again.

"So that void-walker," I said. "What is it?"

I heard a snort from Zadis. "Why do we have to talk about such an unpleasant creature?" He walked in from the kitchen, carrying a tray with an ornate teapot and two cups of steaming yellow liquid.

He handed me a cup, set the tray down on a short table, and sat down again with a cup in his hand. He blew on it.

I looked down at my cup suspiciously. He reached over, took the cup, sipped it, and smiled at me with those glowing green eyes.

"Perfect," he said.

Reassured, I sipped the tea slowly, and the warm liquid calmed me instantly. It was fragrant, like flowers. "What is it?"

"Honeysuckle tea," he said. "I'm glad you enjoy it."

We sipped tea for a few moments, just enjoying the quiet, the sounds of birdcalls in nature.

"Isn't this nice, Cleo? Isn't it better than following that demon around, watching him kill things?"

"He's not a demon," I said.

"He might as well be," Zadis said. "Acts like a demon, so I'm going to call him one."

"How does he act like a demon?"

"He enjoys killing," Zadis said, shaking his head in disgust.

"Maybe he just knows killing needs to happen," I said.

Zadis shook his head. "He enjoys it. There's a difference. I'm not such a fan of celestials either, but they have morals and ideals. Sam... I'm not sure he thinks of anything but what will benefit him next. Yes, he walks with the celestials. But those of us aware of his history know he's more of a merc than anything else."

"Merc?"

"A mercenary. A killer for hire. Just because he has wings and celestial blood doesn't make it better. He uses slayer swords. *Uses* them." He shuddered violently. "I can't imagine."

"Why is that bad?" I asked.

"Let's talk less about him and more about us," Zadis asked. "How pleasant life would be here, with me. I'd respect you. Court you. Love and take care of you. Bond with you. What can Sam do?"

I flushed, thinking about what Sam could do. What he did to me for hours.

Zadis caught the look before I could hide it. "You've already been with him, haven't you?" He shook his head. "I'm too late. You're tainted."

I sat up straight. "Tainted? Excuse me?"

Zadis set his cup back on the tray and faced me seriously. "Cleo, if he has been with you, it means nothing. He has no honor. If you stay with him, you will fall for him. He's handsome and charming. I'll give him that."

"Charming? Are we talking about the same person?"

"He charms people, regardless," Zadis said. "But he doesn't care for them. His heart is ice-cold. I promise you that. If you are starting to get feelings for that monster, Cleo, it's all the more reason you should leave his side as soon as possible. Because he will only bring you pain."

"I don't think so," I said, thinking back over our experiences together. "He hasn't... done anything I didn't want."

Zadis's cheeks flushed, and something I didn't like flashed in his eyes. "Even if he makes you a slave to his body, you will never have his heart, Cleo. He doesn't have a heart to give. Stay with him. Watch him slay, and you'll see. But it will be too late by then. You'll have fallen for him, and he'll betray you. That's all there is to it."

He was probably right. My heart already beat fast just thinking about seeing him again. But was that fear or something more?

Besides, I had more than drama to think about. I needed to survive in this new world, and Sam was my only real ally.

And yes, he himself had said he didn't have a heart.

I just didn't know if I believed him.

"He told me all of this as well," I muttered. "He warned me that he can't feel for me."

"Then leave him," Zadis said. "Such a warning is only manipulation. He knows you'll fall for him anyway, and by then, you'll be stuck."

"Why?"

"Because I might be the only one who can free you from him. No one else is going to challenge him in the mid-realm, if you need help later."

"I don't need you to challenge him," I said. "He's not imprisoning me."

"Can you shift?" Zadis asked.

I nodded.

"What is that collar?" His green gaze fixated on it.

I grazed it with my hand, and the cabochon was cool to the touch. "It's... private."

"He is keeping you prisoner, isn't he? He used sparing you from execution to make you his slave, didn't he?" Zadis's gaze darkened further. "He's manipulating you, Cleo. He'll use you, waste you, and it'll be too late. I have a soft spot for you, and I'm willing to fight him to have you. At least think about it."

I did, and all I could picture was Zadis's bloody body and Sam standing atop it, smiling.

"It's best if you don't intervene," I said. "That said, I'd still love to get to know you. Hear more about fae customs... and bonds."

He cocked his head. "And I don't know if I want to get closer to you if it means I have to watch and know he's going to hurt you."

"I barely know you," I said.

"I know," Zadis said. "But I can tell we were meant to meet. It's fate." He moved off his cushion and knelt in front of mine, holding my hands in his. "I'm just so drawn to you, Cleo. I want you. I know I would always treasure you. I know you're only in my life for a short time if you leave with him. And that you'll be hurt. Can you blame me for trying to save you? For trying to give you a better life?"

I shook my head and pulled my hands away. Zadis

was kind and beautiful, but I felt nothing when he touched me.

Just my luck that I was already falling for a sadist with an inner incubus who loved killing above all else.

"I can't convince you, can I?" Zadis asked.

"No," I said. A part of me did believe Zadis that I was in trouble if I stayed with Sam. Another part said I was safe. But I knew one thing for certain. I didn't want a bloody fight, and there would be one.

"You're afraid, aren't you?" Zadis asked. "You don't think I can win?"

"I also don't think I'm in danger, for now," I said. "He needs me for something."

"Your heart is in danger every day you're with him," Zadis murmured. "I can see it in your face."

I shrugged. "My heart has been in danger since I was born."

Zadis shook his head. "Be that as it may, Samael treats you like a belonging. He snarls at me like a dog guarding a bone. He doesn't want a good man to court you, but he tells you not to get feelings." He took my hand again, holding it gently. "Cleo, that is not a good man."

I stood, yanking my hand away. "I get it. I'm in trouble. But look, I've been in trouble my whole life, and if Sam is truly endangering me, I'll deal with it when the time comes. But I don't know you, and I don't want you to fight him, and I'm irritated that you won't let this go."

I turned to leave, and he grabbed my hand again, stopping me. I whirled to look at him, and he put up both hands.

"I'm sorry. I'm already bonded to you, Cleo. There's something in me that doesn't want to stop fighting for you. But I understand. I won't touch you again, or talk to you, unless you want me to. But my door is always open."

I stared at him. "I'll stay if you shut up about Sam."

He gave me a repentant look. "I'll try."

"Okay," I said, walking back to my cushion. "But just so you know, I am strong as a shifter. If you try something, I'll throw you into your own wall."

Zadis grinned. "I would expect nothing less from a pure-blooded celestial shifter." He rubbed his hands together. "Now that I feel I've done my duty in warning you about Sam, I have so many questions about your life above the veil."

"Shoot," I said, leaning back and enjoying the cool air in the room and the soft cushion beneath me.

"What's it like, shifting into a wolf? Does it hurt?"

"No," I said, shaking my head. "Well, maybe a little. Like a hard shiver or a long stretch that's too strong."

"Do you end up naked if you shift back?" he asked, wiggling his eyebrows at me.

I liked this Zadis better, when he wasn't just bashing Sam. "No," I said. "You wish."

He grinned. "Nothing against flirting, right?"

"No," I said. "As I said, Sam told me not to get serious feelings, so I consider myself a free agent."

Zadis's eyes narrowed like he wanted to comment, but he decided against it. "I'd love to see your wolf. I'm sure she's beautiful."

"She's a wolf," I said, laughing. "Just bigger than usual."

"Would you shift for me if I took you somewhere there was room?"

"Sure," I said, stretching. "You want me to just do it in here?"

He got up and moved chairs and cushions out of the way, giving me room. "Please." He was moving back and forth in sheer excitement, practically dancing on his toes like a kid on his birthday.

"It's just shifting," I said.

"It's just the power most connected with nature," he retorted. "Fae could only dream of feeling one with this earth like you must in wolf form."

"I suppose," I said. "I do have enhanced senses." I cracked my knuckles. "All right, let's do this."

I closed my eyes and called to my wolf, letting the shift take over. My bones shifted, and I relaxed into it, knowing it was easier that way.

My senses assaulted me as my snout elongated, and I fell onto all fours in wolf form, breathing hard.

So many smells here. The tea. The flowers. The wild. The room. Zadis, who smelled like mulch in the best way. His handsome face was lit with wonder as he watched me. Then he clapped his hands together and came forward, walking around me in a small circle.

"You're beautiful, so beautiful," he murmured, reaching out a hand. He froze, withdrawing. "Can I—"

"Sure," I said. "It's just fur."

His hand reached out, moving down my neck and along my pelt. I shivered slightly at the odd touch, and he grabbed the fur lightly, shook it, then released it. "Amazing. It's really part of you."

"Yes, what did you think?" I asked.

"I never knew. I just..." He stroked over my pelt again. "So soft. So real." He stepped back. "Thank you," he said, bowing his head. "I can die complete now. I've petted a shifter."

I grinned and shifted back into my human form, and he gaped at me in surprise.

"That easy?" he asked.

"Yes," I said. "Then again, I've been doing it since I was young."

He moved forward and caught me in an unexpected hug, and I let him. "Thank you, Cleo. Thank you for letting me touch nature through you."

"Uh, sure," I said. I found all of this slightly confusing, but then again, shifters were apparently rare in this world.

"Is there anything else I can do for you?" he asked, sitting in his chair again, looking as dazed as if he'd seen some wonder of the world, not just a wolf shifting.

I felt flattered since no one had ever reacted like this before. If this was how fae saw shifters, maybe staying here would be nice.

My wolf definitely loved all the wilds and the woods, and the fae all seemed kind to me.

No omegas anywhere.

Maybe I should stay here, I thought, *and not go into the mid-realm with vampires.*

But Sam's face, serious and cold, brought me back to reality.

Zadis didn't know I was a demon, and if he ever did, he'd never look at me as he was now.

The thought killed my mood, and Zadis noticed.

"Did the shift tire you? Surely there's some way I can

pay you back for such a favor. Ask me whatever you want."

"I do have one question," I said. "But don't get offended."

"I'll try," Zadis said with a wink.

"That thing... the void walker—"

Zadis's face sobered instantly. "What about it?"

"What's going on with that? Why did Sam even ask you about kidnapping? What is that thing?"

Zadis sighed. "Since Sam won't tell you, I suppose I will. Though, you may want to reconsider staying with someone who keeps so much from you. The void is a dimension between the mid-realm and the darker abyssal realms, and the inhabitants use portals through time and space to change location. This one invaded our realm, killed our people, and must be stopped before it can do more damage."

Zadis spoke with conviction, but something sparkling in his eyes told me there was more to this than he was saying.

But Sam probably wouldn't give me a straight answer either.

"Why did he say you kidnapped it?"

"Perhaps he spoke with the creature, and it tried to blame us to save its own skin," Zadis retorted. "I said I would tell you. You don't believe me?"

I didn't know what to believe. "It's not that. I just don't know anything about these things." I put on a sad face. "I hate to see anything die, let alone if it's innocent."

That seemed to work on Zadis.

"Well, it's not innocent. Let's just say that. It's something from a realm next to the demon realm, so it's as good as a demon. Children died, Cleo. Screaming in pain, they died. That thing must be killed, because if it's ever set free, with its void-walking abilities, its potential to cause harm is endless."

Something still wasn't adding up here, but I had no reason to disbelieve Zadis.

"All right," I said. "Fair enough. Tell me more about you. More about fae. More about bonding."

His eyes lit up eagerly. "Of course."

And as he spoke, telling me the customs of his people, for some reason, all I could see were Sam's dark eyes, staring with disapproval.

When I saw him again, I was probably in for a fight.

25

I was glad it was Griffin who came to collect me from Zadis's home.

We'd been discussing bonding and drinking tea, and I'd honestly lost track of time. I was enjoying myself so much.

Zadis was charming, kind, and open. He treated me unlike anyone ever had. I'd be lying if I said I couldn't still feel him trying to win me over and get me to stay with him, but I didn't mind it too much.

It just wasn't possible.

Zadis liked to talk about fate and how it brought us together. But in my heart, deep down, it felt like maybe Sam was my future. And I wasn't silly enough to imagine it would be romantic. But there was something between us, and I couldn't focus on anything else until I figured out what it was.

Plus, I was still hiding that I was a demon. But it was fun for a while, pretending I hadn't been born an omega and I could just entertain courtship like anyone else.

Griffin was apologetic, still wearing the red robes he'd had on earlier. "Sam wants to talk to you," he said.

My stomach clenched. "Right." I stood, accepting Zadis's hand when he extended it to me.

His green eyes glimmered in his handsome face. "I had a nice afternoon, Cleo."

"Me too," I replied, almost too eagerly. I released his hand. "I'll talk to you later."

"Soon," he said.

Griffin grabbed my hand and practically yanked me out through the front door. I had to put a hand up to shield my eyes as we stepped out into the blazingly bright sunlight. "Over here," he said, pulling me off the beaten path and into the trees, where we were hidden in shadow.

"I thought Sam wanted to talk to me," I said when Griffin released me and put his hands on his knees, panting.

"He does, but I wanted to check on you first. See how you were doing before he gets to start berating you again."

"Ah," I said. "Thank you."

Griffin's deep-blue eyes glowed. "No problem. We're friends, remember?"

I grinned. Even after I left here and no longer had Zadis, I definitely had an ally in Griffin.

And my adventure was just beginning.

"So you're okay, aren't you? Nothing happened?" Griffin shook his head, releasing me. "Honestly, I don't sense anything bad about Zadis, but Sam and Os keep acting like we should really watch out for him."

"Do you trust them?" I asked Griffin.

Griffin rubbed the back of his neck. "Well, I trust Sam less, knowing he forced a kiss on you."

I sighed. "It wasn't exactly like that. I was in the stocks. Yes, I didn't consent, but it wasn't exactly... forced."

Griffin's nose wrinkled in disgust. "It doesn't sound sexy."

I grinned at him. "That's the messed-up thing. It kind of was."

Griffin shared a look with me. "You like him, don't you? You like Sam!" He laughed. "Poor Zadis."

I flushed deeply. "I don't like him. I'm attracted to him. There's a difference."

"Well, who wouldn't be?" Griffin asked. "He's an

absolutely beautiful specimen of a male. But that personality..."

I kind of liked his personality. But I was also his pet. Was it Stockholm syndrome? Still, despite everything that had happened, I couldn't help feeling excited to see him again.

"You do like him," Griffin said, leading me out of the woods and back onto the bright main path.

"Maybe. I don't know. It doesn't matter," I said. "I'm just his pet."

"I'm Os's pet. I don't mind it."

It was my turn to smirk at him. "So when are you going to tell me more about that?"

Griffin's cheeks resembled strawberries. "I don't... I just... It's complicated."

"I get that," I said.

"Besides, Sam needs you. He's still arguing with the fae, and he wants you to come talk to that void creature. He says he thinks it was trying to talk to you."

My stomach clenched. "I think it did. It asked me who I am. What I am."

Griffin nodded. "It hasn't spoken to anyone else. Maybe Sam, but when they converse, it's in a different language. But he says he's almost ready to execute. He just needs 'one more data point.'"

"That sounds like him," I said, laughing. "By the way,

you want to spar later? I need to release some tension, and I assume that'll be even truer after seeing Sam."

Griffin's eyes widened. "I couldn't hit you."

"You won't hurt me," I said. "We're both shifters. It's good practice."

Griffin shook his head. "I don't know. I know I'm big, but I'm not much of a fighter. Like, I do win the fights I'm in, but I hate fighting."

"I love fighting," I said. "I don't love hurting people or killing them, though. Sparring is fun. You should try it. You just don't hit at full strength."

Griffin still looked immensely turned off by the idea, so I let it go. Instead, I grinned and nudged him in the side with my elbow.

"Looking pretty good in those fae robes, huh?" I asked.

Griffin went even redder, clearly mortified. "I look like... I don't even know what I look like. I'm not a fae. I have no idea why Os insisted on it."

"Maybe he wanted to see you in them?" I asked, wiggling my eyebrows at him. "For his personal benefit?"

"Os doesn't like me," Griffin said somewhat sadly. "He doesn't even remember me." He straightened, appearing to shake off whatever emotion almost overcame him. "But it's fine. I'm just happy to be by his side."

I wasn't sure I could say the same about Sam. Happy wasn't really the emotion I would use to describe the way I felt around him.

Things felt too real for that.

As we reached the main square, and I saw the huge cage, the creature, and Sam behind it, my blood began to pump rapidly.

Sam's eyes met mine, and instantly, my heartbeat picked up, racing against my chest. Tingles went down my arms to my fingertips, and Sam gave a knowing smirk as he moved his gaze away from me and back to Zarris.

Griffin and I reached the cage just as Zarris began to yell at Sam openly.

"You don't get to investigate. You do what we ask. You believe us! The fae and the celestials are allies. You do this, or I—"

"I'm *going* to do this," Sam said flatly. "If you want it done your way, then do it yourself. I have my own methods."

Zarris scowled. "You are offending us deeply by even asking this creature his side of things."

Sam straightened, towering over Zarris with his broad-shouldered build. Huge wings flew out from his back, black and shading everything around us with their immense size. "You offend me by treating me like a dog you can order to kill for you."

Zarris shrank as Sam approached, wings still spread menacingly. "You eternals. Always flexing your power." He gulped. "Your father will hear of this."

Sam threw his head back in a laugh, then faced Zarris with an expression that was dead serious. "You know nothing of my father."

Zarris looked ready to run, so I ran over to Sam and put a hand on his arm. Rather than calming, he jerked out of my grasp.

"Stay out of this, Cleo," he said, pushing me back and stepping in front of me protectively. His curls gleamed with gold in the afternoon light.

"Griffin said you wanted me here," I retorted.

Sam turned to face me, blinking as he realized I was right. He glared at Zarris. "I will do this execution, you bloodthirsty animal. But I will do it on my time."

"Soon—" Zarris insisted.

"On. My. Time," Sam said, folding his arms. "Or you do it yourself."

"Fine," Zarris said. "But I'm not happy about it, and the other celestials we work with are going to hear about it."

"Let them do your dirty work, then," Sam muttered. "I'm an angel, not an exterminator."

"An angel isn't all you are," Zarris said with a sneer.

Sam's wings extended again, and Zarris made a run for it, almost tripping on his purple robes as he moved down the main roadway.

"Don't disappoint me!" he screamed back at us, clearly terrified of Sam but still intent on making his point.

I put my hands on my hips as Sam retracted his wings and faced us. "Well, he's definitely different than the first day I met him."

Sam scowled. "The fae are always polite when they're trying to get what they want. It's when they don't get what they want that you have to worry about them. Otherwise, they're all, 'Look at my jewels! Drink my tea! Participate in our communal mating rituals!'"

"Communal mating rituals?" I choked out.

Sam flushed lightly as he realized what he'd said. "Ah. Zadis didn't mention those?"

"No!" I couldn't believe what I was hearing. "He only spoke about fae mates."

Sam's eyes glittered with triumph. "Well, I did warn you about them, after all. What's wrong, Cleo? You don't feel like bonding?" He looked at Griffin. "Hey, you should try getting an invite to one. You might be able to hook up with Os there."

Griffin's knuckles popped as his hands clenched into

fists. "What are you saying? He goes to them?"

Sam just shrugged, turning back to the cage. "You two are too innocent for words. It's interesting and troublesome all at the same time." He put his hands on the bars, and the creature inside slinked back slightly, still a black swarm of particles that almost made the shape of a man. He pointed to me. "So what did you want with her? I brought her, as you asked."

"Morningstar," the creature rasped in a tone that was too unearthly to sound like a voice. A voice so quiet I knew no one but Sam or I could make out what he was saying. "Queen."

Sam stepped in front of the cage, pushing me back. "This is Cleo. A celestial shifter from the havens."

"Does she know that you search for the Morningstar? For the queen?" the creature rasped again, so quietly.

"She does," Sam said. "All of us are searching."

The creature in the cage vibrated hard and somehow solidified enough to be a man. He had thick black hair, black eyes, and pale olive skin.

And he was beautiful. He had a square face with a V-shape jaw, a straight nose, and a tall, well-built body. At least, what I could see of him appeared that way.

His hands clutched the bars as he surged forward, trying to get closer to me. I realized the bottom of his body was still a swarm of particles, making him look half human, half aberration.

"Cleo..." His eyes met mine, so much darker than Sam's. The darkness in Sam's was warmer because of the gold burning at the center. The dark at the center of this man's eyes was a void. So dark it was like staring into black holes. "Free me, Cleo. Let me be with you."

Sam's brows lowered.

"I was meant to serve you," the creature rasped. "Morningstar."

I thought back to Sam's conversation with Os about the "Morningstar" they were searching for. Clearly, this creature thought that just because Sam was dragging me around, I was somehow involved.

"I'm not... I'm just a wolf shifter," I murmured.

"Not true," the creature hissed.

"Damn," Griffin said. "It really does talk."

The creature sent him a glare. "Celestial." It hissed in distaste, then turned its attention to me. "Free me, queen."

"It's confused," I said to Sam. "I'm not a queen."

Sam just narrowed his eyes, thinking. Then he folded his arms and got as close to the cage as possible, stepping between the thing and me. "Why did you kill those fae? I'm not going to ask again. Zarris isn't going to let me wait any longer."

The creature was quiet but dispersed back into a mist, no longer holding any form that looked at all human.

"Void walker," Sam hissed. "I won't ask again. I have delayed this because I believe your story about being kidnapped and brought here against your will. But unless you explain your killing—"

"An accident," the creature finally hissed. "I was forced to open a void to the hell realm, in a small home where no one would see my portal. The fire blew back and obliterated the family living there. Not my fault."

"Hellfire killed them?" Sam asked.

The creature did something like a nod.

"Who made you do this?"

The creature vibrated, almost becoming human again, then stopped. "I can't tell you, celestial."

Sam rolled his eyes, looking to the heavens for patience. He put a hand on his katana. "You aren't leaving me any options."

The creature stayed silent.

"Cleo, you stay here. See if you can get anything out of him. Griffin, you watch out for Cleo. I'm going to try to get to the bottom of this. Someone is going to tell me the truth, even if it's on the end of a sword."

He strode away, and Griffin and I watched him until he disappeared out of sight.

"Is Sam always like this?" Griffin asked. "Did he hesitate to kill you?"

"I don't know," I said. "This is the third execution I've come to with him. Other than mine, which didn't happen. I mean, he doesn't mind killing, though. I'm just not sure why he's hesitating."

"Why did that thing call you the Morningstar?" Griffin asked, looking nervous.

"What? I think it was just confused."

"You're right. It's just confused. And why not? It's stuck in this cage, its powers confined."

I eyed it with distaste. "It still led to the death of fae. Including children."

"Right," Griffin said.

I moved closer to the cage, then a little closer.

The shape immediately moved toward me.

"Let me out, queen. Let me out to serve you."

"He's trying to trick you, I bet," Griffin says. "He probably says that to everyone to make them let him out."

But I wasn't sure.

Though his eyes had been dark and empty, I hadn't sensed any insincerity in his words, and I was a pretty good reader of people.

This wasn't a person, however.

"I can tell the Morningstar my story, no one else," the creature rasped.

Griffin looked at me, and I nodded, so he stepped back with his hands up. The swarm watched him warily as he continued until he reached a stone bench about twenty feet away and sat down on it.

"Why do you want to talk to me?" I asked. "I'm just... I don't have anything to do with that thing you mentioned."

"The prophecy," it rasped. "You are wrong. Queen, release me. I wish only to serve you."

"They say you're demonic," I muttered.

"I am," it said. "Proudly so. I am aligned with the abyssal realms and everything in them, as any true void walker would be."

"Why won't you tell Sam what's going on?"

"Can't trust him," it rasped. "He has angel wings. Against the void walker code."

So demons apparently hated angels as much as angels hated demons. Or was this thing even a demon?

"I did nothing wrong," the thing rasped. "Zadis..." The swarm moved side to side as if checking around us. "I was brought here. They want the forbidden rubies from the hell realm."

"Why was there a fire?" I asked. "If you want me to

help you, you have to tell me more. Like how you killed those kids."

"I didn't kill them!" The thing vibrated again, nearly taking form. "I was forced to open a portal to the void. Forced inside. The hellfire came out when I was dragged back. He bound me."

"Who did?" I leaned in even closer.

"Zadis," the creature hissed. "Zadis bound me. Pulled me back. Too fast, to close the void. Exposed them all to hellfire. Didn't want to use his own home."

I blinked. "What the hell?"

"Yes," it rasped eagerly. "The fire was from hell. It burned, and I was bound again, unable to portal back to the void. They put me in this cage. They took the rubies."

"Rubies are in the hell realm?"

"Special rubies," the creature replied.

I didn't really get it, but gemstones weren't my thing.

"The fae seek the power the celestials have. To rule. To take. To conquer," the thing said.

I looked around us. "They seem pretty happy where they are."

The void walker slumped slightly. "It is hopeless. No one will believe me. To celestials, the fae can do no wrong. They will capture other creatures in their lust for power. Someone must stop Zadis."

"Why Zadis?" I asked.

The creature simply vibrated again. "Let me out. I will help you escape too."

"I can't," I said. "But I can tell them the truth about you. That Zadis—"

"They won't believe," the thing said.

"Sam does hate Zadis," I said, hoping that was helpful. If this creature was telling the truth—and I got the feeling he was—then he was the one who was wronged.

He shouldn't even be in that cage.

"Sam can do nothing," the creature said. "You are the Morningstar. Set me free."

"I'm not," I said. "I'm sorry."

The thing formed a face again, and its expression was disappointed. "I can't die here. I have a family. I have a future... Do not let them kill me."

"What can I even do?" I asked. "I'll talk to Sam, but I'm his prisoner as well."

"He is binding you?"

I touched my collar. "Kind of. I was in trouble with the celestials."

The creature shuddered. "The angels are the ultimate evil. I wish a slayer were here."

"A slayer?"

"A slayer would see I had a fair trial. Slayers are the only ones strong enough to go against the angels." The creature's face blurred again, forming back into a swarm. "It is hopeless, human. I was mistaken."

"About what?"

"You can't help me," it said. "I will die never having served the Morningstar now. I opened portals, trying to find her. I wish I never had." It slumped. "At least inform my family. Sam will know how to find them... once he kills me."

I swallowed. "He might not if I talk to him, though."

"Zarris will not give up. He will protect his brother."

"Sam isn't known for doing what he's told," I said.

"He is a celestial," the creature replied, as if that were all he needed to say. "I am sorry for mistaking you for someone else and wasting your time. I hope you escape him, someday."

"I don't need to escape him," I said. "I mean, I don't have anywhere else to go. Well, Zadis did offer."

The creature buzzed again, this time distinctly angry. "Do not trust the fae."

"That's what everyone says," I said. "But I gotta say, I was treated really badly before I came here, and the fae have been nothing but pleasant."

"They don't see your real form," the creature said. "I sense demon on you, mixed with celestial, so I mistook you for the child of prophecy. But you are still in trouble here. After I'm killed, make sure you aren't the next target."

I put my hand on the bars, staring at this creature, wondering what I could do for it. If I should do anything. If it was telling the truth.

But the thought of Sam killing it pained me now.

"I will talk to him," I said. "I will tell him what you told me."

But the creature had already moved to the side of the cage, a despondent swarm of black. In that moment, I decided. I was going to save it. I would convince all of them somehow.

But first, I needed to talk to Zadis.

"Griffin," I said. "I'll be right back."

I heard Griffin call after me, but it was too late. I was already jogging toward Zadis's house. Once I confirmed whether this story was true, I would talk to Sam and get to the bottom of this.

Because something deep inside me just said that creature in the cage did not deserve to die.

26

When I reached Zadis's place, he was already walking out, and he stopped to greet me.

He was wearing black robes, looking oddly somber compared to only a little earlier.

He looked down at himself, then smiled. "My execution apparel. I'm sure you saw the slayer had his on also?"

"Slayer?"

Zadis's eyes flashed. "Well, he slays things. All murderers are the same to me." He tossed his long, glossy black hair over his shoulder. "But it's lovely to see you, Cleo. Walk with me?"

"I need to talk to you, in private."

He winked at me. "I'm sure I can spare a few moments when such a beautiful woman is making the request."

I looked down at my jeans, sweatshirt, and ponytail, which was hanging over my shoulder. Beautiful. Sure. "Zadis, can we go inside?"

He nodded. "Don't be so formal, Cleo. You know I'm hoping you stay with me when that monster moves on." He opened the door to his home and led me in, then shut the door. It was cool and quiet and beautifully furnished as always.

Yet a part of me wished I was somewhere else. With Sam.

"You still aren't convinced?" Zadis threw his hands in the air. "I'm rich. I'm handsome. I'll shower you with jewels. You can come on my journeys to gather them."

"It's about that," I said, looking at the jewels on his hands. "Your ruby. Where did you get it?"

He flushed but quickly composed himself. "Why do you ask?"

"I just... That thing in the cage, it spoke to me."

He reared back. "What? Why would you talk to that thing? It killed children."

I sat on a cushion, sighing and intertwining my hands on my knees. "I know this is hard, Zadis, but don't let them kill someone who doesn't deserve it."

Zadis's eyes narrowed. "That thing deserves it, just

by dint of what it is." He took off his ruby ring and handed it to me. It was on a simple golden band.

I turned it over in my hands. "Can I make fire with it?"

Zadis cocked his head. "Depends. What are you?"

"A shifter," I replied. "But, Zadis, I spoke to him. I know you brought him here. But why?" I asked quietly.

Zadis took a step back from me, looking genuinely shaken. "How on earth are you, a celestial, taking sides with that thing? How could you believe a demonic creature trying to save itself from death over someone who has been nothing but kind to you?"

I looked up at him somberly. "I don't know, but I just do."

Zadis let out a sigh, composing himself as he put a hand to his head. "I'm sorry for reacting so strongly." His green eyes met mine. "It's just that I'm already bonded to you, Cleo. I thought you would give me the benefit of the doubt over a known and imprisoned criminal and murderer."

I just stared at him, still waiting for an answer.

"Well, I like that about you," he said finally. "You're sharp." He moved over to sit on a tall cushion across from mine. "I'll tell you what I know, and you can make up your own mind. And if you truly, truly don't want that thing murdered, I will listen."

I sucked in a deep breath, feeling oddly relieved that this wouldn't be so tense. "I swear, I'm not accusing you of anything. It's just that I was recently nearly executed, so I have to be sure."

His eyes narrowed slightly, but he nodded. "What was it you were nearly executed for again?"

My cheeks burned. This was getting too close to discussing the fact that I was an actual demon too. Something Zadis could never know. "Rejecting the alpha's son."

Zadis grinned, flashing white teeth. "Of course. I knew you were powerful. Of course the alpha's son would want you."

"I'm not used to this," I said. "I'm used to being bullied, overlooked. I'm not used to so much attention. Or a guy that likes me that isn't trying to push me down or keep me caged."

Zadis listened intently, the look in his emerald eyes soft. "I'm glad you met me, then. So I can treat you better. I swear, Cleo. Tell me what that demon said, and I'll put your heart to rest about the matter."

I swallowed, my throat tight and nervous. Despite Zadis's reassurance, I didn't really know him that well. He might still get upset.

But that creature had begged me.

"He says you kidnapped him," I finally blurted out,

still clasping my hands over my knee. "He says you used him to hunt rubies and that you forced him to open a portal to the hell realm—"

Zadis's mouth firmed into a hard line, and a muscle in his strong jaw ticked. "Ridiculous."

"But..." I thought for a moment. "Zadis, those fae. Were they killed by hellfire?"

"Yes, when that creature tried to escape," Zadis said.

"So you did bring him here?" I asked.

He looked away. "I had no choice. I need rubies. But I didn't do everything he said. He killed those fae on his own."

I really wasn't so sure.

"I'm a prince of my people," Zadis said. "One of our top warriors. My strength is important. Yes, I needed a void walker to reach the hell realm and get what I needed. I brought him to our settlement, but I didn't treat him wrongly. But I didn't tell him to misfire that portal so it killed a whole family."

"But this whole thing still isn't his fault," I said, standing. "We need to tell Sam you're involved so we can get to the bottom of this."

Zadis moved to stand in front of me, preventing me from leaving. "You can't. That reaper is going to kill the creature regardless."

"No," I said. "Sam doesn't kill things that don't deserve it."

"Anyone he is paid a tithe to kill must deserve it, then."

"So what, are you using him to dispose of your evidence?" I asked, nearly yelling now. "That creature was just doing what you told it to do. I get that you didn't mean any harm and no one should have been hurt, but you can't just—"

"That creature is lying to you, Cleo. It wanted to hurt those fae." He put his hands on my shoulders, firm and warm. "You don't understand how this world works. It's us versus them. My people, the fae, are aligned with the celestials. Void walkers serve the demons. We don't care about killing demons. It's just a service that is performed for us."

I felt a pang at that and tried to push away, but Zadis kept a firm hold on my shoulder. Not wanting to cause more of a scene, I waited for what he had to say.

Looking at the base of his long, pale throat, I could see his pulse racing. He was nervous. Why?

"I like you, Cleo," he said, raising one hand to brush my hair back. "I've done nothing to hurt you. Nothing to make you think less of me. How can you believe that creature when it's condemned to death?"

Because I'd been condemned to death also.

And if Zadis knew *I* was a demon, it looked like he wouldn't hesitate to have me killed too.

Sam was right.

"Cleo, don't let this come between us," Zadis said. "I like you. You like me. We were meant to meet. I'm glad I called Sam here because it brought you. Just give me the word, and I'll fight him for you."

"Thank you, but I don't need it."

Zadis cupped my face in his hands, and despite his handsomeness, I felt nothing. "At least consider me, Cleo. I hate to think what will happen to you in that sadist's hands. He's misleading you; I know it. He has no heart. No soul."

"You don't know that," I said, pushing back from Zadis. "You don't know him at all. And you called him here to murder because you can't do it."

Zadis looked taken aback at that. "You're right. Because it's his job. Because everyone knows he's good at it and likes it. You really want to be with someone like that, Cleo?"

I thought of Sam. His face as he licked me. Seeing him in incubus form. His dark, glittering eyes. Those wings.

There was so much more I still wanted to know.

And deep down, I knew he wasn't as cold and evil as Zadis was saying.

"Cleo, just know you can come to me if anything—"

A loud knock sounded on the door. Then it burst open. Sam was there, wings outspread, hands in fists, still in his executioner's outfit.

His eyes locked on Zadis, and he lunged forward, grabbing me out of his grasp. He quickly shoved me behind him.

"You don't know your place, angel," Zadis said, coming over to sneer at Sam imperiously, eye to eye.

"This is my property," Sam said, gesturing to me. "If I so much as see you fucking *near* her again, I'll slit your throat."

"Possessive," Zadis murmured. "So celestial." He looked over at me. "I think Cleo should be able to make her own choice, don't you, Cleo?"

"I..." I raised my eyes to Zadis. "You don't even really know me. I'm with Sam. I'm sorry."

Sam smirked, folding his arms as he glared at Zadis. "See? She's with me. Stop trying whatever you're trying. It's not going to work."

Sam headed out the front door, grabbing my hand and dragging me with him.

"Can you ever love her, though?" Zadis yelled after us, following us onto the path in front of his house with clenched fists. "Cleo, he can never love you! Can you live with someone so cold?"

I wasn't sure I really had a choice.

For now, Sam was my fate, and I would stay with him until I needed to leave him or saw my next opportunity for safety. That was all.

And Zadis would never be safe for me, if he knew what I truly was.

27

Sam's wings disappeared, and his chains clanked as we hurried down to the square where the execution would take place. His hand held mine tightly, and he practically dragged me along.

"Idiot shifter. Idiot woman. Idiot," he was muttering as he stomped forward down the street. "Now I just need to hurry and get out of here. He's already too bonded to you now."

I tried to jerk my hand away, but his hold was too firm. He was too powerful. "Stop, Sam. We have to talk about the void creature."

Sam glared down at me with stern disapproval, his jaw jutting stubbornly. "There's no time to figure that out anymore. We have to go before that jerk issues me a challenge. The last thing I need is a fight with a fae prince. Os would kill me."

"Wait! A fight?" I asked. "I told him no, Sam. And I don't like him, not like that. Just stop!"

Sam finally stopped, sighing as he released me. He truly looked terrifying in his executioner outfit. Like a chained-up ninja ready to murder with two swords.

I looked down at his boots. "Why do they have spikes on them?"

"Sometimes I have to kick things off me when they're begging for mercy," he said in a way that I couldn't tell whether he was serious. "So what did that creature tell you?"

"He didn't mean to hurt anyone. He was brought here against his will. Zadis admitted it."

Sam put his hands on his hips and exhaled. "That won't be enough to save him. That's all he said?"

I flushed. "He called me queen and said he wanted to serve me. I told him he was wrong."

"He is," Sam said. "You aren't his queen in any way." He clicked his tongue. "Why was he brought here?"

"Zadis needed him to open a portal to the hell realm to take rubies."

Sam swore long and loud in a language I didn't understand.

"What?" I asked.

Sam started forward again, pulling his black-sheathed katana out in one smooth move. The silver metal gleamed in the daylight.

"Sam, please," I said. "That creature. It has a family. It didn't mean to hurt anyone. It was brought here."

Sam turned to me, rolling his eyes. "For the last time, Fae hate demons. They don't care about anything other than the fact that fae died and that thing was involved. It being brought here, imprisoned, killed, they won't care at all about the reason. It just has to die."

I lunged forward, grabbing his sleeve. "If you kill it, I won't forgive you."

His dark eyes flashed down at me, the gold rings at the center gleaming. "You're kidding me right now. Don't make things difficult, Cleo."

"Difficult?" I yelled, my hands making fists at my sides. "Difficult? You made me talk to that thing. You brought me here in the first place. Now, even when I know it doesn't deserve to die, you're just going to kill it anyway?"

Sam just looked at me flatly. "That's my job."

"Why can't you offer it a deal? Like you did me?"

Sam's eyes darted to the side, then back to mine. "Cleo. You have to trust me. This is what has to happen."

I swallowed, my throat tight. "I can't watch."

"Too bad," Sam said. "You have to stay right by me

from now on. I don't trust Zadis for a minute. Especially if he has blood rubies."

"Why does he even want me?" I asked.

Sam paused, running his eyes up and down me. "I can think of lots of reasons. None of them matter, however, because I'll gut him if he so much as tries to take you from me."

"But... he cares about me," I said. "He might even come to love me someday."

Sam's eyes flashed angrily. "You're barely out of your haven, living your life for the first time. Why would you even be thinking about love?"

It stung, though I knew he'd never considered what we did anything but casual.

It was why I'd told him I wouldn't be exclusive.

"You don't own me, Sam."

He folded his arms, and I tried not to look at his flexed biceps, his huge, masculine shoulders and chest. "Actually, I do." His smile was mean. "Don't forget, Cleo. It was me or death. There was no other option."

My heart was burning. We'd done things together... Why was he intent on reminding me I was trapped?

So far, even though I'd been forced to stay fairly close to him, I'd felt like a free woman. No one's prisoner.

It was what made it safe to fantasize with him, to be with him.

But it was clear he didn't care about me beyond whatever he wanted to use me for.

He didn't see me as someone with her own agency.

"Cleo, I told you," he said. "Don't fall for me."

"I haven't!" I shouted back, wishing I had something handy to throw at him.

"Then why do you seem upset?" He looked genuinely confused.

"I just... After what we did..." I looked away.

Sam let out a sigh. "You were desperate. We both enjoyed it—"

"You fed off me—"

"Many would die for the opportunity to have me do so," he said flatly. "Listen, Cleo, I've been clear with you."

"You also asked for exclusivity!"

His cheeks reddened. "A moment of weakness. Jealousy. Primarily, I don't care, as long as your partner isn't Zadis."

"You were upset," I said. "Admit it. You don't want me with someone else."

His jaw clenched. "Because I have a purpose for you. That's all. And I don't share my meals. But I already accepted that nothing more will happen between us.

You're right. It would be stupid to ask for exclusivity when I don't intend anything further to happen between us. I was overwhelmed by your beauty before. I won't make the same mistake again."

I breathed out through my nose, too angry at his arrogance to speak for a few moments.

He'd helped me have my first orgasm. He'd "made love" to me. He'd been so jealous he couldn't see straight.

But beneath all of that, it was clear he was right from the start. He didn't have a heart.

"Any animal can be possessive," he said. "Don't mistake that for what it's not."

"What do you mean?"

"Just that many creatures will guard something for their own enjoyment or use. It doesn't mean implicit care."

"Why are you even making that point?"

Sam snorted. "I'm making it about Zadis. He may tell you things about me. That you're not safe with me. That he can protect you. Don't mistake his silken words for goodness, Cleo." Then he started striding forward again.

"Stop," I begged, walking after him. "If you kill that creature, I will never forgive you. I won't even be able to look at you. It has done nothing wrong. You know this is wrong."

Sam turned to flash a glare at me, looked around us at the passing villagers, then started hurrying in the direction of the cage again, sword still drawn.

No. No. No.

"Why did you even have me talk to it if you weren't going to save it?"

He whirled to face me. "So I would know how a void walker even ended up in this realm." He took a few steps closer to me. "Listen to me, Cleo. Is this fair? No. This world isn't fair. It's about alliances and who wants who killed and who will kill them. It's dog-eat-dog, and the fae are our allies. I cannot spare him. Do you understand?" He seemed too aware that there were fae around us.

But the fae didn't seem to care.

"If I don't kill him... the consequences will be fatal to our alliance with the fae," he said. "What is one little void walker in the scheme of things?"

"What is one little wolf?" I asked, tears biting my eyes. "What is any creature when so many are up against it simply because it fought back against impossible odds?"

"You didn't burn people to death."

"Neither did that thing!" I said. "Sam, if you kill him—"

"I'm killing him," Sam said simply.

And that's when I knew he must be as cold as Zadis said he was. Because he noted my tears, my begging, with not even a flinch and then continued toward the cage.

"I'll make it fast," he said. "It won't hurt much."

"But—"

"Creatures die, Cleo," he said. "And if you want to save your skin, you'll stop fighting me on this. I can't afford to stall this anymore, though I will take no pleasure in killing this creature. We must leave, due to Zadis—"

"Don't blame this on me!" I yelled back. "Zadis would never—"

Sam glared. "You know nothing about the fae. And I'm getting us out of here before you can do something stupid."

"Stupid like staying with a belligerent angel who might kill me one day too, if that's what the celestials or the fae want?"

His expression went dark and cold. "That's what you think of me?"

I didn't know what to think. Sam had even nodded when Gabe told him he'd need to kill me at the end of this.

My hands were clenched into fists so tight I could feel my nails biting into my palm, almost drawing blood.

"Are you going to kill him?" I asked.

He nodded. "It's my job."

"Then, yes," I said. "That's what I think about you. You're someone I can't trust. Someone I could never trust. You have no heart, no morals, you'll probably kill me at the end of this, like you told Gabe you would, and—"

"If you truly can't watch what's about to happen, then go home and pack, Cleo," Sam snapped as he turned away from me. "I'll come for you when the execution is over."

And then he turned and strode away, shoulders hunched, sword shining, muttering curses under his breath.

I was panicked. I wanted to save that thing in the cage, but I was helpless. I ran forward and saw Griffin and Os waiting by the cage.

"Stop him!" I yelled at them as Sam approached the cage.

"Everyone back up," Sam said.

"But—" One of the fae by the cage fidgeted nervously. "Zarris isn't here."

"Out!"

The fae started moving back from the cage, and I couldn't watch anymore. I turned away with a sob.

"Griffin, take her home," Os said gently. "I don't want either of you to watch."

Griffin jogged over to me and picked me up in his arms, carrying me princess style. I tucked my head into his chest and let the tears fall.

Why had I even come here? How could Sam be cruel enough to do this after forcing me to find out this creature's story?

And one day, if a person high enough in power wanted me killed, would Sam do it?

I needed to figure out some way to escape his grasp before he got any deeper in my heart and tore it completely apart.

28

Go back. Save the void walker.

My inner demon's voice cut through my tears as Griffin carried me down the path away from where the execution would be carried out.

I struggled to get away, but Griffin held me tight. The wolf in me growled at being restrained. I felt the shift taking over, bones snapping, fur sprouting, claws and paws overtaking hands.

Griffin was forced to let go of me as the change took place, and I took off as fast as my paws could carry me, my claws digging into the soft dirt of the paths that made up fae walkways.

Dirt flew all around me as I ran, and I was sure I was kicking up a huge cloud. But up ahead, with fae standing as far back as they could while still watching, I saw Sam standing in front of the cage, his sword out and gleaming.

He pulled out his other katana from the red sheath, and I noticed the blade appeared red. Had it been that way when he fought the minotaurs?

His wings unfurled, huge and high, and to my shock, he wrapped them around the cage as he closed in on it, hiding what was inside from view from the waist up. I could see the swarm of particles moving, back and forth, back and forth, as if trying to escape.

I wasn't going to make it. My heart felt like it was going to explode.

Sam sent just one look at me over his shoulder before he turned back to the cage and shoved both swords into the cage, beneath his wings.

An unearthly shriek rent the air, followed by several agonized gurgles, and blood pooled beneath the cage, soaking around the black iron bars. It spread out in reaching tendrils in the dirt, looking like little rivers.

Sam withdrew his swords from the cage, and blood flew with them. When he pulled back, dropping his wings, all I could see in the cage was blood.

So that was how a void walker died. All I could think of was the face of that creature begging me for help.

Even if I'd been faster, there would have been

nothing I could do to stop Sam. That thought haunted me most of all.

I would just have to stay by this murderer's side, complicit in anything he did, never able to stop him while watching him commit cold-blooded atrocities.

Sam said he wanted to take me to his home, but I wasn't sure I wanted to go there anymore.

He'd just proven he was the monster everyone said he was, and I realized, deep down, I hadn't believed he could be that way because he'd spared me back at the jail.

Now I knew he truly just saved me because he needed something from me. That was all, or he would have brutally murdered me too.

I let go of the shift and fell to the ground in my human form, crying openly. I wasn't crying for me. I was crying for that thing. For how unfair all of this was.

I thought I'd escaped my haven into a better world.

My heart was heavy, as though it were weighed down with stones.

I wasn't going back to the haven. I wasn't up for another stoning. But I just knew I couldn't stay with Sam anymore.

Griffin caught up to me, panting, and pulled me up into a hug, but I pushed away from him angrily.

"You didn't even try to stop him."

"Me? Stop a celestial executioner?" Griffin let out a frustrated laugh. "Cleo, be reasonable. Look, Sam hasn't hurt you, has he? Let's trust him that it had to be this way. It sucks, but—"

"How could you just trust him?" I asked, tears biting my eyes. "After seeing him do that?"

"That thing killed children," Griffin said. "I'm not sure why you're so eager to believe it."

"I could feel it's fear. I remember... feeling that afraid." I was shaking. "I think, in my heart, even though Sam threatened me with death, I hoped he would still have been unable to kill me. That he wouldn't want to hurt innocent creatures just because it's his job." I lifted a shoulder, the pain in my heart a physical, heavy ache. "I guess I was wrong."

"Cleo—" Griffin said.

I knew I was taking this hard. I hadn't ever seen anyone die before, other than Zane and the minotaurs, who definitely deserved it. I liked fighting, but apparently, I hated killing, even when someone else was doing it.

I suppose I understood what Sam was in concept, but not in reality. And now that I understood, I wanted to run.

"Don't," Griffin said, seeming to read my intentions.

"Don't even try it. He'll find you. And, Cleo, you're better off with him. I still believe that—"

"I don't care what you believe, Griffin," I said, instantly regretting how nasty it sounded. I met his hurt gaze and realized I was being a jerk. It had clearly affected him as well, but there was nothing to be done.

Os had been willing to stand there too.

I gave Griffin a quick hug. "I'm sorry. This isn't your fault. But you don't understand. You're with Os. He isn't heartless."

Griffin gave me a sad but understanding look as I pushed back from him. Even he couldn't say Sam had a heart.

"I have one other option," I said. "Perhaps Sam was just supposed to get me out of the haven. Now I have to do the rest myself."

"He will find you," Griffin says. "He won't let you go. I don't think he means to harm you, but there's no way—"

"Tell him I'm with Zadis now. Permanently."

Griffin's blue eyes went wide. "Will you be?"

"No," I said. "But how else will Sam give up?"

Griffin frowned. "I don't think he's going to give up no matter what we tell him."

"Fuck," I muttered. "Well, I'm going to talk to Zadis anyway."

"But isn't he...? He wanted that creature killed," Griffin said. "Cleo, I don't trust him."

"He's my only option," I said. "And I don't believe he'd murder anyone. True, he hates creatures like that void walker, but he only did all of this because he was trying to protect his people." My mind was racing, and even I couldn't tell if this was a good idea. But I didn't have a better one.

No one else would stand up to Sam to keep me, and Zadis had already agreed to.

"I know you're upset, but I don't think you're thinking straight," Griffin said. "I know that was traumatic, but I believe you're safe with Sam. He's a celestial, and—"

"A celestial who puts swords through things that don't deserve it!" I yelled, my hands clenching into biting fists.

Besides, I knew Sam was far more than a celestial.

I'd discovered one of his secrets, but he probably had mountains more.

Who knew what he was planning?

I was better off escaping his grasp, even if it meant going to a fae prince I barely knew.

It was my only option.

29

Zadis was home when I knocked rapidly on his door, still panting from exertion.

"You didn't watch the execution, did you?" he asked, his green eyes filling with worry.

Seeing his handsome, comforting face should have alleviated the worry in me, but it didn't for some reason.

A stupid part of me, probably my inner demon who wanted to feed his incubus, kept telling me to go back to Sam.

"This is a wonderful surprise, regardless," Zadis said, ushering me in with an arm around my shoulders. "Here, let me get you some tea. You look ready to pass out."

I was shaking slightly as I sat on the cushion, and

when Zadis came back with tea, I cupped it with both hands, savoring the heat as it seemed to bring blood back into my digits.

"I saw," I said. "As much as anyone did. Sam blocked the gory part with his wings." I swallowed. "He made it fast."

"He had no choice," Zadis said, looking sympathetic. "I hate the man, but he had to kill that creature." He cocked his head. "Don't get me wrong. I'm the one who benefits from you abandoning him. But why? Why for that creature?" He wrinkled his nose. "Cleo, it was a demon."

"I know," I said. "I suppose because I can relate."

He straightened. "Why?" His tone was sharp enough to cut glass. "How can you relate?"

"Because I was almost executed," I said.

"Yes, but that was for an unfair reason," Zadis said. "Not for being a demon."

"Right," I said, still trying to regulate my breathing.

Don't let him find out you're a demon. Keep the collar on until you escape him too.

Escape? I wondered why my inner demon thought we had to escape right now. We'd just escaped Sam, as we needed to.

Idiot.

Argh, it was like Sam had even tainted my inner demon's voice.

Run.

Zadis was still studying me intently, watching me drink the tea. It felt so soothing.

"I'm glad you came to see me. But what exactly is it you're wanting?" He sat upright with one leg crossed gingerly over the other, still wearing his black robes. "I can't bring that thing back."

"I know," I said, twisting my hands together. "But before, you offered... you know."

"To protect you from that psychopath?"

I nodded. "It's not that, so much. I think I could defend myself. But I have nowhere to go." I raised my eyes to his. "I know no one outside my haven, and I'd rather die than go back there."

Zadis studied me thoughtfully. "You seemed irritated with me earlier. You were angry with me for kidnapping that creature. How do I know that won't come up again? Are you holding it against me, but you just see me as a safer option than Sam?"

I raised my eyes to his. "I don't know. But you've been kind. So when I was panicked, I came here."

"As you should," he said, pouting in a way that was slightly condescending as he stood and pulled me into a hug.

His arms were warm and strong, but I felt nothing as his hand brushed my hair back and he lowered his head for a kiss.

I pushed away from him, shaking my head before our lips could touch. "I'm not ready," I said.

Impatience flashed in his eyes. "We haven't even had a chance to bond properly, and you want me to be your protection against that insane angel?"

"You said you would be," I retorted. "But if I'm to be your whore, then it's time for me to go. I'll run into the woods first."

Zadis moved in front of the door to stop me. "I'm sorry. I was being hasty. I just wasn't expecting you to change your mind like that. Or for the execution to take place so fast. I realized Sam was going to take you out of here as quickly as possible. So I wouldn't have much opportunity to win you over." He reached up to stroke my hair back, and I let him. "I just... This is faster than even I thought."

"So you don't want me?" I asked, confused.

"No, of course I want you," he said. "You're beautiful, a celestial shifter, and unknown power just radiates off of you." He walked over to a small golden container with odd symbols on it. "You're everything I've been looking for in a primary mate. My other consorts—"

"What?" I gaped. "What consorts?"

Zadis gave me an impatient look. "We really should have spent more time together so I could explain things. I am serious about you, Cleo. I will always fight for and protect you. But also, I am a fae prince. I have many lovers, and always will. But you will be my primary mate."

I swallowed, realizing this had been a big mistake. "What does that mean?"

"You get your choice of days of the week?" He wiggled his eyebrows at me like his joke was funny. "In all seriousness, Cleo, my other mates know that a newly bonded mate gets top priority. In fact, we can start the bonding process almost immediately." He opened the container and rummaged inside, then pulled something out. Looking closer, I saw it was a ring with a clear cabochon stone and blue glow that seemed to dance over the surface.

"What is that?" I asked, taking a step forward.

"I just need to see what other magic you possess. Before letting you see the rest of my home."

My eyes narrowed, and my heart began to beat fast. "What do you mean, the rest?"

He eyed the stairs. "My menagerie. My pride and joy."

I swallowed. "That's not where your mates are, right?"

He laughed, a little too jovially. "Oh, no. You're funny, Cleo. No, my fae mates live around this village. But the pride and joy of my life is my menagerie downstairs. Anyone who wants to truly bond with me must see it."

I blinked.

"So just put on this ring. I just need to make sure none of your magic is... unexpected."

I wondered if it would detect a demon.

"Zadis," I said, my throat tight. "I'm not... exactly what you think."

His eyes narrowed. "I know." The jovial mask seemed to slip by the second. "I sensed something from the start, but I thought it was some kind of shifter-related power. But the way you reacted to the angel killing that void walker... it made me suspicious. I've been sitting here thinking what to do about it. I could have kissed you and detected it through a bond. Now we'll have to use the ring."

I took a step back from him, wondering how fast I could get out through the door and run for help.

If I was even in danger right now. There was no reason I should be. Zadis had only been kind.

I could fight him, probably, in my wolf form if something happened.

I just didn't know what would happen if I put that ring on and he found out I was a demon.

"I changed my mind," I said quickly. "I'm going back."

He was in front of the door again, blocking it, almost faster than I could blink. It appeared fae had supernatural speed.

He smiled down at me, extending the ring. "Just put it on. It'll alleviate any... concerns I have, and we can go back to my prior plans for you."

"Which were?"

"Making you my own and spoiling you rotten," he said, smiling. His dark hair hung at both sides of his face, providing a frame for his pale, handsome face and glittering eyes. I noticed his pointed ears sticking out of his hair for the first time.

Why had I never truly looked at him until now?

I suppose because I'd only had eyes for Sam.

It was hard not to fall for a guy who stabbed your attempted rapist and then gave you the orgasm of your life.

But looking up into Zadis's green eyes, really looking into them, I saw what the others did.

Coldness.

He idealized me and nothing more. I tried to push around him to leave, but he was stubborn and hard to move. "Cleo. The ring."

I looked up at him, heart thumping like a drum pounded by a barbarian. It felt hard to breathe.

He reached out and grabbed my hand, and I nearly shifted, but he was too fast, and he shoved the ring on my pinky before I could pull away.

The stone almost immediately lit up pink, and Zadis grabbed the ring back and simultaneously shoved me away from him so hard I hit the ground on my butt.

"Deceiver!" he shouted, growing before my eyes as I looked up at him. He'd been about six feet tall, so a few inches shorter than Sam. But he grew at least half a foot taller. His shoulders grew broader, and his hair lengthened.

His ears were even more prominent, and his eyes were larger, giving him an exotic look.

"My warrior form," he said. "The natural response to finding out a demon is in my home." He advanced on me. "I'm going to blood-bind you with my ruby so that nothing can ever set you free, you monster."

"I'm not a monster!" I yelled, dodging back out of his grasp and running for the stairs. If I couldn't go through the front door, maybe I could hide.

I realized I wasn't thinking very clearly as I ran down

the steps into a musty smelling cellar with a dirt floor and looked around to see glass cases everywhere, floor to ceiling, spaced out about ten feet apart from each other.

Inside, creatures stood, stock-still and waiting, as if posed like still life.

I tried to hide behind one of the cases, which held something that looked like a unicorn, and tried to stifle my rapid breaths.

The animal inside was gorgeous, a black-pelted horse with a shining purple horn. I would have died out of pure excitement that such a thing existed if I wasn't horrified that it was here as taxidermy.

But as I stared at it, waiting for Zadis to come down, I realized it wasn't dead. Just still. Like something was binding it in place other than the cage, which merely surrounded it. Its sky-blue irises darted down to meet mine.

A grotesque animal exhibit.

I should have known there was something wrong with this guy. How obsessed he was with my shifting.

There were dozens of creatures down here. I put my hand on the glass, staring sadly at the unicorn. "I wish I could free you."

The unicorn's blue eyes merely widened, and I got the sense it was trying to warn me, even if it couldn't.

Footsteps announced Zadis's entrance into the basement, his huge, booted feet stomping down into the room.

I peeked out and saw him standing there, and his eyes instantly flicked to mine.

"There's no reason to hide, Cleo. I'm not going to hurt you," he said, his tone falsely gentle. "I've taken a moment upstairs to calm myself and consider the situation. It's not your fault you are... what you are." He looked around him. "These rare creatures couldn't help their demon taint either. So I sealed them here, where they can hurt no one and no one can ever hurt them."

I looked around, seeing what looked like a half-shifted werewolf with gleaming yellow eyes and huge claws and a half-wolf, half-human body, semi-covered with fur.

Another case held a tiny creature that seemed to be made of shimmery light-blue liquid in the shape of a little droplet, a small flower on its head. It had tiny blue eyes and little black feet in tiny shoes that sat a few inches below where the water stopped.

I had no idea what it was or how it floated above its own feet like that.

"You'll have plenty of time to get acquainted with everyone here once I've bound you," Zadis said.

"I'll fight you," I said.

He just grinned, cocking his head at me. "Cute. But you don't know how to fight a fae. Shift, Cleo, so I can bind you."

"No," I said. "I refuse. Let me go. Whatever I am, it won't be your business once I leave."

"You're too rare, Cleo," Zadis said. "I must have you in my collection. Besides, I would be a poor warrior if I released you to deceive anyone else. I'm fond of you. Bonded to you. After this, you'll always be where I can find you."

"You psychopath," I growled. "My friends will never allow this."

"They can't do anything about it," he said, touching a red stone on one of his rings. "Blood ruby, the stone of blood-binding. After I do this, no one will be able to release my hold on you but me. Unless I die, you'll be trapped forever." He looked around at the other creatures. "And that's the plan."

"I told you, my friends won't stand for it. And when they see this creepy place—"

"Everyone here knows I'm simply protecting my community. These things trespassed in our woods. Or I found them while hunting gems. Either way, they are mine, and I have blood-bound them, thanks to the rubies from that void walker. And I will find more." He smiled. "It's my duty and privilege as a fae warrior. Nothing but a celestial can challenge us at all."

"And you think it's okay? Keeping them prisoner?"

"They're all tainted by demonic influence, like you," he said. "If I claim dominion over them, it doesn't matter. At least I'm not letting them be killed. I couldn't blood-bind that void walker, so I made sure to trick him into killing that family by forcing him to make a portal so the celestials could come deal with him instead."

"You suck," I said, walking out to face him. "A lot."

He smiled at me. "And you deceived me, so I suppose we are even." He pointed his finger with the red stone on it toward me, and tendrils of red smoke shot out of it.

I gasped and tried to stumble back, but the tendrils were winding around my arms, my hands, my legs. I looked up to see Zadis engulfed in a cloud of red mist hovering around him. Was that blood?

I screamed, knowing no one could even hear me, and felt the tendrils work their way into my skin. As they did, I lost control of my muscles. I couldn't move anymore as the tendrils sank into my skin and disappeared, locking me in place like they were controlling me from the inside out.

I looked up at him in terror.

"Don't worry about food," he said. "Once a day, I

come down to feed everyone. Give them a short respite from immobility." He smiled gently at me. "I'll look forward to seeing you then."

I could still move my eyes, and my mouth, though stiff, could speak, even as I felt my lips pulling closed. "Sam will—"

Zadis whirled to face me. "No, he won't. Even if your friends wanted to, they couldn't do anything about this. Even if they found you. Because in order to free you, they would have to kill me. And no celestial is going to kill a fae prince." He laughed. "Such an issue would go all the way to the ninth realm. We are allies. If an angel killed a fae prince for a demon... let's just say even that reckless waste of space celestial with black wings wouldn't be immune to the consequences."

Zadis walked over to the stairs and started to jog up them. "See you tomorrow, Cleo," he called back. "And every day after that."

I could hear the grin in his voice. That psycho.

Was he right? Was this the end for me?

As he disappeared upstairs, the light went out, leaving me in darkness, utterly still. I hadn't ever been so afraid. I didn't want to die here, yet living in this situation seemed almost worse.

I could only pray my friends would find me.

It was clear Zadis had only wanted me when he thought I was something other than a demon.

Sam and all the others had been right. The second Zadis found out about what I was, it was all over.

And I'd been stupid enough to think I had somewhere to run for help.

30

Almost as soon as Zadis disappeared, leaving me in darkness and closing some sort of trap door to hide the stairs, I heard a loud thud shake the ground somewhere above me, sending dirt falling onto my head.

Then I heard a huge *boom* of an explosion, as if something made of cement were instantly blasted apart.

Then I heard a voice that was unmistakable.

"Where is she?" Sam growled out in a yell. I heard another smaller explosion, and then the trap door must have been opened because light streamed in, hurting my eyes against the pitch black.

I slid my eyes to the side and could just make out a figure in black in my periphery, stalking down into the basement and toward me.

"Stop!" Zadis yelled, running down behind him.

"This is private property! You've destroyed my house. You've—"

Sam stopped in front of me, looking straight into my eyes before moving down my body. When he was convinced I wasn't hurt or in any imminent danger, his eyes returned to mine again.

Those dark depths gazed into me, then flashed with even more rage as he turned to face Zadis, standing in front of me in the center of the dirt aisle that led between all the glass cases.

"You blood-bound her?" Sam practically shrieked at Zadis, leaping forward to catch the fae by the throat and then throw him savagely into one of the walls of the basement.

Zadis slumped then stood again, brushing his robes off, and Sam moved in front of me again to face off with him.

"She is a demon," Zadis said. "How dare you intrude on fae matters by bringing this creature here—"

"If I took that collar off, she'd finish you in an instant!" Sam snapped.

Zadis smirked. "Not much incentive for me to take it off."

Sam huffed and turned to look at me, then turned back to Zadis and punched him, right through the face, sending him sprawling backward and into a glass case, which shattered, sending tempered glass all around the droplet creature inside, unmoving and unharmed by the disruption.

Like me, he could only be freed by Zadis's death.

Looking into that creature's eyes, I saw fear that mirrored my own. How long had he been here?

Zadis recovered again, looking a bit shaken. "Where is Zarris? You can't just destroy fae property and fight a fae prince. You're a celestial—"

"Right now, I'm just someone so pissed I could hold your beating heart in my hand and not be satisfied," Sam growled back at him. His hands were in tight fists, and I could hear the knuckles cracking.

"You can't kill me," Zadis said, going even paler as he looked to the stairs where light was still streaming, as if he expected backup to come.

Sam unsheathed his red katana, holding it out to the side where it gleamed dangerously in the light, the blade no longer red. "I can't wait to taste that filthy blood you used to bind my property, you fucking prick."

Zadis reached behind him and, to my shock, pulled out a long, elegant sword, not a katana like Sam's. "I will fight you, but you must not use your ninth-realm celestial powers. Make this hand-to-hand."

Sam grinned in a way I found scarier than his grimace. "Good. I want this to be personal. It would be pointless to simply obliterate you with energy. I want to hear you beg." He pulled out his other katana and ran the blades together, making an awful screeching noise. "I want to hear you scream."

"You'll be fucking yourself over," Zadis said, though his voice sounded somewhat shaky now. "Even the ninth realm won't tolerate this. You and I both know this. So why bother? It's just a demon. A special demon that I'm proud to have in my collection, but a demon all the same. Surely, it's not worth—"

Sam lunged forward, swinging his red blade in a hard, fast-as-lightning diagonal strike, and Zadis spun, catching it with his own blade, which he held with one hand despite its size. In his other palm, he built a small ball of blue flame, which he sent at Sam the second he blocked his attack.

Sam spun faster than I could see, dodging the magic, and I saw his black sword lash out in a diagonal strike that slashed across Zadis's upper leg, making the fae let out a grunt of pain as blood spurted from the wound.

Sam raised his sword, his eyes manic and glowing red, though I hoped Zadis wouldn't notice. Holding the blade in front of his face, Sam licked it with one long, ominous motion, then gave Zadis a maniacal grin. "I know your blood now. So you hate demons, but you want to fuck with demon powers? You want to hunt rubies, but you can't control hellfire? You want to blood-bind someone else's property?" He swung his sword out to the right, and Zadis's blood gleamed from it.

Zadis was looking down at his wound but kept his sword up with a shaky hand. His other hand came forward with green fire in it this time, which shot at Sam, who ducked backward, easily evading it.

Sam held both swords and spun toward Zadis. The first sword missed, but it was just a feint, so Zadis didn't see the second coming, right for his ribs.

Sam's sword cut through Zadis's robes and skin with a tearing noise, and Zadis gasped as he fell forward, dropping his sword and putting his hand up to catch the blood falling from his chest.

Sam approached, one katana over his shoulder with the dull side of the blade down, one dragging behind him ominously. "Get up, prince. I'm not done yet. Or are you ready to beg?"

Zadis's hands were covered with blood as he looked up at Sam, and he nodded. "Please, I—"

"Too bad," Sam said, placing a booted foot in Zadis's chest and kicking him backward so he rolled a bit on the dirty floor, leaving a trail of blood before he landed on his face with a thud. "I want to hear you scream instead."

Sam advanced on Zadis, the chains on his outfit

clinking, his swords catching the light, now both soaked with Zadis's blood.

Sam kicked Zadis's sword back to him. "We aren't done fighting, fucker. Pick that up. And don't bother with any spells. They won't work on me."

Zadis let out a scream and lunged at Sam, swinging his sword at head level, but Sam ducked back as though Zadis were moving at a snail's pace, even though it was almost too fast for me to see.

Zadis sent another ball of blue fire at Sam, and this time, Sam caught it and tossed it back. Zadis was consumed in blue fire for a moment before he was frozen instantly.

Sam walked over to him, smirking as the fae stood there, frosted over and only moving his eyes.

Sam smacked the top of Zadis's head with the hilt of his katana, and the ice broke. Then Sam shoved him back again with a boot in his gut, which made him fall to the floor, still shivering and cold.

"So you'd have to freeze me to beat me?" Sam taunted. "Good to know."

"This is sick," Zadis said, shivering and muttering. "My brother—"

"Can't do anything," Sam said. "I have an illusion over this whole house. No one will even know I've destroyed it until we leave. No one will know until you're dead." He swung his sword so that the handle rolled in his hand, and then he caught it again, grinning. "Use a ruby to warm up if you have to. But I don't recommend using the kind the void walker brought from the hell realm. Not unless you want to—"

"What are you?" Zadis's voice was raspy and lost, like I'd never heard it before.

And he deserved all of it for trying to lock me and these other creatures up for all eternity.

"What do you mean?" Sam asked, cocking his head with a mocking smile as he advanced on Zadis, who was using a red glow from one of his rings to warm his body. "I'm a celestial from the ninth realm. What you've done is forbidden. I'm here to deal punishment."

"No," Zadis hissed. "This is a violation of the treaty. No angel would ever do this to me over a demon. What *are* you?" Zadis's voice rose, almost hysterical now, as he stood there dripping blood.

"Pick up your sword and fight," Sam said, running his blades together and getting back in a combat stance. "We finish this, now."

Zadis was practically shaking as he picked up his sword again. He circled with Sam for a moment, then attacked. This time, unlike the others, he was desperate. Before, he'd almost been testing Sam, as if he hadn't thought they were truly fighting to the death.

Now he seemed to understand what was happening, and he was doing his best to take out his opponent.

His sword moved wildly, fast and with a bigger reach than Sam's. Sam was quicker, though, easily spinning out of reach of a strike, only to follow through with both swords, the second one catching Zadis across the shoulder. Zadis seemed energized by his impending doom and slashed forward harder, faster, lunging at Sam as Sam dodged back and then attacked. This time, Zadis dodged him.

They moved almost too fast for me to see what was happening, parrying and dodging back, slamming their swords together and breaking apart again.

Their hard breathing and pants, the scuffle of their boots on the ground, and the clashes of their swords were the only sounds for several minutes.

Finally, it appeared Zadis was tiring, only barely managing to block, while Sam fought him back, hitting against his defense with strike after strike against his sword.

Finally, with one huge slice, Sam cut Zadis's sword in half, and the top flew to the side and clattered on the dirt floor.

The men stood there, Zadis holding his broken sword, Sam staring at him with two blood-soaked katanas.

Then Sam lunged forward, catching Zadis in the gut with his red sword, and I felt my entire body clench at the horror of it.

Sam dropped his other sword and grabbed Zadis by the shoulder, holding him up as he shoved his katana farther in. It slid into Zadis's gut like butter, and Zadis let out a choking noise as his hands moved to the sword, touching it blankly as if he could move it.

Then Sam twisted the blade to the side, and Zadis let out an unearthly scream of pain unlike anything I'd ever heard.

Sam slammed him on the ground on his back, and Zadis slowly slid down the sword to rest on the dirt.

He was still alive, still struggling, as Sam picked up his other sword and knelt over Zadis, looking as calm as if he were simply checking on a friend.

"Why are you doing this?" Zadis gurgled.

Sam froze, glaring down at him. "Because you dared invade her skin with forbidden magic. Because you dared to bond these creatures with your blood. But, most of all, because you dared to take what's fucking *mine*."

Then Sam raised his other sword and shoved it into Zadis's chest right next to the first blade. Based on the cracking sounds I heard right after, he was using them both to wedge Zadis's ribcage open. The fae continued to scream, and I wished I could be free to close my ears.

"Only a moment longer, Cleo, and you'll be free," Sam said in a raspy but assuring voice.

Then he shoved his hand into Zadis's chest and pulled out something red and bleeding, and Zadis continued to shriek.

Sam crushed the thing in his hand, and Zadis's screaming stopped abruptly. The second he went limp, I felt his hold on my body loosen, though I was still too frozen by fear to move.

Sam threw what he'd had in his hand back into the hole in Zadis's chest.

He turned to face me, covered in blood, semi-shaded by darkness, and sighed. "You're free now."

Around me, other animals began to move stiffly, but none seemed to want to break out or draw Sam's attention.

I was shaking, afraid if I took even a step, I would fall. I moved one foot slightly forward, feeling nauseous.

But I was also relieved because I was saved.

Sam had saved me.

Against my better judgement, I glanced down at Zadis. Then I gagged, turning away as quickly as I could, covering my eyes so I couldn't see it.

"I won't blame you for this," Sam said. "Because he

was worse than I even imagined. But I did warn you that this would end in death." His voice was quiet and low.

I glanced at him, not knowing if I should fear or trust this person after what I'd seen.

Though, I knew without a doubt I now owed him my life.

Who knew what would have happened if he hadn't come here, if he hadn't risked everything?

Sam turned away from me to yank his swords free from Zadis, and I had to bend over and resist vomiting at the sound of the blades pulling free of his ribcage.

Sam pulled a black cloth out of his pocket and began to clean off his blades. Then he sheathed them both in one smooth motion and came over to me. I felt him lightly touch my back with his hand. "Cleo?"

I shoved forward and threw my hands around his neck, burying my face in his shoulder, not caring about the blood.

My legs were shaking from not moving for those minutes I'd been frozen. My hands were trembling.

Sam stood there as if he didn't know what to do for a moment. Then slowly, his arms wrapped around me, holding me closely but lightly like he was afraid I would break.

I hadn't known he could be tender like this. Especially after what he'd just done. His chest was still heaving from exertion, and I didn't know what to say.

I'd been so afraid, and despite him being a murderer I was still angry with, I was just glad he'd come.

I didn't know if I should thank him.

Did thank you really cover cutting someone else's heart out for you?

We stayed there for several quiet moments, and Sam pulled back to check me over, holding me up by the shoulders while he did.

Before I could figure out what I wanted to say to him, light flickered at the stairway, and I saw someone else coming down. I tensed but relaxed when I saw it was Griffin, followed by Os.

"Sam!" Os said. "What the fuck are you doing?"

"You weren't supposed to get him," Sam growled at Griffin.

"I wanted to help Cleo," Griffin shot back.

"We need to get out of here," Sam said, grabbing me by the hand and pulling me forward. When I tripped, he swept an arm under my knees and picked me up like I weighed nothing.

He handed me over to Griffin. "Go. Fly to Cayne's sanctuary in the mid-realm. I'll join you there."

"Will we be safe?" Griffin asked.

"There's nowhere else we can go now that he's killed a fae prince," Os said, putting a hand to his head.

"He blood-bound her," Sam grated out. "Now go, Griffin. Fly. I have to fix this."

"You can't fix it," Os shouted. "We're all fucked! The treaty—"

"I don't fucking care!" Sam shouted. "I couldn't let them have Cleo!"

Os just stared at him. "Have you lost your mind? You could have spoken with him."

"A blood bond can't be removed by anything but death," Sam said. "But I can save him still. Not that he deserves it."

"You cut out his heart!" I yelled from Griffin's arms. "There's no coming back from that."

"She's a bit hysterical," Sam said.

"You have to destroy a fae's heart to kill him," Os said quietly, looking somber and upset now. He looked at me. "I'm sorry, Cleo. I never thought a fae prince would resort to something so low. So demonic."

I shrugged. "Me neither."

Griffin let out a growl. "We need to go."

"I'll meet you there," Sam said. "I'll explain this to the fae, with Os. You take Cleo." His dark eyes met mine. "You'll be safe now."

"Sam, we need to fix the body," Os was saying to

him. "And deal with the rest of the creatures. Even if we explain this, the fae aren't going to..."

His voice faded out as Griffin jogged up the stairs with me, and I saw Zadis's house was completely ruined.

"Where are we going?" I asked.

"To the center of the mid-realm," Griffin said. "A place I've only heard of. Maybe the only safe place. But it should be easy to spot from an aerial position since I know what I'm looking for."

"But what about Sam? Os?"

"They can handle themselves. They're celestials," Griffin said. "The fae are going to be upset about this. It's best if you're gone before they know."

I leaned into Griffin. "This is all my fault, for going to him."

Griffin was quiet for a moment. "We all would have come for you, Cleo. That fae's heart would have come out one way or another." He set me down and shifted into his griffin form in the ruins of Zadis's top floor.

When I climbed on again, grabbing onto his fur firmly, Griffin launched into the air, carrying us up and over the tree canopy that overlooked the fae wilds.

Up ahead, dark clouds hid our destination as we flew straight into them. All I could think as we soared up and up was that I hadn't even said thank you to Sam.

And I had no idea when I would even see him again.

I was still mad at him for killing that void walker.

But in the end, he'd come for me, and no one else ever had.

I leaned into Griffin's fur to rest and closed my eyes, but the wind beat against my skin with a sure but frightening realization.

I was already losing my heart to an angel with demon eyes.

31

I fell asleep at some point as we flew through the gray clouds and didn't wake up until we landed.

The thud made me jerk upright, my hands still twisting in Griffin's fur as he let out a grunt.

I slid off of him, rubbing the sleep out of my eyes, and he shifted back into his human form. The first thing he did was pull his red fae robes up and over his head, tossing them to the side right after. He wore a white tee shirt with a sports logo and jeans, Converse sneakers on his feet.

I looked up at him, wishing I could explain to someone what I just saw Sam do.

What I just witnessed...

But then I was distracted by observing the place

where we'd landed, which was unique compared to any place I'd ever been.

The air all around us was smoggy or foggy, making it difficult to see past the property we were on and the ruined streets around it. The asphalt was cracked and pulled up in lines so that no car could ever go past.

The grass I was standing on was green and lush, and the air was humid around us. I looked up to see an old cathedral, Gothic style, with a huge arch over a large stained-glass rose window with small sections of colorful stained glass arranged like the petals of a massive flower.

Below that stood huge, worn cherry double doors that looked heavy enough to crush a dozen people if they ever fell forward.

I looked around me and saw that old iron gates blocked the entrance to the property, and a tall, old-fashioned iron fence with elaborate metalwork surrounded the entire plot.

With a little shiver, I noted that, to the right of the cathedral, guarded by a giant willow, there was a small cemetery with crumbling headstones and monuments shaded by mist and fog.

On the other side of the cathedral stood more gravestones, giving a haunted feeling to the whole place.

Everything felt gray, from the smoggy sky overhead

and the thundering storm clouds approaching to the mist in the yard and the worn gray stone of the Gothic cathedral.

Above the doors, a wooden sign had been mounted, and it looked the worse for wear.

But in old script, carved deep in the wood, I could read the message.

Cayne's Sanctuary. All peaceful creatures welcome.

I stared up at it blankly. You'd have to be truly desperate to think this place could offer you respite.

And what did it mean, all peaceful creatures? Was I a peaceful creature? And who was Cayne?

All of these questions circled in my mind as I rubbed my arms and tried not to think of how Sam cut Zadis open.

"Come on. This place gives me the creeps," Griffin said, leading the way up to the stairs. "You good to walk?"

I nodded. Though I was shivering slightly from the shock of everything that had happened, it was nice to stand on my own.

Griffin walked up to the door and knocked with a heavy fist. The door creaked open a crack.

"We are not accepting new applicants until Cayne returns," the deep, silky voice murmured. "You may wait at the nearby vampire keep. They are accepting—"

"Sam sent us," Griffin blurted out. "We have nowhere else to go."

The door opened slowly, and a tall, elegant man with dark skin stood there, gazing at me with almond eyes in a startling shade of blue. Like ice on a frozen lake. He wore a dark cape that hid the rest of his outfit, except for his fitted leather pants that were tucked into polished leather boots.

His hair was white and cropped short, and he had a white mustache to match. He cocked his head at us. "Well, we do hate to turn anyone away. If you were truly sent to us by Samael—"

Griffin nodded, but he looked nervous about this place.

The man dipped his head respectfully. "My name is Orpheus," he said in that smooth, velvety voice. "I am Cayne's valet, butler, and assistant. I am also the manager of this sanctuary. How long will you need to stay?"

"I don't know," Griffin said quickly.

"Will Samael be following shortly?" Orpheus asked.

"I don't know," Griffin said again. "Look, can we find her a place to lie down? She's been through a lot."

Orpheus nodded, welcoming us inside. The floor of the cathedral was intricately tiled, though here and there, a few had broken from wear. The cathedral inside was beautiful. The empty pews stood in rows. Light streamed through the stained-glass windows at the front and back. Beautiful Gothic arches curved up into the ceiling, meeting every ten feet or so. At the front was an altar.

Orpheus walked up to it, knelt in front of it, and pressed some kind of button at the side of the crimson velvet cushion.

To my shock, with a rumbling jerk, the altar began to lower, disappearing out of sight.

Orpheus stood and beckoned to us. As we walked over, I saw the platform continuing to go lower and lower, making odd grinding noises until it stopped twenty feet down. Orpheus reached into the opening where it had lowered and pulled something out from the side. It looked like a rope ladder.

Griffin swallowed, staring at it nervously. "Is there somewhere up here we can stay?"

"Samael has never personally sent me a visitor," Orpheus said. "You must be in grave danger. This is the most secure place to hide. There are some rooms above ground, where the master sleeps and where certain guests are allowed to live. We also have some separate cottages and staff quarters out on the grounds. But this is where you'll want to be right now."

Griffin eyed the ladder skeptically, still not convinced.

But I was done not trusting Sam's advice. He might be a murdering psychopath, but so far, everything he'd told me had been trustworthy.

And the last time I went against what he said, I ended up frozen in a basement with Zadis.

I put my hands on the cold stone and began lowering my foot to the first step of the ladder.

"Be careful," Orpheus said. "Watch your step."

The ladder swayed slightly as I put my foot on the first rung. It was dark beneath me, save some dim candlelight from nearby corridors, so I felt a shiver go down my spine as I took another step downward.

"You okay, Cleo?" Griffin asked. "I should have gone first." He shuddered. "I hate dark spaces. Especially caves."

"This is merely the catacombs," Orpheus said. "Cayne has outfitted it handsomely. You should feel privileged to have access to it. No one can hurt you here."

"Where do the others stay?"

Orpheus sounded confused. "What others? As you know, Cayne likes to help relocate or find work or homes for the creatures who seek him here. We don't have many long-term guests." There was a pause, during which I took another step down. "And if we did, we wouldn't speak loudly or publicly about them."

"Right," Griffin said, sounding unsure about this whole idea.

On the fifth step down, my foot slipped off the small rung of the ladder, and I lost my hold completely. I screamed, as cold air was all that existed between me and the ground.

However, almost instantly, I landed on a huge, soft cushion of some kind.

"Cleo!" Griffin shouted, and I looked up in the dim light to see his huge body hurrying down the ladder. "Are you okay?"

I rubbed my ass, looking up and wondering how often people fell off the ladder like I had that they had put an actual cushion here to break the fall.

When Griffin lowered himself and jumped the rest of the way to the cushion, he lost his balance and landed on his butt across from me.

Before we could even look up to wait for Orpheus, he jumped down to us, landing on one knee comfortably and standing with the same imperious grace with which he seemed to do everything.

Then he held out a hand to both Griffin and me to help us up.

Orpheus was strangely strong, pulling us to our feet

smoothly. Then he turned and walked to the wall and grabbed a torch that was burning there.

I looked around to see stone beneath our feet and elaborate murals on the walls on either side of us. We were looking down a long hallway with doors on either side.

"Cayne had this place outfitted for those needing a safe haven. I will show you to a suitable room to rest."

"Who is this Cayne guy?" Griffin asked. "How does he know Samael?"

Orpheus didn't answer, leading us down the hallway and stopping at a large wooden door on the right with an iron knocker. He drew a ring of clanking skeleton keys from within his robe and selected one from the others, which he placed in the door.

He opened it and led us into a spacious but old-fashioned bedroom, complete with a huge four-poster bed with a rich red and gold velvet canopy at the top.

On the floor was a rug in gold, red, and navy.

There were lamps on the walls, and as Orpheus moved past them, raising a hand, they lit up, glowing a warm yellow, casting the fine details of the rug and furnishings into high relief.

"I presume Cayne will join us shortly," Orpheus said. "He likes to greet new arrivals and show them around. Or, rather, explain the rules. I will have food delivered to you both. Would you prefer a shared room or separate?"

"Separate," Griffin and I both said quickly. I liked the guy, but we weren't close like that.

Orpheus looked somewhat surprised but nodded and motioned for Griffin to follow him back into the hall. "I'll put you side by side. Cayne may move you when he returns."

"I'll be right next door," Griffin said. "As soon as I'm settled, I'll be over."

Orpheus paused, then removed the huge, pitted iron key that he'd used to unlock the door. He handed it to me. "The only one."

I gaped at it. "Thank you."

Orpheus gave a polite nod and moved out, leaving me alone in the room.

I walked over to the bed and sat on the edge of it. The rich silk and velvet cover crackled beneath me, and I smoothed my hands over it.

Then I pushed back and flopped down on the bed on my back, staring up at the canopy over my head.

Compared to my tiny little room at the haven, this room was huge. I loved the feel of it. The covers sank in beneath me, and my weary bones and muscles relaxed at the sheer luxury of it all.

There was a knock on the door, and Griffin poked his head in.

"Come in," I said, and he did.

His blond hair was mussed from running his hand through it, and his blue eyes were somewhat hectic, but he smiled as he walked over and flopped next to me on the massive bed. "How are you doing?"

"Good," I lied. Things had improved, but until I saw Sam and Os again, and knew both of them were fine and that no one had to pay for my stupidity, I couldn't relax.

"It's not your fault," Griffin said. "It really isn't, Cleo. Blood magic... that's only for demons. I think the fae will go easier on Sam, knowing that."

I looked at Griffin, panicked. "Could they do anything to Sam? Since he's ninth realm?"

Griffin looked up at the canopy as if searching for the answer there. "I don't know a great deal about the fae. I'm sorry. But I don't think they can do anything to him. They can report him to the ninth celestial realm, though."

"Even though Zadis imprisoned me?"

Griffin let out a growl. "Those stupid fae don't see demons as creatures worthy of anything, let alone freedom or life. I worry that, even with the blood-bonding, they will not be happy to have lost a prince."

"I don't blame them," I said. "Even though that guy was more psychotic than Sam."

"No one is," Griffin said with a shudder. "Did you see what he did to that guy?"

I swallowed, throat tight and sticky. "Yeah. I watched the whole thing."

"Dear gods, Cleo. He did it in front of you?" Griffin asked with wide eyes.

"I was frozen at the time. I couldn't move."

Griffin cleared his throat. "You want to talk about it?"

I smiled because I knew he would have, for me, but I didn't think he had the stomach for it. "I'm okay for now. I just want to forget about it."

Zadis's begging. His staring eyes after he died.

I'd never seen Sam lose it like that. Even when he killed, it was cold and calculated. When he exploded Zadis's house and came to save me, calm was the last thing he'd been.

But what did it all mean?

He needed me for something. It could just have been because of that.

"I don't trust him, Cleo," Griffin said. "This Cayne guy. I've heard he associates with vampires."

I shuddered. "Perhaps. They live in the mid-realm. But the guy is giving us shelter. We should give him the benefit of the doubt."

"I don't know," Griffin said. "This feels like some kind of trap." He glanced around the room. "This place is creepy."

"Well, you used to live in the most gorgeous place ever," I said, thinking of the lush-forested mountains where the cougars roamed.

"So did you," he said. "The first thing I noticed flying down here was the pollution. In the havens, everything is green, and the air is so clean." He let out a sigh. "I bet it's even better in the sky kingdoms, where the celestials live."

"It probably is," I agreed. "But I'd rather be here, personally, given how the celestials feel about demons."

"Me too, given how they feel about my friend," Griffin said, putting his hand on my arm and giving it a small, reassuring squeeze. "And don't worry. If this Cayne person shows up before Sam does and causes trouble, I'll protect you. I promise."

"I'll protect you too," I shot back, making him grimace.

"Again, I didn't mean it wrong." He looked up at the canopy again. "Os gets mad at me too. I'm just a protective person. I always have been."

"Nothing wrong with that," I said. "As long as you accept it when someone wants to protect themselves."

"Of course."

We were quiet for a moment, and I truly was glad to have Griffin by my side. It felt odd to be away from Sam, to know he wasn't even close.

He could be anywhere.

"Do you know anything about this Cayne guy?" I asked. "You said you'd heard of the sanctuary."

Griffin scratched the side of his neck. "I mean, I know what most people do. We get more news of the mid-realm than you wolves do, I suppose. All I know is there's this notorious slayer no one wants to mess with, and he set up a safe zone for creatures no one else would want. So many hybrids popped up after the great divide, and a lot of communities reject anything that isn't pure. Someone passing through my village told me about it, since he'd noticed I wasn't like the other cougars. He said creatures like me, who don't quite fit in, can come here. And there are few who would risk Cayne's ire."

"A slayer," I said. "I've heard them mentioned. They're demons, right?"

"Right," Griffin said. "You'll usually not see them above the abyssal realms. If they're in the mid-realm, it's near lesser demon settlements that need protection. Slayers are like the—"

"Like the archangels are to the celestials, right?"

"Right," Griffin said. "They protect demons for free

and others for pay. They're killers. Trained for years with the best of the best to murder anything. You typically don't want to meet one. But I hear Cayne is benevolent to anyone not trying to harm demons."

"He better be," I said. "I'm not in the mood to see anyone gutted."

"You think Sam could beat a slayer?" Griffin asked.

I looked over at Griffin. "He has two slayer swords already."

Griffin grunted. "I knew that guy was crazy." He let out a pouting sigh. "I miss Os. He isn't practically insane."

I laughed. "Right. Tell me how things have been going between the two of you. I need a distraction."

"I'm not ready yet," Griffin said. "I mean, Os doesn't really even like having me around. I'm not sure he'll even come to get me. He tolerates me as a pet, but you can tell he's bothered at having to drag me around. Sam will probably be the only one to come here, and I'll just be another one of Cayne's lost creatures."

I swallowed. "Cayne does seem to help them find homes, according to Orpheus."

"I'll stay with you and Sam," Griffin said, frowning. "I don't like you being alone with him."

I snorted. "I don't think I'm in any danger from Sam. I know I should be, and I've seen what he can do. But at this point, I've accepted that he needs me for something. Until that time, I'll survive."

"So odd, a celestial so obsessed with a half demon," Griffin said. "Do you know what type you are?"

I shook my head.

"Maybe we'll find out more here," Griffin said. "Maybe Sam is looking to Cayne for info."

"Maybe," I said.

A knock on the door startled both of us, and a voice with a slight rasp called out.

"Hello, hello? Cute little humans? I vant to suck your bloood. Come play with me."

Griffin's eyes went wide, but before he could jump from the bed, I pushed up and got ready.

"What the fuck was that?" I asked.

Griffin shook his head next to me. I realized we hadn't locked the door behind us, though Orpheus had given us the key.

The door opened slowly, and a pale face with dark hair peeked around the opening.

"Boo," it said.

32

"Shut the door," I yelled to Griffin as we both tried to sit up, but before we could, it swung open, and a dapper figure appeared, leaning against it with a smile. In the lamplight, long canines with sharp points glistened.

A vampire.

The creature had silky black hair to collar length and exotic, almond-shaped eyes in a shade of blood red. Its lips were pretty and naturally dark, and its skin was as white as the moon.

It seemed a few years older than me, maybe mid-twenties, and its face was beautiful and heart-shaped.

He was a few inches taller than me but much shorter than Griffin, and he wore a black cloak over a white dress shirt and black pants, with shiny dress shoes. "I didn't know we had visitors. I would have dressed up even more."

Griffin stood in front of me, but I pushed in front of him.

"Who are you?" I tried to keep my voice from trembling since this was my first time facing a vampire.

"Simon Card at your disposal," Simon said, sweeping a bow that made his hair shimmer in the light. When he stood, he reached out a hand for me to shake it.

I stared at it for a moment, and he laughed.

"You didn't think I was serious, right? About the sucking your blood thing?" He chuckled. "I was trying to give you a special introduction to vampires. But, no, we don't do that anymore." He smiled. "Not without permission."

I swallowed. "You're not going to get it."

He came closer to me, sniffing the air. "Interesting. I don't want it from you anyway." His red eyes slid to Griffin, and he fluttered his eyelashes prettily. "This one smells amazing, though. Top tier blood."

Griffin took a step back from Simon, looking unimpressed.

"You both smelled amazing at a distance, like freshly baked sugar cookies. A vamp could smell it from miles away." He raised his nose in the air, inhaled deeply, and sighed. "Mm. Delicious." He cocked his head. "Just a hint of something I don't want." His gaze went to mine. "Something tainted in yours, eh? Good thing this guy has enough to go around. Look at the size of him."

I moved in front of Griffin, blocking the vamp's path. "You need to get out of here. Orpheus said we were alone—"

"You are," Simon said, clasping his hands behind his back and stepping back with a smile. "Except for me. I'm a close friend of Cayne's, so I come and go as I please."

"You say we smell good?" Griffin sniffed his armpits. "Does that mean other vampires will come for us?"

Simon flashed his fangs. "Not with me in the vicinity. Besides, everyone's too afraid of Cayne, even if it's just his reputation protecting this place most of the time now."

"Who is he?" Griffin asked.

"You don't know the most famous slayer of all time?" Simon clicked his tongue. "Too bad for you." He rocked back and forth from foot to foot. "Hey, what about just a taste? You have plenty to spare. I won't turn you into a vampire, you know, and—"

"Bothering our guests, Simon?" Orpheus's deep voice cut into our conversation, and shortly after, he appeared at the doorway. "Dinner is served. Let us all head upstairs."

"I wasn't bothering anyone," Simon muttered. "Just meeting the new inhabitants. It's been a while since—"

Orpheus shot Simon a look that shut him up and turned to leave the room, a torch held in his hand, illuminating his white hair in the darkness.

"Should we?" I asked Griffin.

"I'm starving," he said, putting a hand on his stomach.

"Me too," Simon said, looking at Griffin hopefully.

Griffin just went red and shook his head once again.

Simon shrugged, rolling his eyes, and turned to go out. I followed him. He seemed to be less of a danger to me than to Griffin.

Griffin stayed behind me, his hands on my shoulders so we could stay together in the dark, humid passageway we were led down.

Orpheus turned to a stone wall, pulled down on a light fixture, and we heard the loud rumbling of a wall moving.

Orpheus stepped forward, through where the wall had been, and his torch lit up old stone spiral stairs leading upward.

I ran my hand along the cold, humid stones that made up the walls of the stairwell as we climbed higher and higher. We came out into some sort of dining room with a long table and many chairs.

Three places were set at the table.

Two had plates that were full of human foods I recognized.

At the third, a large goblet of what looked like blood sat alone.

"Dinner is served," Orpheus said. Then he whirled to leave, walking out of the room and into a nearby corridor.

Silence fell over the room, other than Simon picking up his goblet and drinking noisily.

When he'd finished, he sat back with a sigh, patting his stomach. "Amazing. This place always has the best blood store."

He said it as though he were complimenting a fine wine.

Griffin looked pale enough to worry me, his royal-blue eyes stark in his face. So I pushed his fork toward him, encouraging him to start on the steak and potatoes on his plate.

He cut into the meat aggressively, glaring at Simon, who didn't seem at all worried about his animosity.

I cut into my baked potato and took a bite with a sigh. The food was hot and good, and I trusted it enough to eat all of it.

Simon stayed quiet while we ate, and based on his moans of enjoyment, Griffin enjoyed the food as well.

When we were done, Simon sat forward, putting his elbows on the beautiful red tablecloth, leaning forward on the heavy wood surface of the table.

"So tell me what you two are doing here."

Griffin cleared his throat. "We were sent by Sam—"

"Samael?" Simon cocked his head. "Interesting. Any thoughts about why he sent you here? Weird thing for a celestial to send his friends to the home of a demon."

"Cayne is a demon?"

"All slayers are," Simon said, looking at me like I was an idiot. "Where are you from? You don't know anything."

"A celestial haven," I said.

Simon's eyes widened, and the beautiful red in them looked slightly purple, like rubies. "I have never met someone raised in such a place. I suppose it must have been like when other humans met the Amish."

"The Amish?" I asked.

"A dead religion," Simon said. "Many religions went extinct after the great divide. The Amish weren't shifters and didn't have any special powers, so the celestials weren't interested in saving them as some of the chosen humans. Celestials saved who they wanted, and vampires got most of the rest."

I swallowed. "And you're a vampire?"

"At your service," Simon said pleasantly. "So what are you?"

"I just told you—"

"No, you told me where you were from. Not what you are," Simon calmly retorted.

"I'm—"

Griffin interrupted me with a hand over my mouth. "Cleo, don't. We don't know him. We shouldn't tell him anything."

Simon smiled, flashing a fang. "He's probably right about that. Can't blame a guy for trying."

Griffin scowled at him. "I do blame you."

Simon slumped, resting his chin on his arms and pouting like a small child. "So not even a tiny taste of your blood, then? Just a small—"

"No," I said. "Stop trying to get Griffin's blood, and maybe we'll trust you more."

"If you were hanging out with a Twinkie and it refused to give you a bite, you'd be irritated too," he said, still pouting.

I laughed. "So we're like Twinkies to you?"

He nodded.

Twinkies were a common human treat that was still being manufactured somewhere in the mid-realm. They sometimes got to the havens even.

"I'm not your Twinkie," Griffin said, still working on finishing his meal.

"You could be," Simon said. "It would feel good. You might like it, and—"

We heard a loud slam from elsewhere in the cathedral, like heavy doors closing, and the stones around us seemed to vibrate from the noise.

"Get help! He's bleeding," a smooth, high-pitched masculine voice said.

"Get Orpheus," another voice, more familiar to me, said.

Os?

"I'm fine," a deep voice grated out. My heart nearly jumped out of my chest. That was Sam.

I heard rapid footsteps running down the hall, and somewhere in the entryway, the talking continued.

"He's hurt," Orpheus said. "What has happened? Master Samael never returns injured—"

Injured? I pushed my chair out, causing it to screech against the stone floor, and bolted toward the door that led out of the dining room, heading for the sound. I took a corridor under a Gothic archway, and it led me to the front of the cathedral where Sam was being brought farther into the main room, helped by two figures.

"Give him here," Orpheus said, moving forward as

Os and a black-haired man in white robes handed him over.

Orpheus picked up Sam's huge body, carrying it like it was nothing, and walked in the direction of the altar.

"Is he okay?" I asked.

My heart felt squeezed like someone had a fist around it. Sam's body and face were shaded by black robes, but I could sense there was something very wrong about him.

"I don't know," Orpheus said. "I will have to tend to him. All of you go. Now." Based on the way Orpheus looked down at Sam, I could tell he cared deeply about him.

But how did they know each other?

Still, what mattered to me more at this moment was Sam.

"I'm coming with you," I said. "This is my fault."

"There's nothing you can do about this, mortal," Orpheus snapped at me. "I doubt this is your fault because master Samael can't be forced to undertake anything. But we must be alone for now."

He then turned at the front of the room where the altar was and disappeared into a hallway that led to the right and out of sight.

Os turned to me, along with the other figure, whose

white robes were streaked with blood, and I realized it was one of the angels I'd met the day I'd been in jail.

"Mor?" I asked.

The handsome face that was almost too delicate gave me a worn smile. "Ah. The wolf shifter from the prison."

I frowned at that.

Mor folded his arms and walked closer to me, frowning and moving in an intimidating circle around me. "What does Sam see in you that he would go so far for you?"

My face burned with embarrassment because even I didn't know.

Mor leaned in close, deeply scenting me.

"Back off," Griffin said. "Or face me."

Mor turned to him, and his face was instantly amused. "A pet!" He walked over to Griffin and put a hand in his hair, ruffling it. "Good doggie. You being a good guard dog, boy?"

Griffin went red, whether from anger or blushing, I wasn't sure. He swatted Mor's hand away, and Mor stepped back.

"Things sure got interesting for Sam while I was away," Mor said, shaking his head. His eyes met mine, a sharp silver. "So why did you almost get him killed?"

I swallowed.

"It wasn't Cleo's fault," Griffin said. "She was tricked."

"Hm," Mor said, not convinced. He snapped his fingers, and his outfit changed to a blue tunic and flowing blue pants, plus soft slippers. He faced me again. "I don't trust you at all. Sam stuck his neck out for you, even though you're just a lowly demon, and the next time I see him, he's a beaten pulp of a man. Tell me why I shouldn't kill you now and get this over with."

"There's no need for that," Os said, nudging Mor back from me. "Also, I wouldn't threaten Cleo if I were you. Sam doesn't like it."

"Yeah, well, I don't like seeing my friend beaten to a pulp because someone didn't follow his advice about staying the fuck away from a fucking fae prince. They're fucking treacherous," Mor said.

"Hey, watch your language," Os said. "Zadis doesn't speak for all fae. He was much more messed up than any of us knew. Dabbling in demon powers. Cleo couldn't have done anything to stop this."

But deep down, guilt was making it almost too hard to breathe.

I hadn't listened. I'd let my fear of Sam, after that execution, ruin everything for us.

I'd run to Zadis. It was all my fault.

Even now, I wanted to run to Sam, beg his forgiveness, and ask why he went so far.

"I didn't think that guy could get hurt," Griffin said. "He killed Zadis without even getting scratched, and Zadis was a prince."

"Zarris is a high priest, equal to a king in the fae realm," Os said. "With his gems, and his grief over the loss of his brother, he was a strong opponent. Also, Sam had used most of his energy on the previous fight."

"Why didn't you help him?" I asked Os.

Os pinned me with an amethyst glare. "I couldn't. What Sam did was forbidden. Had I intervened, this would have been even worse. Sam knew there would be consequences." Os's eyes ran over me. "He just decided it was worth it." He studied me with calm coldness. "For some reason."

"Don't talk about Cleo like that," Griffin said. "She's a good person. Don't take this all out on her."

Os sent him a glare.

"He's right," I said, sighing. "I fucked up. I didn't know who to trust. When Sam killed the void walker—"

"What?" Mor asked.

"Just... I'll work it out with him. Make it up to him somehow."

"He'll take at least another day to heal," Mor said. "Don't bother him in the meantime."

I stared into Mor's astonishing silver-blue eyes, wondering what his relationship to Sam was to make him this protective.

He'd been the most jovial with Sam when I met the archangels back in the jail.

"For what it's worth, I truly am sorry," I said.

Mor sniffed. "Your sorries mean nothing until my friend is okay. So stay away while he—"

"Samael would like to speak with you, Cleo," Orpheus said, cutting Mor off and making him flush violently.

Mor took a step forward in protest. "But—"

"No buts," Orpheus said. "Sam's request."

"Fine," Mor said, turning to walk away toward the kitchen. "I'm going to go eat and get my strength up. You watch it, girl. I'm not done with you. It's my job to watch out for him, and I'm going to do it whether he likes it or not."

Mor disappeared, and Os looked at Griffin and me apologetically.

"Mor is just upset," Os said. "Sam was truly in bad condition when he arrived."

My heart squeezed painfully at the thought. "I'm going to go see him. Coming, Orpheus!"

Orpheus, who stood at the other end of the cathedral, nodded and disappeared out of sight once again.

"How are you two doing?" I heard Os ask Griffin. "Are you safely settled? No one has bothered you?"

"Just me," Simon said, his voice ringing out as he joined the room. "Your friendly neighborhood vampire."

I glanced back to see him hanging on Griffin's arm and grinning at Os.

"I'm hoping this 'snack' will let me have a snack," Simon said.

I took that moment to make a quick exit because I had a feeling drama was about to break out, and all I cared about right now was seeing Sam and making sure he was okay.

No matter what else had happened, I owed him my life, and I would do everything I could to pay him back.

33

When I reached the place where Orpheus disappeared, I heard voices and followed them down a stone corridor filled with natural light and toward a large wooden door with an ornate doorknob and lock.

I raised my hand to knock, and the door opened, Orpheus's face behind it.

He pulled it all the way open with a creaking sound and revealed a beautiful old-fashioned bedroom with a giant cherry-wood four-poster bed even bigger than mine. Elegant, expensive antique couches and chairs sat in a small sitting area in front of the bed.

At the side of the room, huge windows reached up to the high ceiling, giving a view of the graveyard and the willow outside. A large stained-glass window topped the room, showing a beautiful view of a lion and a deer amidst a forest.

The windows were somewhat hard to see through, due to age and the foggy weather. On the opposite side of the room from the bed, a large fireplace stood, unlit.

"So what do you think of my brother's home?" Sam's voice startled me, and I turned to see Orpheus helping him into the bed. He was naked, except for small black boxers.

I looked away to give him privacy and heard a snort of amusement from him.

"Oh, Cleo, so innocent, so sweet. Good to see you haven't changed."

"This human is the reason you are hurt?" Orpheus asked disapprovingly.

"No," Sam said sharply. "A fairy prince dabbling in blood magic is the reason I was hurt." He sighed, and I watched him melt into his incubus form before my eyes, his hair growing long and red, his large horns growing from his head. The slight white and pink shadows on his face.

His red eyes.

But what stood out more were the deep bruises all over his body, covering his face, shoulders, neck, and chest, at least what I could see of it.

He sighed, slumping back in the covers, letting out

what sounded like a low groan of pain. "Cleo, come over here. I want to see you."

Orpheus moved back. "Will you need me, master?"

"No," Sam said. "See that Os and Mor are given a place, if they're staying."

"Of course." Orpheus made a slight bow. "It will be done."

He disappeared, closing the door behind him, and I heard the click of a lock shortly thereafter.

We were locked in. Maybe Sam wanted to kill me to punish me?

I cocked my head at him. "I just don't understand. You handled Zadis like it was nothing. Why did you let Zarris hurt you like this?"

Sam didn't say anything, just turned his face, which was still gorgeous despite the bruising, to look out his window at the willow. "I missed this place. What do you think of it?"

I looked around me. "Honestly?"

He nodded.

"It's so beautiful," I said. "I could stay here forever."

"Don't tempt me," he muttered.

"What do you mean?"

"Don't tempt me to lock you up here forever, where fae princes can't blood-bind you."

I flushed, and my hands tightened into fists as I took

another step closer to the bed. Sam was already looking out the window again, his expression somewhat peaceful.

"Sam, I'm so sorry—"

His eyes met mine sharply, and the red there was so much richer and brighter than Simon's. Like the petals of a red rose but liquid. "What? You're going to apologize for betraying me? For running to the exact man I kept warning you about? For nearly getting yourself into a fate worse than death?"

I nodded slowly. What was the point in denying any of it?

"I suppose there haven't been many men you could trust," he said.

I nodded.

"Still, I saved you from execution. I gave you pleasure. I don't know what I did to earn your mistrust—"

"You killed that void walker," I said.

He frowned. "You know why I had to do that." He started to sit up, then winced and immediately sank back down. He let out a raspy breath. "I don't have the energy to argue with you. Not until a few of my ribs heal."

I took another step forward, worry pushing me closer. "Your ribs are broken?"

He smiled at me. "My everything's broken. Zarris was really unhappy with me for what I did to his brother. Not that I blame him." He glanced out at the willow again, face slackening slightly.

But his gaze was sharp as usual when he looked back at me.

"So this is your brother's place?" I asked.

He nodded.

"I'm guessing he's your brother on the demon side," I said.

He nodded. "Our family is quite complicated." Then he looked out the window again. "I'm sorry, Cleo. I'm tired, and I need to rest. I just wanted to see that you were okay." He flushed lightly. "Because, as you know, I still need you for something."

"Right," I said, twisting my hands together. "And that's why you fought Zadis, right? Because you didn't want him to take someone you wanted a favor from?"

Sam just stared at me without answering, his jaw jutting stubbornly despite all the bruises on it.

I probably wasn't ever going to get an answer to what I truly wanted to know.

"If there's anything I can do to make it up to you, let me know. Since this is my fault, I want to—"

"I'll have you give me a sponge bath later. You can

scrub me down naked as punishment," Sam said, grinning and then wincing as if the expression hurt. The desire to go to him, tend to him, was almost unbearable when he was hurt like this.

But I could tell from his stubborn face that he wasn't going to let me in yet.

"I'm going to come check on you later," I said. "Regardless of whether it's for a bath or to see you're okay."

His lips firmed into a line, and his eyes narrowed in confusion. "So worried about me, even though you tried to escape my company?"

I moved back toward the doorway. "You scared me, Sam. I won't pretend you didn't. But I want you to know I trust you from now on."

His eyes narrowed farther. "I don't know if I would recommend that, Cleo."

"Why not?" I threw my hands in the air in frustration. "You did this for me! You fought Zadis for me. It wouldn't have happened if I had trusted you."

He cocked his head. "It probably would have, just differently. I do blame you for some of this, but I knew I would have trouble, taking you on." His eyes darted to my collar. "You aren't a typical demon. I knew that when I found you."

"You said you didn't know what I was."

"I'm not positive," he said. "And what I suspect is something I couldn't dare tell anyone. But now we're in the mid-realm, where most celestials wouldn't dare to tread. In the morning, I'll have my blacksmith make you a more accurate restraining device. Those collars the celestials use are fairly weak." He coughed, made a choking noise, then sighed, leaning back in the bed. "But as I said, I need to rest now."

"Right," I said. "I just wanted to thank you. Again. For saving me."

I expected some rude comment in return, but instead, he simply nodded, and I bowed my head and reached for the door behind me. Then I realized it was locked.

Sam raised a hand, turned it sideways, and I heard a click behind me. "It's unlocked now."

I opened it and left because I had no idea what to say to this odd creature any longer. I knew what to do with angry Sam. With rude Sam. With violent Sam.

I didn't know how to react to an injured Sam, sitting in his bed, staring at a willow with guarded eyes.

But I could at least give him the privacy he wanted so he could rest and get better.

The rest of what lay between us could wait.

But a tiny, demonic piece of me really was hoping he meant it about that bath, if only so I could see him again soon and make sure he was all right.

In the meantime, I'd go see Griffin and make sure hell hadn't broken loose in my absence.

34

After a hot bath in the antique tub in my room, provided by Orpheus who had made the steaming water appear as if from nowhere, I felt refreshed and ready to go see Sam.

Dinner had been an awkward affair, with Mor glaring at me angrily while Os tried to soothe the tension. Meanwhile, Simon kept making attempts at convincing Griffin to let him drink his blood.

I had to admit I kind of liked the vampire. He wasn't like anyone I'd met, but his bluntness made me trust him more than someone smoother who could hide things easier.

I pulled on a blue silk strappy nightgown, a bra, and a blue silk robe that had been delivered to my room with other clothing and went to the mirror to finger-comb my hair.

It was drying in dark waves, silky and lustrous despite everything I'd been through. Looking at my oddly delicate features and burning blue eyes, for the first time, I liked facing myself.

I liked seeing the woman who had survived so much. Who had escaped the haven and found a new world.

I touched the collar around my neck, wondering if it would come off tomorrow. Then I pulled my hair back in a low ponytail with a band from my wrist and looked myself over once more.

The silk looked amazing against my pale skin, and my heart beat a little more rapidly when I wondered what Sam would think when he saw it.

We hadn't been alone for a significant amount of time since that day he'd nearly made me pass out from pleasure.

I didn't know if he was expecting to do something again.

I didn't know if things were different between us after what had happened.

A knock sounded on my door, and I sighed and went over to it. When I opened it, Simon was standing there, leaning against the doorway.

"My favorite human," he said. "Thought I would

check in on you." His eyes roamed over me, taking in my outfit. "Hm, thinking of visiting our resident incubus?"

I gasped and grabbed him inside, shutting the door behind him. "What are you doing? Not everyone knows that—"

"Right, Griffin probably doesn't," Simon said. "The others are playing stupid if they claim not to. It's obvious. The boy is *hawt*."

My flush probably confirmed his point, but I gave him no words to do so.

Simon swished his cape over his shoulder and sat on my bed. "But you aren't a human, are you? I call you my favorite human because I don't know what else you are. Are you a shifter like Griffin? Maybe with a little bit of demon?"

I glanced at him, not sure what I should say.

Simon landed back on the bed, both of his palms resting behind him to prop him up. "Show me yours, and I'll show you mine." He grinned.

"What do you mean?"

"Tell me more about yourself, and maybe I'll tell you more of what you're wondering. After all, I know almost everything there is to know about Sam and his brother."

I swallowed. There were a million questions I wanted to ask, but I wanted to give Sam the chance to tell me the answers himself.

But would he ever? The proposition Simon presented was tempting.

"You have too much dignity for gossip?" He folded his arms. "That's boring."

I laughed. "Well, I can tell you I'm a wolf shifter. Because you'll probably see me running on the grounds."

Simon's eyes widened, and he shook his head quickly. "No, sweetheart. Don't even leave these walls without someone with you. Don't go outside of the fence. Don't run in the graveyard either. It's rude, you know."

"Why can't I leave? There's no one anywhere in this mist."

Simon raised an eyebrow. "You can't *see* what's there in the mist. Look, wolf shifters are a rarity that no one has seen. The chosen creatures of the celestials. People here like things that are rare—"

"Then why—"

"They like to own them like toys and gut them like fish for potions," he said. "Keep your blood safe and stay here with Sam."

"How do I know you're not working with him to convince me?" I asked.

Simon just started laughing. "You wouldn't be here if Sam needed my help convincing you of anything." He studied me, and I felt my cheeks heat. "So why did you go with him? Why did you leave your precious haven for this forsaken place?"

I swallowed. "This place is better for me than the haven was."

"Ah, were you an omega?" Simon asked.

I nodded, surprised he knew about it.

"Hm, unlucky draw," he said.

"How did you know?"

"Cayne spent some time in the celestial realms, and he's told me stories about how backward some of the communities have gotten. Figures."

"But you think it's worse here?" I asked.

"Well, no vampires or demons or dark mages could have reached you there, so since you're a sweet little fluff of fur, yes, it's worse for you here. Stay with Sam, sweetheart. Till he gets sick of you."

"Sick of me?"

"He's not the type to stay, sweetie," Simon said, giving me pitying eyes. "That man's heart is as cold as that graveyard outside is in winter."

"We're not like that," I said, though my cheeks gave me away. "He's helping me, and I'm going to do him a favor later."

Simon sat up slightly, his red eyes taking on a dark glow at the centers. "Interesting." He glanced at my collar. "Doubly interesting." He stood. "Well, since you won't gossip, I'm off to find someone who will. Plus, based on your apparel, I'm assuming you're going to see him?"

I nodded.

Simon grinned. "Good for you. You should help him heal after he fought that hard for you. Not to mention, it must have been hard for him to kill someone's brother."

"Why?" I asked.

Simon's cheeks sucked in, and he frowned slightly. "No reason in particular. Anyway, go feed him. You won't regret it, if you haven't already tried it. That boy fucks as well as he slays, which is immaculate. You'll enjoy it."

Jealousy flooded me. "How do you know that?"

Simon laughed lightly. "I told you. I've known him and his brother a very long time. And he's an incubus. It's easy to infer."

"Right," I said weakly. "Anyway, I'm just going up to help him with whatever I can since he's injured. I'm not even thinking about... you know."

Simon walked to the door and opened it, then shot me a speculative glance. "But just for your information, an incubus does heal faster if well-fed. Something to think about." Then he disappeared, leaving me gaping at what he'd just said.

A part of me would have loved for him to be right, to have an excuse to touch the only man I'd ever wanted.

But Sam's health would come first. So I left my room, locked the door, and headed up to Sam's chambers.

Who knew what the night would hold?

35

When I knocked on Sam's door, Orpheus was the one who opened it, and his disapproval showed in the minute twitch of his white mustache before he showed me into the room.

"I must say I don't approve of this," he said. "Master Samael needs rest, not company. But as it's his request—"

"Stop bothering Cleo," Sam called grumpily. "You're overstepping your place."

Orpheus shot him a look that said they would be having a discussion about this later, but he left the room.

"You didn't have to be rude to him," I said, following the sound of Sam's voice toward a door at the end of his bedroom. "He was just trying to help."

I opened the door to see a huge copper tub filled with steaming, soapy water. Sam was in it, his shoulders and arms exposed above the water, his head back in a relaxed pose, his tousled golden-brown curls already wet.

He looked over at me, and I noticed the bruises on his face had already lightened quite a bit. They did nothing to deter from the natural beauty of his high cheekbones, full lips, and strong brow.

The tattoos on his arms caught my attention, and I had to admit I found them sexy.

I winced at a huge bruise on his chest, the size of a foot.

He looked down. "Yeah. He stomped on me a few times." He grimaced as he propped his hands on the edge of the tub, moving and trying to get comfortable. Then he rested the back of his head on the lip behind him and turned to look at me. "Well? What are you waiting for? Sponge bath?"

I breathed in through my nose, inhaling the fragrance of the bathwater as I came closer. Jasmine and woods, unexpectedly.

I knelt by the side of the tub, grabbing a sponge that had been placed in an attached delicate silver tray and next to a bar of elegant soap.

I picked up the soap and lathered it against the

sponge, heart beating as I realized this was really happening.

This demigod incubus was really going to make me wash his body.

The worst part was I couldn't wait.

Sam sent me a glance as I wrung the excess soap out of the sponge, then looked forward again with a smirk as I leaned over him, unsure what to do. "Well? Wash me," he said flatly. "I'm too sore to do it myself."

I summoned all my courage and put the sponge on his defined, huge shoulder, scrubbing lightly as he let out a little laugh.

"You can push harder than that," he murmured, closing his eyes as he leaned back.

I did, scrubbing over his shoulders and chest, pleased as I saw dirt and blood wash away. I knew he could have had Orpheus do this, but I was glad he trusted me to take care of it instead.

It felt like he was letting me do this to make things up to him, to help with my guilt.

But I knew if I asked, he'd deny it. Plus, I was probably giving him way too much credit.

But it was hard not to give someone credit when they'd saved your life and paid so much for it.

His eyes opened as my sponge paused on his bicep,

and he sighed as he looked up at me. "You don't actually have to do this, Cleo. I just wanted to see you."

I smiled. "I like doing it. I still feel really bad."

"I thought you would," he said. "It's not your fault, though. And believe me, I'd be the first to blame you if it were." He sighed as I rubbed the sponge over his collarbones, gulping as I moved down into the soapy water to his abs. I had to lean over the tub to do so, and something inside me clenched as his abs flexed under my hands. I couldn't see them, but I could feel them.

That was almost worse.

Sam at least didn't seem to notice. He kept his eyes closed, head tilted back to the ceiling, utterly relaxed. "At worst, I thought we'd have to do a bonded mate challenge in the underground arenas. I could have gone easy on him then. I still might have murdered him, but it wouldn't have been the same. But what he did, it's forbidden even to demons." He shook his head. "So, no, it's not your fault."

"It's my fault you had to get involved," I said.

He opened one eye to peer at me, and my hand paused at the bottom of his abs. "I chose to get involved with you. As I said, I think you're special. And I need you. Pets sometimes need watching. That's all. And if someone else tries to take your pet, or threatens your pet, you protect them. That's all." He closed his eyes and leaned back again.

My hand, and the sponge I was holding, inched closer to forbidden territory. Lower. I glanced up at him, unsure if he really wanted me to wash him all the way.

His full lips turned up in a smirk, and I could see he wasn't going to help at all.

I put aside the sponge, causing him to open his eyes and look up at me.

"What, reneging already?" He smirked. "I thought so."

If he'd thought to simply make me blush and cower, he was wrong.

"No, it's just..." I stood and faced him down. "I wondered if there was something more I could do to help you."

His thick brows came down in consternation. "What do you mean, more?"

I fidgeted, still trying to summon the guts to do what I wanted. What I wanted and what might also help make him well.

"Simon said... he said I could feed you. That it might help."

Sam's eyebrows went straight back up, and I could tell I'd genuinely surprised him. "Just a warning, don't listen to everything that vampire says. He can be dangerous when he wants to be."

"He seems nice," I said. "He says he's your friend."

"He is," Sam said sharply. "I have many dangerous friends. You should be cautious around all of them."

"I'll keep it in mind," I said, sitting on the edge of the heavy tub.

"See that you do," Sam said, leaning his head back again. "Though, I'll be here to protect you anyway."

"Sam, I want to learn to fight. Like you fought Zadis. I want to be strong, and—"

"You will be," he said. "We'll start your training tomorrow, when you get your new restraining device and meet my metalsmith."

"And you'll be better by then?" I asked.

Sam's lips turned up wickedly. "Depends. How eager are you to help?"

"You said not to believe Simon about everything," I said nervously.

"Well, he's right about the healing," Sam said, grinning. "And I'm not above using things to my convenience."

I faced him boldly. "I'm not either."

A light flush tinted his cheeks as he caught my meaning, and his big body shifted slightly in the water as he caught my eyes.

His eyes narrowed to dark slits. "This thing between us, it's dangerous." His eyes roved over my body. "That silk looks gorgeous on you, as I knew it would. Matches your eyes."

"Thank you," I said, feeling like my knees would knock together if I had to stand.

Just the thought of him doing things to me again was making me weak inside.

I wanted him. I wanted to feed him. I wanted to pleasure him. I wanted so many things, and I knew that he would probably not need to do any of them to feed.

But as long as it helped him get better, it was a win-win situation.

He peered at me, as if he could read my mind, and grinned. "Well, you know, there's room in this tub for two."

"How?" I looked at it and thought that, despite its depth, it was fairly narrow. "There's no way we'll fit in there side by side."

"Not side by side," he said, pulling his legs up so his knees breached the soapy surface of the water.

Damn it, even his knees were sexy. Stupid incubus.

"Step in," he said, putting his hand up for mine. When I put my hand in his, his fingers and palm felt huge. He helped me step into the tub so I was standing between his bent legs.

He smiled up at me. "Not a bad view."

I shrugged out of the silk robe, tossing it to the side so it couldn't get wet. Then, audaciously, I reached under my silk slip and undid my bra, which I managed to toss aside before pulling the blue silk down over me again.

My nipples pressed out in hard peaks, and as Sam reached up to take my hands, guiding me down to him, I felt myself get wet between the legs.

He helped me lower into the tub, then, to my shock, raised my legs onto the ledge of the tub on either side of his head and grabbed me under my back, pulling me in toward him.

Instantly, I realized what he wanted. Shock moved through me as he moved my arms up to brace on the side of the tub and guided me closer, closer, till my underwear was almost at his mouth.

I felt utterly exposed, facing him, supported by him, floating in the water except for his thighs helping to hold me up and his huge hands gripping my hips in front of him like a feast he was desperate to eat.

"Sam," I said uncertainly. This felt so wicked. So exposed. I'd never thought of anyone doing this to me. Self-doubts flooded me, but lust was even stronger, and a tingle of anticipation shot up my spine as his mouth came close.

"Don't drown," he said, keeping his eyes locked on mine. Then he pulled my underwear aside, and his lips closed over me, so hot I bucked against his hands, holding tight to the side of the tub.

Gods, his mouth felt amazing. His hand had been incredible before, but his lips, his tongue, flicking out to explore and taste, were so wet and hot the sensation was immediately almost too strong.

Almost.

He dug in voraciously, licking every part of me, his eyes watching fiercely for every movement, moan, or buck. As he had before, he adjusted, twisting his tongue this way or that, sucking down just where he knew I wanted it.

An orgasm was already building, faster than I'd ever imagined. The steamy water engulfing my body, his hold on me, the scent of jasmine in the air, and even the knowledge of what he'd done for me all increased the intensity of what I was feeling, like natural aphrodisiacs.

"Sam," I murmured, breathing hard as the tension got stronger, tighter, knotting me up inside and making me thrash against his hold slightly.

But he was resolute, and his hold on me didn't waver as his lips caught my clit in a deep kiss, tonguing and sucking till the pleasure in me was rising like water in a flooded room.

"Oh gods." I bucked, but he held me as the heat built and built, the tension inside me nearly unbearable. "Please, I can't—"

He paused, lifting his mouth above me to look at me triumphantly. Cool air brushed across me, and I shuddered at the loss of his mouth even as I felt the tension ebb impatiently inside me. Then his tongue darted out to flick me again, and I jolted in his hands.

"Close, little wolf?"

I nodded jerkily, and he lowered his mouth to kiss me again deeply, engulfing my clit in his lips and stroking it over and over with his tongue.

The heat was back again, the tension twice as strong, rising twice as fast, and my whole body felt as if it were about to be struck by lightning, based on the way all of me was bracing, my muscles all painfully tight.

He was keeping me up in the water, but as his tongue flicked over me and my head went back, my hair dipped into the soapy, gorgeous-smelling water, and when I jerked my head up, I saw Sam watching with a grin.

"As I said, don't drown."

Looking into those wicked black and gold eyes, I almost wondered if I truly could.

He lifted his head after another long, languid,

utterly irresistible kiss to my clit. I was panting, huffing, squirming against his firm hold on my hips.

"You taste so amazing, Cleo. Every taste of you only makes me hungrier." His long lashes lowered as he kissed me again, and this time, he sucked hard, and I came.

I screamed and then tried to muffle myself with one hand, which made me lose purchase in the water.

But Sam's hand was there, his large palm supporting me despite his threats that I might drown.

And the hot water surrounded me as the most powerful orgasm of my life burst through me, nearly buckling my entire body under the intensity of the waves of pleasure washing through me.

I looked at the beautiful, ornate ceiling and tried not to cry at how good this felt and how long it had taken me to learn my own body, what it was capable of.

But then again, Sam was an incubus, and I could tell from his every expression, the attention he paid my every move, and his smirk every time I came that he was very, very good at what he did.

"Oh gods. Oh, Sam," I said, knowing he wanted me only to speak of him, which was fair since he'd done this to me.

I'd come to him with the hope of helping him, but truly, he was also helping me, awakening my body, awakening my pleasure, and making me come alive everywhere.

And based on the way his eyes flickered red as he looked at me and the way he seemed to be holding his breath and not blinking so as to not miss a moment of my pleasure, it was making him come alive too.

"Oh gods," I murmured as the last aftershock rumbled through me, making my toes twitch as it ended. My body felt limp, and I realized Sam was supporting me completely.

To my shock, he was also looking slightly better, as if some of the bruises on his face had faded.

But as his hands came around my waist, pulling me upright to sit on his lap, and his eyes dipped to my breasts, barely covered by wet silk, his irises flashed to red and stayed there.

"Fuck," he said. "You make me lose control, Cleo." He dipped his head to my wet shoulder and placed a searing kiss there that made me arch back. "I can't stop when it comes to you. I want to please you senseless." His hands gripped into me. "And what scares me is it isn't even about feeding. I want this. I want you... like I've never wanted anyone before."

I gaped at him, watching his beautiful eyes study me like a puzzle he couldn't fit together.

"I want everything with you," he said, leaning in so

our lips were close together. "When Zadis had you..." He shuddered slightly against me, his huge shoulders slumping. "I couldn't breathe... Everything I've been working for would have gone down the drain, true. But you... Ever since I met you, everything has been upside down."

"What do you mean?" I asked. I had no idea what he was talking about, but I wanted to. I wanted to know everything about him.

And while I couldn't take what he was saying as a pronunciation of feelings, I did understand what he meant.

There was something between us. Something we couldn't run from no matter how hard we tried.

"There's so much to tell you," he murmured, his lips almost brushing mine, making me crave the heated curve of them. The things he could do with his talented tongue.

My desire was on his lips, and I saw him lick them carefully, tasting all of it.

"I must have more. I'm sorry, Cleo." His hands cupped my ass, and he suddenly stood in the tub, picking me up with him so I wrapped my legs around his waist and held on.

"Why are you sorry?" I asked as he carried me into the bedroom easily, tossed me onto the bed, and got on with me. We were dripping water everywhere, but neither of us seemed to care.

"Because I can't stop. Because you're probably going to pass out, and it's all my fault. I knew my incubus side couldn't resist you. I won't let him out all the way, but I must have more of your pleasure." He sounded more desperate than I'd ever heard him. "It feels like I'll die if I don't."

"Um, this really isn't a problem to me," I said, looking over at him as he flopped onto his back in the middle of the bed. "I want to heal you, and..."

"And?"

I knew my cheeks were blood red, but I didn't care. The way he wanted me, the way I wanted him, everything had brought us here.

"I've been wanting more of you ever since you touched me," I said. "I've been craving your touch."

The corners of his lips lifted, just for a second, but his red eyes stayed intense. "Someday, you just might end up with my incubus."

I blinked, wondering what that meant.

"But for now, you get Sam," he said, gesturing for me to come over to him. "Come here. I can feed on you easier this way. And again, sorry if you pass out."

"What do you mean?"

"I'm going to give you pleasure until you can't take

anymore," he said. "Unless you fight me in earnest, unless you truly can't take it, I won't stop. So tell me now and leave if you truly don't want this." His eyes flashed, and I could tell from the hardness in his stubborn jaw that he was dead serious.

My eyes roamed down his naked body, and I was disappointed to see black boxer briefs soaked from the bath. So I supposed he had been going easy on me when he'd been teasing me about sponge-bathing him. Still, I could see something hard and tempting and absolutely huge pushing against them.

Talk about weapons of mass destruction.

I reached for his waistband to pull them down, but he pushed my hand aside and grabbed me by the thighs, pulling me forward on top of him.

As he kept pulling me up, over his abs, then his chest, I felt his muscles graze against my wetness.

Then I saw his chin, so close to the apex of my legs. My silk slip was still on. His underwear was on. We were soaking the bed.

"I can't wait. I'm sorry, Cleo. I must have you." Then his hands grabbed my ass, tore my underwear away easily, and pulled me over his head so I was sitting on his face. His tongue flicked out wickedly against my bare skin, now trapped against him, and I let out a moan, realizing what he intended.

Gods, this man was too good.

I was too turned on to be self-conscious, my body too aware of the pleasure his mouth could bring to care about anything but that.

My knees were on his shoulders, and my hands were braced behind me on his chest. Every part of him I touched felt amazing.

But it felt so wicked, so forbidden, to feel my wetness dripping into his mouth, to feel his tongue reach up to tease me before playing along the seam of my folds, then returning to my clit. I felt his face rise so he could press fully into my sex, and his nose, his chin, everything stimulated me.

"Sam," I moaned again as I arched back, maintaining my balance as his hands came up to pin my thighs, pulling me even closer into his mouth.

I was worried I might smother him, but as his tongue and lips lazily explored, licking, flicking, and torturing, all thoughts of everything but how amazing this felt flew away.

Fully supported, I arched against the foreign sensations of his entire face moving against my most vulnerable place.

But then he began to kiss me again, using the weight of my body and his utter access to me to own me completely.

I buried my hands in his hair, leaning forward, and his tongue moved slightly inside me, giving me a unique sensation I immediately loved.

I wanted more.

I moved against his mouth, mewling, and he let out a growl, grabbed both my ass cheeks in his hands, and pulled me so tight against him there was no escape.

I bucked. I jerked. I nearly passed out because it got hard to breathe as the pleasure built, but Sam didn't stop.

As I reached the apex, I felt him licking and sucking, voracious, and when he let out a little growl and commanded me to come, I did, my body releasing instantly.

But his tongue stayed against me as I came, trapped against his mouth. He stroked me, sucked me, urged every wave higher and more intense.

It was almost too sensitive to take, but the second I was coming down, he was starting again, building another intense release.

And all I could do was hold on through the greatest storm of pleasure of my life.

When I came again, I shuddered against him, nearly losing my balance, but he merely readjusted me and muttered that he wasn't done.

When I pulled back, wondering if he could even

breathe right, he let out a little growl and pulled me back, licking me again.

And, gods, I couldn't bring myself to want to stop.

If both of us died like this, so be it. My body wanted *more*. And gods help me, my heart did too.

Sam continued to feed on me until my body was exhausted from orgasm, till I could barely breathe, my body so was enervated from pleasure, until each release was so strong I didn't know how I could survive.

He fed on my desire, licking and slurping as though I were the best thing he'd ever tasted, and the firm, reassuring grip of his hands never failed. I rode his face, enjoying every sensation, lost to the pleasure of the moment.

"Breathe, Cleo," he murmured against my vagina, making me choke out a gasp. "Breathe. I don't want you passing out... yet."

"But I..." I panted, my whole body ready to go limp from so much release. Yet my muscles were tensed, ready, and my inner demon felt awake and like she would never have enough.

We should keep him, she said suddenly when Sam was sucking on my clit at a particularly delicious angle.

I pushed the thought away. I would never take a mate if I had any say in it.

This was enough. This moment of pleasure. This hurricane of feeling *so* good.

I came again, then again, and Sam adjusted his position, never seeming to get tired of licking, sucking, tasting, and making me buck, writhe, and moan.

"Cleo, so gorgeous," he'd say against me, still sounding ravenous. "More, I need more."

The thought that I was somehow helping him alleviated any guilt, and I lost myself to the pleasure, the moments flying by, my vision unimportant as all I could do was focus in on the intense pleasure of his face between my legs.

If only I could have stayed there forever.

It got harder to breathe due to how many times I'd come, due to the rising intensity of every sensation. I was gasping, panting, as I felt a strong release building in me again.

This time, Sam moved slightly, and I could see his eyes watching me as his tongue flicked down over me, once, twice, and then from side to side, and I released.

I felt it wave over me like crushing pressure that felt better than anything in my life, and then everything went black.

36

When I woke, Sam was lying on the bed in his incubus form, watching me with those beautiful rose-red eyes.

He looked relaxed, content. As if he'd been the one pleasured to the limit of existence.

He gave me a lazy grin as I pushed myself up, realizing he'd changed me into a soft, fluffy white robe. "Couldn't let you catch a cold."

"Right," I said, wrapping the robe around me nervously as I met his eyes. "How long have I been out?"

"I did tell you to breathe," he said. Then he smirked. "Two hours."

"Wow." I sat back on the bed, then looked over at him tentatively. The bruises seemed less bad, though perhaps that was his natural healing too. They'd said he'd be better in a day.

When I moved, my sex ached, and I couldn't help smiling, remembering what would probably be the hottest moment of my life.

Sam, writhing beneath me, feeding on my pleasure.

It probably didn't get any better than that.

His expression went solemn as he cocked his head at me. "Incubus is my preferred form," he said. "As long as I'm not hungry, I'm no danger to you or anyone."

"And if you are hungry?" I asked.

"Then I go kill something," he said as simply as if he were mentioning going to the butcher to pick up some meat.

"And it feeds you? Like this does?"

His eyes ran over me. "Nothing feeds me like this does."

I flushed, not knowing what to make of it.

I also didn't know if I should leave or thank him for the orgasms or offer reciprocation.

I was a bit embarrassed that I'd been asleep for two hours.

"I'm going to rest now," he said, but there was warmth in his eyes as he said it. "I enjoyed that, Cleo. Thank you for feeding me."

I swallowed. "I... enjoyed it too. It's me who should thank you."

"No," he said. "I'm the one who got the steak dinner."

I giggled. "Happy to help."

He went solemn again, and his hand reached out to my hair, which had dried in unruly waves. But then he dropped it, seeming to come to his senses. "We shouldn't... This still isn't..."

I nodded. "No feelings, right?"

He nodded but watched me warily, as if he expected me to be upset.

"That works for me," I said, drawing my knees up to hold them. "What we've done together, I like it. And I want more. At least, I think I will. But I'm not looking for someone to control me. To mate me."

"I control you now," he said, eyeing my collar.

"No," I said. "You may call me your pet, but you treat me like your equal. You fight for me. You come for me."

He sucked in his cheeks. "Maybe I would do that for all my pets."

"Then anyone is lucky to be your pet." I put my hand over his, just for a moment, and he went paler, looking like he didn't know what to do.

So I gave him a light pat and pushed off the bed, making sure I was steady before standing fully.

"Stay down," I said, waving him away when it looked like he wanted to escort me to the door. He was wearing red pajamas and appeared ready to sleep, and I wanted him to rest and get better.

And I needed some time alone to think.

I also didn't want another fight like we had before, about being exclusive.

I now knew he was possessive, but since there was no one else I wanted, for now, I didn't mind.

"Tomorrow, you'll start training. I'll be catching up with matters here and arranging for transfer of the creatures Zadis had."

It felt so odd to be talking normally after I'd just ridden his face until I passed out, but I realized that was just how things went in his world.

Too much to do for any breaks.

"You're taking them?" I asked, thinking of the black unicorn and pausing by Sam's door.

He nodded. "They're 'tainted,' meaning demonic influenced. But that doesn't mean they can't find a place. My brother used to run this place. Now I run it for him instead. I'll still take any creature that cannot find a home."

I wanted to ask him more about that. I wanted to spend time with him.

But he'd said he needed rest.

"I will see you tomorrow, Cleo, after you get fitted for a new restraining device. We can start training your inner demon." A wicked glint lit his tired eyes. "She should be more awake now, after all."

She was. I could feel her.

Then again, being around someone like Sam, who did what he wanted when he wanted, had helped as well.

I was no longer the omega from my haven, fighting helplessly but never allowed to be fully strong.

Here, I could become strong like him. Learn to fight like him.

"I want to be able to fight like you did against Zadis," I said quietly.

He grinned at me. "We'll see, little wolf." But I could tell he was affected by the compliment.

"Good night, then," I said, putting my hand on the doorknob. After what we'd done, it felt odd to leave him.

But we'd both gotten what we needed.

"Good night, Cleo," he said. "And thanks for the meal."

He'd infuriated me with that phrase before, but this time, I just smiled at it.

"You're welcome," I retorted, seeing a flash of surprise on his face at my audacity, before I jerked open the door and shut it behind me, smirking as I left.

37

In the morning, I got dressed and ready and headed out into the courtyard behind the cathedral.

There were overgrown weeds and grass and trees around the edges. But in the center, there were flat paving stones making up a large standing area.

To the back right, there was a worn-looking shack, and Sam had said that was where I'd be going.

Because he had some things to take care of at the sanctuary, he'd stopped by early this morning to tell me to head over to the smith.

Presumably, some new pets were coming in. I hoped I could get dibs on that unicorn.

I tromped through the weeds, noting the moody, cloudy sky and the fog hanging low over the ground.

When I reached the shack, I walked up to the old

wooden door and knocked.

I heard it creak as it was pulled open, so whoever it was had been waiting.

To my utter shock, it was the face of the void walker Sam had "executed."

How could he be here? I'd seen his blood go everywhere. He had to be dead.

I gaped at him, and he smiled.

"Surprise," he said, sticking out a hand to shake mine. His dark eyes sparkled with his smile. "I'm Nic. Thank you, by the way. If you hadn't begged him like that, I doubt he would have freed me."

"Hi... Nic." It was hard to even speak, seeing someone I thought was dead. "I—I saw him stab you."

"Come in, dear. You're wasting heat, and I'm in the middle of forging," an unknown voice called out.

My eyes widened as the void walker pulled me in, and I looked around a room that was much too big to fit in the space the shack took up. "What in the...?"

"It's enchanted," a stocky person with gray hair and a black leather apron said, facing away from me. "Sam put an illusion on the outside so it looks smaller than it is. People only walk around to this door, so they don't notice." The person was currently hitting something on an anvil, and a fire was glowing in a nearby forge contained within the stocky stone hearth.

The room wasn't as warm as one might expect, and I assumed that was due to an enchantment as well.

"I'm a metal mage," the person said, finally taking off their welding helmet. As they turned to meet me, I realized she was a woman in her late sixties or early seventies in human age, with gray hair lit with white strands. Her face was heavily lined, and her light-blue eyes, diffused from age, sparkled as they looked over at me.

"Name's Betty. Betty Silver. Nice to meet you." She put out a weathered, calloused hand, and when I put mine out, she shook it firmly. Then she held on to it tightly, jerking me forward to look into my eyes. "Hm. Interesting." Her eyes wandered down to my collar. "Even more interesting."

"Why?"

"May I?" she asked, pointing at my collar.

I hesitated for a moment, because Sam had implied there might be danger if I removed it, but the frank look in her blue eyes assured me, and I nodded.

She took it, unbuckling it carefully and lifting it away, staring at it with narrowed eyes. Off of my neck, the stone was no longer yellow but dark brown.

"I'll be right back," she said. "I have to examine this." She walked to a nearby desk, pulled out a chair, and grabbed an odd-looking pair of glasses that would probably help her magnify what she was looking at.

Though, for all I knew, they had another purpose as well.

"So," I said, looking at the void walker. "How are you alive? I saw your blood everywhere."

"Not my blood," Nic said, brushing his black hair off his pale face. "You must have convinced Sam to spare me at the last minute. When he put his wings around the cage, he said he was going to use an illusion so they didn't notice the cage opening. He told me to come here."

I gaped. Just how good were Sam's illusions? "How was there blood, then? Was that an illusion too?"

"No, the red slayer sword Sam carries has the capacity to store the blood of those it kills and release it at will," Betty called to us from where she was sitting. "It helps us fill up the blood stores here and also helps him fake executions as needed. Those stupid death-loving celestials haven't noticed yet, and I doubt they ever will." She shook her head. "I still don't approve of him working with them."

"Did you make his sword for him, then?" I asked. "I thought he stole it off some slayer he killed?"

Betty gave me an odd look, then shook her head and turned back to her work, not eager to say anything more.

Nic peered at me. "He hasn't told you much, has he?"

I shook my head.

"He will, Morningstar," Nic said.

Betty gave him a sharp look. "You watch your mouth about that. That's sacred. We don't know that applies to her yet."

I looked over at Nic. "I'm really glad you're not dead. I'm just confused... He said he had to kill you."

"He had to make it look that way," Nic said. "The fae thirsted for my blood. But here I am, alive."

I felt overwhelmed by the whole situation. Nic was sitting there in jeans and a gray tee shirt, casual as could be.

And he'd called me the Morningstar. Like he had back when he was imprisoned.

"What is this Morningstar everyone keeps talking about?" I asked.

"Very powerful demon," Betty said in a hushed tone, still studying my collar. "The most alpha demon of all."

"Alpha demon?"

Betty nodded. "The celestials likely stole the alpha and omega system from demons. Demon power hierarchies are innate rather than assigned at puberty. Anyway, all slayers are alphas. Some of them have even higher powers than other slayers though. Based on the color of the brimstone on your collar, you're high-level something. I'm just not sure what."

My jaw dropped, and my heart instantly started hammering in my chest. "High level? Alpha?" I shook my head. "What?"

"Mm-hmm," she said. "Brimstone doesn't lie."

"But Sam does," I said. "He said it was yellow, which is common."

"Was he in front of celestials at the time?" Betty asked.

"Yes."

"Then he couldn't tell them," she said. "They've been hunting and killing high-level demons and slayers for years, just to prevent the rise of the Morningstar."

"The what?" I felt like I was speaking another language. Ever since we'd reached this sanctuary—since I'd left the haven, really—I'd been thrust into an entirely new world.

"The prophecy," Nic said. "You don't know?"

"That's only in demon circles," Betty said. "Only the angels at the top know about it and only because it's in their best interest to stop the prophecy from coming true."

"What prophecy?" I asked, frustrated.

"I'll let Sam tell you the rest," Betty said.

Nic looked like he wanted to say more, but with a stern look from Betty, he decided to keep his mouth shut.

He gave me an apologetic glance.

"Anyway," Betty said. "He had to tell them you were low-level or they would have taken you and had you killed by a ninth-realm celestial, or someone who would have made sure you stayed dead. So be grateful he didn't tell the truth."

"But it *was* yellow, which is common," I said. "I've been wearing it. I *saw* it."

She grinned at me. "If it were truly yellow, yes, it would be common. And that was a very clever way for Sam to get you out of that situation. He's been incredibly smart about working with the celestials and making it work for him. Unlike Cayne." She made a *tch* sound and shook her head.

"So it's not yellow?" I asked, confused.

"No. It's gold." She grinned. "That tells me you have immense power. It's the highest level of demon. But there are other high-level demons who aren't the Morningstar." She peered at me. "You come from a celestial haven, correct?"

I nodded.

She ran her eyes up and down me, appraising me. "And you're a wolf shifter, so I have to ensure your new collar doesn't restrict it?"

I nodded.

She focused back on the collar, picked up a tool I

didn't recognize, along with a hammer, and worked on it for a few minutes. Then she stood and walked over to hand it back. "You can keep this on until I have your new one. It should provide protection from you destroying anyone or anything with the worst of your powers, for now. I'll start working on a new collar as well. And a sword, in case you need one. Since you don't have your slayer sword yet."

"I need a sword?"

"Of course," she said, looking at me as if I were stupid. "Everyone needs a sword when working with Sam. Even if you aren't the Morningstar, there is plenty of work to be done. Plenty of creatures who need killing."

I swallowed. "Sam did say he wanted a favor one day. But I don't want to kill anyone."

Nic took in a shocked breath, and Betty turned to face me with a gasp.

"You don't want to kill?" Betty asked. "But you're a slayer. I can feel it in you."

I shook my head, raising my hands. "I've never killed anyone. I don't want to. I won't be needing a sword."

Betty shook her head. "In this world, it's kill or be killed, little wolf. You'll soon see that. I will make the sword, and Sam will train you to be ready to use it. You'll be a slayer we can all be proud of soon enough." She smiled at me like she was telling me I'd get good grades in school or something.

I genuinely felt sick even thinking about killing someone. I'd been so busy thinking about escaping the haven and the alphas that I hadn't even thought of what would happen when I got to a destination with Sam.

What he would want from me.

Nausea rose in me, and suddenly, the room felt too hot.

"I'm sorry, I have to go outside," I said, stumbling to the door and pushing it open. I sucked in a breath of cool, foggy air and tried to process what Betty had told me.

That I was a slayer. I wasn't a low-level demon. I wasn't a succubus. I was something special, and Sam had known all along.

I supposed it made sense, since he wouldn't have stuck his neck out for me otherwise. But a slayer?

Did all high-level demons have to slay? Sure, I loved fighting and martial arts, but to actually end someone?

I didn't know if I could do it.

Deep down, I knew it was selfish, that people like Sam had borne the burden for me in that way.

But he liked it, so what was wrong with it?

Nic came out to check on me, and it was odd to see him with legs in the open air rather than black mist below the waist. He was tall and peered down at me curiously.

"Is there anything I can do to help? I will serve you in any way I can, Morningstar."

"Why do you call me that?" I asked. "Why does everyone keep talking about it?"

"You should ask Master Sam," Nic said. "I think now that you are safe and in a more private location, he will tell you all you want to know."

I gritted my teeth together. "He better."

I walked to a nearby stone bench and sat down on it.

"Betty will be done soon," Nic said. "You'll feel better when you see what she makes for you. She's the best. Until you get your own slayer sword, that is."

"Will she be making me that one too?" I asked.

Nic bit his lower lip. "Sam really didn't tell you anything, did he?"

I shook my head. "So how do I get it?"

"That's not for me to say," Nic said. "A slayer should tell you."

"Right," I said, head hurting slightly from all the new information. "So why are you here with Betty?" I asked Nic.

"Sam got me a job here," he said. "He told me to find Betty, and she's helping me support my family. I use my void portals to bring her rare materials, and she pays me what I need."

I folded my hands in my lap. "So you're part of the demon world?"

He nodded. "The void realm is to the demon realm as the fae realm is to the celestial realm. Neighbors and allies."

"Interesting," I said weakly. "I still can't believe demons have alphas and omegas like celestials do."

Nic sighed. "Celestials will do anything to get the worship and belief they need to feed. Demons have tight communities like packs. The alphas protect them. And unlike the selfish celestials, the slayers protect their kind for free. No tithe. No worship needed."

I looked at him sideways. "Then why do they do it?"

"Ask Sam," Nic said. "I'm not a slayer. I'm just glad that one saved me when he did."

"So Sam is a slayer?" I asked. "That's why he has a sword? Why does he have two of them?"

Nic looked forward, his expression sobering. "Those things... I think you have to ask Sam about them." His eyes darted to the graveyard and the willow looming over it next to the cathedral up ahead.

It looked even lonelier from this vantage point, the lush grass emphasizing the bleached white stones like bones protruding from the ground.

The willow branches swayed in the breeze, giving me a haunted feeling.

"While you traveled with Sam in the celestial realms —or anywhere they only know him as Samael, the angel of death who walks with the celestials—he surely hid a lot from you. Just in a day, Betty has caught me up. So I could tell you. But I think you should hear certain things from him." Nic blushed lightly. "I think if it's you, he'd want to tell you himself." He smiled. "There's something between you. I could tell."

I sent him a grin. "I'm glad you're okay, Nic."

He looked mildly disappointed that I didn't confirm or deny something between me and Sam, but I wasn't ready to tell anyone.

And for all I knew, Sam saved me only because I served a purpose and fed on me only to heal.

But it didn't feel that way.

"Nic!" Betty's voice yelled from the cracked door to the shack. "Get back in here. I need you to go for some more wood."

Nic smiled at me. "I hope we'll see each other again soon." He stood, brushing his pants off. "And remember, you can come to me for anything."

Then he headed inside, and I sat on the bench for a moment, thinking about all the things I needed to ask Sam.

Slowly, I got up and made my way back through the courtyard and up to the back entrance to the cathedral where there were huge double doors.

But just as I reached the steps leading up to them, Griffin burst through, his huge chest heaving. He wore a blue shirt with jeans, and when he saw me, he let out a huge sigh of relief and leaned forward, putting his hands on his knees to recover his breath.

"I'm glad I found you, Cleo. We've got to get out of here. Sam is crazy. Everyone here is crazy. And there's so much you don't know."

"Calm down," I said, going over to him and rubbing his back. "Hang on a minute. We'll go downstairs and talk, okay?"

"Okay, but it's not safe here, Cleo. We need to get your things and run." He pushed himself up and grabbed my hand, pulling me inside the cathedral.

As we walked down the center aisle, I heard footsteps coming from the direction of Sam's quarters. A moment later, Sam appeared, tall and gorgeous in a white tee and jeans, his golden-brown hair gleaming in the light streaming through the stained-glass windows, his tattoos showing on both arms.

He folded them, glaring at us ominously. "Just where are you two going?"

38

My heart stuttered when I saw Sam there, looking so handsome. Looking so much better.

Glaring at Griffin like he was considering whether or not to kill him.

I grabbed Griffin by the arm and dragged him with me backward, taking him outside.

Whatever had to be dealt with could be dealt with out in the open, in the cloudy afternoon light.

Sam followed, arms folded, expression stern.

When we were standing in the center of the courtyard, Griffin turned to me, exasperated.

"I'd rather talk to Cleo in private," he said. "Then she and I are going to leave."

"Like hell," Sam said.

"You can't stop us," Griffin said. "Cleo's powerful."

"Cleo's not nearly powerful enough to face off with a fifth celestial realm fighter right now, let alone a ninth." Sam's jaw was hard as granite. "Regardless, this is moot. Cleo owes me, and she won't leave until she pays me. Simple as that."

Griffin's blue eyes flashed with rage, and he turned back to me. "Cleo, do you see how crazy he is? You can't get feelings for him. He's a..."

"I already told her not to get feelings for me," Sam said flatly, squaring off with Griffin in a way that made me nervous. The two tall men moved closer, and I grabbed Griffin by his hefty bicep, pulling him back to me. He was practically snarling.

"What am I?" Sam asked sharply.

"A demon," Griffin blurted out, face reddening. "Os told me. Before he left."

Sam's lips lifted in a mean smirk. "Oh, he left, did he? That's what you're upset about?" He shook his head. "Look who shouldn't have gotten feelings." He let out a short, mean laugh. "I mean, Cleo and I had to play master and pet as a disguise, but you would have done it for real with Os, wouldn't you? You would have followed him to the ends of the earth."

Griffin's face went blank. Then he shook his head. "I do have feelings for him. I won't deny that. I don't know what you mean about master and pet, though."

Sam's eyes narrowed meanly, and he took another step forward, backing Griffin up.

I didn't think there was anyone Sam couldn't scare if he wanted to.

"Yes, I'm part demon. A lot of beings are hybrids in this world. However, you want to go back to the celestials? They would have killed you just on the chance of you being the Morningstar."

"That's just it!" Griffin yelled. "When were you going to tell Cleo you're just waiting to use her as a weapon of mass destruction?!"

Everything went quiet, and Sam cocked a hip, glowering with his folded arms but not saying anything.

"Is that true?" I asked him.

"You're something," Sam said. "I'm not sure what, and I'm not willing to state you're the Morningstar yet. You're just the closest I've found."

"Betty said you lied to Gabe and the other celestials about me," I said.

"I did," Sam said.

"Why didn't you tell me then? All that time together."

Sam's glare was cool. "Until you're strong enough, you're in great danger. If I'd told you, you probably would have gone off and told someone like Zadis. You didn't trust me yet, so I couldn't confirm my suspicions to you."

That made an odd amount of sense.

"So you brought me here because you want me to kill for you?" I asked, my hands making fists. "Because that's what Betty said, and I don't think I can do that."

"I said you'd owe me a favor," Sam said, lifting his head imperiously. "I never mentioned what it would be."

This was the Sam I met in my village. Immovable. Haughty. Above all of us and not needing to involve us in the plan.

Yet he'd saved me over and over.

"You should have told her," Griffin said. "She's—"

"I know what she is and isn't far better than you do," Sam said, practically twitching as he walked forward to get farther in Griffin's face. "And what are you going to do about it?"

"Turn into my winged form and get her out of here," Griffin spat back at him, hands in tight fists.

"Where would you go?" Sam asked. "You don't understand the mid-realm, and you'll be killed, and she'll be taken from you faster than you can snap your fingers. The safest place for you both is here."

"Yeah right," Griffin said. "Where you can keep manipulating her for your own purposes."

"If she is the Morningstar, then every creature will be drawn to her. Are you ready to protect her?"

Griffin swallowed. "With my life."

Sam barked out a laugh, stepping back from him. "See? As expected, all creatures want to follow the Morningstar."

"So it *is* Cleo?" Griffin asked.

Sam shook his head. "I told you. I don't know. I don't owe you any answers. I brought you here. I spared your life."

"Why?" Griffin asked. "Why, when you kill so easily?"

"Because you're rare, and I kind of liked the idea of having a ninth-realm pet to myself. Kind of amusing." He smirked, looking Griffin up and down. "You can also detect high-level demons, which is useful. The fact that you could scent Cleo confirmed my suspicion."

"I couldn't scent you," Griffin asked. "Why is that?"

"Because I'm not a high-level demon," Sam said. "As an incubus, you could say I'm something of an omega. I'm just very good at what I do, and my ninth-realm blood makes me unstoppable as a slayer." He folded his arms again. "So consider what you do next very carefully because I'll kill anyone who takes her out of my sight. Including you, Griffin."

I stopped between them. "Stop it. This is crazy. We're on the same side. Griffin, Sam saved us."

"What's the good of saving us if he's going to use us?" Griffin asked. "Cleo, he's manipulating us. We should leave."

"Sam has been honest with me," I said. "As he could. And where else do we have to go?"

Clicking footsteps echoed onto the courtyard steps, and I looked out to see Simon walking down them, adjusting the cuffs of his white dress shirt to roll them upward.

He wore no jacket today, and his straight black hair lifted slightly in the cool afternoon breeze. He wore black dress slacks and dress shoes that made a clicking noise as he made his way over to us, hands in pockets.

"Pleasant party we're having," he said, red eyes darting between us. "Why wasn't I invited?"

I looked up at the sky, then at Simon in shock. "You can be in the sun?"

"Oh yes, vampires got that ability after we first bred with humans," Simon said pleasantly. "Those who didn't burned up pretty fast. Unnatural selection, you might say."

"Stay out of this, Simon," Sam snapped at him, pointing a finger aggressively.

"Cleo, trust me. Sam's manipulating you," Griffin

said. "I know you've been getting closer. I know you spend time with him late at night. I don't blame you. He's seductive, but I don't want you to get hurt."

Irritation moved through me at Griffin's unwanted interference. "Griffin, Sam has been honest with me from start to finish about what we do in private. It's none of your concern."

"He can't help it," Sam said. "It's in his nature to be protective. In the ninth realm, they're bred that way. As pets."

"Bred?" Griffin asked, eyes bulging.

"Exactly," Sam said, narrowing his eyes. "You know nothing of this world. So shut up before you start corrupting Cleo. I have many faults, but not the ones you're accusing me of. I'm your only hope of help in the mid-realm, and I'm losing my patience."

"You could live with me, Griffin," Simon butted in unhelpfully. "Probably feed a lot of vampires with that huge body."

Griffin sent him a shocked glare, then looked over at me. "I'm sorry, Cleo. I know I shouldn't interfere. But after what I heard, I can't help it. I tried to come to your room last night, but you were already asleep." He sent Sam a mean glare. "We could have just left and avoided all this."

Sam threw his head back, laughing with an arm over

his taut midsection. "You have to be kidding if you think I'd let you leave. If you think I don't have a way to stop you."

Griffin let out a snarl. "So you'll keep her here, no matter what?"

Sam stared back. "Absolutely. There was never a choice."

His words seared into me, and I froze, silent, for a moment.

He'd never meant to give me a choice. He'd been honest from the start about wanting to use me.

Why had I ever thought anything else?

But when I came to bathe him, to talk to him, and he'd pleasured me, I saw another Sam. Different from the hard, cold one I saw here.

I didn't want to believe what Griffin was saying, but I wasn't sure who to believe.

"Griffin, why do you keep saying he's manipulating me?" I sighed. "I knew he was a demon. I just kept it from you because I was grateful he saved my life. I knew he was using me for a favor, but I thought it a fair price. Now I don't know. But do we really have any other options?"

Griffin looked between me and Sam, panicked. "Cleo, remember how hurt he was when he came back? How he made you take care of him all last night?"

I flushed, hoping Griffin was only imagining sponge baths and nothing else. I nodded.

"That's all a lie," Griffin said. "He's one of the most powerful slayers of all time. No way Zarris could have taken him on. Sam was trained directly by Cayne, the most legendary slayer ever."

Sam went rigid, shooting an accusing look at Simon, who raised his hands, trying to look innocent.

"How was I supposed to know you'd bring them here without telling them about your brother?" Simon asked. But I could see something less than innocent in his eyes.

Griffin kept his focus on me. "Cleo, I found out more about the fight from Mor and Os. Sam didn't even fight back against Zarris. He lied to us. He stayed totally still and just took every hit. Why the fuck would he do that if he wasn't just trying to manipulate you? To make you feel bad and owe him for the entire situation. What other reason is there?"

Sam sent Griffin a look of rage so fierce it was actually scary, which told me that at least part of what Griffin said was probably true.

"Why?" I asked, turning to Sam, betrayal flooding through me. "Why would you do that? What kind of trick are you trying to pull?" I thought back to his bruised, broken body, how bad I had felt. "Did you just want me to feel guilty? Did you want to ram home that I made a bad choice? I already feel bad you had to murder Zadis."

"I don't owe anyone any answers!" Sam spun away from us, huge shoulders hunching as he stomped away at a brisk pace. He looked back at me fiercely. "I'll come find you to train at three. You'll pay me back, Cleo. You don't have a choice."

I gaped at his back as he walked in the direction of the cemetery.

Simon moved over to me. "There, there, Cleo," he said, putting his arm around my shoulders comfortingly. "He's just being an angry ol' demon. He doesn't mean it."

What happened next happened so instantaneously I could barely comprehend it.

Sam's wings were out, and he cleared the distance to us in a split second, getting up in Simon's face, wings flaring threateningly like huge black clouds to either side of him.

Simon let go of me with a hiss and moved to meet Sam's challenge. Huge black wings unfurled from his back, but instead of feathers, they were glistening with an oil slick of purple and green over what looked like black leather.

Or bat skin.

In size, they rivaled Sam's, or were even slightly bigger.

"Showing me your wings like that," Simon said, a scowl taking over his normally cheery disposition. "Threatening me. Cayne would be ashamed of what you're doing right now."

"She"—Sam pointed at me—"is fucking mine. It's best for your health if you never lay another fucking finger on her."

Simons's lips turned up in a grin. "Ah, getting feelings finally? Cayne would have loved to see that."

"He's fucking gone, and he lost that right!" Sam practically shouted in Simon's face. A vein was bulging at the side of his temple. He leaned in even closer and said his next words loud enough for me to hear him. "And I'll never care deeply about anyone, ever again."

Sam gave Simon one more harsh glare and whipped around, retracting his wings as he stormed away, disappearing around the side of the cathedral somewhere by the willow.

Why was he going there?

Simon looked over at me. "You should go find him."

"No, you shouldn't," Griffin said. "You and I should go. I don't know where but anywhere you don't have to be with that demon. He took a beating to make you feel guilty, Cleo. He won't even explain himself. You can't trust him."

Simon shook his head. "You're mistaking something, though Sam is definitely someone to watch out for." He took Griffin by the arm. "Let me tell you a few things, and you can decide if you still want to take Cleo from Sam."

Griffin looked dubious, but I nodded.

"I need to go talk to Sam," I said. "I need to know why he did that and what he intends for me. And then, if you're right, I'll think about whether we should go."

Griffin sniffed. "I doubt there is anything that you could tell me that would make sense to me."

Simon sighed, rolled his eyes, and put a hand up to cup Griffin's ear as he leaned in to whisper to him.

Griffin's eyes went wide at whatever Simon was telling him, and he slumped with a nod as Simon finally pulled back.

"Well, what do you think now?" Simon asked Griffin. "You still want to fly away from here?"

Griffin blinked, looking confused, and his hands moved into fists. "That explains the Zarris fight, yes." He swallowed, looking as if his throat felt tight. He looked over at me. "But I still don't want my friend to be a weapon if she doesn't want to. You can talk to him, Cleo.

But if you decide you don't want to stay, we'll figure a way out of this. I promise."

I nodded, grateful to have found such a good friend. I walked forward to pull Griffin into a hug, and, to my shock, I felt Simon join us, locking his arms around us.

"Mmm... human energy. Almost as good as blood," Simon said happily.

"Get off me," Griffin said, shoving the vampire away. "I'm going inside to get something to eat." He stomped back up the stairs to the cathedral.

"Ooh, I do like a chase," Simon said. "All that self-righteous, judgmental celestial in him is so easy to get riled up. Looks like this will be fun."

I just gave Simon an odd look, and he laughed.

"Well, aren't you going to go after Sam?" Simon asked. "I think if you approach things right, you'll learn something new about him. He's a difficult boy, but I can tell you feel something for him."

My chest and throat felt tight. If he hadn't even fought back against Zarris, why hadn't he told me the night I took care of him?

Simon let out an exasperated breath. "I shouldn't say this, but I can tell you don't even know where to start." He looked down at the ground for a minute, then up at the sky. "Sam lost his brother a year ago. He hasn't been the same since. Whether that played into his fight, I don't know. But it's worth considering."

A heartbreaking picture slowly came together in front of me, and I immediately knew I needed to see Sam.

I took off, jogging in the direction he'd disappeared.

Behind me, I heard Simon softly mutter, "Atta girl. Go get him."

39

I had to be careful not to step or trip on any gravestones as I jogged along the open paths in the cemetery to find Sam.

I slowed down as I approached the willow and saw him standing under its shade.

The gray day cast the tombstones in sharp relief. Some were very old, the corners worn, the letters barely visible. Some were newer, with dates from this century.

I cast my eyes around for a certain one but didn't see it.

Sam was standing beside the willow, staring at the ground, saying nothing. His curls lifted slightly in the wind, and with his back to me, the world silent around us, he was the very picture of loneliness.

"Sam?" I asked, startling him slightly. I figured he must have been lost in his thoughts.

When he faced me, his face was slightly paler than usual, the color high on his elegant cheekbones.

This was the man who'd fought for me. Saved me. Teased and tortured me.

And maybe, at this point, my best friend.

Or maybe he just saw me as a weapon, as Griffin had said.

Either way, I owed him.

"I'm not letting you go," he said, folding his arms and glaring at me. "I told you from the beginning that leaving me wasn't an option." His jaw ticked. "But I didn't trick you with the bruises. I never had such intentions at all."

"Griffin is overprotective," I said. "We know that."

Sam seemed to calm slightly at those words. But his sharp dark eyes held a slight vulnerability. "Do you hate me, Cleo? For lying to you about what I suspect you might be?"

I shook my head slowly. "No. I think everyone lies in this world. You lied to protect me, I think."

"I did," he said. "You're the most important thing in the world to me." My heart almost leaped at his statement, but he wasn't done. "But it's because of what you might be. What my brother and I spent our lives searching for." His eyes were dark like wells. "So I can't give up. I can't let you go. Not until you've achieved your purpose."

"You mean your purpose?" I asked.

"The purpose of the Morningstar," he said.

"Which is?"

"To bring balance to the world," he said. "To kill even the highest corruption." His eyes met mine. "You're the most powerful slayer in the world." His eyes dipped to my collar. "Or you will be once you're trained."

I thought about that for a moment and couldn't help being a little bit excited. Power had been taken from me all my life, and now I was realizing I had more of it than I'd ever imagined.

It was an odd feeling. But I still didn't want to kill.

"That's why I called you an idiot when I met you," he said, facing me. "I felt power radiating off you. You were either the Morningstar or some other very powerful hybrid. Yet you cowered before bullies because you accepted their view of what you were. You attacked with only a fraction of the power you could have used." He shook his head. "I called you an idiot for not listening to the demon inside you. For not seeing how powerful, and how beautiful, you are. And for ever letting anyone mistreat you."

My heart clenched at his words, and I wondered if he even knew how sweet they were.

Based on the stubborn jut of his jaw, I didn't think so.

But this all lined up with the Sam I knew. Sometimes withholding information but usually telling me the truth when he could.

"I saw the void walker at the smith," I said. "Nic."

His lips lifted in the faintest of grins, but there was still pain in his eyes. "Ah. Yes. I lied about that too. But when you were desperate to stop me, there was no way to tell you with all the fae watching. And I wanted to get out of there before Zadis could get any closer to figuring out what you were."

"I get it," I said. "I don't like being lied to, but I get it. As I said, everyone lies. It's just about why. Do you lie to get ahead? Do you lie to take advantage?"

"I'll lie whenever I need to, Cleo," he said solemnly. "I have a mission. As I mentioned back in your haven, I am seeking revenge. The need to achieve it has burned inside me from a very young age, and I won't stop until I've gotten it. You should remember that."

I nodded. "I get it. So what is it you need from me? What do you want?"

He blinked, then shook his head. "I can tell you more once you've trained. Once we know for sure that you're the Morningstar. You don't even know how the abyssal realms work, so there is a lot you wouldn't understand yet. But I won't ask anything of you until you're ready."

"So this is all part of this mission you have?" I asked.

Sam nodded. "And understand, Cleo, I won't stop until this is done. This is what means everything in the world to me. The reason I went to work with the celestials this year at all."

My eyes widened. "What?"

"They needed a new executioner," he said. "No celestials wanted to get their wings dirty. I used my ninth-realm blood to get the job, though I could tell Gabe would have rather worked with a dirty towel than a slayer with half-demon blood. Still, they're desperate to find the Morningstar."

"Why?" I asked.

"To kill it," he said simply, folding his arms. "To stop it from being able to take down the most corrupt, most powerful of their kind." He sighed. "You don't understand, Cleo. The ninth-realm gods have been unstoppable for too long. They can invade the abyssal realms, cause so much pain and torture. The Morningstar can—"

I put up a hand. "I don't think I can handle any more information about the Morningstar for now. I'm willing

to train and at least consider doing what you ask of me."
My eyes met his shyly. "Because, truly, you've saved my
life. It's been better since you've been by my side. But
that's not why I came to talk to you."

He stared at me in confusion.

I looked around the graveyard. "It's beautiful here,
isn't it?" I moved over to the willow and placed my hand
on the trunk, feeling the bark. "Your room looks out on
this?"

His expression was neutral, but I could see how
tightly he was holding himself to keep from showing a
reaction.

"Kind of weird, watching a graveyard," I said.
"Unless someone is there."

His face went a little paler. "I have to go."

"Wait," I said. "Simon told me about your brother."

Sam whirled, white as a sheet. "That stupid vampire.
I'm gonna—"

I moved in front of him, stopping him with a hand
on his chest. My heart jumped at the feel of his hard,
warm muscles and his heart beating against my hand.

Gently, he removed my hand and pushed me
backward.

"I don't need your pity," he said. "My brother made
the right choice. It wasn't his fault it went wrong." Sam

sucked in a breath that looked painful, and his eyes were slightly wild.

"But?" I asked.

His eyes met mine. "But it hurts every day."

I came forward then, unable to resist holding him, and I felt him freeze in my arms. Then his hands came around me, and he let out a breath of surrender combined with annoyance as he enfolded me in a hug.

"You're making me too soft, Cleo," he said.

"You let Zarris beat you, didn't you?" I asked against his shoulder. "Not because you were manipulating me, but because you couldn't hurt someone like you."

His jaw tightened, and he pulled back to peer down at me as his hands found my shoulders. "You have a soft heart, Cleo. Too soft to be a good slayer. We'll have to harden it up." He let me go and turned away from me.

"Am I right, though?"

He turned around to meet my gaze with haunted eyes. "Yes. But it's not as intentional as you think. I simply recognized the pain in his eyes and knew what he felt, and for some reason, I couldn't bring myself to hurt him after that." He gave a soft shrug of one large shoulder. "That's all."

"That was kind of you," I called after him as he continued to walk away. I got the feeling this had already been too much for him.

All I got was a vague nod as he left. When he reached the side doors to the cathedral, he turned and held up his hand with three fingers, which I instantly took as a reminder to come train with him at three.

Then he disappeared, leaving me with only an empty graveyard, the wind whistling through the willow's branches, and the echo of the fathomless heartache I'd seen in Sam's eyes.

40

There was a challenge in Sam's eyes when he met me in the courtyard at three for practice, as if he were daring me to mention the things we'd talked about beneath the willow.

Though I would never forget that moment, that secret look into the deep recesses of his heart, I understood and respected that he didn't want to go any further in talking about it.

Even if I was dying to know more.

I wanted to know everything about his revenge, about what his brother had been trying to do when he died, and about what had happened.

But I knew I would have to wait. Information came from Sam in a slow drip, never a torrent.

"I didn't say everyone could watch," Sam muttered to Simon, Mor, Griffin, and Nic, who had all gathered.

Simon was dressed snappily as usual, sitting on the remnants of an old stone wall, legs crossed gingerly, pale face lit with excitement. "Cleo's first training? I wouldn't miss it."

Griffin, wearing a red sweatshirt with jeans, folded his huge arms. "I'm here to watch out for Cleo."

Nic, wearing a black tracksuit with white stripes down the sides, was seated next to Simon. "Me too."

Sam rolled his eyes, then looked over at Mor. "And why are you here?"

"I'm curious as well," Mor said. He was wearing a gray sweatshirt over black lounge pants, with tennis shoes. I'd never seen him looking so casual.

Mor was taller than Simon, and his dark hair was shorter and more lustrous, his skin pale but fresh with life, rosy in the right places.

Simon looked like someone had dug him up, washed him, and put him in fancy clothing. His skin was such an eerie shade of white.

Out here in the cloudy sunlight, he looked far more undead than he had inside. But still almost eerily beautiful.

Sam got into a fighting stance. He wore a black sleeveless tank that showed off huge, muscular shoulders, plus black shorts that revealed the best calves I had ever seen and tennis shoes on his larger-than-average feet.

Apparently, incubi looked crazy hot in workout gear.

But who was I kidding? Sam looked crazy hot in everything.

His hair was tousled as always, and his dark eyes were sharp.

He stepped back with one hand and gestured for me to approach.

"What, like you want me to spar with you?" I asked.

He nodded, gold glinting at the centers of his dark eyes.

I was wearing a white tank top with black leggings and Converse, which were easy to move in. All the same, the thought of sparring with a slayer was daunting.

"Hit me," he said. His lips lifted in a grin. "At least try."

I took a step forward uncertainly. "But my collar, will it still protect everyone from me?"

Sam nodded. "Right now, you have access to half your physical strength and some of your demon abilities. Not safe to have certain ones yet. But I need to see how skilled you are with basic hand-to-hand fighting. If you know techniques, then your demon power, as you unlock it, should do the rest."

I cracked my knuckles. "Okay, here I go."

I ran toward Sam, who stayed in a relaxed fighting stance until I got close. He gave a slow practice swing of a left hook to test me, and I ducked quickly under it and came up with an uppercut aimed right at his jaw.

He dodged it in the speed of a blink and shot out a leg to hook me while I was unstable. I dodged back, lifting my leg to avoid the trap, and snapped my foot upward in a roundhouse kick that paused right at the level of his eye, forcing him to stop as he came forward with a heel strike.

He stepped back from me, and we circled. A smile lifted his lips. "Who trained you?"

"Some alpha wolf back in the haven," I said. He didn't deserve even being known by name after kicking me out just for being an omega.

Little did he know I still looked in on classes, practiced moves on my own outside or in my room.

I'd loved sparring and had always been good at it. The alphas who'd lost to me were so glad I was banned after being labeled an omega that no one questioned the decision to throw me out.

Perhaps it had even influenced it.

Power surged through me. I wasn't an omega anymore. I could fight as much as I wanted.

No one was here telling me I needed to be weak.

I lunged toward Sam and, when within range, spun and aimed a back kick at his midsection. He'd been preparing for a roundhouse with both arms up protecting his face, so my foot caught him in the middle in a speedy but not-too-damaging kick.

I followed with a spinning hook, and he ducked this time. Then he took advantage of me needing to bring my leg back down to grab it and trap it against his middle.

I just grinned at him. Using all my strength, I jumped off my ground leg and, using his hold, spun my free leg up toward his head.

He let me go to dodge the hit, and I stumbled backward, barely able to jerk my legs down and recover in time.

It felt fucking good to be able to do that. I wasn't sure I'd even had the strength before.

I lunged at Sam with a punch, enjoying this now, and though I could tell he was at times taking it easy, I knew I was giving him more of a challenge than he'd thought.

He would duck, then give me a strike to dodge. I would dodge, then attack back. We went through kicks, punches, and then groundwork as Sam swept my leg and took me down to the grass, sitting on top of me.

I thrust my hips up hard and reversed the mount, staring down at him with a grin.

He grabbed my arm and shoulder and rolled me over again. I slammed a fist toward his groin, making him dodge back long enough for me to pull my knees up and kick him back with both legs.

As we both rolled to our feet, the fighting only intensified. All the skills I'd practiced were suddenly doable with more speed, more precision. I couldn't help but smile as the speed of our moves increased. It was probably hard to tell from an outside angle who was doing what.

Finally, Sam dodged back, breathing heavily, and held up a hand. "I'm satisfied on the sparring."

"You should be," Griffin said. "Shame on you, trying to hit a girl."

"Let me try," Mor said, cracking his knuckles together.

Sam looked at me and raised an eyebrow, and I nodded.

"I should warn you that Mor is the top brawler on our team," Sam said. "I'm the executioner, but Mor takes care of the fights that don't need to end in death. Our strongest fighter."

Mor grinned and stepped forward until we were face

to face. Gods, his face was even prettier up close, those silver-blue eyes looking almost like mirrors.

Mor's eyes flicked to mine, and I saw a sneer in his gaze as he looked me over. Clearly, he was still mad at me for getting Sam hurt by Zarris.

But I was just happy to be fighting. I couldn't imagine killing, but I loved fighting a lot.

Mor stepped into a fighting stance and gestured for me to come forward. As I did, attacking with a right-left combo that usually worked, Mor easily raised a hand to block one strike, then the other. Then I saw a fist coming straight at my face, faster than I could stop it.

WHAM!

I flew backward, pain exploding through my face, rolling over the grass.

Holy shit, Mor was good.

Mor came to stand over me with folded arms. "Not so good now, are you, demon wolf? If that's even what you are."

I pushed myself up, narrowing my eyes. "I just won't hold back with you."

But right before I could attack Mor, a blur struck him from the side, removing him from my vision and taking him to the ground.

As the two men rolled, I made out a red sweatshirt and blond hair. Griffin.

Griffin had pinned Mor beneath him and raised a fist. Mor punched him off of him and pushed up to stand.

They faced each other, chests heaving.

"What the fuck is wrong with you?" Mor yelled at Griffin. "I'm trying to help train her. Sam was going too easy. I'm showing him she's not ready yet."

"You fucking hit a girl!" Griffin yelled back.

"Who else is supposed to train her?" Mor asked. "Sam would have to hit her if I didn't."

"Men... shouldn't hit girls," Griffin said.

Mor threw his head back in a laugh, and Sam shook his head warily.

"I'm not a man," Mor said. "Who said I was?"

My jaw fell open, and my eyes darted to Sam, who just shrugged one shoulder lazily.

Sam walked forward, still shaking his head. "Let's get one thing straight, Griffin. We don't do celestial rules here in the mid-realm. We go by strength, not gender. Female demons are often stronger than males. Other supernaturals, it varies. Cleo is stronger than all of us, and if we take it easy on her, she'll fail at what she needs to do. She needs good opponents if she's going to take on someone in the ninth realm one day."

Griffin just blinked in shock, staring blankly at Mor, while Simon laughed, holding his middle.

"I'm glad you brought these creatures back with you, Sam," Simon said, wiping tears from his eyes. "I do so love watching them."

"I'm glad you're entertained," Sam said flatly.

The two seemed to have made up at least.

Still, looking at Mor, I saw no sign that would have told me she was a woman.

Mor caught me. "What are you looking at?"

"I... You just..."

"What, don't look like a girl?" Mor asked.

"Yeah."

Mor ran a hand through her short hair. "I'm a professional fighter for the celestials. I look how I look."

"Actually, the higher you go in the celestial realms, the less difference there is between the sexes," Sam said. "Mor looks like a normal female from the sixth realm."

Mor just lifted a shoulder. "What I am isn't your issue unless I'm trying to fuck you. So anyway, let's fight." She made a gesture for me to come to her.

Now that I knew she was female, some things did make sense. The pretty face. The higher voice.

But it didn't matter, compared to having a good sparring partner.

Sam stepped forward. "No. I think Cleo's hand-to-hand skills are fine. We can do more practice later. Mor, you and Cleo can practice daily for the next week. Get her even faster."

Mor nodded.

"There are two aspects to even basic slaying," Sam said, walking to the middle of the courtyard. "Combat, which you're good at. And ending life, which you probably never have."

He snapped his fingers, and a bag appeared in the middle of the courtyard. It was burlap and dirty, and wriggling, while whatever was inside it made hissing noises and shrieks.

My stomach dropped like I'd swallowed a rock, and my chest felt like it was caving in suddenly.

"No," I said. "I don't want to."

Sam grabbed the bag and opened it, letting it fall aside as a tied-up creature fell out.

I gasped as I saw a humanoid creature tumble out of it. Its eyes were black holes surrounded by sickly yellow, it was basically skin and bones, and its skin was the sick bluish-green of someone left under water for a very long time.

It saw me and tried to lunge at me, hissing, but I stepped back out of the way, and it couldn't go farther because it was tied up.

Sam's black sheath appeared at his side, and he drew his long katana from it. "Since you don't have your slayer sword yet, and Betty hasn't made you a replacement, you can use mine."

I put both of my hands up, shaking my head. "No. No way."

Griffin looked at me like he wanted to help, but he was also still dealing with the utter shock of attacking one woman to defend another one.

I was growing really fond of the guy. Misguided but always trying to help me.

Just like Sam was misguidedly trying to help me now.

I took another step back, my hands still up. "I can't. I'm sorry."

"It's a ghoul," Sam said. "It's practically dead already."

"Not yet it isn't," I said. My heart was racing. "No. I'll fight. I'll figure out a way to do it without killing, but—"

"Disgusting," Mor said. "How dare you be a coward after all Sam has done to get you here?"

I looked at Mor, shame waving through me. "That's not my fault. He made his choices."

"A ghoul kills anything it can find, brutally," Simon said from the wall. "It's truly a creature you would do the world a favor by removing."

I looked at the ghoul, but it simply bared yellow, inhuman teeth. "What is it?"

"A half-turned vampire," Simon said. "A human that was continuously fed off of until their life source was drained but who never made the transition into a vampire."

"Why?" I asked.

"Are we going to stand around all day talking about ghouls, or are you going to kill something?" Sam asked, looking impatient.

"Of course this would be easy for you," I spat, still taken off guard by this whole ghoul thing. "I... I can't. I'm not ready."

Sam's eyes shuttered momentarily, and I could see disappointment on his face as he turned away.

In his next step, he turned back, still holding his sword, and cut the ghoul's head off.

Black blood flew into the air as the creature fell backward, and blood continued to pump from the open wound of its neck.

I swallowed, looking at Sam, who watched the ghoul impassively before turning to look at me.

"I'm not a killer, Sam. I'm sorry. I'm not cold like you." I knew it was a mistake the moment I said it, but I couldn't take it back.

Sam's jaw was clenched. "I killed many creatures to bring you here. If you have such a problem with killers..." He turned away with a *tsk*, then walked back to the cathedral without even finishing his statement.

The large wooden doors slammed shut behind him.

Mor was watching me pensively as Simon climbed off the wall to come to her side.

"So female? Interesting. I've never met a female celestial. And you're staying? Unlike Os, you aren't afraid to hang out a bit with the undead?"

Mor looked at Simon like something that crawled out from under her shoe. "I'm here for Sam. He's my friend." She looked at me. "And as a half void walker, it wouldn't make much sense to hate demons, or those they keep company with."

She turned and followed Sam inside, sending me a mean glare before she disappeared.

Simon came over to me, almost putting his arm around my shoulders and then thinking better of it, probably remembering Sam's anger before.

"It'll be okay," Simon said. "You'll figure it out."

"Void walker?" Griffin asked. "So she's half demon, like Sam?"

"They aren't demons. They just ally with them," Simon said. "And it's common for celestials to be hybrids. The elder gods love to fuck around." He sighed. "You two have so much to learn."

Griffin eyed me, appraising whether I was okay.

Then he looked at Simon, and for once, he wasn't defensive. "Maybe over lunch, you could tell us more?"

Simon lit up like it was his birthday. "Oh goody. Lunch!" He moved forward toward Griffin's neck.

"*Normal* food!" Griffin said, and Simon's face fell.

Then he smiled.

"Well, company is good too," he said. "Come on. Let's eat."

As we followed him inside, I wondered how I was going to get through this.

Sam had every right to want me to be a slayer.

But I didn't know how to make my heart willing to kill.

I didn't know if I ever could.

41

After lunch, where Simon was pleasant enough to make up for Griffin's stunned silence and my inner turmoil, I headed downstairs for a nap in my room.

Griffin was behind me as we took the stone stairs downward, and when I heard him let out a heavy sigh, I decided we needed to talk.

I unlocked my door and held it open for him. "Come in."

His round, puppy-ish eyes went wide, and he nodded, following me in.

I sat down on the bed, patting the spot beside me.

But he took the chair across from me so he could face me better.

I didn't like how pale he looked. How drained.

"Are you okay? You seriously don't look like you're doing all right."

He clasped his hands together nervously, looking around at anything but me. "I don't know is the answer."

"Talk to me," I said.

He raised his blue eyes to mine. "You have enough on your plate. Having to become a slayer. Or the Morningstar. Whatever you may be." He scratched his head. "Apparently, I'm just some kind of dog." He laughed ruefully, then leaned back in the chair. "I was the pet all along."

"A bit ironic," I said. "But you're no one's pet now. Don't let Sam get under your skin. Who cares what the celestials think you are? They don't get to own you."

"And they tried to kill you," Griffin said. "So obviously, they have bad judgment." He frowned. "You're too kind to even kill that ghoul."

I looked down at my hands folded on my knees. "I guess so many have used their power against me that using mine against someone weaker, especially to kill them... it just feels wrong."

"I agree," Griffin said. "We should get out of here." His lips turned up in the corners in a teasing expression that was nonetheless defeated. "We could go find Os."

"Why did he leave?" I asked. "I was, um, busy, and when I came back, he was gone."

"He only came to see Sam here safely. He's not in favor of any of this. He couldn't believe Mor wanted to stay. He doesn't know you're the Morningstar, but I think he has some suspicions, based on how far Sam went for you with Zadis."

I put my head in my hands. "Everything's a mess. Griffin, how am I supposed to be some epic killer?"

Griffin shrugged one massive shoulder. "I don't know. But I'll be here by your side the whole way." He grinned. "We condemned creatures from the havens have to stick together, after all."

He fidgeted a bit, and I could tell he was trying to get up the nerve to say something.

"What?" I asked flatly.

"I'm sorry if it ever felt like I underestimated you. I never thought you weren't cool... or strong. Yes, I was raised never to hurt women, but it's not because I thought you were weak. Mor has me rethinking all my past beliefs."

"Not a bad idea," I said. "I need to rethink mine also."

"It's just... maybe this whole Morningstar thing is true, because from the moment I met you, Cleo, I wanted to protect you. I wanted to follow you. I don't even know why. I mean, you're nice—don't get me wrong—but it goes beyond that."

"I'm flattered, Griffin," I said. "But yes, apparently, I don't need protection that much." I leaned forward to pat his knee. "But a friend is always welcome."

His smile was bright enough to light the dungeon. "Friends forever."

"So now tell me what upset you so bad about Os leaving."

Griffin scratched the back of his head. "I mean, finding out Sam was a demon was a shock since I hadn't sensed it at all. But finding out I couldn't be with Os anymore... I wasn't expecting it."

"What is he to you?"

Griffin picked at the side of his nail, then went to bite it, and I lightly tapped his arm to make him stop before he hurt himself.

"Sorry, nervous habit," he said. "I've known him a long time. Since I was little. In fact, I was actually up for execution a long time ago."

"What?" I had to keep myself from yelling. "When you were a kid?"

He nodded. "As I grew, people started to realize I wasn't their type of lion. Maybe some noticed before, but they liked me. Maybe none of us wanted to see that I was different. But then my mane came in and my wings showed up, and—"

"And they thought you were a satanic demon who needed to be killed?"

He shrugged with both hands in the air. "You know how it is in the havens. The celestials make us report everything that stands out or is different in some way. Different is always dangerous."

I snorted. "True."

Griffin sighed. "Plus, anything with celestial wings can technically reach the sky kingdoms, and the celestials can't allow that."

"They have to keep their secrets to themselves, true," I said. "But anyway, anyone who doubted you was an idiot for not seeing how awesome you are. You're one of the most moral, upright, loyal people I've ever met."

"Thank you," he said, his blue eyes glimmering warmly. "I really appreciate that, Cleo. Truly." He let out a heavy sigh. "I suppose I can tell you the whole story, since Os is gone and I doubt I'll see him again."

"Did he say where he was going?"

"Back on patrols," Griffin said. "I'm disappointed, but I get it. After all, I first met him on a patrol. He was there at the time I was scheduled for my first execution."

"What?"

"He was young like me," Griffin said. "Training."

"Ah."

"Anyway, I don't know if it's because I'm the creature Sam thinks I am, and not a demon, but Os told the celestial he was with, a tall guy with ashy hair and cold eyes, to spare me. The other guy seemed to think it'd be easier to get it over with, but Os interceded for me. He actually hugged me tightly, so the executioner's blade couldn't fall." Griffin smiled at the faraway memory. "After that, the town came to their senses and stopped the whole thing. Seeing a celestial defend me turned them around."

"Until you got older," I said.

He nodded.

I tried to picture Os like that. Caring rather than aloof and diplomatic. He was kind and gentle outwardly, but I'd always sensed a cold hardness to him as well.

Like he wouldn't tell you if he thought badly of you.

"That's why I waited for another execution so calmly. I could have flown away, though that would have dishonored my community. But a small part of me, a shameful part of me, wanted to see Os again. I thought he would be the one to come."

My heart went out to him. "I'm sorry he didn't turn out to be the man you deserved."

Griffin shrugged again. "I figured out things were pointless when he went out with the fae the whole time we stayed together in that hut in the fae realm. But it still hurt when he left."

"Simon likes you," I said, somewhat unhelpfully.

Griffin laughed despite his frustrated expression. "That's true. Should I try a walk on the vampire side? Simon said vampires give great sex in exchange for blood."

"I..." I sucked in a breath. "I don't know. The heart wants what it wants."

"Does your heart want Sam?" he asked.

My face went red and heated. "No," I said a little too quickly. "He made it clear that no feelings should be involved."

"I don't think he can decide that. I don't think it's that simple," Griffin said. "I got feelings for Os after he saved my life. Sam has saved yours, like what, five times now?"

"Like three," I muttered. Still, the point was made. "But I wouldn't fall for someone just because of that. Maybe a crush, but nothing I can't keep a hold on."

"But you go to his chambers," Griffin said. "Cleo, don't let him use you."

"He isn't," I said. "I mean, I'm using him too. What we do benefits both of us." I refrained from telling him sex helped empower my inner demon. "Plus... it isn't bad. Being with him. I try to just live in the moment and enjoy what I can. It's all better than living in my old haven."

Griffin stayed quiet, studying my face. I felt uncomfortable being watched so closely and made a face at him.

He laughed. "Cleo, you're one of a kind. Oh well, if you like that sexy demon, I guess you're getting what you want."

"I am," I said, though I wasn't fully certain. All of this was going really fast. "I'll try and be careful."

Griffin's eyes were full of warning as they met mine. "Sam isn't the type to bullshit, not about this, I think. Truly, if he says not to get feelings, try not to."

"Don't have feelings for Os, then," I shot back.

"Touché," he said, a blush tinging his cheeks.

"I'm sorry. I just don't know," I said. "I've never had feelings for anyone. I don't think I would even know if I did. But I like Sam; that's for certain. Probably more than most, having seen some different sides of him. I'll try and keep things surface level."

Bullshit, my inner demon said. *We've already gotten too deep.*

Maybe she was right, and I should stop letting him feed on me.

Now, let's not be too hasty.

I sighed, then decided to focus on Griffin and ignore my own uncomfortable feelings. "At least Os didn't say you couldn't have feelings," I said. "Who knows? He might be back at some point. You don't have to give up yet."

He fidgeted with his hands. "But at what point is hope hurtful rather than good?"

"I don't know," I said. "I guess it's up to you whether you want to decide to hope or not."

"I think not," he said, standing and stretching. "Anyway, I'm going to go nap. Thanks for talking, Cleo."

I could tell he was still upset about Os, but I respected his need for space.

I pulled out my void sac and dumped some books out onto my bed. Perhaps reading would make me forget that I was a completely incompetent killer and probably an utter disappointment to the man who'd saved my life.

42

"Cleo? You in there?"

I opened my eyes groggily, blinking at the utter darkness all around me. Thinking it was a dream, I turned over and pulled my covers in, trying to get back to sleep.

A loud knock made me sit up immediately.

"Yes?" I called out to whoever was outside my door. Who would bother me in the middle of the night?

It wasn't Sam's voice. I hadn't seen him since training, and I'd spent the rest of the evening in my room, going to bed early.

"Meet me in the courtyard, Cleo. I have something you want."

Mor. I recognized the voice now. But I didn't know if I should follow.

"Something bad might happen to someone you care about if you don't."

Fear flooded me, and I rushed for the door, but when I swung it open, no one was there. Just dust lightly falling as if someone had moved by quickly.

I sucked in a breath, then went to change into different clothes. I pulled on black jeans and a loose white sleeveless tank top, along with a sports bra, and slipped into my Converse and walked out into the hall, locking my door behind me.

My footsteps echoed eerily in the darkness as I made my way upstairs.

No one else seemed to be awake, and the cathedral seemed to be truly abandoned. I walked down the aisle toward the back doors, looking around me at the moon-light streaming through the stained-glass windows.

An owl cried outside, making me jump.

A shudder of anticipation moved through me, and I wondered what Mor could be calling me out for at this time of night.

I knew she was Sam's friend and angry with me for letting him get hurt by Zarris. I knew she didn't like that I hesitated to kill.

Her punch to my face had shown that.

I didn't hold it against her. I actually respected that she treated me like an equal and didn't hold back.

That didn't mean I felt awesome meeting with her at night.

For a moment, I wondered if I should go call Sam to come out with me, but then I thought better of it.

He still needed to heal, and he'd need sleep for that.

I could handle this. I was the Morningstar.

That's the spirit, my inner demon said.

I smiled, glad that I was finally beginning to trust her.

Sam was right. My inner demon had been correct all along. I was the only one holding myself back. I fought back against being an omega outwardly, but in my heart, I followed the rules and believed them about who I was.

I wouldn't make that mistake again.

I pushed open the back doors quietly and slowly closed them so they wouldn't creak.

But as I walked out and down into the courtyard, I froze, unsure if I was hallucinating or really seeing what I was seeing.

The moon was full and high, casting eerie shadows over the shaggy grasses growing up between the broken slabs of concrete. Trees swayed along the borders of the courtyard, their branches grasping creepily at the cool night winds.

And in the center of the courtyard, on a large, black

object that looked like a huge standing X, Sam was hanging, unconscious.

Shock moved through me, tightening my chest and making it hard to breathe, let alone think straight as I approached the odd... cross?

Sam was chained there, shirtless, tattoos and skin bared to the moon. He wore only black boxer briefs, like he'd been taken from his bed. His wrists were chained by cuffs to each of the top tips of the X, and his legs were chained to the bottom.

He was breathing, I noticed, his abs gently moving with his inhalations. He was drenched in sweat, possibly in pain.

Blood flowed from the cuffs cutting into his skin as they bore his weight.

And then, in a puff of wind, Mor appeared behind the cross, walking out from behind it to glare at me.

"Half void walker, remember?" she asked. "It was enough to gain Sam's trust, to make him think I was on his side in finding the Morningstar. Like I would betray the celestials for some half demon." She smiled cruelly. She was clad completely in loose black clothing perfect for fighting, including black tennis shoes.

As she glared down at me imperiously, she looked competent as hell.

I walked forward, hoping to free Sam immediately,

but she blurred and then appeared in front of me, getting right in my face so I could feel her breath on my cheek.

"I'll finish you off. Then I'll find Os, and we'll take Sam to the ninth realm for execution," she said, folding her arms and walking forward, forcing me to back up.

My heart was still racing a million miles a second, and sweat was breaking out on every inch of my skin. My hands were twitching, and my neck burned where the collar was every time I looked at Sam.

Whatever was inside me didn't like this situation at all.

"How did you capture him?" I yelled at her. "He trusted you!"

"I'm a void walker. I have my own abilities. Why would we be on the same squad if I wasn't at his level? Are you going to fight me, then?" Mor asked, lunging forward as I lunged backward. "Show me what you are, Morningstar."

We'll show you something, fucker, my inner demon replied.

Then lightning-white heat burst through me, and bright light shone through the clearing as something shot out from my chest in a wide beam, barely missing Mor.

It hit a wall behind her where it left a sizzling, melting hole. In stone.

Mor just stared at me, frozen, then looked from the stone wall to me and back again.

Then she put up both hands, backing away from me. "All right, I never said I'd fight a laser. Your collar needs an upgrade."

Rage still pounded through me. What she'd dared to do to someone who trusted her. Someone who had done so much for me. "Cut him down!" I yelled at her. In my chest, I could feel heat building again. Intense, roiling heat that I couldn't control.

She put her hands up. "Wait, Cleo, it's not what it looks like. Hold up—"

You're gonna die, my inner demon roared.

One more look at Sam hanging there, bleeding, and I knew destroying her was inevitable.

A part of me was shaking, holding back. We didn't want to kill. We weren't ready. It felt like I was being torn in half inside.

Mor hurt Sam. Mor wanted to hurt us.

And yet... and yet...

She took what's ours. She harmed what's ours. We kill her, the demon said. And that was that.

I felt the cabochon break on my neck, and another bright light shot out of me, feeling like it was tearing out my entire chest with it, though when I looked down, I was fine.

Another place in the stone wall sizzled, but Mor had narrowly dodged, using her void powers, and was standing there looking shaken, both of her hands up.

"Hey, wait," she said desperately. "I need to explain something."

But I didn't know how to calm the demon inside me.

"Cleo, stop!" A voice rang out from the steps leading up to the cathedral, and I turned to see a figure there, standing in a black bathrobe.

I blinked in shock because, based on the tousled, golden-brown hair and tattoos showing on his chest and the disapproving glare, it was *Sam*.

"Just what the actual fuck is going on right now?" he yelled before he noticed the cross, where another version of him was still tied up. "Mor, what is the meaning of this?" He jerked a finger at the X. "You have two seconds to explain yourself."

Mor just looked up at him like a dog caught digging up bones in a backyard. "Well, shit."

43

Sam stared at us, and the wind whipped at his bathrobe, which he pulled tighter around him, tugging on the belt.

He walked forward then, and the demon in me tried not to lick her lips at the sight of him. The gleam of his skin beneath the moonlight. That utterly handsome face.

Then I looked from him to the cross, where he was still hanging.

I felt like reality was being torn in half.

"Mor has always been good at illusions," Sam said, shaking his head as he walked over to us. "Take it down. Right now."

Mor sighed, rolling her eyes. "Fine." She snapped her fingers, and the cross disappeared in a puff of gray smoke. "There."

Sam looked around us at the two smoking, blackened places where my "laser," had aimed. "So now you're trying to destroy my brother's home? Everything he spent his life to build?"

Mor shook her head rapidly. "Hell no, you know I would never—"

"Then explain yourself," Sam said, his tone low with a deadly note to it despite the calm there.

Mor fidgeted. "I just... I was trying to teach her how to kill. For you."

Sam, who was standing there with folded arms, cocked his head. "And why did that involve stringing me up half naked and putting me on a cross?"

Mor shrugged. "I was just trying to get creative."

"And why a Saint Andrew's cross?" Sam asked.

Mor grinned. "You know I like BDSM."

Sam put a hand to his head. "This is a mess. Mor, I don't need help training Cleo to kill. That's something she'll have to deal with when she's ready. For every slayer, it happens at a different time."

Mor slumped slightly. "I know. It's just... I saw you get beaten because of her. I know how far you'll go for her. I wanted to see how far she'd go for you."

My heart was slightly touched by that, her love for Sam.

Then jealousy whipped through me as bitter as a cold winter wind.

I got up in front of her. "Don't touch him again," I said. "Don't even think about—"

She put a finger out on my collarbone and poked me backward. "Oh please, put the jealousy away. He's not my type."

My eyebrows jerked up. "Really?"

She took a step in closer, putting her hand on my chin and tilting it up. "You are, though, if you're interested."

"Mor!" Sam's yell was loud and fast, and he was immediately there, pulling her back. "What the hell? Now I have to worry about my friend too?"

"You two don't have any deals," Mor said. "I heard you told her not to get feelings. That means you aren't exclusive."

"Like hell," Sam said, getting in Mor's face.

I got between them, pushing them apart, because it looked like they were going to start scuffling.

Mor laughed, putting her hands up. "Fine, fine, I've lost. I'll let you two talk, I guess." She saluted me. "Thanks for not killing me, Cleo. You've got some cool lasers."

"First you don't trust her. Then you've got a crush on her?" Sam sighed in utter exasperation.

"I didn't say a crush," Mor said. "I was just letting her know my type." She shrugged. "I can't help it if I'm attracted to power. But well, if she's yours..."

"She's mine," Sam said.

Mor sighed. "I thought so." She looked up at the sky. "At least I now know she deserves you." She gave me a wave. "Thanks for the fight... and the entertainment. I'm sure we'll train again later, when you get that new collar." She blew me a kiss, and Sam caught it out of the air, threw it on the ground, and stomped on it.

"Hmph," she said. She disappeared into the cathedral, and Sam turned to me.

"I'm sorry," he said. "For all of this. Mor has been like an older sister to me ever since my brother died. She worked with him. She's a little overprotective."

"She's batshit crazy," I said.

"No," he said. "She's a little weird and moody. Most void walkers are. But she knew what she was doing." He looked at the place where the cross had been. "That illusion, kinky as it was, must have taken a lot of energy. Remember that, Cleo. Celestials love illusions, and the more power they have, the better illusions they can do."

"Like when you put that illusion up so no one could know you'd been at Zadis's house?"

"Yes," Sam said. "Here, from now on, if there's ever a question, just ask the illusion of me something I would know." His eyes narrowed, and he put his hands on his hips. "Or actually, I'll give you a code word. Halo."

"What?"

"If you ever need to know that you're talking to me for sure, just ask me the code word, and I'll say halo."

"What about you?" I asked. "Should I give you a code word?"

"No," he said. "I know how to see through most illusions. I should be fine." He smirked. "Plus, I can read your every expression. I'd know if it wasn't you." He frowned. "So what the fuck was up with you thinking that Mor could actually capture me and string me up like that? And what was with the lasers?"

It all seemed so stupid now that I'd ever believed he was in trouble.

My hands tightened into fists, and I turned to stride away from him, cheeks flaming. I'd just been in a fight where I found out I had literal lasers inside me. I didn't need to feel stupid right now.

His hand on my shoulder stopped me gently. "Wait, Cleo. I didn't mean it like that."

I turned around with a sigh. "You want to make fun of me. Sorry, I didn't see through it. Sorry, I thought she could take you. I guess you must think I'm stupid, because it never even occurred to me that it wouldn't be possible or real. I just saw it, and I couldn't... couldn't—"

He looked around at the burn marks. "Couldn't hold back?"

I nodded.

"We'll need to get a stronger collar on you, then," he said, grinning slightly. "Can't have you destroying my brother's house." He looked down. "Oh, it broke."

"I know," I said sadly.

"If you think you can handle restraining yourself tonight, I'll take it over to Betty and have her upgrade it. No lasers. Though, I guess we can say you're definitely the Morningstar now."

I frowned. "But what if I need my lasers?" It had been kind of cool to see light shoot out of my body.

"It's not something you should use, even in a fight, right now, Cleo," Sam said seriously. "If you couldn't aim, if you lost control... you could hurt someone you aren't meaning to."

"Hm." He was right. What if I'd tried to divert the laser and someone else had been in its path?

"It's not that I don't trust you," Sam said. "You have powerful weapons inside you, and I know it would destroy you to hurt someone if you didn't want to. You have a really soft heart."

"Right," I said, kind of wishing that wasn't the case.

"More importantly, there will be opponents who can

reflect that right back at you or direct it to your team-mates or friends."

"I don't want that," I said, sweat breaking out on my forehead as I realized the implications.

"Most importantly, you don't need that. Not yet. You have so many other powers and ways to fight that have fewer risks. Fight with those. I'll make sure the collar allows it."

"Fine then," I said, folding my arms, as the night air was starting to bite through my tank top.

He snapped his fingers, and the air moved and swirled in front of me until a black piece of fabric appeared. A blanket. He plucked it out of the air and put it around my shoulders.

"Always making me use my celestial powers," he said. Then one corner of his mouth lifted. "I still remember when you made me build that house in minotaur territory."

I laughed, thinking about how mad I'd been. "Yes. You were a jerk about it, calling it a doghouse."

"I'm a jerk in general, and I was doing my best to push you away," he retorted. Then he pursed his lips. "Though, I am sorry."

I shrugged. "Forgiven."

"Come with me," he said, waving for me to follow him

into the cathedral. He pushed open the heavy double doors, and it was empty and quiet, the dust catching the moonlight as it drifted quietly through the air.

He led me through the main hall and down the turns that led to his chambers. But instead of his bedroom, we turned right and went through an ornate door into a little sitting room that had ceiling-high windows in a semicircle.

Ornate, cushioned chairs with elaborate carving in their arms and legs awaited us. Sam sank into one, gesturing for me to take the other.

"I'm sorry I walked out on your training today," he said, frowning and keeping his gaze trained on the willow outside the window. "I shouldn't have gotten frustrated. This is all new to you, after all."

"I shouldn't have been defensive and insulting," I said, twisting my hands in my lap. "I do appreciate what you've done for me. I don't judge you for killing at all."

"Don't you?" He raised an eyebrow, and in my heart, I knew he was right to doubt me.

"Maybe it's the celestial in me," I said. "I was taught life is sacred." I sighed. "I've never had trouble fighting back or breaking a nose if I had to. But those things aren't permanent. People come back from them. I hate the idea that I could take everything from someone, and it would never be given back." I swallowed painfully, then met his dark eyes, focusing on the gold at the centers. "I just don't know how I can have the right to do that."

"Not only the right, but the responsibility," he said. He exhaled, looking over at the window again. "If this world were different..." He shook his head, ruffling the curls there. "There are bad things and bad people. They will try to hurt you and others. They won't stop, and they will sense your unwillingness to hurt them back. They will use it against you."

"I hate that," I said. "I don't want to hurt anyone, and—"

"That is a disadvantage," he said. He let out a long exhale. "Look, I was like you. I think that's why I was drawn to you from the start. When I was younger, before I got my celestial powers, I was weak. As an incubus, I had no power, other than feeding. Celestials grow at a different rate, and so my powers didn't manifest for a long time. My brother was my protector. His father was a powerful slayer, and he grew into his skills before me."

I nodded, listening intently.

"Gods, I never thought I'd be talking about this," Sam said quietly, more to himself than me. "Anyway, he taught me something important when he would share skills with me to help me learn to fight better."

"I hear he was truly a legend," I said.

"He was," Sam said, eyes growing misty. He jabbed at them with the sleeve of his bathrobe, remaining composed. "Anyway, that's not the point. The point is, one day, he said something that really stuck with me."

"What's that?"

"That the killing is better than the dying."

"Huh?"

He rubbed the back of his neck. "As a slayer, he had to kill to protect others. If he hesitated, he got to see those he was trying to protect die or suffer horribly. He told me it is better to love the killing than to see the dying."

I shook my head, my throat tight and painful. "That's awful. It shouldn't have to be like that."

"But it is," Sam said, leaning forward to tilt my chin up lightly. "Cleo, how many people would have hurt you if I hadn't killed them?"

I blinked, tears filling my eyes. "I don't want that, though. That choice…"

"I know," he said, dabbing at my tears gently with his robe. "I know. You're gentle. That's why I know you'll make good choices. You'll only kill when it's absolutely needed." He relaxed, sitting back again. "You have others with you to take care of the rest."

Warmth filled me, and I realized how right this felt, sitting alone with him in the moonlight.

I wanted to get closer to him, to know everything about him.

But I knew deep down that it would only result in him pushing me back.

He'd told me what this was at the start. He'd told me not to fall for him.

I just hadn't known how hard that would be.

"Cleo, I'm going away for a day or two, maybe longer," he said. "I need to get my head on straight. I need to go back to slaying for a while."

I straightened, panic moving through me. "No, you can't. What about—"

"Mor can train you," Sam said. "Simon can protect you. Despite how he looks and acts, he's one of the most powerful vampire kings in existence."

"Simon's a vampire king?" I nearly yelled in shock.

Sam laughed softly, a sound that resonated in my heart. "Yes. He was close to Cayne. They ran this place together. I think he's glad to see creatures here again."

I nodded. "He has been very welcoming."

"He gets lonely," Sam said. "Some vampires treasure their deadness, but Simon likes to feed on human emotions and feel alive. You should be able to trust him."

"Is that why you nearly got in a fight with him?" I

asked. "Because it sure seems like you don't trust him at all."

Sam put his hands in his hair, leaning forward so I couldn't see his face. He let out a huff of frustration. "That's just it. I'm so possessive I can't control myself. And I was too impatient to stay for your training. Cleo, you'll be better off without me. I'm not a good coach, like Cayne was. We at least need a break."

My chest felt tight, like the walls were closing in around me. "No. You can't go. I need you."

He eyed me stiffly. "No, you don't. Cleo, you're more powerful than I'll ever be. You just don't know it yet. Even without your lasers, you'll be able to protect this place. Until you're ready, others are here to help you."

I swallowed. "I'm not good at killing yet."

"You will be when you need to be," Sam said. "When someone is truly in danger, I don't believe you'll be able to hold back. That's why I was angry with Mor for pushing you." He sighed. "I know what it's like to be at the stage where you don't want to kill."

I raised an eyebrow at him. "Whereas now you love it."

"I have to," he said. "Because I have to do what needs to be done either way." He grinned. "But yes, after the first time I killed and bloodlust took over, feeding me without sex, I did come to love it more. But I also love the feeling of being powerful. Of knowing that I'm strong enough to protect myself and others. For so long, I felt so weak and couldn't protect even myself. So I know the luxury of having strength, and I don't take it for granted after being powerless for so long."

"I see." The more I came to understand this amazing person, the more I couldn't help the squeezing feeling in my heart at the thought that he would leave.

"I got you to this place," he said, folding his hands together. "That was all I ever planned for. And I will need a favor from you, when you're ready. But in the meantime, we can only cause each other trouble. I can only distract you."

"What trouble?" I asked. "Sam, we've been together in this all along. Without you—"

"You'll be fine," he said, shooting me a wan smile that didn't reach his eyes. "You'll be better off without me. I was only supposed to find the Morningstar, not get involved with her."

"No—"

"You have things you need to do," Sam said. "Things far more important than I am. I'm just a slayer, and it's best if I focus on that for a few days to remind myself. As it is, I'm not able to keep myself away from you." His eyes met mine, burning. "This thing between us, it's dangerous. I would have died to bring you here, Morningstar. But now, it's not up to me any longer. Between Simon, Betty, Griffin, and Mor, you'll have everything you need."

"Why is it dangerous?" I asked. "Why is it dangerous, just because we're getting closer?"

He swallowed, and his face was pained when he looked back at me. "I can't seem to stay distant from you, which is dangerous to me. I can't do it again. I can't care for someone and lose them. And I don't want to disrespect your feelings either, if I can't return them."

I looked up at him. "So you know how I feel for you?"

"I'm an incubus," he said softly. "I almost always know what you're feeling."

"Hm."

"Cleo," he said. "Look at me. I'm not abandoning you. I'll be back. But I... need space. To come back and be in the proper position in your life."

"You don't have to leave, though," I said. "All those things you did for me, they were just because I'm the Morningstar. I'm not taking it wrong. I promise. I just... I want to be with you. You're my best friend."

His eyes widened in shock, but he was silent for a while. "Cleo..."

"I get it," I said. "You have to go because you're afraid

I'll get feelings. Fine." I waved a hand. "Then go soon, so I can forgive you."

"I'll be back," he said. "It's my brother's house. Once I have space—"

"It's fine." I waved my hand again. "Hurry up and go, since you don't have feelings and it won't hurt you." I faced him, eyes welling. "I'll just be here, training to be the Morningstar like you want. No pesky feelings to bother you."

He let out a frustrated hiss. "Cleo, it's not like that." He sighed. "Look, I've done more for you than you think. Things I shouldn't have…"

"What do you mean?"

"I lied when I took you from your haven," he said. "I had no idea if you were the Morningstar. I felt you might be, but I'd been wrong before. But there were no rules in your haven about me being able to take you. I bluffed to Os, and Mor backed me up. She has been on my side since I started working with them undercover."

I blinked. "What?"

He nodded. "That's why we took off so quickly. I fucking made up rules and took off with you, no idea what I was going to do next."

"Why?"

"The same reason I fought Zadis," he said.

"Because I'm the Morningstar and you need me for revenge or something?"

Sam looked at me like I was purposefully trying to misunderstand. "That's why I *killed* him. Why did I *fight* him? I could have made it fast. I didn't have to utterly dominate him first."

I swallowed, my heart pounding. "What do you mean?"

His eyes met mine, looking guarded. "I wanted to impress you. I wanted to show you why you should choose me. Though I didn't realize it consciously, I wanted you to watch me prove I was better than Zadis. Stronger."

"Ah," I said, feeling lightheaded now at what he was implicating.

"That's mating behavior for demons, and we both know I can't have a mate."

I swallowed. "Why not?"

He shook his head. "I'm a slayer. It's a bad idea." He exhaled. "Besides, it's not the feelings you deserve. What I feel is just possessiveness. Obsession." He shook his head. "Demons make bonds, but I don't think I can ever make them again after my bond with my brother was brutally broken. All the same, I'm ashamed of myself. I was supposed to find the Morningstar, not keep wanting to make her mine so much I can't think straight."

My eyes slid to him. "You want me to be yours?"

His eyes were panicked, but he nodded. "I even threatened Simon. He was right. I'm out of control." A corner of his lips lifted. "Everyone wants the Morningstar, right?" His lips fell into a line. "But it's not what you deserve. You can love, Cleo. That part has been burned out of me, but it's possible for you. So I need to give us both a moment of space so we can think straight. It has only been a few days for us. Once I'm out of your sight, you'll be fine."

"I don't want to be *fine*," I said. "I want to be with you."

He raised his head, appraising me.

"I won't have feelings. I won't even pressure you to feed on me," I said, knowing that I was begging now. "Just stay. As my trainer. As my friend."

"I can't," he said. "I just can't." He stood, moving to the window. "I'm in too deep already," he murmured so I could barely hear. "If I bond again, and it goes wrong again, I might well die. And I need to be here for you in the future. When you're ready to finally rise as the star you are." He nodded to himself. "This is the best way to go forward. The bandage must be ripped off."

"So you're going to be gone for how long?" I asked. "A day? A week? A month?"

He just stared at me. "I don't know."

"Why are you pushing me away? Because we're getting closer? Damn it, Sam. Don't do this!"

"You'll be fine, Cleo. No matter who would have found you, you would have been fine." He pulled me up and enfolded me in a hug. "Your powers would have saved you even if I didn't. You only think I'm important because I was the one to find you."

"That's not it," I said. But he was already pulling away, and I could tell I should have taken this half demon's advice and not fallen for him.

Because in the end, he was always planning to leave.

And come back when he needed me.

Perhaps he was just trying to be nice about it.

"Fine," I said, turning away from him with folded arms. "Do what you need to do, then."

He turned to go. "I'll be back, but try not to think about me too much. It would be best if you moved on and considered me just one of many friends."

I stayed silent, too angry about the one-sidedness of the situation to talk anymore.

It didn't matter what I said. He was leaving.

And it hurt since he'd been on my side all along.

I knew he thought he was protecting me, but I also knew he was protecting himself. From having to feel again.

Because no matter what, I could tell this was hurting him too.

"I left you a letter with a map to something special that you can enjoy when I'm gone," he said. "Orpheus has it."

I sucked in a breath. "So you were already planning it."

"Immediately after training," he said. "I realized I'm getting too close. That I have no idea what I'm doing. I can't help you the way you need."

"You're just afraid," I said bitterly. "Afraid you might fall for me."

His eyes met mine. "Afraid I already have, and it's the worst thing that could happen to both of us." One corner of his lips lifted ruefully. "But maybe, with some time apart, after we've been through so much together, we'll both be able to focus on what matters."

My nails bit into my palms. "Fine, just go, then. Who needs you anyway? I'm sure Simon can give me anything I want—"

Sam made an angry sound, then turned away again. "Good-bye, Cleo. I'll be back... when I can."

"When you've killed enough creatures to numb whatever you feel for me?"

He whirled on me, his face red and angry. "When

I've become the man you need to help you achieve your destiny. When I've recovered my senses."

"I think you have them now," I said.

"I don't," he said, putting his hands up. "What was I thinking even getting as close as I did to you? You're warm. You're light personified. Your destiny is to rule over everything. But I'm cold. I was cold even before Cayne died. I was a cold fucker after my childhood and a killer for most of my adulthood. You deserve better, and despite these violent feelings inside me, I don't think I can ever give you what you want. I'd only be in your way, Cleo."

"You aren't," I said. "You've been... everything."

"And now you need to be everything to the world," he said. "And I need to leave so you can feel that you are fine without me."

"But I want you here by my side," I said softly, brokenly. "I can't do it without you."

"That's where you're wrong," he said. "You can, Cleo. Just believe in yourself like I always have, from the moment I met you, and you can."

I stood there, heart slamming into my chest, wondering what I could say, what I could do to change this.

Then I realized there was nothing. He was right. I had to stop relying on him.

I had to start standing on my own.

And I needed a break from my feelings too.

Then a stupid, desperate suggestion rose inside me.

Since he was leaving anyway, why not?

"Feed from me one more time, then," I said quietly. "Awaken my demon once more before you go, and be strong so you'll be safe on your journey."

His eyes met mine, and the longing in them took my breath away. "Just tonight?"

I nodded.

"You won't hate me?"

"Does it matter?" I asked.

His chin dipped.

"I won't hate you," I said. "Just once more. So we'll both be stronger apart. Just to say good-bye."

"I should tell you no," he said. "I should pull us both out of this whirlpool that is slowly dragging us down. But I can't. I want you too much, Morningstar. So just don't hate me when the morning comes."

"I won't," I said. And I wouldn't. I would simply be grateful for everything he had done.

Then he took me in his arms and settled his lips gently over mine.

44

The kiss started gentle, and I felt his hands smooth down my arms until he found my fingers and entwined them tenderly with his own.

He kissed me softly, nipping at my lower lip before his tongue swiped out to lick my bottom lip, then my upper. Then he dove inside, stroking softly, then harder, twisting against my tongue, enticing me into a heated dance that had us pressed tight together, our hands clenched.

It wasn't enough, the feel of my breasts against his powerful chest, my nipples rubbing against his hard muscles. It wasn't enough, the spicy scent of his musk, the taste of him in my mouth, the way he was holding me.

More, more, more, was all my demon wanted.

I thrust my tongue against him, trying to get into his mouth and take control, and he let out a little growl and broke apart from me, our hands still entwined. Then he separated our hands and grabbed my wrists, jerking them behind me and pinning them there with one hand.

His other hand came up to brush my hair away from my cheek.

His eyes flashed red in the darkness, and slowly, his hair began to grow, falling lower and lower over his shoulders and onto his chest and back. Large, twisting black horns grew up and out of his head.

When he smiled, there were fangs.

I'd awoken the incubus in him.

"Think to top me, little wolf?" He shook his gorgeous red hair back over his shoulder, then gave me a fierce smirk.

I just stared at him. As beautiful as he was normally, there was something extra captivating about this form.

Something so sensual it felt like the air was filling with pheromones. The slightly pink tinge to his skin glowed in the light of the moon, streaming through the nearby windows.

Keeping a hold on my hands behind my back, he slowly walked forward, pushing me backward and into his bedroom with a keen look in his eyes. I had to strain just to look up at him.

Finally, I could look deeply into the eyes of his incubus form, and I let out a little gasp when I saw rings of gold at the center of his pupils.

"I hide them," he said. "I use shadows to hide the red from the world. It's a sure giveaway that I'm a demon. The gold almost always shows through."

I nodded. "Your eyes are beautiful either way."

His eyes flashed with something, and I felt the heat in the room intensify.

"Cleo..." He brought one of my hands forward, cupping it against his face as he leaned into it. "I wish we could be together. I wish things were simple." He kissed the inside of the palm, and the skin there practically sizzled. He licked me gently where he'd kissed, and I let out a moan as a shock of pleasure moved over my hand.

I hadn't known my hand could get me turned on.

"There are a million sensitive places you don't know about," he said, pinning my hand back again. He lowered his head to kiss the side of my neck, then moved to the edge of my shoulder, pushing the blanket aside and off me to kiss me there as well.

I sighed, arching back to give him access to my neck.

Instead, he tore my white tank top open down the front with one hand, his red eyes pinned on my face.

I gasped as the night air touched my bare skin.

I felt something move around my hands, locking them together behind my back, cool and silky.

As Sam moved both of his hands in front of me, I realized he must have tied me with something.

He put up a hand, and to my shock, sharp talons extended from his fingers. He dragged them forward, cutting the center of my sports bra open and making it fall apart to the sides without even grazing my skin.

He picked me up and tossed me on the bed, still fully tied. I looked up to see that even though he'd tossed me like I weighed nothing, he was about ten feet from the bed.

As I lay there with tied arms, pushing myself up slightly so I could watch him, I saw him start to slowly untie his bathrobe. As he shrugged it over his shoulders and let it fall to the ground, he was revealed in only a pair of tight black boxer briefs.

And what was in those briefs was way more than I even remembered.

Holy shit. He really is a sex demon.

My inner demon licked her lips.

It was impossible not to feel slightly afraid as he

took a step closer, then another one, looking like an evil king of hell approaching his captive.

But my fantasies were rough, and I was wet as hell thinking of him fulfilling them.

I struggled slightly as he got a little bit closer, and it only seemed to excite him more, as I saw a twitch at the side of his mouth.

"The powerful Morningstar, at my mercy," he growled. "What will it be, my queen?"

I just stared at him, running my eyes over his beautiful skin, his gorgeously shaped pecs, his narrow hips, his rippling abs.

His strong, muscular legs.

And... was that a tail?

My eyes went wide, and he looked back at it, a long red rope with a slightly pointed end. He grinned. "Not tonight."

"Not tonight *what*?"

He smirked. "We can have a lot of fun with my tail." He moved his hand to the front of his briefs, grazing his member. "And this." Then he dropped his hand and took another step forward. "But not tonight." He scented the air. "Not with a virgin."

"What? You know that by smelling the air?"

"No," he said. "I know *you* by smelling the air." His gaze met mine, hot enough to burn. "Hm, time to feed."

In a blink, he was on top of me, kneeling over my abdomen on the bed with me still tied beneath him.

I didn't even know how he'd moved that fast, but he leaned over me, licking over the shell of my ear, his hands planted on either side of my face as I lay on my side.

"How does it feel to be tied?" he asked. His lips found mine in an awkward angle that became amazing once our mouths were both open. I moaned as he stroked inside my mouth, and I struggled against the silky bonds on my hands. "You get so turned on being restrained, pet. There's no way I can hold back."

I felt the tie around my wrists fall away and almost cried out in frustration, but immediately, I was flipped on my back. As he knelt atop me, his arms folded, I felt something wrap around my hand and then pull it out and to the side. Looking over, I saw something black and smoky winding around my wrist, the other hand tying itself to one of the tall wooden bedposts.

My other hand followed, and then both of my legs, until they were spread-eagled. I could move slightly, enough to stay relaxed against the bed.

But other than that, I was totally helpless, utterly exposed except for my jeans and underwear and the hanging remnants of my bra.

He put up a hand again, extending the claw on his

forefinger, then lowering it to my body without even looking. Slowly, moving as he needed to, he cut through one side of my jeans along my hip, my knee, my calf. Then the other. Then he yanked the jeans away from me. He also unhooked the back of my sports bra and pulled it away.

He moved so that he was kneeling between my legs and looked down at my underwear and licked his lips. Then he leaned down and, as I watched from my trapped position, put a fang at the waistband of my underwear.

I shuddered at the sharpness of it next to such a vulnerable area. He smiled as he put it down on the skin, a cool, poking feeling that made me afraid to even move. My heart was racing, my skin breaking out in sweat, and I was so damn wet it was embarrassing.

What was he going to do?

With his eyes locked on mine, he slowly dragged the fang down, cutting through my underwear. When he reached my clit, he stopped for a second, kissing it, then he tore the rest of my underwear away with his hand.

"Fuck, Cleo, you bring out the demon in me."

"The feeling is mutual," I gasped out, utterly caught up in the feel of his breath over my mound, my entire body trapped and at his mercy yet totally available to him.

"Let's see if you like internal or external orgasms better," he said, putting his finger up to his mouth to lick it. Then he lowered it over my clit, stroking over it softly, back and forth. Cool air alternating with his hot touch made me buck against him, as much as I could with my tied hands and legs.

Gods, I loved feeling helpless like this.

With him.

Somehow, it was safer than anywhere else in the world.

"I don't want to choke you," he said, still moving his finger all too lightly against me as I bucked. "It's too risky when I'm caught up in incubus mode." His hand moved up to my neck, caressing it lightly. "Besides, I have so many other amazing things to do with your neck."

I gasped at the lightness of his touch, the teasing getting me going when I was caught up like this.

"If I'm going to make you feel like you're dying, it's going to be through orgasm." He moved back again and leaned down to put his mouth where his hands had been. He flashed a fang, running it super lightly over my clit, and the pinpoint stimulation sent a sensation through me unlike anything before. It was heightened because of the risk, because I couldn't move at all or it might hurt.

He just smirked, and I saw him pull back slightly and use his tongue on me instead.

Oh gods, here we go, I thought.

I wanted my hands free to pull his hair. But everything was more sensitive being tied. The bonds didn't hurt, but they ensured there was no way I could escape the absolutely delicious things he was doing with his mouth.

I bucked against his tongue, which only made him growl and swirl harder. There was nothing I could do. My release was coming. I could feel it like the moment before a tsunami when the sea pulls back and holds before it unleashes.

He sucked hard, just once, and I came, screaming, as my bound body couldn't thrash against the extreme pleasure flooding my limbs all the way to my toes and fingertips. Behind my eyes, I saw stars. All my mouth could do was call out his name.

And when I opened my eyes again, I saw him watching, waiting patiently, as though he'd only just begun. He probably had.

"That was good," he said. "Let's make you squirt. See how your demon likes that."

"What? What does that mean?"

A devilish smirk was all I got in return. He stroked a

hand down to my slit and gently moved through my folds, caressing and opening them. "May I?"

I looked at my bonds. "Seriously?"

His eyes grew a deeper shade of red. "I like my consent enthusiastic. Especially when my prey is tied."

I swallowed. "Of course. Whatever you do to me, I want it." Fuck, I wanted it so much.

He sat up a bit, propped on his knees, and lowered his hand to my entrance. I loved being able to see him, his powerful shoulders and beautiful abs and the flexing muscles in his arms as he pushed one finger forward, gently penetrating me.

Oh, it felt so good. Like it was right. Like I needed something inside there. It was tight, and I squirmed against his finger, and he went still, allowing me to adjust to it. Meanwhile, his free hand stroked over my thigh and knee, caressing my skin and relaxing my body.

All I had to do was lie back and let him take control.

And I would because I trusted him. Incubus, angel, I would always trust this man.

My heart twisted at that, but Sam inserting a second finger distracted me, pushing me back into the space where pleasure was all that mattered.

I could deal with emotions later. All I wanted right now was to feel.

I loved the stretching feeling of his two fingers as he gently pushed them apart, taking up more space.

"Ah," I breathed, and the corners of his lips turned up.

"You like that, little wolf? You like my fingers inside you?"

"So good."

He pushed in a third, and I made a little whimper.

"Breathe. You'll like it. Fuck, you're so wet, baby."

I nodded and relaxed and found he could put three in, though it was a tight fit. But as I felt my sex clench and release, adjusting to him, I felt something else building, a certain kind of pressure I'd never felt before.

It was so strong it made me shudder.

"Mm, found the spot," he said. He removed one finger, and with the other two, I felt him make a hooked motion, stroking the spot in me a few inches above my entrance.

Sparks moved through me, making my body jerk against the bonds.

"Oh gods, what's that?"

"I told you, internal," he said, starting a steady rhythm of stroking and pulling, moving back and forth against that spot, his hungry eyes watching me all the time.

It built fast. It felt too good. So wet, so warm. His

strong hands. Unable to move, unable to escape the powerful feelings building in me, all I could do was pant and hold on and pray that he never, never stopped what he was doing.

A pressure, almost like needing to pee, moved through me. Something even stronger than my orgasm before.

"That's your G-spot," he said, hooking against it again. "I could hit it better with my dick. Or my tail."

I gasped at the forbidden image of that.

"But not tonight."

He continued to stroke as my moans and gasps got more and more frantic. Unlike my orgasm before, I felt myself trying to hold back from this one, like it was going to be too strong.

"You love penetration," he growled, red hair falling partly over his face as he continued to patiently stroke. "You'll love how the orgasm feels."

I thrashed side to side, unsure of it. My whole body was becoming so tightly wound, and pressure was building in that intensely sensitive inner spot.

"Oh gods, oh gods... Oh Sam," I cried out as the pressure finally crested and my body felt crushed in a vise of utter pleasure and then released into waves of it.

Something squirted out of me, totally out of my control given how strong everything was happening.

Some of it shot right into his face, and he simply grinned, sticking out his tongue to lick at it.

I was breathing heavily, semi-humiliated, but the triumphant gleam in his eyes showed that he couldn't have been more pleased.

His eyes roamed over me, hot as hellfire. "Told you you'd like it." He licked his lips. "Mmm, tasty. Good girl."

I felt myself flush down to my toes.

He leaned down and ate me out again, licking against my sex, kissing my clit, and thrusting his tongue up and into me until I was thrashing again, lost in an utter cloud of need and lust.

I came over and over, and every time I came from my clit, he'd then use his fingers inside me, wringing even more of me out.

When I finally couldn't take any more and was practically lying in a pool of my own fluids, utterly exhausted from so many orgasms, he released me from my bonds, and my hands and legs fell flat to the bed.

He got off the bed and paced at the foot of it, a sexy incubus with his tail whipping impatiently as he sent me another look.

It seemed that though he'd wrung everything out of me, he still wasn't done.

There was something I hadn't seen yet, that I would

have given everything to see, but I didn't know how he'd take it.

Since it wouldn't technically be feeding, it wouldn't be awakening anything. It would just be about my feelings, which I wasn't supposed to have.

But I wanted it nonetheless, and I knew Sam had so far given me most things I wanted.

And tomorrow he would leave, and we would both have to try and move on. Put this behind us and focus on more important things.

But right now, the only important thing to me was this unbelievably sexy incubus and that huge thing at the front of his briefs.

I wanted to see him lost in pleasure.

I looked down at him, making it obvious what I wanted, then extended my tired arms to him.

I saw the doubt flash in his face, but then something else, something wicked and hot and desperate, and I knew I had won.

He jumped onto the bed, pinning me with his hands and kneeling over me easily. "No one has ever tempted me like this, Cleo. No one has ever made me want so much."

My arms wrapped around his neck, pulling him down to me. He moved slightly back and then pulled my legs up and around his waist.

"I can't take you," he said. "It would hurt you. But I can show you what I know you want to see, even if it takes everything from me."

"What do you mean takes everything?"

He put a hand to my face, and the look in his eyes was pained and desperate. "Because it's already so hard for me to leave."

Then he put one hand on either side of my head and thrust forward against me. Even in his briefs, I could feel his huge length pushing against me. With my legs around his waist, I could put my sex right against his hardness. He thrust up, brushing my clit, my folds, with his hard length, moving back and forth, making me moan just at the thought of having it inside.

But he was right. It was enormous. There was no way...

But it was enough, looking up at him propped on those strong, tensing arms, hair falling over his face, which was focused in pleasure, damp with sweat. His lashes lowered, then raised to look at me with those flashing crimson eyes.

It was the hottest thing I would ever see. I was sure of it. And he was building the pleasure in me again, just moving carefully against me. I was so wet that the fabric was easily soaked and glided smoothly against him and me.

The tension got tighter, tighter, and with one last stroke of that hard length, I came, my clit ringing like a bell, over and over, my body thrashing in response, my nails digging into his back.

When I was done, panting and shaking, I shook my head against his shoulder.

"No. No. I want to see *you*," I said desperately. "I want you to—"

His eyes widened, and he pulled back slightly. "Tell me what you want, sweetheart. I'll do anything."

I pushed myself up onto my elbows, trying to catch my breath. The demon in me was awake, fierce, and very clear about what she wanted.

"I need to see you come," I gasped out.

He swallowed as if this was something he hadn't expected. "I don't need to feed that way. I told you."

"It was wonderful, feeling you against me," I said. "And it's amazing that you give me pleasure." I jerked him down so I could growl in his ear. "But I need to see you come. Just once. Please."

My plea undid him. I could see it in his face as he pulled back.

He looked me over. "You're exhausted. If you want to see it that badly, I'll do it myself to save you effort."

He got off of me, and cool air moved over my naked body. It felt good after so much heat.

Already, post-orgasm bliss was drifting through me. But I couldn't rest until I had even more.

As Sam moved to the corner of the room, moonlight streamed over him.

It seemed so naughty, watching him push down his shorts, soaked from my wetness. His huge length sprang free, so huge I literally gasped at it.

Sam was a tall, muscular man, but even so, he was incredibly hung. My mouth watered at the perfect shape of him, the slight upward curve, the defined head with a beautiful ridge.

The veins running up the sides, the heavy balls beneath. My hands ached and my body begged me to go to him, to take him in my hands.

But this was what he wanted, so I would take what I could get.

He moved his hand down to grip himself, then leaned his head back so that his hair fell behind him. His whole body flexed, and I realized he was literally going to do this standing.

For me to see.

His fierce eyes met mine as he stroked himself, and he seemed to be asking me, *Is this what you want?*

I mewled as a new rush of wetness hit and couldn't help reaching down to touch myself.

I'd thought I was done, but when I saw him like that, so gorgeous, I couldn't stop myself.

He let out a growl when he saw that, and his head arched back as he bucked against his hand.

Gods, he was beautiful. Those horns, that hair, that body.

That face, which was all Sam. The Sam I'd known. The Sam I'd been with through everything.

The Sam that I could never truly have.

I pressed down on my clit, watching him, and came just from being so sensitive, and that instantly dragged him over the edge with me.

His legs nearly buckled, but he stayed up, stroking, liquid spurting from his perfect dick, his gorgeous face tensed with pleasure but pinned desperately on mine, drinking in every second of my release.

No matter how much he gave me, he seemed desperate for more.

There would never be another man like this for me. I knew it.

I leaned back through my own orgasm but kept my eyes on him, his orgasm a sight so beautiful I couldn't look away.

"Cleo," he called out raggedly, still watching me come. "Cleo, you're breaking me. I don't even know who I am anymore."

His hand fell away, and he walked over to me, picking me up and holding me close as he sat down on the bed.

He brushed my hair back, placing kisses all over me from the top of my head to my cheeks to my lips, which he claimed fiercely.

I could feel his heart beating hard against my hand, and I never wanted that sound to stop.

I looked up into his eyes, which were red but still shining. His cheeks flushed from release.

My body was wrung out, tired and satisfied. But my heart, my heart was reaching out, grasping at something it could never hold.

I had thought having him once more would be enough for me.

Now I knew it never would be.

As I sank in against him and let him hold me, murmuring as he stroked a hand through my hair, I knew I was in greater trouble than ever.

Because as much as I had tried never to get feelings, I was definitely in love with this man.

45

Sam spent the night with me in his arms, much to my surprise.

But in the morning, he was gone.

Orpheus had come at breakfast to give me the letter Sam left me, but I wasn't ready to open it.

I wasn't ready to acknowledge that he really had left and that things were over between us.

Still, life had to go on, so after breakfast, I went outside with Simon, Mor, and Griffin to keep training.

As I walked into the courtyard, the wind seemed to bite at my skin. Perhaps fall was ending soon.

I could still remember the smell of my haven in autumn. The crops. The grass. The apple cider.

The air here smelt like crisp nothingness with a tinge of ash.

Mor was wearing black leggings with an oversized tunic and flashed me a smile as I walked into the middle of the courtyard to meet her.

"How are you doing?" she asked, and I could see the hint of pity in her eyes.

I shrugged. "Ready to get started, I guess." I was wearing a black tee shirt with ripped black jeans and combat boots.

Moody as hell and ready to fight.

"I have something for you." Betty, who had been sitting on a rock wall by Simon, walked over to me, holding a shiny wooden box.

I took it from her gingerly and, when I opened it, saw a thin, silver necklace with a small red stone.

"Pure, natural brimstone. Nothing like the synthetics those celestials use. Nic brought it to me. It should suppress your light beams."

I took it gingerly from the box, and Griffin walked over to help put it on me. I could feel his large fingers fumbling with the clasp, but he got it on.

Then he unclasped and handed me my old collar. I looked at it for a moment, studying the cracked brimstone.

I didn't want to let it go.

Betty seemed to sense this and put her hand out. "If you're attached to this, I can fix it. Even add extra suppression. I assumed you'd want something more subtle."

"I should," I admitted, turning over my old collar in my hand, unwilling to give it up yet.

I still remembered the day I'd been given it, the day I left the haven with Sam. It felt like my life had begun that day.

The stone no longer glowed any color, just a dark amber with a crack down the center.

Betty gently removed it from my hands. "I'll take care of it. Repair it. Get it back to you."

"But—"

She shook her head, gray hair bouncing. "I can see it means something to you. Objects are always more powerful when they have meaning to a person." She raised a hand, muttering to herself as she jogged back to her workshop.

Simon stood and came over to where I was standing, peering at my new collar. "Looks nice." He pointed to a field across the road from us. "Want to go see the creatures Sam had delivered from Zadis's basement?"

I nodded, and Simon grabbed my hand before I could say no to jerk me across the street with him.

An old wooden fence enclosed a pasture, and I saw the black unicorn with the purple horn I'd seen in

Zadis's basement, along with an odd winged tiger and several other creatures standing in the mist.

"The enclosure is enchanted so no one but me can open it."

I looked into the mist. "What about the werewolf? I saw one when I was in Zadis's basement."

Simon nodded. "I took him to my keep. We like weres."

I stared at him. "You have a keep?"

"Yup." He leaned on the fence, looking at the unicorn as it grazed. The creature raised its head, looked at us, and scraped its hoof against the ground, making an angry huffing noise. Then it charged us.

I took a step back, but it rammed into something invisible that lit up with blue light when the unicorn hit it and went tumbling back.

It got back up, shook itself off, and took a jog around the enclosure, looking for openings.

"Was it trying to attack me or you?" I asked Simon.

"I don't know," Simon said, sighing wistfully. "Beautiful though, right?"

"Mm."

"I'm sorry Sam left," Simon said.

"It's fine," I said. "He saved me. He's already done so much, and—"

"That boy was always coldhearted. Always a sullen

little shadow following Cayne around. When he came into his powers, he became strong but conceited and even more closed off. An incubus who only fed by killing."

I just listened, watching the animals move in the mist. Out of the corner of my eye, I saw the water droplet creature approaching, little black shoes beneath it carrying it over to me. It was only about a foot tall.

Small black eyes looked up at me, floating at the top of the droplet. It began an elaborate dance, pointing its little shoes forward one at a time, and I couldn't help smiling even as Simon put a hand on my arm and pulled me back.

"Water sprite," Simon said, glaring at it. "Don't let it complete its dance. It wants you."

"What?" I blinked, turning away from the enclosure with a sigh. "Dang, so much to learn."

"Did Sam say why he was leaving so abruptly?" Simon asked. "I was surprised. It's clear he cares about you. And even before Cayne died, he pretty much cared about no one but his brother. Since Cayne died, Sam's been totally closed off, until you."

"He said it was because we were getting close," I said. "Because he was getting possessive, which can't happen because I'm the Morningstar." Pain lashed through my heart. "He was hurt when his brother died, and I don't think he ever wants to face that again."

Simon let out a hiss of impatience. "We were all hurt when Cayne died, but he'd be pissed at Sam getting everything so wrong after his death. The lesson in losing someone is to hold on tight to those who are still with us, not let them go in order to avoid pain."

Simon's red eyes flashed with something and looked extra glassy. I remembered suddenly that Cayne was his friend, that they ran this place together.

He swiped at his eye with the sleeve of his black coat, then laughed. "Good thing vampires can't cry, right?"

I put an arm around him and pulled him in for a side hug, and we stayed there for a moment, both taking comfort in having someone there when the one we wanted was gone.

"What happened to Cayne, Simon?"

"Murdered while working with the celestials," Simon said. "No one knows how. They dumped his body here with no explanation. I don't know if Sam knows more than me, but he made it clear he wanted to take things into his own hands. Both to continue Cayne's work of trying to find the Morningstar and to figure out his death. I have no celestial in me, so I can't even pass through the veil to investigate."

"Ah."

"I do think of him often," Simon said wistfully. "That's why I visit this place. It's like I think he'll show up and just be here if I come."

I was quiet because I had no idea what to say. But I kept my arm around Simon's shoulders because I could tell it steadied him.

He looked up into my eyes. "Comforting a vampire. There really is something special about you. Do you really think you're the Morningstar?"

"I don't know what it even is," I said.

"A prophecy," Simon said. "About a being born in the celestial realm, with both celestial and abyssal blood, gifted with the power to bring balance. And right now, with the celestials going to the demon realm to do whatever they want, unstopped, there's no balance."

"I don't know if I truly am the Morningstar," I said, letting go of Simon to run my hands through my hair. Using my teeth, I pulled a ponytail holder off my wrist and tied my hair up, leaving it in a messy bun. "I'm ready to learn if I am and try my best to live up to the prophecy, though. I won't let what he did go to waste."

"What Sam did or what Cayne did?"

"Both," I said.

"It's a legend to us. Sacred to demons. Cayne was always obsessed with it." Simon moved his neck to the side, cracking it slightly. "I don't even know what I believe about the whole Morningstar idea. It seems too good to be true." His gaze narrowed on me, long lashes shading his red eyes to bordeaux. "But there is something special about you, Cleo. That's for certain."

"You aren't drawn to me, though, are you?"

"I don't feed on demon blood anymore," he said. "I'm interested in Griffin because he smells amazing."

I just laughed. "Good luck with that."

"Come on, tell him it'll be good. No feelings involved."

I shook my head. "That won't work for Griffin. He's *all* about the feelings. Plus, he's already in love with someone else."

I looked over to the courtyard where Griffin was talking about something with Mor. Mor threw her head back in a laugh at something Griffin said, and he just looked at her in confusion.

"Come on. Let's go back over. I need to train."

"Sure," Simon said.

We crossed the road, gravel and broken pavement crunching beneath our feet.

"Some interesting creatures, huh?" Mor asked. "I told Griffin he should see if that winged tiger is a shifter like he is. They could make ligers." She laughed again heartily.

Griffin narrowed his eyes. "It's just a tiger with wings."

Mor tilted her head cockily. "And you're a lion with wings. It's perfect." She pouted. "I want to see a liger."

Griffin just shook his head and came over to me, putting an arm over my shoulders. "She's so weird. How are you doing?"

I shrugged him off, not feeling like being pitied any more than I already was. "I'm fine. Ready to get stronger."

To show Sam he was right about me.

To show him I could still fight without him around.

After all, I'd been fighting alone my whole life. I could get used to doing it again. Sam had gotten me here. The rest was up to me.

Mor looked at my collar, nodded, and walked back a few paces from me, getting into a fighting position with her hands up guarding her face. "Come on. Let's spar a bit. Get your speed up."

I put up my hands, ready to guard.

She motioned for me to come at her. The second I moved forward, I felt a burst of power unlike any before. I was in front of her in a split second, as though I'd flown. My fist moved out, hitting her in the stomach and making her fly back, rolling over to land on her face.

As she pushed herself up, she flashed a thumbs-up. "Wow. You really improved."

I touched the thin chain at my collar. Was it the lack of suppression or the way Sam had awakened my demon last night?

Either way, happiness welled within me at the power I had. Finally enough to fight back.

"Super speed," Mor said, cracking her neck back and forth to stretch it. "I should have expected that. How's your strength?" She put up a hand, made a gesture, and something huge formed in the air, growing bigger and bigger.

A giant boulder.

She hurled it at me, and terror struck me as I realized it could obliterate Betty's hut. Before I could think more about it, I lunged forward with a perfect punch aimed at the center of it.

My fist made contact with the cool stone, and I felt unbearable pressure just before it exploded against my fist, sending chunks flying every which way and coating the air in a thick powder.

"Excellent," Mor said. "Sam told me not to go easy on you. He said you need to learn fast." She cocked her head. "You should have telekinesis."

"I did at my execution. It was kind of beyond my control."

"A lot of strong powers are like that," Mor said. "Even those wielding them don't fully understand them. But you have to trust them, and yourself, and use what you have."

The dust from the boulder finally settled to the ground, but as I felt something tiny and cold land on my cheek, I looked up at the sky and saw small white flakes falling from the sky.

"Snow?" Griffin put his hand out, then his tongue, catching something small and white on it before turning to smile at me. The red sweatshirt he wore had several small white dots on it as well.

Simon frowned up at the sky. "It's too early to snow."

Mor looked up as well, then down at her hand where several snowflakes had fallen. "Shit."

"Why shit?" I asked, tilting my head so a little flake could fall on my tongue. It melted in a little flash of cold that I loved. "Snow is awesome."

"This isn't normal snow," Mor said, whirling around to face the cathedral behind us. "This is—"

The doors to the cathedral burst open, and Os strode through them. He wore a dark-purple tunic over black pants and black leather boots. His purple hair was tied back in a braid, like he was ready for battle, and his right hand was in a glove, his left covered in an assortment of blue rings.

I hadn't seen him like this before, and I didn't like it.

Something about the tight way he held himself and the slight shame in his eyes made me nervous.

The snow began to fall more heavily, surrounding us like a blizzard.

"Os, no!" Mor yelled as the snow fell faster, harder, and then began to swirl around us, getting colder. I couldn't even see Griffin and Mor and Simon anymore. They were just shadows as the snow fell so heavily I couldn't see anything but blankets of white.

Then the snow stopped falling, and I stood, looking around me.

Griffin, Mor, and Simon stood stock still, eyes wide and staring, their bodies like frozen statues covered in a thick sheet of ice.

Betty's shack was frozen too, and so was everyone inside probably.

"I just need everyone to stay calm for a moment, Cleo," Os said, walking forward and looking over Mor. "We don't need anyone getting hurt who doesn't have to be. It's too bad I can't even trust Mor, though. She knew what Sam was doing." Os's eyes met mine. "He had no right to take you."

"What?"

"Or haven't you found out he was a liar yet?" Os

asked. "There are rules, Cleo. Rules that have to be followed."

"What do you mean?"

Another figure walked out of the cathedral, folding his arms and glaring. I recognized the dark hair and gray eyes, the confident build.

It was Bran.

"You have to come back, Cleo," he said, sneering at me. "You never had permission to leave."

I took a step back. "You don't have any authority here."

"Unfortunately, that's not true," Os said. "The celestials don't like to come to this polluted, desecrated realm, but they will if it's important. And when one of our havens is robbed by one of our own enforcers, we have to get involved."

I blinked. "They tried to stone me. They abused me."

Os looked at Bran. "Is that true?"

"She hit me in the balls," Bran said. "I told you."

Os cocked his head, his braid falling to one side. "Then we will deal with it in a pack court, and I will oversee it to ensure a fair outcome. But either way, you'll have to come with me, Cleo. Rules are rules. Do you want everyone here to get hurt?"

I glanced around me. "What did you do to them?"

"Don't worry. I put a layer between them and the ice.

They'll be fine for now. Long enough for you to come with me and Gabe."

"Gabe is here?" I asked. "That conceited jerk from the prison?"

"Don't talk about him like that," Os said. "This isn't his fault. He raised me, so don't act like you know him." He closed his eyes to gather his composure. "Cleo, I like you. You know this. But this is out of my hands. If you don't go back with him, the ninth realm is going to send someone else to take you back anyway."

I shook my head. "I'm just an omega. I'm part demon!"

"You're still the property of our haven," Bran spat. "And we want you back."

"There is one other option," Os said, looking pensive. "If you take it, and win, you're free to stay, and your friends won't be in any danger."

Os folded his arms, waiting for my reply.

"What option is that?"

"You could issue him an alpha challenge," Os said. "If you win, you become alpha and can make new rules for the haven. That's what alphas do."

I thought about it a second, afraid for my friends, afraid for the animals across the street.

Afraid to leave and not be here when Sam came back.

"I'll do it," I said. "Come on. Let's move somewhere out front. I won't fight at Sam's home and damage it."

Os's eyes darkened. "He would deserve it after lying to me. But fine. We will go see Gabe, who is waiting out front, and tell him you've accepted the challenge."

I eyed Bran, who slid a mocking look at me as we all walked to the front of the cathedral.

But deep inside, I was more excited than scared, despite the stakes here.

I finally got to fight an alpha from my haven, no holds barred. My inner demon was more than ready.

46

As we trudged through the cathedral, I tried to remember what Sam had told me.

To believe in myself. To remember how strong I was.

But it was harder without him there.

When we walked out into the cold air again, I saw Gabe standing there in a crusader outfit.

He wore a loose white tunic with a blue lion on the front over silver armor beneath. His ashy-blond hair matched the gray of the sky, and his light-brown eyes had no sparkle.

He eyed me like I was something beneath his notice. "We meet again, demon."

I lifted my chin. "Fuck you."

His mouth tightened. "Not even with someone else's dick."

My eyes widened at his crudeness. Before, in the cell when I'd been awaiting execution, he'd said I shouldn't even talk because I was just going to die instead. At my most terrifying moments, this "angel" had treated me like garbage.

As Os moved to his side, I wondered what he possibly could see in this man that he would serve him so loyally.

"Good job, Os," Gabe said, patting Os on the shoulder. "Did she accept the challenge, or are we just dragging her back?"

"She accepted," Os said, but there was something in his eyes I didn't like.

Something like defeat.

"Os, why are you doing this? Do you know how they do things?" I pointed to Gabe. "They lie. They make up whatever suits them to keep everyone in line and believing."

"Obviously," Gabe said, folding his powerful arms. "We feed on belief. But keeping our haven safe above the veil ensures that everything runs smoothly. You, Cleo, are disrupting everything. People are starting to question things. Like how you disappeared and how effectively we really deal with demons."

"Demons aren't what I was told they were," I said. "They've only helped me."

Gabe laughed, raising an eyebrow. "Because you're also a demon."

"Better a demon than a jerk like you," I retorted. "Os, listen to me. They are brainwashing you."

Os just shook his head. "Cleo, you're the one being brainwashed. Sam is not to be trusted."

"Why?" I asked, but Os simply looked away.

"We can start the fight now," Os said.

"Come on." I gestured to Bran, who was watching sullenly, and then I jogged across the broken street to a large square that held the remnants of what must have been a huge building. "We'll fight here, away from the others."

"I promise they'll be safe," Os said. "I wouldn't kill any innocents."

"Why should I believe that when you were willing to freeze them?" I yelled back.

"I'm a diplomat," Os said, following behind us with Gabe. "Sometimes things get too hot, and I need to cool them down." He held up his hand. "My sapphires do that."

I rolled my eyes and continued jogging to the ruins, climbing over the low remnants of a cement wall. Looking up at the gray sky, I asked for patience.

For strength and the ability to win this fight so that

Gabe and Os could leave and I could prove to Sam he was right to trust me all along.

I didn't pray to some god or the celestials, but to the demon within me, who had been my hidden ally from the start.

Together, we could do this. I could feel it in my heart.

Gabe and Os stayed on the outside of the remnants of the building while Bran walked inside with me.

We had a fifty-foot by fifty-foot fighting area amongst the rubble, which Bran appraised skeptically.

"So how do you want to do this?" I asked, my collar burning at my neck, warning me not to overdo it.

Bran was just a wolf. Just a childish, pampered alpha who'd been given everything from birth. Then again, he'd probably been given a dispensation of increased power when he was ordained an alpha.

That made him a bit more dangerous.

And any pure-blooded wolf shifter was strong.

"As wolves," Bran said. "The way we were meant to fight."

I focused on the shift, telling myself we would get this over quickly and then be able to go back and help our friends.

I glanced at Gabe and Os, hoping they would make good on their promise to make this go away if I won.

In my haven, no omega was allowed to challenge an alpha, so little did they know that this was a privilege.

Bones cracked and popped and rearranged, and I felt the familiar lengthening in my nose and face, the fur covering my entire body until I dropped onto all four paws.

My wolf was dark brown, and Bran's was silver. He paced in front of me, slightly larger than me, his eyes narrowed and his lip curled.

"You're larger than a typical omega," he said.

"You're small for an alpha," I shot back, glad we could talk in wolf form.

I'd heard weres couldn't.

His eyes narrowed, and he began to pace in a circle, trying to intimidate me as his huge paws crushed through the fallen debris beneath him.

We were both easily twice the size of a normal wolf, Bran maybe three times.

But I wasn't afraid.

"To submission?" I asked.

Bran nodded. Apparently, alphas valued their pampered lives. Who could blame them?

"Why didn't you just stay back in the village?" I asked as we continued to circle, watching each other with hackles up. "Why bother to come for me? I'm just a demon."

"You undermined my authority," Bran said. "Nothing is the same. No one trusts me as alpha."

"They shouldn't," I said.

"When I bring you back, and kill you in front of them, they will."

"Won't happen," I retorted. "Because I'm going to win, and you're going to leave with your tail between your legs."

"Like I'd lose to an omega," Bran snarled. "Even this fight is beneath me. But to keep order and regain my status with the pack, I will do so."

"How noble of you," I shot back. "Make your move."

Bran raised his head, and his eyes began to glow an unearthly yellow. The air buzzed around me, and when he opened his mouth, I knew he was going to use his alpha powers to try and force me to mentally submit.

"Bow," he growled, his eyes glowing.

The words hit me like a shock wave, making my wolf legs want to buckle. But I felt my inner demon pacing, annoyed.

Ignore him. We don't have to obey.

But it hurt as I tried to resist it. A part of me felt it was hopeless. We were overwhelmed. We should bow. We were made to...

But then Sam's face came to mind. He'd be so angry if I lost here, after all he'd done for me.

I raised my head, feeling like I was pushing back against the force of a jet engine as I walked forward. "I will never submit to you."

The pressure broke, and I knew I had beaten his command.

"Then you'll die," he snarled. "In front of everyone, like you should have." He lunged forward, leaping into the air, claws and teeth bared, a truly terrifying sight.

I skidded to the side, dodging, and grabbed him by the scruff of his neck as he flew by.

Then, harnessing all my strength, I dug my claws into the ground and twisted, throwing him as hard as I could in the opposite direction of the cathedral.

To my shock, he flew about thirty feet, hitting the skeleton of the wall behind him, the last part of the building still standing.

With a loud creak, it fell back due to his weight and landed in the rubble with a crash, sending dust into the air.

Bran let out a growl as he rolled to his feet, looking shaken.

"You don't obey my commands," he said, panting. "You have unbelievable strength. What are you, Cleo?"

I saw fear glimmering in his icy gray irises, and I couldn't bring myself to feel bad.

"I'm not your mate," I spat back at him. "That's all I

know." Then I lunged, picking up speed and bolting over the ground, opening my jaws to grab him by the scruff again.

He dodged, rolling to the side, and I jumped on him, fighting to keep him down. He jerked his scruff out of my reach and used his back paws to kick me off, hard.

I went flying backward and landed in the rubble, rolling a couple times before I stopped.

He leaped up, and I had just a second to see his huge wolf body soaring over me, teeth flashing, drool flying. I dodged, quicker than any wolf should be able to, and ran to the side, making a circle to come back to where he was.

He ran as well, and we circled each other, planning our next attack.

If I wanted to win, I needed to get his neck to the ground and keep it there until I earned his submission.

Suddenly, he skidded to a halt and put his head in the air, making a high-pitched noise that made my eardrums scream in agony.

I howled and darted to the side, stopping to cover my ears with my paws.

What the fuck was that?

He used the opening to pounce on me, and I felt his jaws close around my scruff. I tried to shake him off, but my ears were still ringing from the sound.

"My alpha power," he growled against his closed teeth, which were painfully cutting into me. "I can use it again. Don't test me, Cleo."

I struggled, still disoriented. But this couldn't be the end of it.

I kicked at him with my back legs, but he still didn't let go, and then the sound started again. He could make it without even opening his mouth.

I screamed this time, feeling like my ears were bleeding, and Bran stopped the sound.

"Give up, Cleo. This is the strength of an alpha."

He's killing us. I'll do what I have to, my inner demon warned.

Then heat flooded me, overwhelming me as flames from somewhere within me burst out and covered my body, hissing and crackling against Bran's mouth.

He let out a shriek of pain and jumped back, then rolled on the ground to put out the fire burning his pelt and face.

He continued to shriek as the fire burned, but no amount of rolling would put it out.

"Hellfire," I heard Gabe say. "I thought so."

I had no idea what that meant.

Bran was still burning, the silver parts of his fur growing smaller as the blackened, burned, fire-edged parts spread. "Make it stop, Cleo. Just make it stop!"

My wolf was still covered in flames, and as I looked down at my paws, I could see that the fire wasn't damaging me in any way. I could make out the perfect dark outline of my claws beneath the flames.

I stepped forward, fire crackling over me.

Bran began to scream again, batting at the parts of him that were still burning.

"Do you submit?" I growled, furious for my friends who were still frozen. Furious at Bran for using cheap tricks like that howl. My ears were still ringing.

Furious at myself for letting alphas like him control my life for so long, when it turned out I never had to listen to them at all.

I thought back to all the times I'd been beaten and hurt, all the times I'd thought I couldn't fully fight them.

Bran let out a choked sob but shook his head, then glared at me furiously. Raw red skin was showing where the fur had burned through, but there was still spite in his eyes. "I'll never submit to a fucking omega."

I bit down on his neck, and the flames there did nothing to me since I was already covered with them.

"No," he growled, struggling weakly to get away from me. He made that sonic howl again, and I felt blood trickle from my ears but ignored it.

"Submit," I urged, the smell of his burning flesh tickling my sensitive wolf nose. I closed my teeth harder, breaking the thick skin of his neck, tasting the char of his flesh. "Now."

Bran let out a choked cry of pain. "This isn't possible," he grated out, struggling to get out of my hold even as new parts of him began to burn from contact with me. "No omega wolf can beat an alpha."

"I'm not an omega wolf," I growled against his skin, biting even harder, feeling blood gush into my mouth. "I'm an alpha demon."

"You'll have to kill me, for I will never submit," Bran rasped, beginning to grow weak. "I'd never lose... to a girl. To an omega... to a demon."

"Then you'll burn to death," I growled. But deep inside, I didn't know if it was a threat I could make good on.

I wanted to hurt him. I wanted him to submit to me. But kill him? I didn't even know how.

I shook him by the scruff, trying to convince him, but he went limp, having lost consciousness, either from the fire, the pain, or the bleeding. His neck was pumping blood into my mouth, but the wound was nothing he couldn't recover from with alpha healing.

I opened my jaws, letting him fall to the ground in a heap. The fire slowly went out.

I hated that I was slightly relieved to see he was still

breathing, the burnt fur on his chest rising and falling slowly.

I shifted back into my human form, covered in blood but at least dressed, and faced Gabe and Os, who were watching intently.

I stomped over the gravel and stepped over the wall to join them, leaning over to put my hands on my knees.

"I won, right? I mean, passing out has to count as submission."

Gabe stared at me with those cold eyes, and for a moment, I thought he might refuse, but he nodded. "It does."

"Great," I said, brushing my hands off. "Then I want to abolish the omega program. Os, can you do that? Just go back and tell them I want different rules. Pick some fair ones, from another haven, and..."

I trailed off as I saw Os shaking his head slowly, staring at me and then looking at the ground in shame.

Gabe began walking toward me, pulling something out of a sheath on his back. A longsword, gleaming and silver, with a blue hilt. "I'm afraid that won't be possible," he said.

"What?" I took a few steps back from him, putting up my hands, which were still bloody. "But Os said—"

"After I heard about what Samael did to save you, I told Os I needed to see you fight to tell whether or not you were the Morningstar." He frowned. "I should have suspected this sooner."

I looked at Os. "Traitor!"

Os's hands made fists at his sides. "You don't understand any of this, Cleo. Sam is trying to take down our entire world. If the Morningstar rises, the world as I know it will end. Everyone I love will die horribly, by murder, and—"

"That's a lie," I shouted. "Why would I kill everyone?"

"You don't understand anything," Os said. "That's why I kept asking Sam if you were the Morningstar. The whole reason we needed an executioner was to find you and end you before you could destroy our world. I like you, Cleo. But I can't let everyone I love die because of you." Pain flashed in his eyes. "I can't let demons take over the world."

"Who told you that would happen?" I asked. "Him?" I pointed at Gabe.

Os flushed but nodded. "Gabe has trained me almost my whole life, and I trust him implicitly. Cleo, our kind has feared your birth for many years. I swore an oath to protect my people as a celestial enforcer and have been doing so almost all my life. All I've done would be for nothing if you were allowed to go free and ruin everything."

"I'm not going to ruin anything!" I shouted. "*They* ruin everything." I jabbed a finger at Gabe again. "And they use fear to keep you in line!" I shook my head. "Even the demons don't think I'll murder everyone. They think I'll bring balance. Os, I don't want to kill anyone. I'm definitely not going to commit genocide."

Os looked stymied by that, but a glance at Gabe only had Gabe shaking his head in disgust.

"I'll kill you, Morningstar," he said as his wings flew out from his back, gleaming white under the gray sky. "I'll kill you and be the strongest angel the fifth realm has ever seen."

I swallowed, stepping back into a fighting stance and wishing I had a weapon as well.

"You said you would take her back to the haven and suppress her powers, not kill her," Os said, stepping forward. "I didn't agree to this."

"It isn't about you," Gabe said. "Or have you forgotten that?" He pointed a finger to the heavens. "We serve the elder gods, and this thing can kill them." His lip lifted in a sneer. "But not yet. She's not strong enough. We came just in time."

Os shook his head. "No. Just suppress her and let's get out of here. Killing her is wrong. She hasn't done anything bad yet."

"That's because demon powers take a while to truly

awaken," Gabe said. "The more she is alive to use them, the more powerful she will get. She already can use hellfire, something only a celestial with high-grade abyssal blood could do. We will get permanent dispensations from the ninth realm if we can do this."

Os shook his head, raising his hand. "No, Gabe. And I'm seventh realm. So if I say no, that's what goes. I told you I would help you prove it was her, and you said you would leave the others alone. Take her into custody, and we will have a trial in the celestial court."

"She's a demon," Gabe said, shaking his head. His sword gleamed as a ray of sun burst through the clouds for a moment, then disappeared again. "There will be no court." He stared at Os coldly. "Are you really going to fight me when I'm just trying to save our people?"

Os dropped his hand, looking confused.

"This guy is a piece of shit," I yelled, backing away from Gabe still. "He just wants some kind of reward for doing this. Come on, Os. Look at me. Do I look like I'm a demonic murderer? Like I deserve to be killed for what I may do one day? Think!"

"I think a lot of creatures have already been killed for you," Os said softly. "So I'm not sure what to do."

Os put a hand to his head, looking pained by the entire situation.

"Stop!" A loud, angry roar interrupted us just before

I heard bounding footsteps, and Griffin flew into the clearing in his lion form with his wings out.

Os looked over at him, shocked. "How did you—"

Griffin just roared, lunging forward and leaping into the air to land on Gabe, pinning him before he could get to me.

Griffin snarled in Gabe's face, but Gabe just stuck a hand up, grabbed Griffin by the neck, and tossed him to the side like so much garbage, despite his huge size.

Griffin landed in a puff of dust and pushed himself up to face Gabe again.

"I'm sorry," Os said to an irritated Gabe. "I don't know how he—"

"A ninth realm pet?" Gabe's eyes widened as he fully took Griffin in. He raised a hand, and out of nowhere, an iron cage formed in the air above Griffin. When Gabe lowered his hand, the cage dropped, locking Griffin in.

Griffin slammed against the bars, but nothing happened. Then he let out another roar.

Gabe walked closer, peering in. "Fae powers can't hold a creature like this very long. High immunity to almost everything." He smirked. "Except iron. That's what the ninth realm celestials keep them in when they aren't using them."

Os and I shared a baffled look as Gabe paced around the cage. He raised a hand, made a gesture at Griffin, and Griffin let out a cry and instantly shifted into his human form.

He backed up against his cage, looking at Gabe as if he were a monster. "How did you—"

"Force you?" Gabe laughed. "Any celestial can decide what form you're in at any time, pet."

I grimaced at hearing the word from Gabe's mouth.

"So what, he's like a guard dog?" I yelled, trying to distract Gabe and bring his attention back to me.

"They do detect certain demons, yes," Gabe said, crouching by the cage to study Griffin. "But there are other uses." As he studied Griffin this time, his gaze was lascivious. "This one is especially beautiful. I think I'll keep him for myself since, after I kill the Morningstar, I'll be ascending to the ninth celestial realm anyway."

Os's mouth fell open. "You can't just *keep* him. He's..."

Gabe stood, snapping his attention to Os. "He's what? A glorified sex slave and guard dog in one convenient package? An extra blessing from the gods for being obedient? Whatever he is, I'm taking him." His lip curled up in a mean sneer. "Or did you want him for yourself?"

Os took a step back, looking shaken. "I didn't agree to any of this. You told me to draw out the Morningstar and get her to fight Bran, to prove what she was. You didn't tell me anything about kidnapping. No one is supposed to get hurt!"

Gabe straightened. "That's your fault for staying to comfort your fae half brother instead of coming to the mission briefing with me and the higher celestials. I simply chose to give you whatever information would make you help me."

"No," Os said. "I won't let you do this. You can't take Cleo or Griffin either. This is wrong."

"She's the Morningstar," Gabe said. "The demon you have feared all your life. And he is just a stupid animal who was made to be used."

Os shook his head, resolute. "No. Something is wrong about this. It isn't by the rules."

"This mission is straight from the ninth celestial realm," Gabe said. "You think they care about rules? They make the rules." He raised his head haughtily. "And when this is over, they'll make me more powerful than I could have ever hoped."

"That's what this is to you, isn't it?" Os asked. "It's not about saving the world or helping anyone. Just your stupid ego."

Gabe just stared at him. "I can't believe you'd go against me after all I've done." He let out an aggrieved sigh and walked over to where Bran was lying.

Before any of us could do anything, Gabe raised his

sword and sliced it down, cutting off Bran's wolf head in one smooth stroke.

As it rolled to the side, blood spurting, something emanated from Bran's body, a golden mist rising into the air.

Gabe stood over him, breathing in deeply, putting his arms out to the side as he did, still holding his sword in one hand.

He appeared to glow for a moment, then turned to face us, breathing heavily.

"The celestials gave Bran a fourth realm dispensation, which I have now absorbed," Gabe said. "I naturally have a fifth realm dispensation. That puts me at a ninth celestial realm level of power. So you can't stop me, Os."

Os lifted his chin. "I'm going to try."

Gabe strutted over to stand in front of Os confidently. "I'll put you back in your place after this. I'll claim that pet in front of your face, since it means that much to you."

Os let out an angry shriek and threw his hand forward, letting out a blast of ice that hit Gabe and split into millions of icy shards that flew in every direction.

Gabe stood there, unaffected. "Was that it?"

Os threw another icy blast at him, but Gabe seemed immune to it, no matter how many Os threw.

As Os attacked, Gabe simply walked toward him. Then, as Os stepped back, looking down at his hands in shock, Gabe shot his fist forward, punching Os right in the face.

"No!" Griffin yelled, grabbing the bars of his cage and shaking them. "Cleo, what is going on?"

I looked at Gabe, wondering how to answer. Then I glanced at Os, who was lying on the cement, still.

"Why would you do that?" I asked. "He trusted you."

"Until he didn't," Gabe said. "Unlike him, I see the higher purpose in all of this." He brandished his sword again. "Fight me, Morningstar, if you can."

Then his wings withdrew, and before my eyes, he multiplied into eight versions of himself, curving around me in an intimidating semicircle.

An illusion, but one I couldn't see through at all.

Each version brandished a sword, and I had no idea which one I should strike. Panic was making my heart pound like a tarantella.

All eight angels pointed their swords at me, armor gleaming, white tunics whipping in the cool wind.

All eight versions of Gabe grinned. "Your move, demon."

47

I had no idea what to do, what version of Gabe to fight.

These had to be illusions, so seven of them were probably not him. But how I was going to keep track of that once he started moving eluded me.

For another moment, I wished Sam was here because he would know what to do about it.

But no, he trusted me. I would have to trust myself too.

I focused, feeling heat warm me from the inside out, growing and growing from the force of my anger. For what Gabe had done to my friends, for what he had tried to do to me, for what he was going to do to Griffin.

Fire exploded over my skin, covering my body but not burning me at all, like the day of the stoning.

The fire felt like a part of me, like my energy burning outside of my skin. I put out a hand and studied it, watching the flames lick out and around my fingers.

"It'll take more than hellfire to kill me, amateur," Gabe sneered. "I've been fighting demons since long before you were alive." All eight versions of him moved in a circle around me. "But go ahead."

I threw my hands out, focusing on throwing my energy toward him, wanting my fire to hurt. To my shock, two screaming balls of red and orange fire shot at and engulfed two of his illusions, and they burned up in a puff of smoke.

I moved to send more fireballs to two more illusions, but before I could, I felt something sharp in my back, then a sudden wetness.

When I looked down, I saw the tip of Gabe's sword poking through my chest.

I let out a choking gasp and fell forward, and he yanked his sword out of me as I dropped.

My blood pulsed out beneath me in a puddle, and the remaining illusions disappeared, revealing only Gabe walking out from behind me with his bloody sword over his shoulder, flat side down. He didn't seem to care that it was dripping on his perfect white tunic and over his armor.

I tried to push myself up, put a hand over the gushing wound on my chest, but I couldn't even think straight. I felt like I was going into shock.

Dead. I'm dead, right? I thought.

Gabe laughed. "That was easy. How could Samael leave after not even training you well?"

"You bastard," I grated out, trying to stand up again. "You fucking fuck."

Gabe raised an eyebrow as I fought to stand again. "Such language. Befitting a stupid demon like yourself." He knelt and caught me by the chin, forcing me to face him even as I could feel blood pumping out of my chest. "This is the end for you, Morningstar. Just accept it."

But just when I felt I would faint, I felt something knitting together inside me. I felt my heart pull together and begin to beat, the feeling echoing in my chest. I felt my skin close together painfully, the slash in my shirt and the blood all over the ground the only signs that I'd ever been hurt.

He can't kill us, my inner demon said. *Not like that.*

Believing in her, I forced myself to stand, though I felt shaky. I'd never been good around blood.

But she was right. I was strong. She'd been right about not having to obey alpha powers, so she was probably right about this.

Gabe jumped back from me as he stood, and his illusions spread out from him again, almost blurring my vision as I tried to keep track of where he was.

My eyes darted between the different versions of him, trying to make out any difference.

I needed to attack the right one.

The wind blew, and I noticed no difference between them. Each had blood on his tunic, each held his sword to the side, and each looked at me with cold eyes as they waited for me to discern which was real.

I couldn't afford to attack the wrong ones again. I didn't know how many times I could heal from a fatal attack.

One version of Gabe shot out to attack me from the front, swinging his sword. This time, I anticipated an attack from behind and jumped, using my strength to go above the two figures who met in the middle, impaling each other on their swords.

One dissolved in a puff of smoke, revealing Gabe had attacked from the front this time. I landed, shoved my booted foot into his gut, and kicked him back as hard as I could.

He went flying back but managed to stay on his feet. But I was there in an instant, this time swinging my leg high in a perfect roundhouse kick to his face. My technique mixed with my demon speed combined to hit him in the head with a cracking noise that echoed in the empty courtyard.

He stumbled back, holding his head, where his hair was on fire thanks to its contact with my flaming leg. Flames still licked over my entire body, and there was fire where I'd hit him with my boot too.

The other illusions disappeared, and Gabe reached into his tunic and pulled out a small bottle of water. He opened it, muttered something, and dumped it over himself.

Instantly, my fires burning on him went out. He glared at me—his outfit muddy from burns and my own blood, his head sporting a nasty bruise and some missing hair—and just smiled.

A nasty smile that creeped me out down to my toenails.

"You won't kill me, will you?" He smirked, extending a hand as his illusions spread out again, blurring which one was him. "You don't even have your sword."

"What are you talking about?"

He cracked his head to the side, and I noticed his hair regrowing, the bruise already beginning to disappear. "I'm a god, Cleo. You aren't going to kill me with fire or by kicking me."

"Then how?"

"Like I would tell you that!" Then his illusions closed in on me, and while I couldn't make out who was who, I felt something punch me hard, in the back of the head. Everything went black for a moment, and I pitched forward onto my hands and knees.

My entire head was ringing with pain, but I felt Gabe behind me, ready to thrust his sword, and forced myself to move out of the way.

As I rolled, his sword stabbed into the pavement, cutting into actual stone.

Holy shit.

I stumbled to my feet, feeling the flames on my skin rise as the healing inside me took effect once again, this time healing my brain.

Gabe moved back into his illusions, and they circled and moved around and through each other, utterly confusing me.

Come on, Cleo. There has to be a way to do this.

Then I realized. I didn't just have my inner demon. I had something else, something I'd been born with.

My wolf.

Backing up from Gabe, keeping my eyes on his illusions, I took in a slow breath, trying not to make it obvious that I was scenting the air.

I assumed the illusions were only visual, not olfactory, so I closed my eyes just for a second to focus on Gabe's smell. Smoky. Bloody. But also... spice. Pine.

My eyes opened, and I focused on the clone on the far right, aiming a fireball at it so fast it didn't have time to move.

It erupted in flames, and the other clones disappeared. The holy water quickly doused the fires, but it had proven my point, and I launched toward Gabe, throwing my fist out in the hardest punch of my life, aimed straight at his nose.

His face caved in with a crunching sound, and he flew backward, rolling over the ground, covering his already tattered clothing with dust.

Still, he pushed himself up, his face quickly rearranging itself back into place, nose pushing back out to where it was, albeit somewhat crookedly.

He reached up and shoved it into place, his brown eyes flashing at me. "We finish this now, demon."

He raised his sword and ran at me, no longer using clones, and, with his speed, reached me in a millisecond.

I dodged to the right, missing his sword, and managed to use my speed as he continued to swipe at me, but without my fire doing anything to him and without a sword and knowing he could heal any injury I gave... what could I even do?

I continued to dodge until I felt tired. On one long swing, I spun around, missing his sword, and managed to whirl and hit his face with a spinning hook from my back leg.

It made him stumble, but he was back immediately, slashing at me with his sword.

I sent more fire at him, but it was quickly extinguished by his still-soaked tunic and didn't even slow him as he attacked.

I sent fireball after fireball as I dodged. Finally, I found an opening and kicked in his knee as hard as I could from a vulnerable angle. He went down, and I grabbed his sword from him, swinging it over my head to bring it down on him.

He was on one knee, glaring up at me, one hand above his head, and I swung the blade down at him.

But it was as if time slowed as the blade moved toward him. Was this going to kill him? Was this the end?

Could I stand that?

And in that moment of weakness, he punched me in the stomach so hard the air was knocked out of me, grabbed his sword back, and shoved it through my neck.

I gurgled as he pulled it out again, unbearable pain echoing in me as blood spurted out of me once again.

This isn't over, my inner demon said.

I felt my healing take over, my skin and internal parts quickly pulling together again. But I was tired, and what's more, I didn't know how much fight I had left. Or how to kill him.

Gabe pushed to his feet, holding his sword over me. "Idiot demon. I can feel you holding back. You don't truly want to kill me. I do want to kill you. That's what will decide this fight. Your indecision makes you *weak*."

He stabbed the sword down at me, but I rolled, missing what probably would have been a finishing blow. I kicked upward, knocking the sword out of his hand.

We both lunged for it, but he got there first, and I could still feel something in my heart that had almost let him.

Because I didn't truly know what I'd do when I got the sword.

How I'd feel if I killed him.

There had to be another way out of this. But as I looked into his cold eyes as we circled, still holding the sword, I wasn't sure.

My fists tightened, and I tried to ignore the pain in my chest and neck as Gabe and I circled, his sword ominously reflecting the clouded sunlight.

He was breathing heavily, so clearly, the fight had taken a toll on him as well.

I glanced at Griffin, wondering just what it would take to save him, and Gabe took advantage of that split second of inattention to slide his sword right into my thigh, making me cry out and lose the ability to stay up on my leg.

I felt magic surging from his sword, suppressing my healing, and then he yanked it out, making me nearly scream in pain, though I wouldn't give him the satisfaction.

He circled me as I struggled to push myself up, hoping my leg would heal faster. But perhaps fighting a celestial like this took a lot out of me, or perhaps his sword was special, because I was finding it harder to heal as this went on.

My skin was weakly, slowly knitting together, but I had lost so much blood, and it was hard to think for all the pain.

Looking up at Gabe as he walked closer, triumph in his eyes, his sword raised for the final blow, I felt utter despair run through me.

I'm sorry, Sam. I couldn't do it. You believed in me for nothing. I'm not a killer. I'm just not.

Don't give up, my inner demon roared, and I struggled to stand again.

Gabe raised an eyebrow, almost amused by me. "I'll give you credit. With the killing power in this sword, you should have succumbed to the first blow. Your power to survive is truly something, Morningstar. It's too bad you can't be allowed to live and see your powers awakened to their full extent. But I'll behead you now, and even you can't survive that."

He put a boot to my face and pushed me back onto the ground on my back. Holy fuck, he was still so strong.

"This is the power of the ninth realm," he said, glowering over me. "Now die, demon."

The sword swung down to my face, and I reached up to grab the blade, not caring as it cut through my fingers to the bone.

I have to live. I have to live.

I pushed as hard as I could, but the blade moved closer, closer.

The pain grew unbearable, and I realized as the blade came within inches of my face that this was it.

I was going to die.

I struggled, but it was pointless.

I'm sorry, Simon. I'm sorry, Mor. I'm sorry, Griffin.

I sucked in a breath, still trying to push the blade back as it lowered to my neck and began to cut.

"I'm sorry, Sam," I murmured, as if he could hear. "I just can't do it."

"He's not here, you idiot," Gabe said. "Too bad. I would have liked for him to see you die."

A whistling sound interrupted us, and I looked up to see something speeding down out of the sky.

Something with black wings.

Sam, I realized as my heart leaped with joy.

But then I felt the blade cut farther into my skin and realized he was probably too late.

48

To my shock, the blade against my neck paused as Gabe looked up, now aware of the whistling noise and the blur of black flying at us.

It was coming toward us at almost supersonic speed, and when Sam landed, a huge explosion of dust and broken cement flew up under his feet, hiding him from sight for a few seconds.

When he walked out of the dust, wearing his black slayer outfit with the chains over his chest, he had both swords out and wore an expression that was more furious than I'd ever seen.

"You fucking bastard!" Sam spat at Gabe. "You coward. You waited for the moment I left, didn't you?"

"Just a lucky coincidence." Gabe stood, pulling his sword away from my neck. "Actually, I'm glad you're back. You can die too, for betraying us. When you're bleeding to death, you can watch me kill her." Gabe pointed a finger at me. "Stay there."

I crawled backward, looking up at Sam as pain still radiated through me, blood still leaking from my leg, which was struggling to heal.

"You okay, Cleo?" Sam asked, keeping his eyes, and swords, trained on Gabe as Gabe walked forward to fight him.

"Yes," I rasped in a hiss. I could feel my healing taking over, my strength slowly returning, the demon in me cheered by him coming to my side.

Something in us was definitely connected because just seeing him made my heart feel stronger, made the fire inside me surge again, licking over my skin.

"You did amazing," Sam said. "I'm sorry I wasn't here sooner. I felt you through our bond."

"Bond?" I asked, dazed.

"I'll tell you more later," he said, stepping back into a fighting stance. "I just have to take out some garbage."

I lay back, trying to gather strength so I could push myself up to watch.

Two celestials with ninth realm power fighting was definitely something I wanted to see.

"Cleo!" Griffin shouted. "Cleo! Don't die!"

"I won't die," I called back, waving a hand faintly.

"So," Sam said, slowly circling with Gabe as I looked over at him. "You've gotten an upgrade." He scented the air, then looked over at Bran's body lying in the wreckage of the skeletal ruins. "Ah, I see. You took his dispensation."

"And if I kill both of you, it'll be permanent," Gabe said, grinning.

"So celestial," Sam said with a sneer. "You'll do anything for power."

"Wouldn't you?" Gabe asked.

Sam slid a look at me. "Not for power. But I would do anything for her." Then Sam leaped forward, aiming a diagonal slice across Gabe's body with his black katana.

Gabe's sword countered the blow, and he pushed Sam back with a hard parry. "Your slayer swords can't beat me," Gabe said. "I've even seen that one before." Using his free hand, he pointed at Sam's red sword. "Let me guess. Cayne was your brother?" Gabe looked up at the cathedral. "Of course. How did I not see it sooner?"

Sam was silent, pacing with both swords at his sides. But I could tell Gabe's words had affected him.

"I saw him fight," Gabe said haughtily. "I expected more from the renowned slayer. No wonder he died like a dog."

"Keep your lying mouth shut about my brother!"

Sam let out a war cry and leaped at Gabe, striking at him with both swords in a flurry of blows.

Gabe parried the red sword, but the black katana caught him in the shoulder, cutting deep and sending blood out in a spray. Then Sam yanked his sword out, dodged to the side, and lunged in again, attacking once more with both swords.

Gabe tried to strike but was much slower, and Sam moved easily out of the way of his heavy sword.

Spinning around Gabe's back, Sam slammed his red blade into Gabe's side, then jerked it out again, sending blood arcing into the air and splashing on the pavement.

Gabe snarled, looking at the two bleeding holes in his body, and sent his hand out. A blast of light burst out of it and hit Sam with a flash, sending him rolling back into the road.

Sam was back on his feet in a moment, leaping through the air with both swords, yelling a feral cry.

His eyes were practically glowing, his hair taking on a red tint, as he continued to strike at Gabe, who had used Sam's momentary stumble to pull out a smaller sword to dual wield and parry Sam.

Metal struck metal, making screeches and bell-like sounds as the men fought, striking with both blades, whirling, parrying, dodging back and forth.

It was so fast I could barely catch it. And unlike

when Sam had fought Zadis, Gabe didn't seem to be tiring.

"You can't kill me with that slayer sword," Gabe said. "I have ninth celestial realm power. Only an Evernight sword can kill me, and you don't have one."

Sam just roared and swung one katana to distract Gabe while he spun and swung the other into Gabe's calf, cutting deep into the muscle as blood poured around the blade.

Gabe howled and fell to one knee, grabbing at his torn flesh as Sam yanked his sword back.

He spun toward Gabe again, slamming his sword deep into Gabe's back as he bent forward. Gabe let out a scream and turned to punch Sam, but Sam dodged back, then came forward with his red sword and cut Gabe's right ear clean off.

Gabe stared down at it, bleeding from multiple places. "What are you doing?"

Sam's face was dark with fury. "If I can't kill you, then I'll just have to cut you to pieces, bury you where no one can find you, and get an Evernight sword to finish you off!"

Sam swung his red katana toward Gabe's neck in a powerful, deft move I was sure would take his head off.

"Do you know how Cayne died?" Gabe spat just as the sword stopped right at his neck.

Sam froze, looking tempted but unwilling to be distracted. "It doesn't matter. I wouldn't believe what you say anyway."

"You sure about that? You know it happened after he came to work with us." Gabe looked over at Sam, ignoring Sam's sword still at his throat. "I don't know how I didn't see the resemblance when you signed up. You don't look at all the same, you know."

Sam's hand was trembling slightly, I realized. His face was neutral, his composure solid, but I could tell from the slight twist of his mouth and the sweat on his forehead that he was in pain. His gaze darted toward me, and then he looked resolutely back at Gabe. "It. Doesn't. Matter."

"Do you even know if he died to an Evernight sword?" Gabe asked, and as Sam froze again, more versions of Gabe appeared and he stood, shoving Sam's sword back.

Sam looked unlike I'd ever seen him. Frozen, staring at Gabe, his sword swinging down to his side.

"It must torture you," Gabe said. "Not knowing if Cayne's waiting somewhere in hell... or just gone."

Sam sucked in a breath. "You shut up about him. You don't deserve to speak his name."

Gabe laughed. "He was a demon. A slayer. He tried to fuck around and trick celestials, and he got what he deserved. He was hired to take out the Morningstar, but in truth, he was trying to find and protect it. We couldn't have that."

Sam was quiet but got into a fighting stance again, even as eight versions of Gabe moved around him.

My heart raced in panic because it was hard to see through illusions normally, and I could tell Sam was emotionally flooded.

Who wouldn't be?

Suddenly, I hated Gabe more than I'd ever hated another person. He was the cause of Sam's pain.

He was the cause of all of this.

And he was causing more pain now as he continued to torture Sam with details of his brother's death.

"I hear he screamed and begged for mercy," Gabe said. "Imagine the pain such a powerful demon could have felt to be losing it like that."

"You're lying!" Sam said, hand still shaking, as Gabe's clone illusions spread out in a semicircle in front of him.

"Don't you want to know what it was like?" Gabe asked. "Well, it won't matter if I tell you because I can kill you, even though you can't kill me. See, you're half demon, and sending you to hell won't be a problem now that I have ninth realm power."

Sam sneered. "I don't believe anything you say about my brother, you piece of shit. I'm here for Cleo, and I'll fight until I die to see her safe. For Cayne. For myself. For the whole demon world." He got into a fighting stance and appraised the illusions. Then he gestured for Gabe to attack.

As the clones moved forward, Sam jumped to slash at one, cutting straight through it so it disappeared in a puff of smoke and then straight through another.

He dodged one's attack, nearly missing Gabe's sword, and destroyed another illusion, but another appeared nearby.

I could tell he was getting harried, that hearing about his brother had taken more out of him than he expected.

I could see the weariness and confusion on his face.

He'd fought so much for me. To get me here. To bring me to my purpose.

And what could I do for him?

I tried to push myself up, but my leg, though healing, felt weak, and my body felt drained of energy.

Sam destroyed a few more clones, and they disappeared in puffs of smoke, leaving only Gabe standing across from him. The two men faced each other, swords in hand, breathing heavily in the wreckage.

"You truly don't care how he died?" Gabe gasped out.

Sam froze. "I know it wasn't you who killed him. It

must have been someone from the ninth realm. No one lower could have bested Cayne."

"You think a lot of him, for a demon," Gabe said. "But you're wrong, and..."

I zoned out to what he was saying because my eyes caught something moving in the air behind Sam. Like the air was shimmering as something was moving closer to him.

I scented the air and quickly realized what was happening. It might have looked like Gabe was facing Sam, but it was only an illusion to disguise what he was really doing.

From his scent, I could track that Gabe was invisible but right behind Sam, sneaking up on him. To kill him.

Heat instantly filled me. The thought of something happening to Sam made energy erupt from my every cell. From the center of my heart, I was burning, hotter than ever before. I got up on both knees, looking straight up at the sky as I felt something hot building in my chest and something hard and solid rising out of me.

Like something was being forged in my heart and now was forcing itself out.

I tried not to gasp, but I had no idea what was happening. As I looked down, I realized there was fire in my chest and a sword was appearing straight out of my body.

I stared at the handle as it floated in front of my face, the rest of the sword still inside.

Take it, my inner demon urged. T*ake it and finish this. Take it and claim your destiny.*

I grabbed the hilt and then drew it out of my chest, marveling at the fact that it didn't hurt.

The sword was huge, like a longsword, but felt light in my hand. I didn't even have time to look at it because Gabe and Sam had turned my way.

Desperately praying to hit my target, I raised the sword like a javelin and threw it as hard as I could at the shimmering space behind Sam.

It flew straight and true, and I heard the sickening wet, grating sound of a sword going through someone's chest.

The next second, Gabe appeared around the sword, standing behind Sam, staggering and looking down at my blade in his chest.

His illusion quickly dissipated into smoke.

Gabe let out a gasp of pure shock, and his swords fell to the ground with a clang.

Sam whipped around to face him, then looked at me.

As Gabe stumbled back, I got a moment to study my sword at a distance. The blade was black and inlaid with swirling red runes. At uneven intervals, white shimmers of lightning moved over the blade.

Gabe stared at it, trying to move it, but his face was turning gray before our eyes.

He was dying, and I couldn't bring myself to feel sad about it.

Not when I'd done what I had to in order to save Sam.

Sam looked at me, shock making his eyes wide and wild.

Gabe fell onto his back, holding the sword and staring vacantly at the sky. "An Evernight sword." He looked over at Sam. "Your brother wasn't killed with one. We don't even have access to one, but the Morningstar does. Who knew?"

Then his eyes rolled back, and everything went still, and with one last gurgling moan, he died.

49

Sam and I stared at each other for a moment, and then relief washed through me, cutting through the agony like light streaming after a hurricane.

I ran into Sam's arms, shocking him, and buried my face against his chest.

I couldn't help it. My inner demon was just too glad to see him again.

Slowly, he put his arms down around me, looking awkward about it. He brushed back a lock of my hair, looking down into my face as if to see if I was okay.

"Hello? Can someone get me out of here?" Griffin yelled.

"Ugh," Os said, slowly pushing to a sitting position, holding his head. "What just happened?"

"I ought to kill you!" Sam snarled, turning on Os and

picking up his swords, which seemed to have fallen to the ground in the shock of him seeing Gabe die by my hand.

I grabbed Sam around the waist, stopping him. "He was brainwashed. I promise. He tried to fight Gabe at the end, when he realized he was evil."

"She was your friend!" Sam yelled, still trying to get to Os. "How could you do this?"

Realizing I wasn't going to let him fight Os, Sam turned away and pulled out of my arms, running his hands through his hair as he looked up at the sky. He let out an exhausted sigh, then turned back to face me. "I'm sorry, Cleo. I never should have left." He looked around. "Where is Simon?" His face went ghostly pale. "Oh gods, are he and Mor okay?"

He spun and looked toward the back of the property.

"They're fine," Os said, pushing to his feet. "I'll free them."

"You imprisoned them?"

"Just my ice spell," Os said. "No one will be hurt from it."

"Cleo could have been hurt! Cleo could have been gone!" Sam's eyes were wild. "I should kill you just for what could have happened."

"I'm sorry," Os said, coming forward and taking a knee and bowing before us, looking unsteady and holding his head. "I just... I thought she would destroy everything. When Gabe decided to take Griffin, I realized everything was a lie, but it was too late. But it's hard to go against what you were taught as a child." Os's purple eyes were pleading. "I swear, Sam. I didn't know he wanted to hurt her, though. I didn't. I always feared and hated the Morningstar, but before we came here, I negotiated Cleo's safety because I didn't want her to be harmed. Gabe agreed."

Sam raised his sword in the air.

Os simply bowed his head. "You would have every right. This is my fault."

"I thought you would protect this place, not harm it. Fairies are Simon's only weakness, and I never thought a fae other than you would dare set foot here."

"You should have known that if I knew the Morningstar was here, I would come, if only to protect my family," Os said quietly. "Now do what you must."

Sam let out a hoarse curse, pausing with his black sword in the air over Os's neck as if he didn't know what to do.

"I swear, if you let me live, I will change," Os said. "I will serve the Morningstar to the end of my days. I will... try to make up for this."

"Why? Don't you still hate her? Don't you think she would destroy the world?" Sam asked.

Os shook his head. "I don't hate her. I never did. I truly thought she would only be suppressed."

"That's naive as hell, and I don't believe you," Sam spat.

"It's the truth," Os said. "I even attacked my mentor. The one who took me from the fae and trained me in celestial ways. That should mean something. Over the years, I've stopped many executions, and Gabe has been merciful. I thought this would be the same, though I did know we would need to take Cleo back to her realm. For that, I am sorry."

I could see in his eyes that he was.

"He's right!" Griffin yelled at us, holding the bars of his cage. "He saved me when I was younger! Give him a chance."

"He almost got you assaulted," Sam grated out. "And you're going to defend him?"

Griffin slumped against the cage. "I no longer admire him, but I don't think he should die. And if he's truly on our side, he can help Cleo with his powers."

Sam stared down at Os, who was looking at Griffin in shock and then remembrance.

And then regret as he realized what he'd lost. The respect of a child he'd once saved.

Griffin no longer looked at him with shining eyes, though he was still trying to save him.

I walked over to Griffin's cage. "How do I get him out?"

Sam snapped his fingers, and the cage disappeared, and Griffin fell forward.

I ran to him and caught him in a hug. When he pulled back, his blue eyes were shining.

"Thank you for trying to save me," I said. "It must have been hard breaking out of the ice."

He rubbed the back of his neck. "I'd die for you, Cleo." He shook his head and smiled ruefully. "And I saw how hard you would fight for me."

I smiled back. "We're square."

I turned back to look at Sam, who strode away from Os to approach Gabe's body.

My sword was still sticking out of it, and he went to grab the handle but let out a hiss of pain as his hand made a sizzling sound.

"Only Cleo will be able to hold that sword," Os said. "I've seen only one before, and it was bound to its creator. All Evernight swords are."

Sam stepped back. "Interesting." He set about picking up his swords and cleaning and sheathing them and then watched as I walked over to Gabe.

To get my sword.

My sword.

I blinked, then reached for the black hilt. It was cool

and soothing to the touch. As I pulled it out, Gabe's body dissolved into a dark puddle and then evaporated into the air, leaving only a vague outline on the cement where he'd lain.

"I can't believe you killed him," Os said, looking over my shoulder.

I whirled to face him, shoving him back. "I don't trust you yet."

Sam looked ready to boot him, but Os jumped back, his purple angel wings flying out to carry him back.

"Go free my friends," Sam said. "Then you can spend some time in the dungeon, thinking about what you've done."

"You have a dungeon?" Griffin said, walking with us as we headed around the side of the cathedral and through the graveyard to help our friends.

I winced as I saw Mor and Simon frozen in giant blocks of ice with a layer between them and the ice, their chests moving shallowly.

Os raised his hand, made a fist, and twisted it, and the ice broke apart.

Simon fell out, then Mor, and Simon's huge iridescent-black bat wings shot out, and he flew straight at Os like a homing missile, knocking him back and into the cement wall to his side.

Os slumped down against it, and Griffin walked over to pick him up and put him over his shoulder.

I looked over at him. "Be careful, Griffin."

"It's not that I trust him. I'm still furious with him for what he did," Griffin said, standing tall and looking remarkably okay for everything that had happened. "It's just that both you and I got a second chance, and I think he deserves one."

Sam still looked ready to swallow his own teeth in rage.

Simon looked between us, breaths heaving. "Is everyone okay, then?"

I nodded.

Mor heaved a breath, leaning on her knees. "That was terrifying. Not knowing if you were hurt, not being able to help."

I dropped my sword and ran over to hug her too, glad to see she was all right. She held me tight, and then Simon came in, and Griffin watched with fond eyes, still holding Os.

Sam watched us like we were doing something disgusting. "Okay, okay, that's enough," he said, coming to break us up. "I have to talk to Cleo."

Simon looked at my sword where it lay on the ground. "Is that an Evernight sword?" He walked over to it. "Great hell, what is it?"

I picked it up. "I don't know. It just came out of me."

Simon cocked his head. "Interesting. So it's forged like a slayer sword."

"What do you mean?" I asked, looking at Sam, who just shrugged, motioning for me to listen to Simon.

"According to what Cayne told me, a slayer sword is forged in the heart of a demon when they have their first true desire to kill to protect. It's forged from the will to kill," Simon said.

I blinked, looking back at Sam. "Did you know this?"

Sam nodded. "I knew you weren't ready to kill yet. Telling you would have only put more pressure on you."

I sighed. "You're probably right."

Sam folded his arms, and a light flush colored his perfect cheekbones. "I never thought your sword would come out because of me." He turned away, as if too embarrassed to face us. "Who would forge their sword for a murdering demon?"

I met his eyes, wishing he could see that he was so much more to me than that.

"I'm taking Os inside," Griffin said.

"I'll show you to the dungeon," Simon said, looking more pissed than I'd ever seen him. He wasn't easily ruffled, but right now, he still looked ready to raise hell. He looked at Sam. "I'm sorry I couldn't protect her like I promised."

"It's okay," Sam said, turning back to face me. "I should have stayed by her side. I realized it almost as soon as I had gone." His eyes were hollow as they met mine. "I thought you would be better off with some space from me. If I'd known you would suffer, I wouldn't have left, even for a day."

Mor signaled to Griffin and Simon to leave, putting a finger over her mouth as they gave us privacy and went back inside.

The wind whistled by us, and I felt utterly exhausted, like my legs were ready to give out.

After all, I'd fought Bran, I'd fought Gabe, and then I'd forged a sword and killed for the first time.

A girl had a right to be tired.

I looked down at the sword, then at Sam. "What do I do with this?"

Sam pulled a couple black cloths out of his pocket and walked over to grab my sword with them, shielding his hands. He walked over to Betty's shack and set my sword against it. "Betty will need to make you a proper sheath."

"Should we warn her?" I asked.

He shook his head. "She'll know what it is the moment she sees it."

Sam then came over to me, sweeping his arm under my legs to lift me into his arms, but instead of heading back to the cathedral, he looked around to make sure no one was watching and then walked toward the outer corner of the courtyard.

Toward a large grave with a statue of a mourning angel overhead.

When he stood in front of it, he raised his hand, and to my shock, it moved, making a grinding noise of stone against stone as it revealed an opening with stairs that led down.

"A crypt?" I asked.

"Did you read my letter?" Sam asked.

I shook my head. "I'm sorry. I couldn't. It would have made it real that you were gone."

"I'm a killer," he said. "I'm not a bodyguard. I'm not a saint. All I'm good at is murdering things that need to die without feeling bad about it. I could never deserve you, with your kind heart. I thought it would be better to take even a day away from you, to see if it could break this bond."

"Bond?"

Sam started down the stairs, carrying me into the dark. He murmured something, and torches lit the stairway, revealing we were heading down to a large, open room.

"That's what pissed me off about Zadis and the other fae, talking about bonds. Demons are the ones who bond. The deeper our bonds are, the more we feel what our bonded ones are feeling. When I felt myself bonding to you, I thought I was overstepping."

"Why?"

He paused on the steps, still holding me. "Because you're the brightest star I've ever met, and my whole life has only been darkness."

I put my hand up to his cheek, unsure of what to say.

He stared at me for a moment, eyes softening, and then continued to carry me down the stairs.

When he walked out of the stairwell and into the main room, I was too surprised to speak.

It was a beautiful study with a large leather couch, and where there should have been shelves to hold coffins, there were instead rows and rows of books.

"My book crypt," he said. "I left you the instructions to get here and use this place in my letter. When I saw you liked to read, I always knew I wanted to show you this place."

He walked over and set me on the couch, then moved over to one of the shelves and took out a book. "You might like this one. It's a romance." He tossed it to me, and I caught it.

I stared down at it, dazed, looking at the couple on the front, embracing on the front of a pirate ship.

I smiled. "Where did you get all of these?"

He shrugged. "I spent a lot of time in a human library when I was ejected from the demon realm for having wings. I would stay there when Cayne was fighting, until he built this place for us."

"I love it," I said. "I can't wait to read them."

"There's a reason I brought you here," he said. "I want to share things with you, Cleo. Things I've always wanted to keep others away from. I want to be with you and protect you. I want to kill for you and die for you if that's what's needed."

He moved around the back of the couch and leaned over me, nuzzling into the back of my neck. "I hate being away from you. I thought bonds were impossible for me, but I think what's truly impossible is breaking this bond I have with you."

I looked up at him, putting my hands up to ruffle his hair. "It's okay. I'm just glad you came back for me." I patted the couch, and he walked around it to sit down next to me. "I... couldn't have done it without you."

He was close, so big and so heated, and looming over me, staring at me like I was something he didn't understand. "I still can't believe your sword emerged because of me."

"Why would that be a surprise?"

His eyes were haunted. "You don't understand, Cleo. I've never gotten along with anyone, even when I was younger. Killing always suited me. I assumed that even when I took up the hunt for the Morningstar, only out of guilt for my brother, that I would have little contact with the Morningstar and then move on." He clasped his hands together. "I never expected the Morningstar to be *you*."

"Me?"

"You got under my skin," he said. "You never judged me. I think I would have done everything I did for you even if you weren't the Morningstar."

"Ah."

"When I thought of you as the most powerful weapon, I thought, why would she need a piece of trash like me hanging around? I'm not even the kind of slayer Cayne was. A legend. I just like killing because it makes the pain disappear, both inside myself and in preventing pain to others."

"And I've admired that about you since you killed Zane in that prison."

Sam's eyes flashed angrily. "My only regret there was not acting sooner. I truly thought you would stop him. That it would be the moment you woke up. I hadn't realized until that moment how much you'd been taught not to fight for yourself." He sighed. "I would have taken you from that place either way, just like I took Griffin."

"I know," I said, taking his hands in mine. They were cold, and I wanted to make them warm.

I wanted to make everything about this man warm.

But I knew it would take time.

But he had come back. That was what mattered. We had fought for each other and been stronger by each other's side.

"We should go inside, take a shower," I said. "I'm practically doused in blood."

"I know," he said. "But when we go in, I'll have to share you. Griffin will want to make sure you're okay. Mor will want to know how the fight went. Simon will want to hear about your sword." He brushed my hair back gently, and I could have gotten lost in the soft look in his eyes. "Right now, I don't want to share you. I was so afraid I would be too late. You mean everything to me now, Cleo."

He leaned in, and my lips parted, and his lips closed over mine.

Heat surged through me, feeling like it was healing me from everything that had happened.

The agony of my wounds had already faded, but the tiredness left in their wake was receding as Sam deepened the kiss, pulling me into his arms on the couch. His hand held my neck gently, cradling it, and with his kiss, he told me something I knew he would never say in words.

And as I kissed him back, I told him I felt the same.

There, underground, surrounded by books that made it clear we were more similar than I had ever expected, I could have sworn I had found my soul mate.

But I knew there was so much still awaiting us.

I pulled back, putting my forehead against his and catching my breath. If we went further, I would want so much more, and we both needed time to rest.

But I did want to be with him. I felt healed and strengthened by his presence.

"So you felt me, through the bond?"

He nodded. "I felt your pain. I was far away, on a slaying assignment. I'm so sorry, Cleo. So sorry."

"Don't," I said. "This is unexpected for both of us. Besides, I wouldn't change anything. Gabe's gone, and we're more united than ever before."

"There's still so much to do," Sam said. "If Gabe was telling the truth, then there's a chance Cayne can be brought back. Of course I want to see him again, but also, he knows so much more about the legend of the Morningstar than I do. We'll have to travel to the deepest realms of hell, though."

I brushed his hair back, treasuring the golden-brown curls as they caressed my hand. "If he's there, we'll definitely find him together," I said.

Commotion above had us both sitting up abruptly. I realized someone was yelling, and that someone was Simon.

"I know you're down there, Sam!" he yelled. "Get back up here and tell me if what Griffin told us is really true! Is Cayne waiting in hell? Gods damn it, get out here and tell me what you know!"

Sam let out a sigh. "He deserves to know."

"We can resume this later," I said, reluctantly releasing his curls.

He stood, reaching out his hands to help me up with him.

I couldn't resist leaning up to kiss him once again and feeling that mysterious energy that only came from touching him.

In a moment, we'd have to deal with all the fallout.

In the future, we'd have to go through hell, literally, to save the world.

But I could do it as long as we were together.

After all, stars shine most brightly against the dark.

Thank you so much for reading The Demon's Pet, book 1! If you loved this book, please leave a review to help other readers find it!

The next part will be out soon, so please sign up for my newsletter to find out when it releases!

http://eepurl.com/hHO3on

My Facebook:

https://www.facebook.com/DominoSavageAuthor

My website:

https://dominosavage.com

I have also written as bestselling shifter author Terry Bolryder, so if you want some more sexy fantasy reading, feel free to check out my backlist.

My Awakened Dragons series is a big favorite with sexy fantasy readers, so check it out!

Onyx Dragon (Awakened Dragons Book 1)

The dragons are back, and they're our last chance...

Isaac Morningstar III, or Zach to the few who know him, has hit rock bottom. Once an immortal, nearly-invincible dragon, he's been awakened only to have his powers and his treasure locked away until he can prove himself to be a trustworthy protector of humans. Since Zach has never liked humans, he's pretty sure he's going to end up back on ice. That is, until he meets sweet, curvy Erin, a human hairdresser who might just turn his world upside down.

Warning: contains ferocious dragons, fearsome fights, fiery love scenes and a fiercely cute three-legged kitten that will steal your heart.

Onyx Dragon (Awakened Dragons Book 1)

My fae princes are another huge hit with fantasy readers!

Found by Frost (Wings, Wands and Soul Bonds)

She's his destiny...she just doesn't know it yet.

Avery Williams always knew she was different. But there's no handbook on how to be supernatural, and the last thing she plans to do is go sharing her secret. Especially not with the blonde hottie who just moved in downstairs with his three ridiculously beautiful friends. Even if every time Avery runs into him she feels something powerful she's never felt before.

Boreas Everfrost, or "Brett", didn't come to our world to make friends. He's here to find his soul mate, and destroy the evil fae that have infiltrated human society. He didn't expect fiery, independent Avery who lives upstairs to be the perfect match, but from the first time they meet it's love at first sight. Now he just needs to earn her trust, protect her from the chaos that's after her, and not reveal his true form to the world. All in a day's work for a powerful fae prince.

Found by Frost is book 1 in the Wings, Wands and Soul Bonds series. No cheating. No cliffhanger. Just a fun, sexy, action-packed romance featuring an irresistible warrior prince and the woman he wants forever.

Found by Frost (Wings, Wands and Soul Bonds)

Made in the USA
Thornton, CO
05/07/22 13:18:55

895808d2-0e59-49ff-801b-4b1efb1d6b0fR01